BOLT FROM THE BLUE

Clifford Johnson

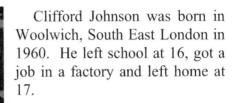

Clifford Johnson was born in Woolwich, South East London in 1960. He left school at 16, got a job in a factory and left home at 17.

During his career he has had many jobs, which provided the wonderful opportunity to meet some unforgettable characters, facets of which you will meet in this, his first book. Clifford has been... an IT training manager, stable boy, riding instructor, labourer, tea boy, mainframe computer operator, office worker, sales assistant, IT helpdesk operator, furniture mover, driver's mate (delivering explosives), security guard and dustman. Temporary jobs included roofer (three weeks), barman (one night), banksman (one day), council worker (one week), soft drinks delivery driver (two weeks), plumbing call centre operative (3 months) and bouncer (one night only).

Clifford has had a lifelong passion for creativity and as an artist has worked in metal, wood, glass and oils, successfully selling his work. *Bolt from the Blue* is his first foray into the art of literature and the most challenging project ever undertaken. Motivated by a comment from a teacher who once told him it was impossible due to his severe dyslexia, he invested hundreds of hours' work over four years to undertake seven re-writes and oil-painted illustrations for the book cover to finally complete the project.

He lives in rural Herefordshire with his wife Sally Boehme, a successful jewellery artist and teacher.

On a freezing December night in 1992, a violent storm rages over London.

In a deserted alley a terrified woman hides in the shadows. Suddenly, she is made visible by a bolt of lightning and at that moment seen by Ron Moon, who resolves to help her. In their attempts to make sense of her traumatic history they trigger a dangerous chain of events. It soon becomes apparent her dark past is closing in fast. They must be ready for it, or it will kill them both.

This book is dedicated to Sally for her love, support and sticky toffee pudding.

CONTENTS

Part One

Part Two

PART ONE
CHAPTER 1
SATURDAY NIGHT

It was something of a Christmas miracle on that December night in 1992 that rain fell at all, for the cold was so brutal and savage, a blizzard was infinitely more likely. But rain it did and London was experiencing the worst storm in living memory. The icy cold gusts of wind, which slammed the city from the east had lost none of their potency in the long journey from Russia. Ear splitting explosions of jagged white-blue lightening stabbed buildings and arced across the black sky.

The air was filled with a low deep rushing noise as torrents of rain lashed the city. At a deserted intersection in a southeast London suburb another sound mixed with the storm, very faint at first but gradually growing stronger. It was the curt clipping of shoes on hard pavement. The footsteps were irregular, as if someone was tripping and stumbling. For a moment it was impossible to determine the direction of the sound as echo ghosts joined the original around the empty crossroads.

Suddenly, the runner burst into view, lit only by the pale light of a single streetlamp. It was a young woman, her clothes drenched and sticking to her. Her

1

blonde hair was short, cut in a pixie style, which the rain had darkened and plastered to her small pale face.

Staggering to a halt, her slender frozen fingers gripped the lamppost to steady herself, breathing hard she gulped back a sob her breath was visible and rose in clouds caught in the lamplight. Tears mixed with the rain running down her face. She wiped the back of her hand across her eyes and looked about wildly.

Rain was hitting the pavements so hard it bounced creating a six-inch layer of freezing wet mist. All around, roofs had been turned into urban waterfalls as rain cascaded into the streets, small drains choked and overflowed.

Clinging to the lamppost the woman stared anxiously back the way she had come. The street was totally deserted; this however, didn't seem to calm her. She chose to go right, hurled herself away from the lamppost and careered on.

The sound of an approaching car seemed to fill her with terror. She immediately crouched down on the wet pavement and crawled under the back of a parked lorry. The car passed without slowing; she let her breath go. After taking a few moments to recover, the woman struggled out from her hiding place, but as she did so her shoulder bag slipped and fell. The catch was jarred open and the contents spilled onto the kerb. A dark oblong shape cartwheeled and came to rest on the brink of the kerb. The woman made a desperate grab for it but her fingers, made clumsy by the intense cold, caught it awkwardly, it slipped and fell into the gutter river, 'No, no, no, no, no, no!' She scrambled after it but was too late. She watched helplessly as her purse was swept along the gutter and swallowed by a storm drain. The woman stared for a moment in misery and disbelief at the dark gurgling hole then returned to the kerb and frantically with numbed fingers scooped up her remaining belongings stuffing them quickly back into the bag. On her way again she tore down the street. Under the lorry something she had missed glinted as it lay in the road.

The more she ran, the more she needed to run. Desperately, blindly plunging on. How long she had been running she didn't know. Totally exhausted and near the point of collapse, her legs refused to run anymore. Slowing to a walk then finally stopping the woman clung to some railings and gulped down lungfuls of air, which came billowing out. Her lungs were painful from the cold air and her body had begun to shiver uncontrollably.

She had come to a halt in a light industrial part of the city and at this late hour no lights shone from the dark buildings that loomed overhead. The only illumination was from the widely placed street lamps.

To the right was an alley, in her desperate state the absolute darkness held no fear, it was only a place to hide, a place to be safe. She felt her way along the alley, keeping close to the wall, then quite suddenly her legs gave out and she slumped against it. She didn't really care any more. An all enveloping, unstoppable tiredness washed over her, it would be safe here, safe from… safe from…? She blinked and shook her head, safe from what? She felt an odd sensation that reality was folding up, becoming smaller and retreating into the darkness. Too weak to do anything, she watched in a strange, detached way as recent memories seemed to dissolve. For a fleeting moment, panic began to well up but then exhaustion took over. Closing her eyes, she turned her face to the wall and began to cry again, this time not even knowing why. The impression that something terrible was searching for her remained in her mind, but its exact form had vanished. She had no idea where she was she knew nothing but fear and misery. Gripping the wall, she sobbed. Thoughts became spaced between nothingness, which gradually lengthened and her mind balanced on the edge between terror and oblivion. A small figure, made even smaller by the monstrous shadows cast by the buildings as lightning ripped the sky apart.

Two miles away, a dark car stopped by the lorry where the woman had taken shelter. A man got out and walked around the lorry. Looking under it, he noticed the silver object the woman had dropped. He snatched it up and took it back to the car, showing it to the driver. 'She's dropped the bug, Micky.' Micky took the pen and studied it thoughtfully for a moment, before tossing it on to the back seat, 'Damn, without that, it's gonna be hard!'

Ron Moon shuddered as he glanced out of the window at the storm, absentmindedly scratching his cat between the ears. Finbar purred and shut his eyes, in a kind of cat heaven. 'It's still raining, Fin,' Ron turned from the window, 'but we don't care, do we Fin? We don't have to go out.' Plopping the cat down on the rug by the fire, Ron walked into his small kitchen. 'Do you want normal food or do you want a surprise?' He peered into the cupboard. 'Let's go for a surprise, eh? Yes, why not.' Reaching in, he rummaged about. None of the tins had any labels; he chose one, opened it, found a saucepan and set it on the heat. Then turning to another cupboard marked 'Finbar', he fished out a tin, which also had no label; this he opened and emptied into Finbar's bowl.

After the soup, he sprawled across one of the large sofas facing each other either side of the gas fire and toasted his feet. Finbar stretched on the rug and purred. Ron poured himself a large brandy and looked at the fire through the glass. Settling back, he noticed that the reflection of rain hitting the window behind him was making a watery pattern on the wall opposite, between the kitchen door and bedroom door with each flash of light. He shivered, 'Oh, it's a bad night to be out...' he raised his glass to the dozing cat, 'Cheers!' He swallowed his brandy, set the glass down and gazed into the fire. Finbar got up sleepily and jumped on to Ron's lap.

Finbar was fully-grown but unusually small; he was completely black except one white forepaw, white whiskers and fluffy tufts of white hair that protruded from his ears. Ron stroked him, Finbar purred and the two of them drifted off.

Some time later Ron woke with a start as a very loud crack of lightening struck some nearby street. The storm was raging directly overhead. It was as if the heavens were being split open by forked lightning and through the cracks in the sky, water poured and then was hurled in sheets down the empty canyon streets by arctic gusts.

He stood up feeling stiff. The sleeping Finbar was dropped unceremoniously on to the rug. Meowing with irritation, he slunk away to sulk under the TV in the corner. In truth, the six inch drop from Ron's knee with outstretched paws to the soft carpet below was nothing, it wouldn't be a long sulk but it had to be done out of principle. Finbar's personal best had been an Olympian leap of over five and a half feet from a table over the vet's shoulder down to the hard floor. In lieu of a medal placed around his neck he had been awarded a red circle placed around his name as a reminder of his abilities. Ron looked down drowsily and wondered where his cat had disappeared to.

He checked his watch; it was four o'clock in the morning, 'Look at the time!' He stretched and yawned then bending, he turned the gas fire from high to low. Smiling, he looked at the glowing coals, 'Very real.' Straightening up, he crossed the room to the bedroom door and flicked the light out in the living room. But instead of continuing through the door, something made him stop on the threshold and look round. He didn't know why but he felt uncomfortable. The room was now in darkness, the sound of the wind hurling rain against the window made him look in that direction. He could see Finbar, who had crept out from under the TV and was sitting on the windowsill staring out into the storm. Finbar wasn't happy. Being tipped off Ron's lap wasn't it, it was something else, something new, something bad. Both the room and the cat were lit by flashes of cold blue light as fork lightning continued to arc across the dark sky.

Ron turned from the room and took a step into the bedroom. He stopped abruptly. Finbar hated storms. Walking back into the living room and moving to the window Ron looked at the cat, who was staring down into the alley below. Following his gaze, he peered down but from the second floor the alley was just blackness. Ron glanced at the cat again, but still he stared down. Finbar's standard reaction was to be frightened of what he didn't understand. He was particularly afraid of storms, which without human company usually sent him quickly to the safety of his basket in the kitchen. Tonight was different, yes he was very frightened but also weaving through his fear, he felt terror. What both puzzled and fascinated him was that the terror he felt wasn't his, it was bigger, deeper, unfamiliar in shape and scent and out there somewhere in the dark.

'I hate it when you stare at things I can't see! It gives me the creeps. Do you hear?' Finbar ignored him and his shining eyes continued to look as if mesmerised by something unseen. Turning from Finbar Ron tried again and stared into the fathomless depths of the alley. He was about to give up and return to the bedroom when a bolt of lightening directly overhead lit the alley.

The image of a woman could be seen momentarily in the flash of light. Ron blinked as he examined the picture in his mind that his eyes could no longer see. She looked terrified, crouching close to the ground and at the time of the flash was looking directly at him. He rubbed the window frantically and strained his eyes to look down, but now he could see nothing but blackness. Swinging away from the window, he went in search of sweater and coat.

A few moments later he stood at the front of the building. It was raining harder than ever. He hesitated for a moment, then thinking of the expression on the woman's face walked down the front steps and cautiously crept around to the alley that ran down the side of the building.

At first, the alley seemed lifeless. Ron stood in the darkness and listened to the rain gurgle down drainpipes and beat on dustbin lids somewhere close by. The tiny feeble light from his own living room window high up on the second floor did nothing to help and indeed, wasn't really noticeable from the ground.

As his eyes became more accustomed to the darkness, he could make out the shape of something hunched against the alley wall. Moving slowly toward it, the vague shape transformed into that of a woman. She had a beige coat wrapped tightly around her and what looked like a shoulder bag on a long strap. In a half–sitting position she seemed to be clinging to the wall, she had turned and was now facing him but with her eyes shut and her head turned slightly to the wall. Ron didn't know what to say for a moment he stood blinking as the rain got in his eyes. She was slender and looked deathly white; in the bad light Ron couldn't see much else apart from the fact she was shaking from the cold.

Eventually, not knowing what else to do, he coughed. The woman's eyes opened and stared at him in terror. He spoke softly, 'It's okay… it's okay… do you need some help? Are you hurt?' The woman continued to stare and still appeared to be very frightened. 'Can you get up?' Ron reached out very slowly, 'Come on, it's alright.' His hand was only a couple of inches from the woman's, when there was another bolt of lightning above them. Suddenly, she let go of the wall and seized his hand. The quick movement made him start but he smiled quickly, 'That's it, you're safe.' He was startled to feel how cold she was, her grip was feeble and her hand shook. Although holding his hand, she now seemed almost unaware of his presence and stared into middle space. It crossed his mind that she may be in shock. 'We have to get out of the rain.' he urged gently.

Slowly, he led her from the alley and around to the front of the building. She seemed in a dream state, not knowing where she was or even caring. Still holding his hand loosely, she allowed herself to be gently led up the steps to the front door of the building and up the wide staircase to his flat. The lower two floors of the building was a printing business, locked and silent. Ron's upstairs flat the only residential property in the building, indeed in the whole area.

On entering the flat, he stood dripping by the door for a moment, not sure of what to do next. Deciding to sit her down, he guided her along the short hall past the bathroom door into the living room to the nearest of the two sofas. 'You just sit down there a minute, I'll be back.' Prising his hand away he went to the bedroom, returning a few seconds later carrying a towelling robe, which he placed in the bathroom.

As he walked back toward her, he noticed for the first time the red smear down the front of her coat. The rain had faded it slightly but it was still obvious, it looked like blood! He glanced at her face, but she gazed at the floor with unseeing eyes, slumped on the sofa like a rag doll, her whole body quivered with the cold. She appeared not to know he was there. Nervously and very slowly, Ron gently lifted the lapel of her coat. The red smear was very faint on the inside; if it was blood, it wasn't hers. He breathed out slowly, 'Come on.' Gently, he put his arms around her shaking shoulders and coaxed her to stand then at the bathroom door, he leaned her against the wall and faced her. 'Look, I don't know what kind of trouble you're in but you're soaked to the skin and frozen stiff whatever the problem is it can wait till morning.' Remembering the lateness he added, 'Well, later on today. Now, you get out of those wet clothes and put on the robe in there. It's OK, you can lock the door.' She looked at him for the first time since entering the flat, but didn't really appear to see him. Ron wondered how much she had taken in. He smiled at her and waved his hand in the direction of the bathroom, she slowly turned, walked stiffly into the bathroom and shut the door.

Ron blew out his cheeks then ran his hand over his face. 'Oh boy, oh boy, oh boy!' He glanced at Finbar who was hiding under the TV; Finbar didn't like strangers. Ron sat down and tried to think, he shook his head, 'It's too late, the morning'll come soon enough.' He glanced at his watch and winced, 4.15. From the sofa it was possible to lean back and look along the short hall that led to the front door. He could see a faint yellow light on the carpet from the crack under the bathroom door. Getting up, he arranged some cushions from the sofas on the floor between them close to the fire. She desperately needed to warm up.

The bathroom door opened, the woman stepped out and stood in the hall vacantly staring at the floor now wearing his robe, which swamped her, her hands hidden by the long sleeves. If he'd stood close, the top of her head would just touch his chin.

'It's not a good fit but at least it's warm and dry,' he spoke as he folded back the sleeves on her wrists, 'come on, don't worry you're safe now.' He gently took her arm and led her over to the fire, it was like guiding a sleepwalker. If anything she appeared more fragile than before, without the shoes she looked smaller and stooped slightly giving the impression that she may fall at any moment. Ron gestured at the cushions, 'I think you need some rest,' he squeezed her hand, 'and you're still freezing. You better sleep here tonight.' Sinking down onto the cushions, the only sound she uttered was a small sigh as she closed her eyes and was instantly asleep. Fetching a spare blanket from the bedroom he gently covered his mysterious guest, switched off the light then paused at the bedroom door and gazed at the dark shape lit only by the glow of the fire. He shook his head and went to bed.

As he lay in the dark, he pondered the strange situation. Had he done the right thing in taking this complete stranger in for the night? What was the alternative? The police? That red stain on her coat; it looked like blood. Surely, calling the police was the thing to do. But he wasn't totally convinced, he felt she had been through a lot and what she needed was a friend. It wasn't that long ago that he had felt totally without hope with thoughts of perhaps it would be better if….. he shivered, someone had pulled him back. He should help her. Just to take her to the Police Station and walk away… no, that wasn't right. He felt he had done the right thing and was sure that after some sleep everything would be explained. Shutting his eyes, before long his breathing was slow and regular.

11

Ron opened his eyes. The room was no longer dark, a thin greyish light filtered through a chink in the curtains. He rolled over and squinted at the clock... one o'clock in the afternoon. He flopped back for a moment, then scratching his head he groped about for his robe.... Suddenly, he opened his eyes wide, 'The woman!' He quickly pulled on jeans and tee-shirt then very quietly eased the bedroom door open. The living room was stuffy, the fire had been turned low all night.

The woman was exactly where she had been the night before. He tiptoed closer and peered at her; she looked very peaceful and her face had a little more colour, an improvement on the frightening white. He decided to let her sleep; she had almost passed out the night before and he felt sure that sleep was best. So he crept off to the kitchen to find some breakfast.

After some food Ron sat down in the living room with a cup of coffee and looked at her. He guessed her to be mid-twenties, the hair was lighter than he had first thought. Now it was dry it sprung up at the crown and was cut close to the face in a pixie style. She wasn't very tall; remembering the night before she had only come just above his shoulder. He wasn't sure if he thought she was pretty. She certainly wasn't ugly but seemed a little plain. Her small face was still paler than normal, there was slightly more colour in her thin lips. He remembered when she had looked up at him the night before she had brown eyes. She held a cushion lightly. He studied her hands; they were slender and like her face, pale.

He sat and considered; she had been very frightened of something and by her general condition, he guessed had been out in the rain a long time. The fact she was sleeping so long meant she had been on the point of exhaustion. He pondered further, what about the inability to talk? That was more puzzling. He decided it was almost certainly some kind of shock, but that raised the question, what kind of shock? Ron glanced in the direction of the bathroom where her clothes were drying and her coat hung with what looked like blood on it. He was sure it wasn't hers, had she hurt someone? Looking at her again, somehow it didn't seem likely but you could never tell. He puzzled on this for a time then finally decided that all he could deduce so far, was something had happened that terrified her to such an extent, she had run herself to the point of collapse to get away from it. Even this, of course, was a guess but it was the best he could manage. He shook his head this was no good. The simple fact was, he would just have to wait until she woke up. Or... an idea suddenly came to him, the shoulder bag was in the bathroom. Should he look through it? It may tell him her identity but not what happened to her. He shook his head again, a woman's bag! It was the most private of places. No, he couldn't.

Although it was Sunday, he couldn't relax. It's not easy to relax with a mystery woman quietly sleeping on your living room floor. He sat at his desk. Ron liked his work so for him, it wasn't like real work. Therefore, if he felt in the mood, working on a Sunday was no hardship. He wrote thrillers part time and when he wasn't writing, designed board games and sold them to games companies. He sold them cheap for a percentage of the profits. He had two very successful games: '*Space Gambler*' and '*Attack 5000*', the revenue from which paid the bills while his writing had taken a back seat, at least until recently. One of his books had caught the imagination of a producer and with Ron's help had been adapted into a play. This play seemed to be well received and was running locally. His stories were action adventure types, normally involving gangsters or the Mafia. The main hero was a man called Max Carter, who got up to all kinds of death-defying adventures. Ron's books were starting to sell very well and he was sure that part of the secret was the kind of villains Ron pitted Max against; they were real, real in the sense that they were very credible. This was no accident, he had a secret research source.

Unable to concentrate he gave up on the new story and tried to work on something else, glancing over his shoulder at the young woman from time to time but still she slept on.

As Sunday evening approached, his restlessness grew. Finally, he backed up his work to floppy disk, closed down the word processor and DOS then switched off his PC. After a final glance at his sleeping guest, he donned his coat and slipped out quietly for a walk.

Outside, the worst of the storm was over and only a light miserable drizzle remained. He walked quickly, soon finding himself in the heart of town. Although it was close to Christmas, it being Sunday, of course all the shops were shut. However, the windows were lit up and the coloured lights made abstract patterns on the wet pavements. He turned up his collar and trudged on. All he could think about was the woman. As he walked, he made up a hundred reasons why she had come to be in the alley, and from what she could possibly be running, but each one he rejected and he was forced back to the same conclusion, wait till she wakes up. The thought of her waking up and leaving before he got home made him start back, he must find out her story.

The drizzle was made worse by a light wind and Ron was pleased to put his key in the door. He hadn't sorted out much, but he felt better for the air.

Inside the flat, Ron hung up his coat and looked across the living room. From the front door, he couldn't quite see if she was still lying by the fire. He peeked over the edge of the sofa and was relieved to see she was there but disappointed to see she was sleeping peacefully.

Something touched his leg and made him jump. He looked down. 'Oh, you scared the life out of me... Stupid cat!'

'MMMEEEEEEOOW!'

'Shut up! You'll wake her up.' Ron felt it important she woke gently and naturally, certainly not to the yowl of a cat.

'MMMME...'

Ron snatched up Finbar and ran off to the kitchen, quickly closing the door quietly behind him.

'...EEEOOOWW.'

In the kitchen, he filled Finbar's bowl, 'Now shut up!' The cat made strange noises as he tried to eat and purr at the same time. 'Weird.' He remained in the kitchen and made a snack, then went to sit by the fire looking at the woman's face, wondering why the night before he hadn't noticed she was pretty.

Ron felt very sorry for her she had seemed so lost. He pondered again what kind of trouble she was in. Also, he was growing concerned about how long she had been sleeping, perhaps she might be ill. After considering for a moment, he dismissed the idea and shook his head. She hadn't appeared to be in any pain the night before. No, he was convinced it was only exhaustion and possibly, some kind of shock. If he was right, sleep was the best thing. He decided to leave it till the next day. If she still didn't wake and he was no closer to knowing who she was, he would have to consider going to the authorities. The idea didn't rest well, he felt strongly he should help and handing her over to the police would be the wrong thing to do. She would be just another case. Getting up he yawned, took one last look at his guest and went to bed.

PART ONE
CHAPTER 2
MONDAY MORNING 7:30

Ron woke early the following day but kept his eyes shut and lay still, thinking. Today was Monday, he ought to go out, he had things to do, but he didn't want to leave the woman alone. The question was, should he wake her? Deciding to put off the decision as long as possible, he dressed and slipped out of the bedroom.

Checking on her, he noticed she had moved position, but still slept on so he went to the kitchen to get a coffee. He was coming out of the kitchen when he froze in the doorway. She was in a half-sitting position with her hand across her forehead. Ron stood quite still, not wanting to frighten her, she would almost certainly be disorientated and after all he was a stranger to her.

As he watched she seemed to begin to take an interest in her surroundings. First, she looked down at the cream Chinese rug, stretching out her little hand stroked the soft pile, then looking down at her robe, fingered the material thoughtfully. The heat from the fire made her turn and look at the hearth behind her. She tipped her head back as she glanced up at the soft cheerful yellow walls. Turning away from Ron to the right, she looked at the small round table near the end of the large, comfortable sofa. A little behind the sofa was the bay window that looked down on the alley. The long curtains were drawn back, letting the pale morning light through the window, bathing the room in a soft glow. She continued to move round to her right, now with her back to the fire. Directly opposite the fireplace and in front of her was a wall of white shelves, neat and tidy but laden with books, ornaments here and there acting as bookends. To the right of the wall of books, the short hall started and from her half-sitting position, she could just see what she supposed was the front door. Continuing to turn to her right almost completing her circular appraisal of the room she saw the second sofa that faced the first and a desk in the far corner next to another door which unbeknown to her led to the bedroom. The last quarter turn was made quickly to the right as something caught her eye.

Sitting with her back to the first sofa and window beyond she peered over the edge of the second sofa at a man who stood motionless in a doorway. She immediately pulled her robe around herself more tightly and stared at him like a frightened creature, not knowing if she should run. Looking at him she relaxed slightly, he didn't appear threatening. In fact, he looked a little frightened himself. She guessed he was in his late twenties, stocky, broad shoulders, with thick light brown hair parted vaguely in the centre, swept up and back by fingers rather than comb. He was clean-shaven with thick eyebrows dressed in jeans, sweatshirt and slippers. In one hand, he held a steaming coffee cup and in the other gripped a large packet of digestive biscuits.

Ron spoke first, 'Well, you're awake,' he smiled, 'I thought you were going to sleep forever.' She whispered, 'Where am I?' Ron felt a surge of pity, 'This is my place. I found you out in the rain; you were exhausted, I er... I think you'd been running.' He said the last bit slowly as he wasn't certain he should make any reference to whatever had happened to her, at least before she had time to collect herself. The woman stared at him she seemed to be waiting for more. He noted for the second time her brown eyes her stare was making him feel uncomfortable. He put his coffee down and shrugged, 'That's all really, I couldn't leave you in the pouring rain.' She nodded and looked down at the robe again, slowly lifting her eyes to him. He saw the question, 'Er... you were soaked so I gave you my robe and you changed in the bathroom and... well, you must have been exhausted because you almost collapsed down there by the fire and that's where you stayed' Ron added carefully, 'for close on...' he checked his watch, 'twenty eight hours.' The woman rotated her shoulders and gently rocked her head while massaging her stiff neck. She appeared content with the explanation.

'How do you feel?'

'I'm okay. I ache a bit. Could I have a drink, please?' Her voice was quiet and conveyed the impression of well-educated clear speech. Ron brought her a glass of water and she drank it down in one, 'Thank you. May I use your bathroom?' She rose stiffly to her feet and Ron pointed to the door. Before she entered, he asked, 'Do you feel hungry?' The woman nodded. Ron went back to into the kitchen.

Soon he had eggs, bacon, beans and sausages all sizzling away and a big pot of fresh coffee filling the small kitchen with its wonderful aroma. The woman looked timidly around the kitchen door. Ron glanced at her, 'Sit yourself down, it won't be long.' He gestured to one of the four pine chairs that circled the round table at the window. She sat down and smiled. The smile made him hesitate in his work. Her face wasn't just pretty; when she smiled it was quite beautiful. 'Can I help?' she asked.

'Er, you could butter some bread if you like.'

'I can do that.' Cheerfully, she got on with the buttering as if it was the most natural thing in the world for them to be making breakfast together.

Ron felt he should tread carefully. He was sure she'd been through some trauma and seemed happy not to think about it or discuss it. Whether this was because she simply couldn't cope with it right now, or wanted to get to know him better before confiding in him, he didn't know. For whatever reason, he felt the thing to do was let her talk in her own time, so for the present would be patient.

They sat together and had breakfast. He was pleased to see she ate heartily and smiled a lot, 'I was very hungry, I don't know when I last ate.' Ron smiled, 'I'm glad you enjoyed it. Look, I know this is a funny time to tell you but my name's Ron.' Not knowing what to do he offered his hand, the woman smiled, wiped her hand on a napkin and shook his, 'I'm...' she hesitated for a moment looking frightened, this quickly passed, the smile returned, 'my name's Vicky... Vicky Blaine.' Vicky appeared pleased to have remembered this.

Ron smiled back and nodded, 'Vicky… okay. Well, Vicky, I suppose we better get some clothes on you.' He stopped, and for the first time since adolescence thought he was going to blush. He hurried off to the bathroom where Vicky's clothes were airing and felt the hem of her skirt, 'I think they're dry,' he called, 'and your bag's in here.' She peered around the bathroom door. Ron lowered his voice, 'There's a fresh towel and new soap there,' he pointed, 'help yourself, take as long as you like.'

'Thank you.'

He swiftly vacated the bathroom and left her to it.

When Vicky emerged several minutes later, she found Ron sitting stroking Finbar and staring at the fire introspectively. He snapped out of it as she approached. She'd combed her hair and swapped Ron's thick robe for her own clothes. She now wore a dark brown long sleeved silk blouse and black knee-length wool skirt. To him the result was really quite wonderful, a big change from the dazed little bedraggled creature that had entered the flat.

He stroked Finbar nervously, then being careful not to look at her, ventured, 'I er… I was thinking,' he risked a glance, she nodded, 'Yes?' He looked away, 'Er yes, well… look, don't take this wrong or anything but I thought I'd better let you know. The thing is, if you want to stay here for a while to get yourself together… you can. It would make a change from Finbar's company.' He smiled, but still didn't look at her. Vicky spoke slowly, 'Thank you Ron. If you really don't mind, I think I would like to stay a while,' she added quickly, 'oh, only for a couple of days.' Ron stood, 'Right then, well, that's settled.'

21

Ron walked into the kitchen and began to wash up. He wanted to think. Why had he asked her to stay? He didn't know anything about her. This situation was weird, but then again, it wasn't, it seemed natural to help her. He still felt awkward; he shook his head. Jacqui had been gone now nearly five years. Ron stopped wiping the kitchen surface, was it really that long?

'Ron?' Vicky was calling from the living room.

'Yes?'

'This paper?'

Ron hesitated in his wiping, 'Paper...? Oh, you mean the free one. Yes, it comes every week.'

'This one is this week's?'

'Yes, it arrived on Friday, lucky to get it living here, but the newsagent knows me and passes on his way home.'

There was silence for a moment then she read out the date. Ron wasn't sure where this was going, so he answered brightly, 'Yes, that's right.' There were no more questions from the living room so Ron finished his tidying up. He was wiping his hands on a tea towel when he heard crying. Rushing into the living room, he found her sobbing.

'What's the matter?' Ron snatched up Finbar and began to stroke him. Vicky buried her face in her hands and was unable to speak. Ron patted Finbar frantically, 'Vicky, what is it?' Vicky still didn't answer. Ron patted Finbar so much his head was jiggled up and down.

Putting down Finbar he rubbed the small bite on his hand and looked at Vicky who had curled herself into a ball on one of the sofas. He spoke gently, 'Vicky, sshh, come on now, you can tell me, what is it?' Ron's hand hovered over her shoulder, as she glanced up he quickly snatched it away, looked uncomfortable, scratched the back of his head and pursed his lips.

Her words came out in short breathless sobs, 'I can't tell you… I can't tell you anything.' He looked sympathetic, 'If you don't want to, it's alright, you don't have to,' he shrugged, 'I mean I'm just a stranger to you.' Vicky shook her head, 'No, no, you don't understand. I CAN'T REMEMBER!' The tears flowed again. She waved at the crumpled newspaper at her feet. He stared at the paper, it was only a free local one and the front page was all about a new scout hall, nothing there to upset anyone. Ron put his hand out again to pat her shoulder then changed his mind, he quickly sat on the sofa opposite to wait patiently. Feeling helpless, he looked at her sitting alone and upset. He would have liked to stroke Finbar to give his nervous hands something to do, but Finbar was sulking under the TV set because he didn't like being patted so hard. So Ron had to sit nervously and wait.

As the afternoon wore on, Vicky managed to compose herself and was able to string sentences together without falling apart. She poured out her life story. It seemed she really needed to talk, so Ron sat quietly nodding and smiling, gradually he came to know her.

She was born in Devon, her mother and father had been killed by an IRA bomb blast while on a trip to London. Her father was an academic, a research scientist whose field was blood disorders. He had been invited to London for a seminar, taking Vicky's mother. After the seminar they intended to use the time in London to visit friends and enjoy New Year with them. They weren't targets, just ordinary people in the wrong place at the wrong time. She had a sister called Sara who was a year younger. On the fatal night they had been at home in Devon with an aunt who was baby-sitting them. That was New Year's Eve, 1973. Vicky and Sara were only four and five years old and had been brought up by the aunt. After such a tragic beginning, from what Vicky said, childhood had been surprisingly happy. The aunt was comfortably wealthy and loved the girls very much. The sisters had done well at school, and gained good passes. Vicky was the first to leave, being older. She found a typing job in a small solicitor's office. They couldn't believe their luck when, a year later, just as Sara was leaving school, a position opened up in the same firm. Sara went for the job and was successful so the girls were able to work together.

They moved out of their aunt's house and rented a flat between them. Things went well, until one day a man came into the office. He wanted to speak to Mr Siros, the founder member of the firm. Evidently, the man was on holiday in Devon and had been informed by phone that the police were investigating one of his business ventures. He wanted to find out quickly how he stood on some legal point. Vicky didn't know how the police problem turned out. The important thing was that the man took a fancy to Sara. It began with a lunchtime drink, then lunch and finally out for the evening. Before long, Sara was out every night with the man and when she wasn't out with him, talked about him constantly. Vicky had taken a dislike to him and tried to tell Sara he was trouble. Although sisters, they were very different in temperament, Vicky was thoughtful and by nature cautious, whereas Sara being more impulsive and with the over-confidence of youth, refused to listen. This caused a violent row, and in a terrible rage Sara moved out saying that 'she would show Vicky how wrong she was'.

Vicky heard nothing for two months and was frantic with worry, then received a letter saying that everything was all right and Sara was in London. Vicky could clearly remember getting on the London train but that was all; she couldn't remember arriving, nor the address on the letter.

Having finished her story, pointing at the paper and overcome with emotion she burst into tears again. Ron looked at the paper more carefully but still couldn't see what had triggered the new flood of tears. He didn't dare ask so said nothing, half an hour passed very slowly. Vicky appeared to be thinking hard and stared at the floor occasionally biting her lower lip.

They sat in silence, Vicky red-eyed and upset, Ron at a loss for what to say. When he could stand it no longer, he ventured, 'I doze off on trains all the time and sometimes I go around in a dream all day. Perhaps the letter's in your bag somewhere.' He immediately knew he had said the wrong thing by the way she looked at him. Then, not knowing what he had done, added, 'I'm sorry.' She looked at him raw emotion spilling over into tears, 'Oh, you don't understand… I caught that train *over a year ago!*' Then panicking, 'I've lost a year of my life!' He was shocked, 'You mean it's all a blank?' She nodded quickly, 'From catching the London train to look for Sara, till waking up here is a blank,' then after a moment with greater volume, 'I've lost a year of my life and I'm frightened.' She burst out crying.

Ron switched sofas and sat beside to her and uncertainly put his arm around her shoulder. She spun round and buried her head in his chest and sobbed. He patted her soothingly on the back, 'Ssshhh, Vicky, it's going to be okay, we'll get to the bottom of this.' He hadn't the faintest idea how this could be achieved, but his words calmed her. After a while, the crying stopped. 'I'm sorry, Ron. This isn't me at all... this crying and stuff...,' she shook her head, 'to have a hole in your life a year big, it's so... so...' she shrugged and seemed too upset to continue. He nodded, 'I can't even imagine but it's safe to say, if I woke up and found I'd lost a year, I'd be upset myself.' As he said it, he suddenly realised what the significance of the paper was. What a fool! It was simply the date, it must have been quite a shock, no wonder she was upset.

He suddenly became aware he was still holding her tight and began to let go. Immediately, she reached for his hand and held on tight. That tipped the scales, Ron felt like crying himself. No one had seemed this close to him since Jacqui died. He had been coping better lately but suddenly the aching loneliness was back. Ron squeezed Vicky's hand and repeated, for his own sake as much as hers, 'It's going to be okay.'

After a thoughtful pause, she agreed, 'Mm, you're right in what you said earlier, we should check my bag, maybe there's something there.' She got to her feet and fetched it quickly, but after a careful search it revealed only comb, compact, lipstick, keys, a pack of rain-soaked tissues and a 20 unit BT phone card, in fact nothing that helped and certainly no letters. She looked at him puzzled and concerned, 'Where's my purse, my cards, money, oh....?' There were too many questions neither knew what to say. Vicky placed her elbow on the arm of the sofa and held her forehead whispering quietly, 'What does it all mean?'

It was December so dusk came early, the streetlights had already flickered on. Ron decided it wasn't worth going out now and his business would have to wait until Tuesday. He promised that they would start to try and unravel the mystery the following day. He needed to do a few things in the morning, then in the afternoon they would begin to try putting the pieces together. He left that bit vague as he didn't have a clue how to start and luckily, she didn't press it.

After dinner, Ron opened a bottle of wine and the two of them sat relaxing by the fire. The comfortable flat, the food and the wine weaved their simple magic and Vicky appeared a little more at ease. They talked about music and trivia, it appeared Vicky's taste in music was centred around the seventies and early eighties, mainly middle of the road stuff with the occasional favourite that was even earlier. He was amused when Van Morrison was mentioned. '*Brown Eyed Girl*'s a favourite I suppose?' He asked smiling. Vicky's brown eyes sparkled, 'Yes I've danced to that one!' She laughed and after a moment the thought struck her how ridiculous the situation was, here she sat sharing a glass of wine in this man's home and all she knew of him was his name was Ron, his taste in music was fifties and he seemed kind. 'So, tell me about you.'

Ron understood the reasoning behind the casually asked question he was a total stranger after all. So he explained how he made a living, telling her about the board games, *'Attack 5000'* and *'Space Gambler'* which provided what he called the 'bread and butter money' to pay the bills. She was surprised that just two games could be so profitable and asked if they were hard to create. He explained that it took weeks of work to design a game, figuring out the odds on all the random factors and getting it just right so the game ran neither for too long or too short a time. The difficulty level was hard enough to be interesting but not too hard. A successful games designer needed to consider multiple aspects simultaneously. The two games had sold very, very well and his deal with the games company was a small initial payment in exchange for a percentage on sales, which had proved to be an extremely good idea.

Vicky was pleased not to think about her own situation for a while and found him interesting. It occurred to her that when she had first seen him, she hadn't thought him particularly good looking, but as he talked and smiled, in his well thought-out gentle way, she found herself warming to him. Vicky asked what else he did not expecting the answer. He told her he also wrote thrillers based around a character called Max Carter. He was shy when he admitted to the play but was obviously very proud. Vicky liked him for being shy and encouraged him to tell the full story.

'It was just luck,' he told her. A producer had seen his first book and had approached to ask if he would consider adapting it for the theatre. Ron told him he had never written a play before but was always interested in trying something new. After some research, he'd worked on nothing else but the play. When complete it was accepted with only minor changes and had been running locally for nearly two months. The producer was enthusiastic about taking it to the big theatres. He laughed, 'I owe it all to the games, their success meant I had regular money coming in, so I finally had the opportunity to try writing seriously, which was something I'd always dreamed of. I've written all my life mainly for my own amusement, I even had some short stories published in magazines but to have my first book published was amazing and they wanted more. It's all been quite remarkable! The success of the games led to the books and the books led to the play. Just life I suppose, right place right time, plain old luck.'

As Ron relaxed and opened up, Vicky had a chance to study him carefully without appearing to stare. He was quite stocky with long sloping shoulders. She felt he was by nature a quiet man and needed coaxing to talk, but now he was on a subject he was obviously passionate about there was no stopping him.

Vicky was genuinely interested in the story, especially the play and asked a lot of questions which he answered happily. She told him about some of the plays that she and Sara had seen in Devon then, laughing at the recollection, told him she and her sister had even attempted a little amateur dramatics, 'We were awful!' she admitted, 'It didn't last long but we had fun.' When she asked Ron where he got his ideas for writing, he simply smiled and said he had a secret. Vicky tried to get him to explain, but he just grinned and said she would find out tomorrow morning if she came with him when he paid the calls he should have done today.

The two chatted and laughed like old friends and for a while Vicky tried hard to put her troubles to the back of her mind and enjoy the moment. Glancing around she commented, 'Isn't it quiet here, for London I mean.'

'That's partly why I stay it's not a pretty part of London but quiet at night. There's a print shop downstairs, this is the only flat in the building, the whole area is light industrial but I like it, the print shop don't make much noise, they only run business cards, wedding invites, it's not the mighty presses of Fleet Street or anything. Also, here I'm not far from the bright lights. Since the writing is going so well I could move to somewhere better, but it suits me being a bit out of the way.'

'I was lucky someone found me,' she corrected the statement, 'I was lucky *you* found me.'

At one o'clock in the morning, he said they should get some rest. Vicky went to the bathroom and changed into Ron's robe, while he took the wine glasses into the kitchen. When he came back to the living room, he found her making herself comfortable on the cushions by the fire with the blanket over her. 'Look Vicky, it's not right you sleeping on the floor. The first time was different, you were frozen and near the fire was the best place for you, but now... I'll sleep here, you can take the bed, it's only right.' She looked up at him. When she spoke, though her voice was still soft, it betrayed a certain firmness of resolve that would stand no argument. 'No Ron, you've done enough, I'm perfectly comfortable here near the fire. I won't put you out of your bed.' Her expression confirmed the statement. Ron smiled down at her, he knew when to give up, 'Well, wouldn't one of the sofas be more comfortable?' She smiled, 'I like it here.'

'Goodnight then, I bet we'll sort it out tomorrow.'

On impulse Vicky reached up, caught his sweatshirt and tugged, making him bend down. She kissed him on the cheek, 'Thank you.' Then letting go she turned over quickly. Ron blinked in surprise and slowly walked off to the bedroom. He lay awake for a long time.

Some time later, Vicky heard a puppy crying, it scratched and whimpered. She felt compelled to get up, rubbed the sleep from her eyes and crossed the room to the hall. Glancing over her shoulder at the bedroom door no light showed under it. All was quiet except the whimpering of the puppy.

Vicky walked to the front door, reaching out placed her hand on the lock. As she slowly unlocked it, something made her hesitate. The whimpering persisted Vicky opened the front door slowly and gasped.

She assumed there would probably be a hall. What actually greeted her was a flight of stone steps, damp and cold, leading down and disappearing into blackness. She felt about on the wall and found a light switch. A small dim bulb lit the steps, in the shadows at the bottom there appeared to be another door. The whimpering grew louder. Vicky began to descend the steps reluctantly, but felt compelled to discover the source of the sound.

Reaching the foot of the steps she grasped the handle of the door, which her conscious mind attempted to open, but her subconscious refused to allow it. The conflict escalated rapidly, the subconscious part of her was screaming 'No!' But she must! No! But she must! The voice inside her screamed, 'Don't open it!' Finally, the equal and opposing forces became unbearable, she screamed.

Suddenly, a face only inches from hers was saying something. Wet with sweat, her heart pounding, she fought to comprehend what the voice was saying.

'Vicky... Vicky, Vicky... it's a dream, a dream, Vicky. It's only a dream.' She held onto Ron's arm and began to breathe easily. 'Yes... Yes, a dream. Just a dream.' She sank back on to the cushions, 'A dream, just a dream,' she murmured as she closed her eyes and ran a damp hand over her forehead. Her heart slowed and her breathing became more natural. Ron sat by her and gently held her free hand. 'You frightened the life out of me, that scream!' She nodded, 'There was a puppy whimpering, crying. I had to help it, but it was behind a door and I knew I didn't want to open it. There's something terrible behind that door waiting for me.' He nodded gravely then smiled to reassure her, 'Well, you're safe now, try and get some sleep.' Before he could stop himself, he stroked her forehead. Vicky smiled weakly, 'My mother used to do that, I can just remember it.'

'Will you be okay?'

She nodded.

'Alright, get some rest. Good night.' He stood up and returned to bed himself.

Soon, Vicky was asleep, the rest of the night passed without incident.

PART ONE
CHAPTER 3
TUESDAY MORNING EARLY

Vicky woke to the smell of coffee and toast. All thoughts of the dream were gone. Ron stood at the kitchen door, 'Good morning, Vicky,' he smiled. 'Good morning, Ron,' she smiled. They both burst out laughing. It was totally ludicrous the way they had fallen into this, ever so normal routine. 'Come on, Fin,' Vicky looked around, 'Fin?'

'Finbar... him!' Ron pointed at the cat. Vicky laughed, 'Oh, is that his name? He doesn't come out from under the TV much.'

'Oh, he does usually. The TV is his special gloomy sulk place, he's not been very happy lately.'

'Why?'

Ron shrugged, 'Who knows what goes on inside his head... daft as a brush.'

Finbar stared at his spot by the fire, then through the open kitchen door at his food bowl. He hesitated; the food bowl won.

'There's toast and coffee in here if you fancy some.' Ron nodded in the direction of the kitchen behind him.

'Yes please.'

After breakfast, Vicky got dressed. Ron explained he had to go out to see a few people. Vicky asked if she could tag along and Ron was pleased to have the company. He offered to take her to the shops first, as she only had the clothes she stood up in. At first, she objected saying that he had done enough. Ron insisted, 'It's only a loan, one friend to another. You'd do the same for me.'

In the end, she gave in. Secretly, Ron found it a pleasure to look after someone. He had friends that liked him but 'like' wasn't the same as 'need'. Need made him feel valued.

The optimistic mood was ruined however, when Vicky fetched her coat from the bathroom where it hung facing the wall over the radiator, 'Ron!' Her voice was a horrified whisper, he stopped searching for his car keys and look up quickly. She held out her coat and showed him the faint red stain, lowering her eyes and studying it closely, 'It looks like blood, do you think it's blood?'

'I saw it… I don't know, it could be anything.'

She stood frowning at the stain trying to remember but it was useless.

'Come on let's go, perhaps by tonight we'll have some answers.'

She realised he was trying to be bright to cheer her up, so making up her mind to be optimistic she pursed her lips and nodded, 'Yes, we won't get anywhere standing about here, you're right, let's get going.'

Outside, Ron pointed to his car 'Your chariot awaits, ma'am.' He gestured at a big grey car and added a little defensively, 'I've had it a long time… mechanically, it's really quite sound, not bad at all, 'specially when you think how old she is.' Vicky stared at the car, 'This is yours?' 'Yup!' Ron ran his hand gently over the wing, 'Now the writing is going so well, I'm going to get her sprayed up like new, I think some sort of baby blue you know, fifties pastel, perhaps even get some of the metalwork re-chromed.' Vicky caught the dreamy look in his eye, 'I don't know much about cars but even under all the dirt it looks like a classic.' Ron beamed, 'Oh, it's a classic alright, it's a '57 Chevrolet Bel-Air.' They both climbed in, Ron smiled at her, 'I had to kill a few people for this car you know?' Vicky looked at him sharply. Seeing her face he quickly explained, 'In my books…' he laughed, 'Max took care of some bad guys. I think this car cost me about five chapters' worth.' Vicky laughed and relaxed then tilted her head thoughtfully, 'I think baby blue would suit it.' He smiled, 'Mm.'

Although 'mechanically quite sound', the car pretended it didn't want to start. Ron banged the dashboard and feathered the accelerator in a way that appealed to the engine, the big 265-cubic-inch motor roared into life. 'Loose wire… not a problem really.' Vicky nodded and tried to keep a straight face as he gave an embarrassed cough and selected 'Drive'. The heavy car pulled away. She was genuinely impressed 'It's smooth isn't it?'

'The automatic transmission's called a "Power Glide",' glancing at her he smiled, 'isn't that a beautiful name…? "Power Glide". I really think they built things better in the fifties.'

It was a short drive to the heart of town. Ron parked and the two walked to a cash machine. He withdrew some money and gave a share to Vicky. 'You'll need it to get a change of clothes and some bits 'n' pieces,' he laughed, 'I know a woman can't survive in a bathroom with just a toothbrush and soap.' His face changed as if a sad thought crossed his mind.

'What is it?'

He shook his head. 'Nothing… nothing. Really, I'm okay. Come on, you hit the shops.'

'I'll pay you back, I won't forget this,' she touched his arm and stopped him, 'I mean it, this is a loan.'

He waved his hand, 'Come on.'

She stood her ground so he was forced to walk back. She wasn't smiling, 'I'm serious, you're very kind but this is a loan, agreed?' He realised in his eagerness to help he was hurting her self-respect and making her feel uncomfortable. He matched her serious expression, 'Look, I'm very pleased to help, I can easily afford it and I fully understand you'll pay me back every penny.' She looked into his eyes content he was serious smiled and nodded, 'Thank you.'

Vicky shopped very sensibly, feeling happier spending, now it was understood it was ultimately her money. Jeans three for two, jumpers colours various, lingerie and pyjamas. Ron suggested shoes as her court shoes were not very practical for winter streets, so were replaced by ankle boots. Her biggest purchase was a full length quilted coat that Ron said was essential as the weather was viciously cold. Arguing seemed pointless as she kept shivering.

'Everything's been very practical.' Ron observed.

'Yes.' She agreed.

'Why don't you treat yourself to something pretty? I think you deserve it you've had a rough time lately. I meant it's up to you, you're paying me back so it's your money really.' She considered then smiled, 'One dress!'

'Good.'

After buying the clothes, she tried to give the remaining money back to him but he insisted it was spent on toiletries. It made him smile to see the big bag of perfumes and potions she described as 'the bare essentials'. The only purchase Ron made was a big box of cakes. He explained he always treated the theatre staff if he visited so after the shops, it was off to the theatre for a meeting with the producer, Johnny Mitchell. Vicky was introduced as 'a good friend'. Johnny nodded politely but was far too enthusiastic about the possibility of taking the play from the suburbs to a big London theatre to pay her much attention. He explained that the play was pulling big audiences and had begun to get a cult following. If it took off in one of the top theatres there could be lots of spin-offs, real money-earners like interviews, promotional tee shirts, badges, bags. He wanted Ron to meet a man that was, as he put it, 'a big name up West'. He also wanted Ron to meet a man who was also apparently 'big in advertising'. Ron nodded and glanced at Vicky. A couple of weeks ago, he would have been ecstatic that his very first play was doing so well and people were interested; now, although very pleased, he wanted to be alone with Vicky more than he wanted to talk to 'big people'.

In the end, he agreed to meet these people on Friday, and shook hands with the producer who assured him that 'this was going to be big!'

Ron chatted with some of the stage crew and presented the box of cakes. He introduced Vicky enthusiastically to everyone. She was pleased to note that Ron was popular with the backstage people; it wasn't only because he had a winner and that meant work, they seemed to like him personally. He took Vicky over to meet Tom Anderson who was responsible for the special effects, explaining how Tom had done a lot of film and TV work. Vicky shook hands. Tom was evidently a whiz with electronics and was bursting to show Ron some new toy.

As Ron and Tom talked, Vicky drifted away. She caught the eye of Jane Flutter, the make-up lady, who bustled over always eager to chat. Vicky had taken an instant liking to Jane, whom she thought an odd little package, painfully thin and pale but seemed to almost overflow with energy. Her white face accentuated the copper colour of her wildly curly hair. She peered at Vicky through large, round, red spectacles, 'Hello again, is Ron still dragging you around? Tut! He's a love though isn't he? We all like Ron, he's so... normal. You get a lot of playwrights, oh, they're so loud and show-offey and if something isn't right, they fly into a rage. Ron's not like that, he'll quietly try to help. It's funny the way he does it, he doesn't order people about, but he still takes over. In a gentle way, saying things like "Maybe we should change this?" or "Do you think that would work better?" He has a natural way with people. They say this is his first play; if anyone had the right to be nervous, he does, but no, that's not him. It's unusual for the writer to be so closely involved, but no-one minds because he makes good changes and that makes us all look better; the director, actors, crew, everyone! He's a diamond.' Jane suddenly looked at Vicky, 'Oh er, in a professional way, of course.' Vicky smiled at Jane, 'It's great that he's got such a good team for his first play.' Jane looked relieved, 'Yes.'

Ron waved at Vicky, she glanced at Jane, 'Oh, it looks like we're off, good-bye Jane, it was lovely to meet you.' Jane smiled and waved, 'Bye!'

Back in the car, Ron announced, 'I've got to pop into *The Blue Parrot* to see Shades, then we'll have a bite to eat, okay?'

Vicky nodded, 'Sounds good. Who's Shades? And what is *The Blue Parrot*?'

Ron laughed, 'I met Shades about five years ago,' he glanced at her, 'I... was conducting research for a book and I found *The Blue Parrot*. It's a sort of club, three bars, dance floor, but it's old. You can feel the history, it's been lots of things, theatre, cinema, something about the place, ideas seem to flow and Shades is a real character, I think he models himself on a mixture of Humphrey Bogart, Edward G Robinson and Al Capone. His brother Tony is just the same. They both own *The Blue Parrot*, they're fascinated with crime and gangster films, all old films really. Ha, even the place is named after a bar in *Casablanca*.'

Vicky frowned, 'I thought that was called *Rick's Café America*?'

'No, I didn't say *the* bar, I said *a* bar, there was another one in the film. Don't even bother to argue with Big Tony and Shades, because no one has seen the film more times than them. Unfortunately, reality has crept into the fantasy in that *The Blue Parrot* has become the focal point for all the local hoods and criminals. Shades and his brother Big Tony – that's what he likes to be called – love it. They actively encourage it. They were over the moon last year when someone got shot outside.' Vicky frowned. Ron added quickly, 'Oh, nobody died, just lost a toe and of course Tony and Shades weren't involved. In fact, they never get involved with anything illegal. People think they are and of course, they don't deny it. But I know they're not. Shades and I are pretty good friends and I see the other side of them, so I know. *The Blue Parrot* is a funny place, you couldn't set out to create it in the way it is, it's just evolved. The weekends are different again, the edgy reputation has attracted the young party faction, the place is jumping on a Saturday night.'

'How does Shades help you with your books exactly?'

'Well, if I need a rough, evil character to pit Max against in a story, remember I told you Max was the name of the hero I invented?' Vicky nodded. 'Well, I talk to Shades. He never names names but he loves to talk about the different characters that come into *The Blue Parrot* and I get inspiration. I pick different aspects and make composites or sometimes, the ideas go off in a totally new direction, triggered by something Shades has said. His brother is a fantastic character too, they're very different in a lot of ways. Tony is erm… a little darker.' Vicky shook her head, 'Wow, some research source! That's the secret you said I'd find out today?' He smiled and nodded.

'Is Shades his real name?'

Ron thought, then after a moment, 'It's the only one I've ever heard anyone call him. I think he got the name because he always wore dark glasses, and even though he doesn't wear them now, the name stuck.' Ron laughed. Vicky put her head on one side and frowned, 'What?' Ron shook his head. 'Nothing.' Vicky smiled 'Come on, what is it?'

'Look, if I tell you, you have to swear not to say a word, okay?' She crossed her heart quickly and smiled, 'Swear!'

'One day, Shades was walking up the road to *The Blue Parrot*. I was coming the other way. Shades was wearing his dark suit and even darker shades and...' Vicky nodded 'Yes, and...?'

'And he fell over a bit of uneven paving!'

'Is that all?'

'Tripping over is nothing to you and me but to Shades, image is everything. Can you see Bogart falling over as he walked away from Ingrid Bergman?'

'Suppose not.'

'Well, there you are. Wait till you meet him, he's quite an experience.' Ron smiled, then more seriously, added, 'He tends to know what's happening locally.' Vicky looked sharply at him, 'Do you think Shades may know something that could help me?' Ron shrugged, 'I don't know but it's better than going in to a police station and saying, 'Hey, is there anything happening you think I might be involved in?' As soon as he said it, he wished he hadn't. 'Look, I didn't mean it to come out quite that bluntly.'

'It's alright Ron, I know, it's a strange situation.' She squeezed his arm; Ron felt a little better, 'Oh, I forgot, there's something about Big Tony I should tell you. If he's there, watch out for his shirt.' Vicky was puzzled, 'His shirt?' Ron smiled as he explained, 'Tony doesn't even know he does it, but it's possible to know what mood he's in by the colour of his shirt.

41

If he's in a good mood, he'll wear dark yellow or white. If he's low, he goes for blue, or grey. Remember, if it's a marooney reddy colour, stay out of his way.'

'Oh you're making me nervous, is there anything else about them I should know?' Ron considered then added, 'Yes, if Shades says something that seems odd, it's because he likes to throw lines from old movies into the conversation. Get's a kick out of it if you spot it and can guess the film. But don't be nervous of them they really are the good guys.'

Not long after, Ron drove into the small yard behind *The Blue Parrot* that served as a car park. 'This is really private but they don't mind me. That's Shades' car, no sign of Tony's.'

The yard was big enough for about four cars. The building had doors at ground level leading into the back of the club for the staff and two large fire escape doors. The steps of a metal fire escape rose up to a metal balcony on the second floor. Apart from a wooden lock-up large enough for a car the yard was bare.

He parked. They got out and walked from the yard around to the street entrance. The front of the building sported wide steps like a cinema, leading up to double doors. Something prehistoric stood at the doors, in an evening suit smoking a cigarette. Vicky whispered in Ron's ear, 'I hope it's been fed!' He squeezed her hand, 'Shhhhh, it... I mean, he'll hear you.' He nodded at 'Big Foot' as they walked in. The bouncer didn't acknowledge him it was a management directive to glare at the customers, smiling was frowned upon. This was *The Blue Parrot* after all.

The lunchtime crowd were in. The club's powerful sound system was tuned to local radio and although the volume was set low Ron heard the familiar jingle of '194 Capital Radio coming to you from the rocking tower in Euston'. Chris Tarrant introduced the next record and a well known Christmas song drifted softly across the club against a background of murmuring from people grouped around small tables. The place was dimly lit. Vicky looked about with interest, it was bigger inside than she had expected. It had a New York loft style but scaled up to monstrous proportions. The walls were richly coloured bare brick, girders and bolts exposed here and there glinted gunmetal grey in the subdued light. Despite the modern additions, Vicky understood what Ron meant by its atmosphere, any creative or sensitive soul entering its embrace could not fail to notice the calm depth of history. The fabric of the building was old and therefore had witnessed many things in its long life.

They stood at the top of some broad steps leading down to a wide expanse of floor, a beautiful hardwood herringbone pattern, crowded with tables. There was a bar to the right and a bar to the left, both of which were raised up from the main floor area. In front of both bars were more tables. Curving around the raised seating area was a shiny brass rail. Scattered amongst the tables were great plant tubs containing greenery, a few even had enormous fake palms that rose up toward the extremely high ceiling. Lights set low in the tubs shone up illuminating the towering metal foliage. The lofty heavens were a playground for Victorian girders, ornate and stylish. A sophisticated lighting system weaved its way among them, resting on weekdays, their full brilliance and energy unleashed at the weekend disco nights. Some distance ahead beyond the low tables was a clear piece of floor, used for dancing at the weekends. A small stage jutted out from the wall. High above that, dominating the rear wall was a huge blue neon sign that simply read *The Blue Parrot*. In each corner of the massive room exit signs glowed dimly above the fire doors. Between one of these doors and the edge of the stage stood an enormous Christmas tree in a giant tub, beautifully decorated and lit with richly coloured lights.

Vicky took it all in and smiled as she noticed that instead of the traditional star or fairy, the decorator had opted for a blue parrot to top off their masterpiece. She began to move toward one of the bars. Ron stopped her and pointed to a wrought iron staircase she hadn't noticed before as it was tucked away to the right. 'We'll probably find Shades in the upstairs bar if he's not up in the flat on the second floor.' Vicky followed Ron to the stairs and up to the bar that was directly above where they had been standing, hence the fact she hadn't noticed it from the top of the entrance steps.

In a shadowy corner on the ground floor, a small group was having an unfriendly game of cards. One member watched with sharp attention as Vicky and Ron ascended the metal stairs. The other players were impatient, 'Come on Micky, it's your call, are you in or out?' Micky's hard little blue eyes glanced again at his cards, the best hand he'd had in a long time. In a quick movement he folded the fan of cards and slapped it facedown on the table, 'Out.' The

44

other players lost interest in him and continued with their game. When the others weren't looking, he glanced up at the bar now and then to watch Ron and Vicky.

At the top of the stairs Vicky could see a bar, it had a large blue wooden parrot hanging above it. Behind the bar was a door marked 'Private'. In front were a number of tables with people seated, they glanced at them then continued their conversations. A man seated at the bar turned and watched them carefully. Ron whispered in Vicky's ear, 'Shades.' As they approached, Vicky took the opportunity to examine the famous research source. He was wiry with short black hair well defined features and quick brown eyes. He wore a black suit, white shirt open at the neck with a loosened black tie. They sat at the corner of the bar.

Without looking at Vicky, Shades asked, 'Who's your friend?' Vicky, who believed it was more polite to be spoken to than about, narrowed her eyes and was about to say something when Ron said, 'She's okay, she's with me.' Shades nodded slowly and turned his attention to Vicky, 'Well alright then, if Ron says you're okay, then you probably are, a man like me can't take chances... he has to be...' he paused for dramatic effect, 'careful.' Ron suppressed a smile, he knew Shades was dialling it up for Vicky's benefit, let him have his fun, 'I told her that.' To back up Ron, Vicky nodded. Shades looked pleased, 'Drink?' Both said yes. 'Jim!' Shades called the barman and they ordered drinks.

Ron made conversation, 'This is the famous Shades, co-owner of *The Blue Parrot*, close friend and invaluable source of book material. Doors are open to him that I couldn't even find.' Shades puffed up a little, 'I get around,' he said proudly. Ron overdid it by adding, 'That's right, this man can tell you exactly what's happening at any time.' He sat back and smiled. Shades narrowed his eyes and looked at him carefully then after a sideways glance at Vicky, 'You wouldn't be trying to find out something in your ever so subtle way, would you, Ron?' Ron smiled and shook his head, Shades could sense a mile off that this wasn't a social visit. Ron dropped the playful banter, 'The truth is my friend here may be in trouble. I wanted to know if you had heard anything that involved someone called Vicky Blaine... or in fact, anything that happened on Saturday night or early Sunday morning.' Shades looked quickly at Vicky, 'Vicky Blaine?' His face relaxed into a grin. Vicky was suddenly attentive, 'Does it mean anything to you?'

'No... good name though,' after a moments thought, 'probably suit a hero more than a heroine.... we'll see.' Ron and Vicky waited patiently. Shades continued, *The Blue Parrot* is a funny place and I hear all kinds o' stuff, but I haven't heard the name Vicky Blaine mentioned. As to Saturday night, as far as I know, things were quiet.' Ron pressed it, 'There's been nothing unusual?'

'I suppose that all depends on what you're used to. I had a representative from a certain organisation in here yesterday, with a strong Irish accent. Someone had pointed him in my direction. He said we had a reputation for being well connected, was it true and did it extend to guns.' Shocked, Ron sat back, 'IRA?' he whispered.

'Yeah, an' forget where you heard it, that goes for both of you.' He stared at Vicky who instinctively pulled away a little. Swiftly, Ron changed the subject, 'Can we have a talk later this week? I'm working on a lot of things at the moment and I want to tie a few of them up so I can concentrate full time on a new play.' Shades nodded. 'What do you need?'

'One of the stories I'm working on is about a guy whose brother gets killed by the Mafia and so the guy decides to get even by conning the Mafia out of thousands of pounds.' Shades smiled, 'Like it! And you need my help to create some of the Mafia characters, yes?'

'That's it, I need to bounce some ideas off someone who understands.' Shades nodded, 'Sure, I'll help. Come to 'The Parrot' late tomorrow night, we'll talk. Oh, by the way, Big Tony just got round to reading your last book, he said it was… okay.' Ron smiled, 'Oh, that's praise from Tony, say hi for me.' Shades slid off the bar stool to shake hands. Vicky noticed he wasn't a lot taller than her.

'And if you hear anything, Shades…'

'Yeah, yeah, yeah, sure, I got your number.' Then, glancing at Vicky, 'Could this be the start….?' Ron cut him off, 'Shut up.' Shades chuckled and turned back to the bar.

Downstairs, Micky had seen enough. Standing quickly he shrugged into a thick long wool coat, turned up the collar, put his head down and made a quick exit.

Outside in the car, Vicky put on a false voice, 'If Ron says you're okay, you probably are,' she laughed, 'is he real?' Ron grinned, 'He's okay, most of it is a complete act, he has a really dry sense of humour. He laid it on extra heavy for your benefit. He does know what's happening around here though and believe it or not, helps me with some of the characters in my stories. Of course, I strip out the corny clichés but he is helpful when I'm bouncing ideas around. He's one of my biggest fans.

'Why did you tell him to shut up? And why did he laugh as we were leaving?'

'He knew that I knew what he was going to say.'

Vicky raised her eyebrows questioningly. Ron shifted uncomfortably, 'He was going to do the *Casablanca* quote "Is this the start of"....' Smiling, Vicky finished, '...a beautiful friendship.'

'Mm. Hey! You wait till you meet his brother, Big Tony.'

'What's he like? You said earlier he was a bit dark.'

'Well, a little older, much bigger and like all clever people listens more than he talks. Doesn't have Shades' sense of humour but shares his interest in old movies. I'm always interested in characters, Tony is fascinating, you'll understand when you meet him.'

'Is that all they're interested in, old movies?'

'Virtually, except among other interests of course Tony has *The Grey Lady*'.

'*The Grey Lady*?'

'Yes, it's his boat, he's nuts about it. Goes careering up and down the river. I think he got interested in boats years ago when he saw Bogart in *The African Queen*. Bogart liked boats for real you know, at least that's what they both tell me and they're the experts.'

Micky had followed them around to the yard behind *The Blue Parrot* in his car and was watching the gate in his rear view mirror. The unfortunate mirror also had to reflect Micky's pockmarked weasel-like face with its short brown, slightly greasy hair and sharp features. Suddenly, the Chevrolet pulled out of the yard through the gate. The mirror was treated to Micky's smile, the distinctive '57 Chevrolet would be easy to follow.

They picked up some sandwiches and parked. As they ate them in the car, Ron explained his plan, 'Look, it's like this, you couldn't have run very far that night. If we start at my flat and drive in widening circles, you may remember something. I read somewhere that visual recognition is very powerful, so just sit back, relax, look at the streets, and if something seems familiar, tell me to stop, okay?' Vicky ate her last piece of sandwich, dusted the crumbs off her hands and nodded, 'Mm hum… okay.'
'Right let's give it a try.' He started the car and they pulled away.

Unnoticed, Micky's dark car followed. He didn't want Vicky to recognise him so kept well back. The slow moving Chevrolet was easy to follow so he wasn't overly concerned when two cars dropped in front of him. His plan was to locate where they were staying and report back.
Ron weaved carefully through the London streets, Micky had them clearly in his sights. Suddenly a traffic policeman stepped off the kerb raising his hand.

Ron and the following car had just passed, the car in front of Micky stopped.

Vicky and Ron would never know the great debt they owed to a certain Reggie Diamond, much-loved husband and father, highly-respected and sorely missed London tailor. Family, colleagues and indeed even some long-standing customers spared little to give Mr Diamond a funeral befitting the great man.

Micky clenched his teeth and gripped the steering wheel with equal force as he was compelled to watch the Chevrolet disappear from view. He sat experiencing both horror and frustration as the long, long stately funeral cortège slipped mind-numbingly slowly from the side road to join the main thorough-fair. He had lost them for sure, it was also certain he would keep this to himself. To admit he couldn't find her was bad enough, to admit he'd found and lost her could be dangerous, possibly suicidal, given his boss' temperament. Micky's boss wasn't known for his forgiving nature, quite the opposite.

They drove around for the whole afternoon. Vicky looked at the streets full of coloured lights and cheerful Christmas decorations and concentrated hard but nothing came to her. By the end of the afternoon the bright lights of London and the sound of cheerful Christmas music drifting from shops and stalls had done little to lift her spirits. Ron decided not to push it. In the back of his mind was the thought, she doesn't want to remember and that's a bad sign. Whatever it is, it's terrible and part of her doesn't want to cope with it. When she remembers, it will be because it's time. Best not force it.

'Okay, we may have more luck tomorrow. I've got some other ideas, but we'll give it a rest for today, alright?'

She was obviously disappointed, 'Ron, I do want to know, really I do. I just can't remember. This not knowing is driving me mad. What if I am mad? What if I killed someone, what if I'm a murderer?' Ron managed to slide an arm around her shoulder. 'Vicky, come on, you're not a murderer. Look, I don't know what this is all about, but I'm with you, you're not alone.' He gave her a reassuring squeeze, she nodded and moved closer to him, letting her head fall onto his shoulder.

She closed her tired eyes, 'Thanks, Ron.' He felt glad she had moved closer, the way she put her head on his shoulder pleased him. He glanced at her, he could smell her hair and feel her warm body. He had made himself forget how wonderful all the simple things that having a woman close to you brought. It had been so long.

Vicky was doing some thinking of her own, why did she feel so comfortable with this man? She was naturally wary of strangers and did not give her trust easily, this was a surprise, out of character. She lifted her head and regarded him thoughtfully, 'Ron?' He glanced at her, 'Yes?'

'I don't know you, do I? I mean, we haven't met before have we?'

'No' he paused, then, 'Why?'

'I feel comfortable with you like we've been friends for a long time, I don't normally...' She stopped, unsure of how to convey so many complex thoughts in simple words. It was unnecessary however, for Ron had had similar thoughts, 'I know, it feels normal and natural but strange at the same time.'

'Mm.'

They arrived home at dusk. Vicky cheered up a little when Ron suggested she forget all about it for now and try on some of the new clothes. She hurried off to the bathroom to change. Ron sat down and opened some of his mail. He looked up as Vicky came out of the bathroom. She had applied a little make-up and was wearing the blue dress. 'What do you think?' She did a twirl.

'You look lovely.' Ron said it before he could stop himself. He quickly shut his mouth and swallowed, then began to busy himself with his mail again.

Vicky watched him for a moment and felt surprisingly close to this quiet, shy man, not just because he was kind, but because they had, in the short time she'd known him, become good friends. When this was over she didn't want to lose touch, perhaps....

Vicky walked into the kitchen and surveyed the rows of tins in the cupboard with no labels, 'Do you want me to start dinner? Why haven't they got any labels?'

'Oh, don't use those.' Ron jumped up and stood at the kitchen door looking embarrassed then mumbled something.

'What?'

He mumbled again. This time Vicky caught something about 'surprise'. She smiled, 'Come on what's the mystery?' He became a little sulky, 'Well, if you must know, when I lived with someone, she used to make dinner because I worked longer hours than her. She would keep what it was as a surprise. Now I live on my own, I sort of... miss the surprise, so I... so I...' Vicky finished for him, 'So you pulled some of the labels off.'

'I only did it for a joke, I know they're all different soups, I've been on my own a long time,' He offered as if solitude was a valid reason for odd behaviour, 'Sometimes when I'm with friends, they say 'I don't know what I'm going to have for dinner,' then I say 'neither do I' and everyone in the know laughs.' Vicky smiled and shook her head, 'You're quite mad you know?' Noticing his embarrassment instinctively she gave him a brief hug, it had been unexpected for them both. Ron let go first and looked more uncomfortable than ever, which made Vicky feel awkward too.

'I er... I got some good news in the post.' He waved a letter at her.

She brightened, 'Yes?'

'Yes, it's from the company who markets my games. I sent them one ages ago. At the time they didn't think it was right but now they say they want to launch it. I think, what with that and the possibility of the play going to one of the big theatres, we should celebrate. What do you think?' Vicky was enthusiastic, 'Okay, what did you have in mind?'

'What about dinner somewhere flashy? You can show off your new dress.' Vicky spoke without thinking, '*Nick's* is good.' She stopped and looked shocked. Ron was quick, 'What do you remember about *Nick's*?' Immediately, she looked upset, 'Nothing!' She sounded frightened. Ron downplayed it, 'Okay, forget it, don't force it, you'll remember when you're ready.' She remained troubled. Ron encouraged her, 'Come on, help me celebrate.' She smiled and took a breath as if pulling herself together, 'Alright Ron, this is your night, let's enjoy it.' He nodded, 'That's the idea. Oh…!' he frowned.

'What is it?'

'This close to Christmas, especially somewhere like *Nick's*, I doubt we'll get a table.' Vicky looked deflated, 'Yes, suppose so.'

Seeing her disappointment, 'Well, you never know.' He looked about, 'Where's my Filofax?' Ron tried the number…. engaged, he tried again…. success. Luckily, the call prior to his had cancelled a table for two, they just had time to get there. 'I'll change, but don't expect too much, my wardrobe's a little… er… basic!' He disappeared into the bedroom.

A few minutes later he emerged dressed in his best clothes; white shirt, blue paisley tie, jacket and trousers, given the right light the trousers even matched the jacket. In reality, Ron looked presentable, but to Vicky, he looked very, very smart. 'Now you do a twirl,' she urged. He did, she clapped, 'Very nice, so you have got something other than jeans and baggy sweatshirts.' He smiled sheepishly inside he was very pleased she liked his suit. 'I've never been what you call… smart.'

'Well, you look smart tonight.'

Finbar watched them go then turned around, faced the fire and began to doze.

Before Vicky and Ron had time to swap the South London streets for the Kent country lanes a large dark car passed. If Ron had happened to glance in his mirror he would have observed the car execute an extremely fast and dangerous u-turn, spoiling the good Christmas humour of more than one fellow motorist in the process. Micky, who was on the point of giving up, had been cruising the suburbs for hours. He had persevered, driven by the sure knowledge that his boss did not handle bad news well to the extent that Micky was terrified to deliver it. He was not going to lose them again.

Nick's was well known in the South East, a pleasant drive not far outside London down a maze of Kent country roads. At *Nick's*, Ron and Vicky ordered dinner.

Outside Micky had parked to the rear of the car park but from the shadows could comfortably observe the Chevrolet. He waited fifteen minutes then walked cautiously into the foyer and bar area. The diners were behind the double doors in the main dining room. The concierge stood at a little podium near the door checking reservations. He looked up as Micky entered but went back to his book as Micky ignored him and made for the payphone in the far corner. He lifted and pressed the receiver hard to his ear for privacy and dialled, 'It's Micky..., that's what I've been doing..., I've found her, picked her up at *The Blue Parrot*... no, not now, she had a conversation with one of the brothers and left with some guy... I don't know... at *Nick's*... yes, having dinner. I know how you want to handle her but what about the guy? Same, sure... lot of lonely roads from here back to town, okay.' Micky hung up and returned to his car to wait.

Meanwhile, in the warmth and light of the dining room Ron and Vicky were in good spirits. The opulent dining area was subtly lit, each table glowed with the added warmth of its own candle. In addition, the room was decorated beautifully for Christmas, predominantly with traditional evergreens and complimentary dark red glass baubles. Fairy lights also weaved their pretty way around the room. The overall effect was enchanting.

Vicky steered the conversation round to girlfriends, then casually asked if Ron had ever been married. He put down his fork and looked serious. Instantly she knew she should not have mentioned it and tried to change the subject, but Ron stopped her, 'It's alright, I want to tell you. Yes, I was married, we only met six months before we got married you just know when it's right.' She nodded, 'Mm.'

'Well, it was only a few months later, not quite a year even. It was almost Christmas,' he smiled humourlessly, 'like now. Jacquie was out picking up some last minute shopping. I would have done it on my way home but I was doing some overtime. At the time, I was working for a game design company before I went solo. Anyway, Jacqui was crossing the road, a car came round the corner...' Ron hesitated, he was obviously finding this painful.

'Ron, don't!' Vicky put her hand on his.

Talking about Jacqui while another woman held his hand didn't feel right. He pulled his hand back a little but she held on. He swallowed and continued, 'It wasn't anyone's fault. If I hadn't worked late, if she hadn't crossed the road when she did. If the road hadn't been icy... if, if, if.' He pulled himself together. 'That was five years ago now. It's time I got my life back. Vicky was looking at him with so much sympathy in her eyes, Ron glanced down at the table and carried on, 'that's how I met Shades and Big Tony. Er... when I told you I met Shades because I was researching a book and I spent a lot of time in *The Blue Parrot*, it wasn't totally true. It was where I met Shades but I wasn't there to do any research all that came later. I was there to drink. Actually, I drank quite a bit for a while I spent all my time at *The Blue Parrot*, thought it helped, I couldn't sleep you see, I desperately wanted to sleep. The nights were harder than the days and the days were unbearable... I er...' He risked another glance at her. She was listening intently her brown eyes shone surely it couldn't be tears? Why was he telling her all this? Why was it so easy to talk to her? He hesitated, 'Um... I... you have enough problems without me telling you all this.' She thought then said slowly, 'Ron... I feel you are paying me a great compliment telling me this. You don't usually talk about it do you?'

'No, not usually.'

'If you don't want to say any more it's okay, but if you do...'

Ron was still holding her hand, now he didn't want to let go. He ran his tongue nervously over his bottom lip then glanced about to make sure no one could hear, 'Not long after Jacqui died I did something I'm ashamed of,' he spoke very quietly, she waited for more, there was a long pause, 'I... stepped off the kerb a couple of times without looking... I did it on purpose.' 'Oh Ron,' She squeezed his hand, 'I'm so sorry.'

'I never told anyone,' he shuddered, the rest of the story came a little easier having told her the worst, 'funnily enough it was Shades who helped me. One night he came round the bar and said 'I think you've had enough'. I told him to… Well, let's just say I wasn't polite. People don't talk to Shades like that. He grabbed me and dragged me outside. I thought I was in for a going over, I didn't know Shades that well at the time. He threw me against the wall and told me to pull myself together. He said I wasn't the first guy in the world to be hurt, other people handled their grief and carried on. This drinking was a coward's way of committing suicide. Oh, he gave me a going over alright verbally. He went on and on, how I was letting Jacqui down. He'd heard me talking at the bar, honestly his words were like being slapped in the face. I've never heard him talk so much, not before or since. I'm still not sure why he decided to help me he didn't know me that well then. I think the clue was when he said I wasn't the first guy in the world to get hurt. Shades and his brother run deep for all their tough guy act and Shades' silly quotes you're never quite sure what either of them are really thinking.

That night was the turning point. Before then, my life could have either gone down the toilet or been good at the time I didn't much care. I became Shades' special project, the guy didn't leave me alone. I know he is a bit odd and uses corny lines but when I needed help he was there and I won't forget that.' Ron looked at his wine glass. Vicky was still holding his hand across the table, 'Is that why you helped me, because you understand what it's like to be desperate?' Ron nodded, 'Most people need a hand at some point in their lives, not everybody has someone. Shades was there for me and...' he shrugged.

'You were there for me.'

He looked shy, 'I looked out of the window on a stormy night, that's all.'

'Oh no, you did a lot more than that. Some people would have thought 'none of my business' and gone to bed.'

He looked slightly horrified, 'I couldn't do that.'

'I know, that's why I, that's why I feel so... grateful.'

They sat thinking their own thoughts for a moment neither said anything. Ron broke the spell, 'It's ironic, you trying desperately to piece together your past and me, maybe it would be better if I didn't remember so much.'

'You miss her a lot, don't you?'

'Yes, it would have been different if we had been together a long time. If we had rowed a bit, seen the bad side of each other but it was all so new. I know as a relationship develops, the first intensity of the thing dies down and although you still love each other, it's more... more real somehow. But when it's snatched away from you, before it's had a chance, when it's still at the beginning, you think maybe it would've been fantastic forever. Maybe, it was the most perfect thing, it's taken me a long time to come to understand that I was building it up in my mind. Jacqui was a very beautiful girl and we did love each other but given time everyone rows now and then. She would have been miserable at times or been unreasonable about something, or had an irritating habit. In fact all the normal things that happen to everyone. The curlers... the scruffy slippers... Am I

59

making sense? Human! Not on a pedestal, easier to get over if she hadn't seemed so perfect. Only now after nearly five years I can think sensibly about it. I know now I want to move on, it's time to live again, start my life over or if I'm not careful today may turn into tomorrow's regrets.'

After a moment's reflection, 'Oh look, I'm sorry Vicky, I'm rambling and you've got your own problems.'

'No, you're not rambling, I'm interested. It's good to express your feelings out loud, it helps you to get things straight in your mind, I understand what you mean. Sara thought Hammond was perfect...' Ron looked at her sharply, Vicky seemed surprised at her own statement. He encouraged her, 'Hammond?' Vicky continued but more slowly, 'The man's name was Hammond.'

Ron asked, 'The man who came to the office where you and Sara worked?' She nodded, 'I don't think she loved him in a healthy way, it was infatuation.' He stared at the tablecloth thoughtfully. Vicky suddenly looked distressed, 'Hey, look Ron, I wasn't suggesting that you were infatuated with Jacqui or anything. I just thought of Sara, you know, early days in a relationship.'

Ron waved his hand. 'No, no, I wasn't thinking of that.'

'Oh?'

'I was thinking, you remember everything clearly up to getting on the train. That was a year ago, and the only clue 'till now has been a nightmare that doesn't make sense, right?'

'Right.'

'Well then, the only thing you couldn't remember *before* catching the train was Sara's boyfriend's name. Now that has come back, I think this tells us two things. One, that you're beginning to remember and it's only a matter of time, and two, that Hammond is very mixed up in whatever happened to you when you got to London. I think that, because it's the only part of your life you can't remember before getting on the train, it's part of the thing you're trying to blot out. It's starting to come back, slowly I know, but it's a beginning,' he squeezed her hand, 'this is progress, we'll get there.'

They took their time enjoying each other's company, coffee and dessert. Finally, Ron paid the bill and they moved to the door. The headwaiter nodded at them on the way out, 'Goodnight Mr Moon, Miss Blaine.'

Outside, their breath was made visible by the chilly air and a light dusting of frost had covered the car park. Treading cautiously on the sparkly frozen tarmac they moved towards the car. Ice had formed great swirling patterns across the roof and bonnet. They climbed in quickly, Vicky was thankful Ron had talked her into buying the long puffy coat. He rubbed his hands and blew through them, 'God, it's cold, keep your fingers crossed.' He tried the starter. The motor slowly turned over in a deep lazy way, without much enthusiasm. As it seemed it was on its last turn, Ron thumped the dashboard and miraculously, it fired. The engine ticked over with a low burble. Ron shook his head and laughed. 'She's bloody good for her age you know.'

'Why do men always call cars 'she'?'

'I don't know, I suppose it's because you have to shower them with expensive presents and be nice to them.'

She frowned, 'Expensive presents?'

'Yes, parts for this old girl cost a fortune.' As he got out to scrape the windows, Vicky hit him and he laughed. After clearing the ice he jumped in and they pulled out of the car park.

Theirs was not the only car to leave. A dark car slid quietly from the shadows.

Ron loaded a cassette tape into the player and they cruised along at a steady thirty-five. He was in no hurry, the roads were frosty and there were a few winding lanes to negotiate before they reached the edge of town. Glancing in his mirror he smiled, 'Clear road behind, clear road ahead, that's what I like. Haven't got many vices, but I do love driving this old car.'

Vicky smiled, she felt good the meal had been wonderful. She let herself sink into the comfortable leather seat and stretched out her legs. The heater worked well and warm air played on her feet. Glancing at him, again she marvelled at the closeness of their friendship in such a short time, feeling she had known him forever. The cassette played softly and mixed with the deep purr of the engine, combined with the good meal they both felt relaxed, Ron especially had a feeling of lightness after confiding in Vicky. He had felt ashamed that he had chanced his life and after admitting it, somehow the burden had lifted.

They were still some distance from town, the road curved and twisted through the Kent countryside. Trees were close to the narrow road and above them an intricate network of frozen twigs formed a canopy. There was no moon, the way was lit only by their headlights.

The rear view mirror was totally dark. Suddenly, two pinpricks of light winked on, out of the darkness behind them something loomed up fast. Neither of them noticed until the road ahead was lit by the powerful beams of a car close behind. Ron squinted in the mirror and tutted. The road ahead curved to the right, then straightened. He murmured, 'Good. Perhaps this idiot will overtake.' The dark car had no intention of overtaking. As Ron watched in the mirror the car grew closer still. 'My God, I think he's going to…' There was a tremendous jolt, he fought frantically with the steering wheel as the car swerved and slid on to the rough verge. For a moment, it seemed as if they were going to collide with the high bank. Vicky screamed but Ron managed to hold it and they skidded back on to the road. Ron instinctively accelerated. Although the car was old, when asked the question, it responded by lurching forward. The engine note changed as the big car gathered momentum. Ron checked the mirror, the dark car had lost ground, caught by the surprising turn of speed. Their relief was brief, their pursuer was soon gaining. Concentrating on the road, Ron eased off for the next bend; he couldn't take it at speed. He glanced in the mirror the other car was still closing in. 'Hold on!' Desperately thinking if he took the next bend as fast as he dared, the pursuing car may not make it and if it did, the important thing was to keep some distance; it couldn't ram them if it couldn't catch them.

Ron held the wheel tightly and poured on the power. The heavy machine thundered toward the bend. He came off the power at the last second, hardly touching the brakes. He swung the car into the bend using the whole road, cutting across on to the wrong side. As he came out of it, wheels screaming, he felt the tyres lose grip. Letting it drift across the road to his side he gently tried to correct the skid. The car had lost just enough speed in the turn to hold the road. The rear twitched as he pressed the accelerator to the floor for the next straight stretch. Checking the mirror once more brought only disappointment. Unbelievably, the other car had made it round. He had been sure he would lose it on the bend.

Micky knew he was driving beyond his ability, his murderous desperation to announce success to his unforgiving boss drove him to take reckless chances.

Ron's car was fast but the other car was faster, it tore out of the darkness headlights blazing. 'Hold on, here he comes again!' The world shook and there was a scream of metal as the car slammed into them. Again, Ron had to fight to keep control. His car was punched forward, but not straight forward, at a slight angle, it was all he could do to keep it on the road. He swerved to the left then the right and once more managed to hold it. There was a deep growl from the Chevy's V8 engine as he squeezed the accelerator.

Both cars hurtled down the dark lane at just over eighty miles an hour. It was madness but obviously, the car behind wasn't trying to frighten them, it was trying to kill them.

Having rammed twice, Micky switched tactics and attempted to draw alongside.

Ron swung the car to the left then to the right in an attempt to prevent him succeeding. He knew the dark car wanted to draw alongside so it could be sure to run them off the road. The two machines lurched from one side of the road to the other. Ron's attention was caught by the headlights of an oncoming car, in that split second the dark car got partially alongside and slammed into the rear of the Chevrolet. The force of the impact threw the back of the car to the left causing them to swing across the road to the right and into the path of the oncoming car. For a moment their horrified faces were lit by the glare of its headlights.

Micky having hit Ron with such force, had gone into a skid. Ron, desperate to avoid a collision, yanked the wheel to the left, at the speed they were moving it was easy to over-steer. The oncoming car barely missed them and flashed past with the horn screaming. Miraculously, it also missed Micky, who although still travelling forward was spinning uncontrollably on the icy road. Because of Ron's over-steer they ran partially up the bank then slewed down to the road again, skidding across to the wrong side where he managed to correct the skid and drove on.

It was a fantastic piece of instinctive driving to stay in one piece. The new bend that faced them however, was impossible and there wasn't enough road to stop. The Chevy left the road. In front of them a white gate appeared to be hurtling toward them, lit by the headlights. Beyond the gate was blackness. The Chevy smashed through the gate, spinning wooden splinters were flung in all directions vanishing into the darkness as the car plunged into a black void. They were in a field the car travelled a good distance before finally stopping.

Breathing hard, he looked at Vicky, who was nearly as pale as he was, 'Are you alright?' She nodded but said nothing, obviously shaken. Feeling sick himself, he looked in the mirror, nothing but blackness.

Meanwhile Micky helpless to do anything about it had spun down the road incredibly missing everything. The spinning had slowed the forward momentum and finally Micky, still gripping desperately to the steering wheel had come to rest gently on the grassy verge facing the wrong way. He didn't waste a moment slamming the car into reverse and beginning a three-point turn.

Ron could dimly make out a rough track to the right, it did not appear too steep for the car from what he could see of it. Thinking it may be a track across the farmer's land perhaps leading to another main road somewhere out in all the darkness, Ron definitely did not want to go back the way they had come. He selected 'drive' and they began to crawl up the track. This was only made possible by the hard, frozen earth. Ron would have preferred to turn off the lights but it was so dark anything could be in front of them and to drive without lights could be more dangerous than the probability of being seen.

While Ron and Vicky negotiated the rising track, Micky had reached the shattered gate. There wasn't much doubt that the Chevy had entered the field. The dark car moved slowly through the gateposts, tyres scrunching over the remnants of the gate.

The Chevy's taillights were easily seen in the totally black field. Okay, so he couldn't make it look like an accident, who cares? They just had to die. The dark car surged toward its target.

Looking over his shoulder, Ron could see the other car's headlights, they had been pushed out of alignment by the shunting but still worked. Its beams bounced about as the car ran swiftly over the rough ground in an attempt to catch up. The going was getting steep, he had already shifted from 'Drive' to 'Low' and still the engine was beginning to labour again.

Vicky spoke for the first time since the chase began. 'Ron! Ron! It's getting closer, can't we go any faster?'

'It's too steep, this track is probably only used by tractors.'

'They're gaining on us... Oh God, Ron! I'm frightened.'

He squeezed the accelerator and the rear wheels whined as they lost traction. 'Ron, we're not going to make it!' The car slowed to a near halt and Ron fought an impulse to floor the accelerator. He knew this would do no good and the wheels would just dig in so he eased off the pedal. As he reduced the power the wheels regained traction and the big car lumbered on. Vicky looked back, the chase car was still gaining. In the headlights, Ron could see what appeared to be the top of the track, if only they could get there. Wisps of steam began to curl over the bonnet and a hissing sound could be heard. She turned to him in horror, 'The radiator! It must have been the gate!' He nodded then shouted at the car, 'Come on! Come on!' He thumped the steering wheel and shook it, his hands were sweating in spite of the cold night.

Vicky sat silently and looked straight ahead, she didn't want to look back again. She felt sick, her mouth dry, her body taut, one hand had a white knuckle grip on the door, while the other dug deep into the leather seat. She resisted an urge to leap out and run.

The car was barely moving, the temperature gauge warning light began to glow red, the engine had started to boil. She glanced sideways at Ron who was looking quickly from the rear mirror to the hilltop and down at the temperature gauge. He knew it might seize at any moment. With back wheels skidding and steam pouring from the radiator, Ron's Chevy slowly hauled itself over the crest of the hill.

He took a last look in the mirror as they went over the summit, the other car was close but no longer gaining, the Chevrolet had made the steep ascent slick with the spinning of its wheels. Vicky too was looking back as she felt the Chevy tip over the top. She released all the tension with a yell, 'Yeeessss, we did it. Ha ha!' She clapped her hands and glanced at Ron wondering why he was staring ahead and not cheering, then following his gaze realised why.

Falling away from them was an impossibly steep slope to what might be a road in the distance. The Chevrolet plunged down the hill. Vicky gripped the door with one hand and the dashboard with the other. Despite the seatbelt she was flung about as the car gathered speed. Ron had to concentrate to keep them travelling in a straight line, if they moved to the left or right there was a good chance of rolling.

Ahead, the slope seemed to vanish completely, there was no stopping or turning so they both tensed as the car left the ground. For a moment it was as if reality held its breath then a queasy falling sensation in the pit of the stomach before…. They landed with teeth-shattering force. There was a metallic bang as if something had been ripped off the car. The landing wasn't square and for a moment, it looked as it they were going to roll. The car swayed violently from side to side. Ron only just managed to pull it straight. Slipping and skidding they bounced down the rest of the hill.

Reaching the bottom they could clearly see a farm gate in the headlights, Ron drove for it. This time they stopped to open it. Vicky released her seatbelt, jumped out and fumbled with the catch, which seemed to take forever to open. Eventually, the gate swung wide on its hinges.

Vicky looked anxiously back up the hill as she got in. There was no sign of the other car maybe it would take it longer to get over, maybe it wouldn't make it at all. They weren't going to hang around to find out. Back on the road, Ron drove at speed, he noticed with relief that the temperature gauge had dropped out of the danger zone.

'Will we get back, is the car alright?'

He exhaled slowly, suddenly relieved, 'I think we'll make it. We are losing some water but the cold air makes the steam look worse. Now we're moving faster, the night air has taken it out of the red. The car's doesn't feel right, I think we've got a bit of damage to the rear suspension and judging by the noise the exhaust pipe is not as long as it was. Not a problem, really.' He looked at her and they both laughed as she leaned over and kissed him on the cheek, 'We got away!' He smiled, then with relish, 'Yes!'

To be safe, Ron opted for minor roads as he weaved his way back to town. It was two am when two tired people and an equally tired-looking car swung into the alley beside the flat and they hauled themselves out. He put his arm around her shoulder, it seemed the natural thing to do. As they walked around to the entrance he asked cheerfully, 'So! I hope you won't let our first date put you off coming out with me again.' She laughed as the tension of the last hour ebbed away, leaving only exhaustion.

They entered the flat and wearily hung their coats in the hall. Ron made a beeline for the drinks cupboard in the kitchen to pour two large brandies. They sat down opposite each other on the sofas.

'I think we need this!' She nodded, 'I think you deserve it, the way you handled the car.' He smiled, 'Before I was married, I was mad about cars and shared a rally car with a couple of friends, but even with all of us chipping in we couldn't afford to keep it up. I did drive in a couple of races though, nothing big but it was experience.'

'Well, it certainly paid off tonight.'

'We're being watched.' He nodded in the direction of the kitchen. Slowly, she turned to look, but instantly relaxed and laughed. Finbar was glaring at her. She turned to Ron, 'You scared the life out of me, you stupid sod,' and threw a cushion at him then looked at Finbar again. After a pause, 'Why do you think he's looking at me like that?' Ron shook his head, 'Finbar's always been odd, even for a cat.'

'Have you had him long?'

'Finbar?' Looking at the ceiling in thought Ron reflected, 'Jacqui got him as a kitten not long after we were married. After she died, of course he had to stay,' Ron suddenly laughed, 'he must be around five and a half – that's approaching middle age for a cat – you would think he'd be a bit more sensible at his age.' Vicky looked at Finbar's little face, 'Ah, leave him alone, he's alright poor thing, he thinks I've stolen his favourite spot near the fire, I suppose.'

'You didn't steal it exactly he gave it to you, it was Finbar who found you really.' Vicky, switched her attention to Ron, not convinced.

'He did, he hates storms, usually hides, but he wouldn't come away from the window and kept staring down into the alley.' She smiled at Finbar, 'He's my little hero.' She stood and stretched, her expression becoming serious, 'What do you think the chase was about? Why were they trying to kill us?'

'I don't want to think right now, I want to sleep, we'll talk in the morning.' He yawned, she nodded, 'I'm exhausted too.'

Vicky changed into her new soft warm flannelette pyjamas, covered in a tiny gold star pattern on a pastel blue background, tying the matching belt around her waist glad of the warmth and comfort. Re-entering the living room, she lay on the cushions by the fire and closed her eyes. Ron covered her with a blanket and lingered for a moment looking down at her. Vicky's eyes smarted with tiredness she shut them tight and murmured softly, 'Thank you for getting us back safely.' 'Goodnight Vicky.' Already her breathing was becoming deep. Ron smiled, yawned again and headed for his own bed.

As Ron lay down, he fully expected to follow Vicky and be asleep in moments, he felt so tired, as least his body did, his mind was another matter. Something wasn't right. He snorted, probably getting chased by a mysterious car hell bent on killing them was all it was, ha…. all! But no… no, that wasn't it. There was something else, something he had missed. What wasn't he seeing? What...? He muttered to himself, 'You're missing something… something important… what?' He thought, but the something would not come, it was just out of reach! Something…, something…, no. Perhaps if he slept on it in the morning his mind would be clear. He turned over and after a long time slipped into a light doze.

In Vicky's unconscious state, the compelling sound of a puppy crying echoed through her mind. She moved restlessly, Finbar was curious about the stranger who kept falling asleep on *his* rug and edged closer. She turned over mumbling, 'No, I don't want to.' Her arm flipped over as she turned and her hand nearly hit him, he jumped back and crept away.

Vicky found herself standing at the top of a flight of stone steps. The whimpering was coming from the shadows at the bottom. She fumbled for a light switch. Suddenly, the damp steps were illuminated and she could make out the heavy metal door at the bottom. Sweating and breathing quickly, she descended slowly into the gloom running a shaking hand along the rough wall to steady herself. At the bottom she stood facing the door feeling sick, her heart racing. She reached out with a damp quivering hand and gripped the door handle, cold sweat trickling down her back. There was something in the whimpering that compelled her to open the door, but Vicky knew that if she did, it would start something terrible that could not be stopped. With every nerve in her body screaming, she began to turn the handle. It moved very slowly, she must open the door, *she must*! Vicky also knew with every taught fibre of her shaking body what waited behind was monstrous.

The door opened and white light flashed through the chink, the raw tension was almost unbearable. She had enormous energy as if her body was tensing to run for its very life. Vicky threw the door wide and screamed both in the dream and reality.

For a moment, the surroundings were unfamiliar. Someone was beside her, it was Ron, 'Another dream?' Vicky nodded, 'Oh Ron…' she swallowed, 'it was… it was, like before… I got the door open this time, I just got a glimpse of what was inside before I woke up.'

Ron had his arm round her shoulder and kneeling down, he looked at her intently, 'Can you describe what you saw?'

She spoke slowly, the details were retreating fast into the shadows, 'Light… white light and there were four people standing around a puppy. It was wriggling about on the ground. I.. I.. I think it was dying.' She stared at him, 'What does it mean? Oh Ron, I'm going mad!' She began to cry so he held her, 'Come on.' He helped her to her feet.

Opening the bedroom door, with Vicky still clinging to his dressing gown, he guided her into the room. They both lay on the bed, Ron made comforting, 'Shh, shh, shh,' noises and gently stroked her hair. The sobbing gradually stopped. It was a cold night, he pulled up the quilt and put his arm around her shoulder. After a while, Vicky's breathing became regular and deep, she was asleep.

Ron lay in the dark, thinking. He had to think of something, he had to. He desperately wanted to help her. A thought struck him, would she leave when this was over? The idea of being alone again was disturbing. It wasn't until now he realised how lonely he'd been before Vicky came into his life. Instinctively he tightened his grip, she murmured something and moved closer. Had there really been something between them over the last couple of days? Or was he seeing what he wanted to see? He wasn't sure what he felt, but he knew he was getting close to this mystery woman in a way that would be hard to forget if she were to leave. He smiled to himself as he remembered how she had chatted at the restaurant. For a while she had been happy. When she smiled, it lit the room and her brown eyes danced, she was exciting to be near. It had been a good meal too... He inhaled sharply his eyes widened and he whispered, 'Yes of course, I remember!!' He relaxed, 'Now I can sleep, now I remember.' He lay back satisfied and was soon enjoying a deep dreamless sleep.

PART ONE
CHAPTER 4
WEDNESDAY MORNING

Vicky opened her eyes. Sunshine was pouring through the window and the room was warm and bright. She yawned and stretched then turned over. Ron wasn't there so she sat up for a moment and thought about the night before. She remembered the nightmare. The thought made her frown and shiver then recalling how Ron had comforted her, she smiled. The easy way they had fallen into this odd arrangement was really quite amazing. She shook her head slowly; this kind quiet man who had found her in the street and taken her in. Vicky wasn't sure what she felt for Ron but the attraction was strong. Getting out of bed, she called for him but there was no reply and there was a slight odd smell in the air. Vicky wandered from room to room and began to feel a little concerned. Suddenly, the front door opened, 'Hello! You had a bit of a rough night so I thought I'd let you sleep in.'

'I was a bit worried when I couldn't find you.'

'I've been out in the alley with the car. I phoned a friend of mine early this morning, who does a bit of welding,' he smiled, 'actually, that's an understatement, he does a lot of welding.'

'Is that what that funny smell is?'

'Yes, he's fixing up the car... bit of damage to the back end. He's doing a bit of a patch. He hasn't got the right stuff in his van so I told him to just make it safe for now and I'll get him to do a proper job later. He's a very good welder and doesn't like to do temporary fixes so he's moaning like hell but I haven't got the time for him to fuss over it. We have places to go.' He grinned.

'What's the secret?' But Ron continued grinning and waggled his finger at her teasingly, 'Ah, ah, ah... wait and see.' Noting her irritation made him happier and her more irritated. In every man the boy is just below the surface. He relented, 'I've got good news for you, I'll tell you all about it as soon as Dave's gone.'

Ron made three cups of hot steaming tea, 'I'm just going to take this down to Dave.' Vicky took her cup, 'I'll see you out there.' Ron paused and looked closely at her new pyjamas as if really seeing them for the first time.
'What?' she asked.

'That's a lovely blue.'

She smiled and sipped her tea, 'Do you think it suits me?' Ron appeared distracted, 'Suits you...? Oh.. er.. oh yes.' Vicky narrowed her eyes, 'You weren't thinking that at all, were you?'

'Oh yes..., well partly, I was thinking that blue would suit the car too.' 'The car.' She wasn't impressed. There was an uncomfortable pause, at least for Ron, 'I think your friend's tea's getting cold.'

'Ah, right, see you down there then.'

'Mm.'

Ron hurried out, Vicky shook her head, 'Honestly... suit the car? Men!' She turned and disappeared into the bathroom to wash and dress.

A few minutes later, Vicky in jeans, sweater and coat joined Ron who was leaning on the boot watching Dave work.

'Mind yer eyes.' Dave flicked his goggles down as Ron and Vicky looked away. Giant shadows danced on the alley wall as he welded the last plate on the car. 'Well, it's safe enough... don't look too pretty though. I didn't have the right stuff in the van, I've been doing some work down the docks,' Dave turned on Ron, 'you should take more care of this car Ron, its a classic.' Ron looked a little embarrassed and stared at his feet, 'I know,' he mumbled, then brightening up, added, 'tell you what Dave, as soon as I have time I think I'll spend some serious money on the old girl an' really fix her up. I think she deserves that, she saved our lives last night.'

'It was some kind of maniac you say?'

Ron nodded and glanced at Vicky, who remained silent. 'Yes, tried to run us off the road.' Dave looked thoughtful, so Ron added, 'Case of mistaken identity perhaps.'

'Doesn't seem likely, the Chevy's not exactly common.'

To prevent more questions Ron pointed down the car, 'Do you think we can get the dents straightened out in the front?'

'I was gonna ask ya,' Dave's voice rose an octave, ''ow did all that 'appen?' Ron answered with more mumbling, 'A gate.'

'A gate!' Dave stared at him, then like an adult addressing a child, 'Most people... you know, *normal*

77

people, people who care about classic cars, open gates before they go through them.' Ron was suitably repentant and gazed down at his feet so Dave, slightly appeased snapped, 'Right! Come on Ron, get down 'ere and 'ave a butchers at how I've sorted it. It's only temporary mind!'

'Dave, the ground's all wet.'

'Well it's not as wet as it was.' He turned to show Ron the back of his damp overalls and glared at him, daring him to refuse. With a barely audible sigh of accepting the inevitable, Ron dropped to the ground and wriggled under the car.

Dave looked at Vicky, ''E doesn't appreciate my artistry.' Vicky tried to look sympathetic and pursed her lips. Satisfied, Dave dived eagerly after him.

Vicky could only see two pairs of feet protruding from under the car. She put her hand to her mouth to stifle a giggle because she could hear Dave chatting enthusiastically, his sentences punctuated by Ron's 'Mm, lovely,' and 'Oh yes, really amazing.' On struggling out and up, Ron commented, 'You should think about signing work like that, Dave.' Dave's eyes grew distant as he considered this marvellous idea, Ron watched in fascination then turned to Vicky so Dave couldn't see his grin.

Without taking her eyes off Dave, Vicky hit Ron on the shoulder and hissed, 'Be nice.'

Dave shrugged, he'd mull the idea over later. He began to pack up, 'Oh well, you're safe and sound now.' After putting his own tools back in the van, he stooped to pick up the junk he had removed from the Chevy's boot. 'Bloody 'ell Ron, what've you got in 'ere? No wonder the old girl doesn't do much to the gallon with this lot in the boot.' Ron seized the other end of the large toolbox and helped Dave return it. 'There's not much room in the flat for tools, but you're right, I really must sort this boot out.' Dave straightened up, 'Yeah, I would. Right, now listen, I've welded up the exhaust but it won't last long, so don't blame me if it drops off in a few days. You need a new one. While you're at it, I'd stick a new radiator in too. I've patched the bottom pipe but it's a bit knocked about. I wish you'd let me do a proper job.'

'Sorry, Dave, no time. Now, will you join us for breakfast?'

'Ta, don't mind if I do. But hey, listen... don't tell anyone I patched it up, will ya? I got a reputation for doing excellent work, y'know.' Dave poked a grimy finger at him to emphasise the point. Ron nodded and smiled. 'Sure Dave, don't worry. Come on, I'm starving.' They all went up to the flat where Ron soon had bacon frying and coffee bubbling.

All three of them sat around the kitchen table and conversation flowed. Dave pulled Vicky's leg, 'It's about time Ron had someone to keep him in order. 'E's been left on 'is own too long.'

She looked at this scruffy little man in faded blue overalls. He grinned from ear to ear. His face was grimy and he wasn't exactly in the first spring of youth but his sharp blue eyes sparkled with mischief; Vicky liked Dave. 'Don't worry Dave, I'll keep him in order. He knows who's boss.' Ron smiled at Vicky. He liked the idea of someone being interested enough to keep him in order, this implied she had no plans to leave. He reached for the pot and went along with the joke, 'More coffee dear?' Vicky held up her cup 'Thank you dear.' Dave shook his head, 'It comes to us all in the end, your carefree days are over boy,' he grinned at Vicky, then, 'oh, 'ang on a minute,' he searched through his overall pockets and finally produced a business card, 'there you are.' He presented it to Vicky proudly, she examined it, *'You've Tried the Rest Now Try the Best, Dave London, Master Welder Tel: 317 7979'*. 'Thank you.' Vicky said politely. Dave beamed at her, 'If ever you need anything done, give us a bell, I'll give you a good rate, friend of Ron's an' all that,' nodding at the card, he continued, 'I came up with it meself, good innit?'

'Very catchy.'

''Course, by rights I could 'ave 'By Royal Appointment' on that y'know, with a crest an' everyfin'.'

Eyes sparkling, Vicky looked delighted, 'Don't tell me you've worked on the Queen's car?'

'Not the car no, but the garden fence so to speak.' He was warming to his subject, everyone Dave knew had heard the story and most people Dave knew had heard it more than once. He explained, 'It was like this...'

Ron poured himself another cup, he'd heard it more than twice.

'... tourist steps off the kerb looking the wrong way, big van swerves to miss 'im, goes right up the pavement and smack! Right into the wall and railin's of Buck' 'ouse. Oo does she call? Me, Dave London!'

'The Queen phoned!'

Dave tutted, 'Not personally obviously, she's got people 'n't she.' Vicky looked thoughtful. Although she didn't want to hurt Dave's feelings she also didn't want him to get into trouble for lack of understanding. She compressed her lips then explained gently, 'Dave, you have to work for the Royals on a regular basis for a few years before they grant you a 'By Royal Appointment'.' Dave looked at her sharply, 'Is that right?' Vicky wrinkled her nose, 'Mm.' Dave looked away and stared into space as he absorbed this crushing news. To ease his anguish Vicky added quickly, 'It's still brilliant though. I don't suppose Her Majesty needs much welding done but when she did, you got the job, didn't you?' Dave cheered up, 'That's right, I did di'n't I?'

'Absolutely.'

He glanced at his watch, crammed another piece of toast in his mouth and mumbled, 'I gotta get goin' now, got another job so give us a bell when you want the car done prop'ly and remember, don't tell anyone I patched it. I got a reputation y'know.' Dave looked at Vicky, 'Some artists use brushes 'n' canvas, I use a welding torch and my canvas is the car, course...' turning his attention to Ron, 'some Philistines don't appreciate the art form.'

'I do Dave, I really do, look thanks for coming at short notice, beautiful job, really.'

'It's only temporary.'

'I know, I know.' He stuffed some money into Dave's greasy hand, Dave winked at Vicky, 'Don't forget, keep him in line.' Vicky winked in return, 'Don't worry.' Dave nodded and Ron saw him to the door.

Unseen, Vicky used her napkin to remove the oily thumbprint from the business card. She had a thought that it may come in handy. She crossed to the fridge and carefully placed the card under one of Ron's fridge magnets. She smiled as she read the logo on the magnet, "I'm in Heaven Driving My '57" complete with a tiny picture of a 1957 Chevrolet. It appeared Ron had himself a little collection; "Rallying! A Sport You Can Do Sitting Down!" This featured a small picture of the *Ford Escort Mexican* rally car. "Two Wheels Bad, Four Wheels Good, especially if they leave the ground!" had a picture of a car in the air going over a hump. Still smiling, she shook her head and returned to the table.

After Ron saw Dave out, he joined her and they sat together drinking their coffee. 'He's a true artist, old Dave,' Ron mused as he sipped his drink.

'Where did you meet him?'

'Dave London? Oh, we met at a classic car show then lost touch. One day, I took the old car into a garage to have some work done and there was Dave. We meet up for a drink now and again. He loves talking about cars. He's extremely proud of his work. He nearly had a fit when I told him to patch it for now; he's a useful guy to know.'

Vicky frowned, 'You didn't tell him the full story about me and the car that chased us last night.'

Ron spoke thoughtfully, 'No, I trust Dave but… until we know what this is all about, I don't think we should take any risks. Dave would never do anything to harm me on purpose but his work takes him all over London. With so many questions unanswered it's not easy to know exactly what would be harmful if he happened to say the wrong thing to the wrong person. So I… so I… look, I hope you don't mind. I told him you were an old friend and we had met up recently and we were getting on so well, we were giving the living together thing a chance.' Ron coloured.

Vicky jumped in quickly, 'It's alright, it sounds about right, I am living here and I do feel I've known you a long time, you know as much about me as I do.' He nodded. Vicky lowered her voice, 'Ron, what did you mean earlier about us having somewhere to go, and why do you keep grinning? What's the big secret? Have you discovered something?' He smiled, 'We've had a break. I couldn't sleep last night because there was something nagging at the back of my mind. I thought and thought then all of a sudden, it came to me.' He sat back and looked pleased with himself. Vicky was impatient, 'Spit it out then, what came to you?'

'Do you remember when we left the restaurant last night, what the head waiter said?'

'No?'

'He said, 'Goodnight Mr Moon, Miss Blaine'. When I booked the table, I booked it in the name of Moon and I said 'table for two' so how did he know your name? The answer must be because you're a regular, at the very least been there before, so if we drive over and I tip him I may be able to get something out of him that could help us.' As he spoke she nodded and looked excited, 'Oh, that's great, when do we go?' He drained his coffee cup and banged it down decisively, 'Right now.'

A few minutes later Ron's big car left the alley. At first Vicky noticed he kept glancing in the rear view mirror, 'Anything?' she asked nervously.

He smiled, 'Nothing.' Gradually they both relaxed and began to enjoy the pleasant drive along the country lanes.

It was one of those cold bright days that winter can sometimes produce, as if the world has been washed clean, new and fresh by the rain. The fine day was no surprise to the Met Office, a short respite before the following storm was due to blow in from the east. However, no one could predict how stormy the coming days would be for Ron and Vicky, but for now the sun shone, the sky was blue and the air crisp. The town fell away, replaced by fields and they could see in the shady spots a fine layer of frost clinging to the grass.

Vicky was happy to be onto something although apprehensive about what they might discover. There was also something else on her mind, she decided to approach the question gently.

Tilting her head slightly and looking at Ron she observed, 'Have you noticed how your friends are all... em... unusual characters?' He smiled, 'Yes, they are aren't they,' he positioned the car perfectly for the next bend and as they accelerated smoothly out of it, added, 'If I come across unusual interesting characters I try to hang on to them,' he laughed, 'it's more interesting than collecting stamps.'

'I suppose you can take anything too far. My situation is probably a shade too unusual to be comfortable.'

Ron glanced at her. She was watching him closely. He turned his attention back to the road and smiled, he understood, she was asking if he was sorry he had got involved and was waiting for his answer. 'You are the jewel of the collection.' She had her answer.

They reached *Nick's* at eleven o'clock. Everyone seemed busy getting ready for the lunchtime rush. Ron thought the waiter may talk more about Vicky if she wasn't standing in front of him so went in alone. At first, he couldn't see the head waiter and had the horrible thought that maybe the man only worked evenings. Suddenly, he spotted him organising the positioning of a group of chairs, it seemed a large party was expected this lunchtime. Ron caught his eye and beckoned him over. The waiter spoke to one of his staff; after giving his instructions hurried across. The man was short and fat with thick white hair, his name badge introduced him to the world as *C Johnson*, 'I'm sorry sir, we're not open till twelve,' he informed Ron without any trace of being sorry at all.

'That's fine, I wonder if you could do me a favour.'

The waiter grimaced and glanced at his team busy laying the tables and fussing over the exact positioning of the chairs.

'I can see you're busy but if I could have a quick word, I would be very grateful.' Ron pressed five pounds into the man's hand. The waiter quickly looked about, no-one had seen, 'Come this way, sir.' He led Ron to a small side door, which opened to the car park. Vicky saw them and ducked down in her seat. The waiter wasn't interested in the car park, he was looking at Ron carefully and weighing up how much more he could get, 'What can I do for you, sir?'

'Last night I was here with a young woman. My name is Moon, she was called Miss Blaine. As we left you said, "Goodnight, Miss Blaine," so am I right in thinking you've seen her here before?' The waiter went into an act. 'Err.. let me think... mm.' He pursed his lips and covered them with an index finger in a fake thoughtful pose. Ron pressed another five pounds into his hand. The waiter snapped his fingers, 'I've got it! Miss Blaine often used to come with her sister I believe sir, and a man. Although I haven't seen her lately.'

'Who was the man?'

'Oh, mm,' the waiter stroked his chin with thumb and forefinger. Although Ron was by nature amiable, kind and it was fair to say not moved to temper quickly, greed was a trait that was guaranteed to shorten the journey. He frowned and spoke very quietly with suppressed anger, 'This is very important to me, we aren't trying to be greedy, are we?' The waiter caught Ron's eye and licked his top lip nervously. 'I remember the man's name, it was Mr Hammond, but as I say he hasn't been in for....'

'Do you have an address?'

'We don't take add.... Hold on a moment, he phoned once and wanted a table at short notice. I said we didn't have one and he left his phone number in case we had a cancellation. It was written in the margin of the reservations book, I think.'

'Can you get the number?' Ron brightened, this was a piece of luck.

'If you would wait, sir, I will endeavour to try.' The waiter replied stiffly and disappeared into the building.

Ron stood and waited. He glanced over at the car. A little worried he couldn't see Vicky he stood on his toes. He thought he could see a blonde tuft of hair but at that moment the waiter reappeared holding out a crumpled scrap of paper. Ron took it. A phone number was scrawled on it. 'Oh, this is great!' He walked away, still staring at the paper. *C Johnson*

86

tutted and hurried off to get on with his organising muttering, 'And you're very welcome, I'm sure.'

Smiling, Ron climbed into the car clutching his scrap of paper in triumph, 'Bingo! I've got a phone number. The waiter said you came here with Sara several times and a man called Hammond, but lately he hadn't seen you. Hammond once left his number so they could call him if there was a cancellation.' Vicky was silent.

'What's the matter?' He was concerned.

'Hammond! The man my sister came to London with, he was an awful man. What was I doing going out to dinner with him?' Ron pondered but couldn't think of anything. He patted her hand, 'This is real progress, now I've got a phone number, I can get an address.' She shook her head, 'Then what?'

'First things first. We don't know much, but we do know there are some dangerous people mixed up in this, so we must move slowly until we get some more answers.'

'Yes... Oh God, I wish I could remember.'

They drove out of the car park, instinctively, he glanced in the mirror but no one was there. They headed back toward town and as they rounded a bend a small village came into view. The village consisted of a few houses, a row of shops and a pub. Ron noticed a phone box in the pub car park. They stopped, he pulled out his wallet and examined the contents, 'I've got some change for the phone, I'll ring Directory Enquiries and make up some story why I need an address for the number.'

'Right.'

'Look, we could do with some shopping we're running low, we may as well pick up some supplies so why don't you make a start. Here's some money in case you get to the checkout before I get there.' He crammed some money into Vicky's hand and was about to walk to the phone box when she caught his arm, he turned.

'I do appreciate all this.'

He smiled, 'You've seen in the cupboard, you know what we need.' Vicky's expression changed to mock severity, 'I think I need to pick up something a little more healthy than your normal diet.' Ron chuckled and turned away.

In the phone box, he explained to Directory Enquiries he couldn't read his boss's writing. The woman informed him the number wasn't enough and she couldn't help. He thanked her and hung up. He paused with his hand still on the receiver, tapping it frustratedly, deep in thought. He must help her and finding out where this Hammond lived was the obvious place to start, but how?

Stepping out of the phone box, he surveyed the village; it was a peaceful little place. Stretching away from the pub was the main street. There was a Post Office, which also sold a million other things, a butcher's, a large food shop unimaginatively called "The Store" and not much else. As he walked, it occurred to him it was the first time he had been alone for about four days. He stopped and thought. He had found Vicky in the early hours of Sunday morning and now it was Wednesday lunchtime. Less than four days, it seemed incredible so much had happened. What was more surprising was the way they had fallen into this easy relationship. He wasn't sure what it was. It could be a brother-sister-friend sort of thing, or maybe it was more. He considered…

it certainly was more to him. He hurried on, not wanting to think of the possibility that when this was over, Vicky would leave his life as quickly as she had appeared.

As he passed the Post Office, he spotted a small toy bear in the crammed window. On an impulse he went in and bought it. Outside, he looked at it with no idea why he had bought it for her. It had seemed a good idea, something to cheer her up, silly really. He looked up quickly as an old woman walked around him, staring at the small teddy bear and then at Ron. 'Men never grow up,' she croaked as she shuffled on toward the pub. Ron coloured a little, stuffed the bear inside his coat and walked off to "The Store".

He caught up with Vicky at the checkout. 'Any luck?' she asked. Ron shook his head, 'Directory Enquiries don't give out addresses if you only have a number.' Vicky, looking glum asked quietly, 'What now?' Ron took the heaviest bags. He wasn't sure 'what now' so changed the subject, 'What have you got in here? They weigh a ton!' She smiled faintly, 'Oh, just a few essentials.' She scowled at him with a pretend telling-off, 'I noticed you haven't got any fruit, in fact you haven't got anything very healthy at all, tut, tut.'

'Healthy stuff always tastes horrible.' Vicky shut her eyes and shook her head, 'How old are you?'

'Twenty-nine.'

'And you still need telling to eat your veg?'

'I, er…' He mumbled as he struggled off to the car park. They placed the bags in the cavernous boot and climbed in the car.

'I bought you this, don't know why, I thought it might… cheer you up.' Feeling a little foolish Ron produced the bear from his coat. He wasn't prepared for the reaction. Vicky became quiet, then whispered, 'Thank you.' It wasn't the bear itself that touched her it was the kindness it represented. She had tears in her eyes so he put his arm around her shoulder and immediately she moved toward him. 'You silly old thing, it's just a bear!' She sniffed, 'I know. It's only that... only, I don't know. I think I'm a little bit... you know, tearful. I go around smiling putting on a brave face. I even think I'm coping. Then someone does something touching and I fall to pieces... sorry.' He shook his head, 'Nothing to feel sorry about. Tell you what, let's go home, dump this stuff and have a bite to eat.'

He was about to start the car when Vicky said suddenly, 'I er, I feel strange.' He stared at her, 'In what way?' Struggling to put her feelings into words, she tried again, 'I feel as if... as if time is slipping past and we should be doing something. I think it's mixed up with whatever it is I can't remember. That car was trying to kill us and we're no nearer to finding out why.' Ron was silent and stared at the bonnet thinking. It occurred to Vicky that her statement may have sounded ungrateful, she added quickly, 'I know you're doing all you can, more than I have any right to ask. I just feel I should tell you I have an uncomfortable feeling that they're getting close to us and we're not ready. Perhaps it would be better if I went to the police.'

'No, not until we know what this is about and even then perhaps not, it all depends.' He sighed, tipped his head back and looked at the roof. 'Oh, I wish I knew what to do,' with a humourless laugh, he added, 'Max would know.' She frowned, 'Max?' He turned to face her, 'Max Carter, you know, the hero in my books. He'd know what to do...' exasperation turned to exhilaration, 'yes, yes, of course!' Ron clapped his hands together and smiled. Vicky cheered up, 'What? What?' He spoke fast, 'I'm stupid, I considered this as a possible plot line! In the end, I didn't use it but the idea went like this; Max has a phone number and a name but no address.' Vicky was excited, 'And...?' 'Max is a pretty shrewd guy, he knows that the person he's looking for is probably ex-directory because he's a shady sort, like our Mr Hammond. Anyway, he gets a phone book and checks out the code. The first bit tells him the city, the next three digits tell him the area. Now he has a name, a phone number and an area. The next thing is to go to the library in that area and ask to see the electoral roll. The index is in streets. The names in the streets are in alphabetical order so it'll take time but it can be done. Why didn't I think of it before?' Ron smacked his forehead with the palm of his hand.

'Well, you've had a lot on your mind. Would this really work? What if he didn't register?'

Ron was quick, 'Ah, but he will, if he is mixed up in something shady, he will want to keep a low profile. He certainly won't want any trouble with the law, it's illegal not to register.' He jumped out of the car. 'Hey, where're you going?' She called.

'To the pub to borrow a phone book.'

A few minutes later he was back, smiling broadly, 'Right, I've got the area, it's only the next borough from where we live, let's go.' Spirits lifted, they drove off. Ron assumed she was smiling because they were making progress at last and that was true, but the phrase 'where we live' made the smile broader.

A short time later they arrived at a small library. Ron asked to see the electoral roll. The librarian rummaged about and handed him a box folder containing some computer printouts bound together. They sat in a quiet corner and eagerly went through them. Together they came up with twelve Hammonds. Vicky had eight names and addresses on her sheet of paper and Ron had four. 'Ron, it will take us ages to check out twelve people and we can't rush into it. We have to be careful, this will take forever!' Ron tossed his piece of paper next to Vicky's and rubbed his tired eyes. She looked unhappily at the names and addresses on Ron's sheet and suddenly, made a grab for it and examined it closely, 'Vincent Hammond...! Vinny, my sister used to call him Vinny, I remember. Oh Ron, we've found him... yes!'

The librarian came bustling over, 'Sssshhhh!' Ron apologised in whispers. Stifling laughter, they fled the library like a couple of children. On reaching the car, they were still giggling. Ron folded the address and put it in his pocket. 'Home.' He announced. 'Home.' Vicky confirmed.

A short time later, the Chevy stood outside his flat. Taking two bags each from the boot, they hurried up the stairs to the second floor flat. Since Ron had the key, he was first through the door. This meant he was also the first to encounter the cat, who had dozed off just inside the front door. Ron managed to avoid treading on him but overbalanced, putting out his hands to save himself and releasing the bags, one nipping the tip of Finbar's tail as it landed. Ron hit the floor hard, Finbar yowled and ran halfway up the living room curtains. Vicky entered the room in time to see a cat halfway up the curtains screaming like a banshee and Ron laying flat on his face. He grabbed one of the items that had fallen from the bags – which happened to be a toilet roll – and hurled it at Finbar missing him by a mile. 'Shut up! Bloody stupid cat!' But still Finbar yelled, 'Mmmmmmeeeeeeeeow!'

Vicky put down her bags, stepped over Ron and crossed to the curtains. Patting Finbar, she spoke quietly, 'There, there, there,' She lifted him gently from the curtains stroking him, 'Ssshh, ssshh, ssshh, it's alright, no-one's going to hurt you. Did nasty Ronny drop a bag of tins on Finny's tail? Ah, poor tail… kissy, kissy.' She kissed Finbar on the head. He stopped yelling, glared at Ron and gave a little hiss. He wouldn't forget Ron threw a toilet roll at him for a long time. 'Nasty Ronny' was picking up the shopping, which had rolled all over the floor. 'Don't pat him. He wants a kick up the…' He stopped abruptly watching Vicky carefully. She pulled her lips together tightly then looked out the window and began to go pink in the face.

'You're laughing at me, aren't you?' Vicky shook her head. Not only was she pink but her eyes had begun to water and her shoulders shook slightly. Ron stomped off to the kitchen muttering, 'Could have broken my bloody neck, well, as long as some people think it's funny… great!'

When he returned, Vicky hurried past with her bags of shopping and began putting it away. Ron glared at Finbar who was under the TV glaring back. Ron snatched up the last bag and walked to the kitchen. She looked over her shoulder as she continued to stack items into the cupboard, 'Are you okay?'

'Yes, I'm fine, it did frighten me though. I mean, right behind the front door, why there?' She shrugged, 'Cats do things like that, sleep in weird places, it's not his fault. Hey, there's another bag still in the boot. It's the heavy one.'

'Oh yes, I'll go down and...' The phone rang before Ron could finish, he returned to the living room and picked it up. From the kitchen, Vicky could only hear half of the conversation. 'Hello...? Oh Tony, haven't heard from you for a while... yes I have... mm... oh, what kind of trouble? You think it could be that bad...? Yes okay. We'll come straight away... bye.' Standing at the kitchen door Vicky sensed trouble, 'What's the matter?' 'I don't know. That was Big Tony, Shades' brother. He asked if I'd heard of a man named Hammond, I told him I had. He said there'd been some trouble and we may be in danger, he wants us to get over to *The Blue Parrot* and get this bit, make sure we aren't followed. Mind you, that's nothing to go by, Big Tony always talks like that. I told you, obsessed with crime, gangsters and old movies in general, the pair of them. The thing is, Big Tony is no fool so I think we'd better get over there now and see what's up. It's only ten minutes away.'

The Chevy was soon rolling down the road. 'I think I'll stick to side roads.' Ron said. She shot him a glance.

'You know, to be on the safe side.' He smiled but it was evident he was nervous and had taken Tony's call a lot more seriously than he wanted to admit.

By chance, as Ron's car crossed a set of traffic lights, a silver car was waiting at the opposite set. The Chevrolet passed across in front of it. Its engine roared as it moved through the red light and swung left to follow them. It wasn't quick enough and two cars slipped in front. The silver car attempted to overtake but there was a steady stream of oncoming traffic. It was five o'clock, a weekday and near Christmas so traffic was predictably heavy. The silver car lost further ground when a car in front let in another. Now there were three cars between it and the Chevy.

Half a mile further, Ron turned right. None of the three cars following took the turn. The silver car swept round the corner eagerly ready to close on its target. Ron and Vicky had no idea they were being followed. Ron was proceeding cautiously as it was a very narrow road with lots of warehouses either side. He was taking a shortcut across the new industrial estate to avoid the busy roads.

The silver car was accelerating now and in a few seconds would be on top of them. It thundered down the narrow road behind them.

If Ron or Vicky had glanced in a mirror they would have seen the car clearly as it closed in.

Suddenly, from one of the warehouses a forklift truck lumbered out, the driver was startled to see the silver car moving so fast in the usually quiet road and stamped on the brakes. His load of steel tubing was catapulted from the forks and clattered into the path of the silver car. The scream of brakes was lost in the uproar of steel tubes rolling about. The car missed the tubes and buried itself in a pile of rubbish, mainly soft cartons and packing material, left out for the bin men in the morning.

When Ron looked in his mirror to see the source of the noise all he saw was the fork lift truck and a pile of pipes and cartons strewn about the narrow road. 'It's nothing Vicky, it's only a forklift truck dropped a load of pipes,' he smiled, 'I must relax, I thought it was an ambush or something.' Vicky put her hand on her heart, looked at him and puffed, 'Phew, so did I.'

When they arrived at the small yard behind *The Blue Parrot*, Big Tony was waiting. He waved at Ron and pointed at an open door indicating that he should park out of sight in the large lock-up. Moments later, with the door closed they all stood in the gathering gloom, it was bitterly cold and night was falling fast. If it wasn't for the two bulkhead lights above the Club's fire exits, they would be standing in near total darkness. As Ron and Big Tony talked puffs of steamy breath could be seen in the air.

'Why the lock-up?'

'I don't want the car seen, no point in advertising you're here.'

In spite of the name, Vicky was unprepared for the man who stood before her, or more accurately, over her. She knew she was little, only slightly taller than Ron's shoulder but Tony was at least eight inches taller than Ron so he towered a full one and a half feet higher than herself, and he was wide, broad powerful shoulders. As he talked he gestured with huge strong hands, even in the bad light she could see dark hairs on the back of his fingers. He fascinated her so while Tony was distracted with Ron, she took the opportunity to study the face. The harsh side lighting threw hard shadows across the strong serious features, he appeared to have very dark eyes, possibly brown. His thick black hair was combed straight back. The girl in the woman amused herself by trying to imagine that face laughing, but failed. His voice was a deep baritone. The serious image was complemented by a dark, tailored suit. With the build and mode of dress it crossed her mind if she were a casting director trying to fill a gangster role he would get the job with no argument.

Vicky jumped, realising suddenly he was talking to her. There was an unmistakeable presence about him that gave the impression respect was expected. 'I'm sorry, what did you say?' Tony was unaccustomed to people not listening, he paused and stared at her for an awful moment that felt lasted longer than it did. His unflinching, thoughtful gaze gave the recipient the impression he knew what they were thinking. Strangely enough, most of the time he did. For Tony had the rare gift of being able to read people, to distil the meaning behind the word, statement or action. He spoke again in his low rich voice, 'I said, so you're the woman at the bottom of this thing are you?' Vicky wasn't sure how to answer, glanced at Ron for help and was relieved when he moved slightly closer to her and began to talk again. Big Tony turned his attention back to Ron. Vicky was a little frightened of Big Tony, who didn't seem to share any of his brother's humour. Ron's description, 'a little dark', appeared to be something of an understatement.

Ron had been assuring Tony they hadn't been followed and confirming what he and Vicky had asked Shades about. Big Tony made no comment, but merely turned his attention to her again and looked at her carefully. Though it was impossible to read *his* thoughts, the most disturbing thing was the apparent lack of emotion. At the point his gaze felt unbearable, he seemed to have made up his mind and said abruptly, 'I think you both better come up.' He turned and walked away, not bothering to check if they were following; after all, he had told them to and of course, they would. He led them up the fire escape, the back way to the private rooms above *The Blue Parrot*. It was here Tony and Shades occasionally stayed if they worked late at the Club.

They were shown into a comfortable living room, modern and enormously spacious. The concealed lighting shone upward and was reflected from the ceiling, helping to soften the room, which although extremely tidy and clean, was lacking in personal features, giving it the impression of an expensive hotel suite, rather than a home. Everything looked new as if someone had chosen the room from a magazine.

Big Tony waved at the sofa as he walked past, Ron and Vicky sat down. Tony crossed the room to a rather impressive drinks cabinet. 'Drink?' Ron said he had the car. Vicky bravely asked if she might have a brandy. Tony handed her a large brandy and sat opposite, 'Tell me the story.'

Ron was a little puzzled about the way Tony had taken a sudden interest in him and Vicky. He didn't know Tony quite as well as Shades but felt he could trust him. Ron related the whole story right from the way he had found Vicky in the alley till now, including the chase, the phone number, the way he had obtained the address, Vicky's sister Sara and exactly what Vicky could and couldn't remember.

Tony was silent, he tipped his head back and looked at the ceiling, then got up and walked out of the room.

Vicky whispered to Ron, 'Why are we here?' Ron shrugged. Vicky persisted, 'Why did you tell him everything? And why does he want to know?' Ron shrugged again, it was a question he was trying to work out himself. Vicky prodded him, 'RON!'

'Look, I trust Shades. Tony is his brother. They both know what's happening in the area. Tony rings me and asks if I've heard of a man named Hammond, the man you were seen with. He seems to be the key to this and Tony seems to know something. Why should he help us if we're not straight with him?' Vicky nodded, 'I suppose so. Are you sure you can trust him? He gives me the creeps.'

'I told you, it's an act. The sinister heavy bit, they both love old black and white gangster and detective movies, look.' He pointed to the only thing in the room that betrayed any hint of the personality that owned it. An impressive collection of videotapes filled a good part of one wall. Vicky surveyed the tapes and whispered, 'I hope you're right about the sinister heavy bit being an act.' Ron kept an eye on the door in case of Tony's sudden return and added unreassuringly, 'It's just Tony doesn't need to act much, that's all.'

Tony returned at that moment with Shades, who moved stiffly. He sat down heavily with a slight murmur. Ron was concerned, 'Shades, are you alright?' Shades held up a hand, 'No problem.' Tony took over the conversation, 'I've filled my brother in on what you told me. He's been in there resting,' he pointed to the door they had both emerged from, presumably one of the bedrooms, 'Shades had some trouble last night. You came in yesterday lunchtime.' They nodded. 'Someone must have seen you talking to Shades because later he was grabbed by three men wearing ski masks in the yard. They wanted to know who you were and where you lived. They gave Shades a bit of a going over, but luckily two of the bouncers were coming in to start their shift. There was a scuffle, unfortunately the men got away. The only clue was when one of them said, 'Hammond will want some answers so we better shake some out of this guy.' That was why I asked if you had heard of the name Hammond, there we are.'

Ron stood up, crossed the room to Shades and rested a hand on his shoulder, 'Thanks.' He didn't have to ask if Shades had given his address, he knew him too well. Shades smiled and nodded, it was plain they were close friends. Ron walked to the balcony door and looked through the glass, then without turning spoke, 'I'm fed up not knowing what's going on,' he spun round, 'I'm thinking of paying this Hammond a visit,' he pulled a scrap of paper from his pocket, 'this is the address.' Tony interrupted, 'Take it easy, you can't go blasting in there, you don't know what you're walking into.' Shades leaned forward, 'I'll tell you, Ron, I take it pretty personal when some guy has me roughed up. So, what if we paid him a visit together? I think I could get us in, if you know what I mean,' he winked at Vicky then added, 'we could go through his things, it may give us some answers. We must do something, I think this Hammond wants you and Vicky pretty bad so we've got to find out what this is all about before he gets to you first.' Ron glanced at Vicky. She had been looking from one to the other following the conversation and becoming increasingly frightened, Ron felt compelled to sit beside her on the sofa, 'Don't worry, Shades and I will slip in and have a sniff around. We'll be better prepared if we know what this is all about.'

Vicky spoke quietly without looking at anyone, 'I wish I could remember.'

'Tony, can Vicky stay here for a while?' He nodded, but Vicky said quickly without looking at Tony, 'I think I would like to go home.' Ron was pleased she referred to his flat as 'home' but was unsure it would be safe. Vicky looked upset and seeing Ron's hesitation added more firmly, 'I'd really like to go home.' He gave in, it was decided, Big Tony was to drive Vicky back to the flat in Ron's Chevrolet, Shades and Ron would go in Tony's car as Shades had walked in and his was at home. It seemed a sensible precaution not to use Ron's, as the distinctive, grey Chevrolet was known to Hammond's men and presumably, Hammond. Vicky wasn't very happy about having Tony drive her but kept it to herself.

Out in the car park Ron handed Tony the keys and was getting into Tony's car with Shades when Vicky ran to him and threw her arms round his neck, 'Be careful!' He looked at her anxious face, they all appeared pale in the freezing air but she was a clear winner, 'I'll be careful, promise.' He looked at Shades for confirmation. She turned to Shades, who smiled, 'In and out like shadows, no problem.' Although the unexpected show of concern made Ron feel stronger somehow, at that moment he didn't want to go but felt driven to try and get some answers.

Vicky walked slowly over to the Chevrolet, Tony had reversed it out of the lock-up and was waiting for her. Shades called after her, 'I'll look after him.' She smiled weakly, gave a little wave then disappeared into the car. The two cars made large clouds of steamy exhaust gas in the cold night air as they went their separate ways. Tony happily – although he didn't look it - driving Ron's '57 Chevrolet *Bel Air* with the worried and reluctant Vicky and Shades happily – and looking so - driving Tony's car with the equally worried and reluctant Ron.

PART ONE
CHAPTER 5
WEDNESDAY NIGHT

Shades drove for a couple of miles in silence, Ron was thinking about how they were going to get into Hammond's place and what they might find. Shades was apparently thinking of something else because suddenly he commented, 'You know Ron, I think Vicky could be good for you.' Ron was surprised, 'What makes you say a thing like that?'

'Look, I know this broad is in trouble but women an' trouble come as a package so that's not a problem. You seem a lot happier in yourself the last couple of days, you take my advice, hang on to this one,' he grinned, ''she should be kissed and kissed often by someone who knows how.'' Ron gave a short laugh, 'That's a misquote from *Gone with the Wind*, Jacqui and I saw it on TV. I wouldn't have thought it was your taste.' Shades shrugged, 'I watch a lot of old movies not only the gangster classics, anyway, it was one of Mamma's favourites.'

'I'm pleased to hear your tastes extend to some of the more subtle aspects of the silver screen not involving machines guns... and Shades, don't call her a broad, it's 1992 in South East London not 1942 in South Side New York, what's the matter with you?'

Shades smiled, he was enjoying himself. He had always wanted to be a hero in a story and this was his chance. He was also comfortable in Ron's company and felt he could indulge in quoting as much corny movie dialogue as amused him.

For the rest of the journey neither spoke but Ron did plenty of thinking. Perhaps it would be easier to think about Vicky when she wasn't sitting beside him. The thought of 'hanging on to this one' as Shades so eloquently put it, had crossed his mind too. He hadn't looked for anyone since Jacqui died. In fact, he had made no effort in that direction at all.

Now suddenly life had changed. Vicky had come along, he frowned as he considered the situation; it was difficult to understand. He was perfectly comfortable talking to Vicky, even living with her but he felt very uncomfortable acting as if they were anything more than good friends. Come to that was he ready? He felt a strong attraction to this woman, was he falling in love? Was he just very lonely and making more of it than there was? What did he want? Was he misreading the signs? What did she want? He felt uneasy, maybe it was guilt because of Jacqui. In his mind it was safe to think of Vicky as a girlfriend, what did that even mean? Was she a friend who happened to be a girl? Was he starting to think of her as a girlfriend? Yes, he thought he was but if he told her, she may tell him straight that yes, she was grateful for his help and yes, they would always be good friends but that was it. She was sorry he had got the wrong idea and thought anything else. This was the whole problem; how to let her know he cared but still be safe from being hurt? Did he really want to let her know? Perhaps he was rushing it having known her only for a few days, but he felt so good with her, a mixture of excitement and happiness. If he didn't act it could be a lifelong regret, if he messed it up; same result. So, he thought, to sum up, he wasn't sure what he wanted, he wasn't sure what she wanted and he wasn't sure what he wanted her to want. Well, that cleared that up nicely.

All Ron's troubles of the heart would have to wait because they had arrived at Hammond's place. In the light of the dashboard Shades checked the piece of paper, 'Yup, this is it.'

A few miles away across town, Vicky was assuring Tony she would be all right. 'I'm absolutely sure I'll be fine, really. You don't have to babysit me look the door is big and strong. Anyway, no-one except you and Shades know I'm here.' Vicky was peering around the front door at Big Tony who loomed over her and seemed to fill the hall outside the flat. Tony's voice was deep and to her, menacingly quiet, 'Okay then, here's the number of *The Blue Parrot*. It will ring in the flat above and if no one picks up will be transferred automatically to one of the bars downstairs, phone if there's a problem.' He handed her a small card, 'Thank you,' she added timidly, 'er... will you ring me when they get back?' Tony nodded slowly then turned and walked away. She closed the door and leaned against it for a moment, Big Tony made her nervous and being with him was tiring. He didn't strike her as the kind of guy who just liked gangster movies; he looked liked the kind of guy they *made* gangster movies about.

Vicky wasn't alone in the flat. Someone was going to teach her a lesson. She wasn't going to cause any more trouble. As she leaned on the door, he crept unseen toward her.

Shades had suggested they park a little way from the house and walk back. This seemed sensible so they parked the car two streets away then walked past the house to take a look. It was a grand looking place with a high wall around it. The deserted street was lined with mature London Plane trees, their thick leafless canopies creating large shadowy areas between the widely spaced street lamps. Hammond's house stood in a street with other expensive looking houses, all detached and set far back from the road behind gated fences and walls. Behind the houses lay heathland, a very exclusive area. They walked carefully along the foot of the high wall that protected Hammond's property from the curious. It was only early evening but already completely dark, heavy cloud obscured the moon. The second predicted storm front was closing in, it seemed certain they were in for more rain or even sleet as it was easily cold enough.

Back at the flat, Vicky had been ferociously attacked. However, the attacker was now being cuddled and patted. 'Finbar, you scared the life out of me pouncing on my foot like that. I know you were only being playful, silly old cat.' The silly old cat was carried into the kitchen and the sight of the adored tin opener made Finbar forget his grudges. His eye's shone with delight, it seemed she shared Ron's skill in using this device. He slid his small sleek body against her legs quickly alternating from right to left. This was how Finbar said I really do feel hungry, thank you very much. Vicky opened a can of food and tipped it into his bowl, 'There you are, nice bit of din-din.' Five minutes after eating his dinner Finbar was fast asleep in his basket.

Vicky sat at the kitchen table and smiled at the sleeping cat; to be able to relax like that! Very tense but also desperately tired, she sighed and put her head in her hands. She had been over and over it, the same thoughts round and round. If only she could remember... If only! Ron could be walking into anything. If she could remember then she could warn him. Standing up quickly, she began to pace, 'Think Vicky, think!' After five minutes of pacing, she moved to the living room, sprawled wearily onto one of the sofas and closed her eyes, which ached with tiredness. There was some thought she couldn't reach... almost but no, it wouldn't come, she had no clue what it was, it remained in the shadows but she was sure, absolutely sure it was important to remember and somehow, time was a factor. Ron could be in real danger; she must remember, she *must*.

Meanwhile, the boys had decided to climb the wall at an overgrown part of the garden. Shades had pushed Ron up. Although Shades shared little of his brother's build, for his size he was remarkably strong. In the past this sinewy strength had spelt misfortune for those who underestimated it, for Ron it was decidedly good fortune as Shades' mighty shove had propelled him up easily and now he sat astride the wall. Lying down, he stretched out his hand, 'Shades, grab hold.' Shades jumped, caught Ron's hand and began to scramble up. With feet scrabbling for grip and Ron pulling, suddenly Shades was also atop the wall. It was very dark on this side of the house. Ron looked up at the sky, good, no breaks in the cloud, there would be rain before long. Now Shades lay down along the wall, he gripped with one hand and held on to Ron with the other as he lowered himself into the grounds. Ron suddenly let go and dropped the remaining distance, landing quietly on thick dead bracken below. Shades lowered himself as far as he could by his arms then let go. He landed harder with a muffled 'Oooof'. Ron hissed, 'You okay?'

'Mm ribs! Where those bastards hit me.'

Ron grimaced, 'I'm sorry Shades.'

'I'm okay, I'm okay, don't fuss.'

They crouched in the bracken. All was still and quiet. Somewhere a dog barked then silence again. The bone-chilling cold bit deep. Keeping still, they scanned the area; nothing, then far, far away they heard the distant, moody growl of thunder. Ron tapped Shades gently on the arm, 'Come on.' They pushed their way slowly toward the house, a large white structure of generous proportions. A light burned in one of the downstairs rooms. Unfortunately, there was an enormous open piece of ground between their cover and the house, which would be the dangerous part. Ron gestured for them to skirt round to the darker side of the building before breaking cover. Shades nodded and the two crept off to the right.

The flat was silent. Outside the approaching storm grumbled faintly but the streets were as yet cold and dry. Finbar slept in his basket his ear twitched as a sound from the living room broke the silence. It was a faint murmur. Vicky was dreaming and from her restless movement and mutterings, it was obvious her dreams were not pleasant.

Unobserved, Ron and Shades had worked their way around to the side of the house. Ron pointed at the garage, 'Do you think we could reach that upstairs balcony from the top of the garage roof?'

'I think so.'

'Okay, let's try.' They ran to the garage and stood with their backs against the wall. They glanced about nervously. No one seemed to be around. Ron whispered, 'I'll push you up.' He cupped his hands and Shades put his foot in it, 'Hup.' Ron pushed, Shades jumped and managed to grab the gutter. This gave him the boost he needed to get on to the garage roof. Shades lay flat and reached down whereupon Ron jumped, caught his arm and proceeded to pull himself up. Shades hissed at him through gritted teeth, 'Careful you stupid sod, you'll pull me off.'

Ron struggled on to the roof, 'I never said I was a bloody cat burglar; I'm a writer, meaning I write it, I don't do it, mhhm!' Shades had put his hand over Ron's mouth, 'Shut up moaning or someone will hear you.' They edged along the roof close to the house. Ron looked in dismay at the gap between the edge of the garage roof and the balcony, 'I can't jump that!' Shades encouraged him, 'Yes you can! I can and if I can, you can!' Ron shook his head slowly, 'No!' 'Look Ron, if you don't get on that balcony you'll regret it, maybe not today, maybe not tomorrow, but soon and….' 'Last scene, *Casablanca*!' Ron cut in automatically, then hotly, 'This isn't a joke Shades, I can't make it.'

'It's not as far as it looks, you can make it,' Shades' smile faded and he became serious, 'we have to find out more about this guy Hammond. Think of Vicky, we must find out what the hell is going on, now come on!' Without waiting for an answer, Shades launched himself off the roof and grabbed the balcony. With his arms around the rail he pulled himself up, climbed over the rail and stood triumphant, 'Phew, come on,' he whispered. Ron ran his tongue over his bottom lip, then muttered to himself, 'Come on Ronny boy, think of how Max would do it. I'd write him across in no time… have him fly over with the agility of a cat.' Shades was growing impatient, 'Hurry up!' Ron took a couple of deep breaths, 'Just like a cat… yes, a cat. For Vicky!' He ran and jumped. Ron seemed to hang in space for a peaceful second. Then his catlike leap ended abruptly as the air was knocked out of him when the concrete base of the balcony hit him in the chest. He lost his grip on the metal rail, 'Ahhhmmm!' Ron stifled his cry as he saw to his horror a car coming up the front drive. The car approached fast, but luckily Ron was hanging too high up for the headlights to reach him. He had only one hand on the balcony but not wanting to be seen, he kept still and gritted his teeth. Shades had dived onto his stomach and whispered helpfully 'Hold on!' Ron rolled his eyes at this useful but somewhat obvious advice and said nothing.

Three men got out of the car. One spoke to the other two who moved out of view, the remaining man walked to the front door, momentarily a shaft of yellow light lit the front drive, shrank and was gone. Once again all became quiet.

'Get me up!'

'Okay, okay, don't be such a kid.'

'What do you mean 'kid'? I could break my bloody neck.' Shades pulled, Ron scrambled and between them finally, he was hauled up and over the balcony. They straightened up, Ron puffed, 'I thought I was a goner when that car pulled up. This Hammond guy must have guests and they didn't look too friendly a bunch, two of them are in the grounds somewhere. Hey what are you doing?'

Shades was fiddling with the lock on the balcony door, 'You want to get in, don't you?' He stopped working the lock and looked up sharply, 'I don't know how to do this, right?' Ron nodded quickly, 'Oh, right, right.' There was a click and the door was open.

As the first drops of rain began to fall they cautiously entered the room slipping quietly through the gap in the long green curtains, which obscured the balcony door. The room was smartly furnished and appeared to be an office. There were bookshelves lined with expensive-looking books, the kind people buy for effect rather than for reading. There was a large double-pedestal desk, but it was difficult to make out much detail as the only light came from the hall outside through a crack in the partly open door.

Shades moved to the door and very carefully opened it a little more to peer through. Then he quietly closed it and whispered, 'I think they're downstairs, I can hear faint talking. It's only a hall outside, no sign of anyone. Put the desk lamp on, we can't look around in this light.' As Ron fumbled for the lamp, Shades added, 'This is the place to start, an office. Bit strange, having an office upstairs, extra privacy I suppose. If we can't find out what kind of guy this Hammond is by rummaging through his papers, then I don't know what. Hey, it's funny that he hasn't got any alarms.' Ron's fumbling fingers found the lamp switch, 'Got it…' click.

As the light went on, Vicky found herself standing at the top of the flight of stone steps leading down to a door in the shadows at the bottom. She let go of the light switch and looked down at the door. The pathetic whimpering was coming from behind it. With her clothes sticking to her back, Vicky began to edge down the steps. The tension was so great she had to force her muscles to move. Every step was an effort as if her own body was fighting her. She knew she must go on but was terrified of what lay behind the door.

Finally, Vicky reached the bottom of the steps and the whimpering grew louder. Exhausted by her efforts she leaned her damp forehead on the door and shut her eyes. Vicky rocked her head from side to side and muttered, 'No, no, no, I don't want to… I don't! I don't!' She sniffed and choked back a sob, then opened her eyes, lifted her head and frowned. A strange thought crossed her mind, it didn't seem to belong, 'You must…! You must…! Think of Ron, must find out, must find out… Think of Ron.' Vicky gently placed her damp hand on the door handle then breathing hard her heart beating quickly, she gripped the handle firmly and turned it. Crying out with effort and fear as she threw the door wide, blinding white light struck her. She raised her hand to shield her eyes and edged slowly through the door.

The light was coming from four cars facing her in what appeared to be some kind of underground car park. Edging closer, she could make out some men grouped around something on the ground, it was whimpering. She was close enough now to make out the face of one of the men. Somehow, she knew this was Hammond. He stared at her. She glanced at the other men; they had hard faces. One of them slowly moved his hand out of his jacket as though he had been reaching for something and had changed his mind. They stared at Vicky, who watched Hammond. Slowly she moved her eyes to his hands, he held a gun loosely at his side, tiny wisps of smoke curled from the silencer.

Feeling sick she could feel her heartbeat as it pulsed in her chest. Her hands shook and in the chilled air her whole body stung with the cold as if the sweat on her skin were freezing. Not wanting to, she slowly forced herself to look down. The muscles in her neck seemed to resist. Gritting her teeth as the raw tension gripped her body like a vice, she spoke aloud, 'P... puppy...! It's a puppy.. a puppy...' As she stared down, the image of the dying puppy faded, her eyes widened... it was Sara that lay whimpering. Rushing forward, Vicky fell to her knees, 'Sara, Sara!' Sara's eyes opened, her chest was covered in blood. She whispered, 'It hurts, Vicky... It hurts.' Vicky cradled Sara in her arms and her eyes brimmed with tears. Sara was dying.

Hammond's voice was hard, 'She burst in... she shouldn't have done that. These are very delicate negotiations… she shouldn't have followed me, you should have stopped her.'

Vicky wasn't listening, she was rocking Sara gently from side to side, holding her close and with a free hand stroking her hair. Sara whispered so quietly only Vicky heard, 'Vicky… I think Mum used to do that… I can just remember...' Vicky felt Sara suddenly go limp and the soft whimpering sounds ceased. Vicky held Sara away and looked at her face, Sara's eyes were closed, 'Sara!' The enormity of the emotion was overwhelming, the grief too monstrous to absorb. This was simply too terrible to be real. Sara couldn't be dead. Vicky's breathing grew faster and faster but still she felt she was suffocating. Her eyes were looking at something that wasn't possible, 'No…, Sara…, Sara wake up, please wake up! Oh Sara, don't leave me, please don't leave me.' Then gently, very gently Vicky lowered Sara's head to the floor and for a brief moment, touched her cheek. Still staring at her, Vicky slowly stood and began to back away toward the door.

Hammond was watching her. 'Vicky.' Then more sternly, 'VICKY… Come here!' Vicky tore her gaze from Sara, glanced at Hammond and with one last look at Sara she turned and bolted through the door. She heard Hammond shout, 'Stop her!' She raced to the top of the stairs and out through the door at the top. Clearly, the parking area was on a sub-level because she found herself standing outside the building at ground level.

It was dark and raining hard. She had to get away, reasoning of any kind was beyond her, all that remained was the compulsion to run, the direction wasn't important, to run was important, to run and run.

Finbar stood in the kitchen doorway and peered at Vicky who was muttering and crying out as she squirmed about on the sofa. The sofa was put into silhouette suddenly by a flash of lightening from the window behind, followed a few seconds later by a deep growl of thunder. Finbar was frightened. He ran back to the kitchen and dived into his basket.

Vicky ran blindly down streets, down alleys, on and on. Her pursuers were some way behind as they took time to manoeuvre their cars out of the car park. She crouched for a moment under a parked lorry as she heard a car approaching but it passed without slowing. As she struggled out from under the lorry she dropped her small shoulder bag, which spilled open. Her purse teetered on the edge of the kerb. As her frantic cold fingers tried to snatch it up, it was nudged, fell and was whisked away by the gutter river and swallowed by a storm drain. 'No, no, no, no, no.' Frantically, she searched for the remaining contents quickly crammed them back into her bag and ran on.

She raced into the night, crying, tripping and stumbling. The storm raged overhead. At the point of collapse she spotted a small alley. It was dark and darkness meant safety. She staggered into the enveloping blackness and sank to her knees wretched and confused, staring up at the dark sky with wild eyes. Torrents of rain were falling. The almost frozen water felt like a million tiny daggers on her face and hands. Slowly, this faded as the numbing cold crept first along her fingers and toes eventually enveloping her. Finally, she felt nothing. Soaked to the skin and exhausted beyond belief, not knowing where she was or what was to become of her, she felt as if reality was retreating, moving way from her, falling far away. Looking up at the heavens she whispered, 'Oh God, let me die!' Suddenly, a bolt of lightening lit up a face in a window…. 'Ron!!'

As she shouted 'Ron!' she sat up quickly and stared about her. The familiar but dark flat surrounded her. There was another flash of lightening from the window and a roll of thunder. With a shaking hand Vicky reached out for the table lamp needing to sit quietly for a few seconds, trying to take in what she had remembered. Breathing hard as if she really had been running, Vicky wiped the sweat from her forehead trying to stop her hands shaking. Sara was dead! Hammond had killed her. Vince Hammond was a murderer! Ron and Shades were at Hammond's. Ron was in more danger than he could know. Ron had been seen with her so Hammond would think Ron knew he killed Sara. He would kill Ron to stop him talking.

Vicky jumped up and ran to the door then stopped. No car! If she did have a car, what then? She couldn't go to the police. If Ron and Shades were caught it would mean prison, but prison was better than being shot, but then Hammond would be on the outside and he would know where she was. Did it matter as long as Ron was safe? 'I don't know what to do, I don't know what to do.' A sudden thought struck her. She fumbled frantically in her pocket to find… yes, it was there, Tony's card.

She phoned *The Blue Parrot*, a deep familiar voice announced, 'This is Tony.'

'It's me, Vicky, it's come back! It's all come back. There isn't time to explain now. I'll tell you on the way but we have to get to Ron and Shades, they're in danger!' There was a pause that seemed to last an eternity.

'I'm coming over, be outside.' With that, Tony hung up.

Vicky checked the clock; one-thirty. It was Thursday now. She grabbed her coat and shoulder bag and put her hand on the lamp to switch it off. Then with all her problems, she glanced at Finbar who could be seen cowering in his basket in the kitchen, his little frightened face peering over the edge. 'I'll leave it on for you.' She let go of the lamp and was gone.

'Turn it off. I've seen enough to get the idea what kind of guy this Hammond is.' Ron spoke to Shades who was standing by the desk examining a small worktable in the corner. Shades nodded. 'Hey Ron! What do you think this lot's for?' He pointed to the worktable, which was strewn with small electronic components, a large magnifier and a series of intricate-looking tools. Ron peered at it, 'I'm not sure, looks like… I don't know, bugging equipment? And look at that.' He pointed to the large radio set sitting on the same table. 'That's a funny-looking radio.' Shades shrugged, 'I think we have the picture. I don't wanna meet this character. Let's get out of here.'

Just then, voices in the corridor grew louder. Shades switched off the desk lamp and they both dived behind the balcony curtains, but before they could open the door the light in the room came on.

The green curtains bathed Ron and Shades' faces with an eerie glow as they hid. Ron began to ease the door open but Shades stopped him, putting a finger to his lips and pointing at the sky through the pane in the door. The sound of the rain and storm would be heard even through the curtains. As Ron released the handle, it occurred to him that the wind alone would billow the curtains, even if the storm wasn't heard. It seemed for the moment they would have to keep still and hope.

Vicky recognised the shape of Ron's car as it materialised through the rain swept darkness. She ran down the steps from the shelter of the porch and waited by the kerb. As the car stopped Tony leaned over and opened the door. Vicky ran round the car and was about to get in when she hesitated. She didn't feel comfortable with Tony, not at all, but what else could she do?

'Get in!' Tony seemed irritated, Vicky dropped into the passenger seat and they accelerated fast. As the heavy door slammed shut, she had the uncomfortable feeling of a small creature having been lured into a trap. Tony snapped, 'Which way?' This was good, somehow it was a relief he didn't know the way to Vince Hammond's. She mentioned some street names and Tony nodded, 'Right, you better tell me the full story... *all* of it!' He tacked the last bit on sharply as if he didn't trust her. She took a deep breath to steady her nerves and began, 'I fell asleep after you left and had a dream. Well, it was more of a nightmare, except this one happened, it all came back.' The thought of Sara made her stop, Tony pushed, 'Okay, so you remember, what do you remember?'

Vicky pulled herself together. She had little choice. Ron may be in real trouble, they must get there in time, it couldn't be like it was with Sara. In a stronger voice, she continued, 'My sister Sara was going out with a man called Vince Hammond.' She paused, Sara, oh Sara. The image of Sara's face cradled in her arms filled her mind. She swallowed, 'Sara was obsessed by him. I never liked him. We rowed, she moved out of the flat we shared and went with Hammond. About three months later I received a letter, she said everything was fine but I wasn't convinced. I came to London and found the address on her letter. She was living with Vince Hammond and as I was a visiting sister, he let me stay. It wasn't long before I understood exactly what was going on. Hammond was new to London and had come to expand his business. He was involved in awful things; drugs, extortion, you name it. When I found out the truth I begged Sara to leave with me, but she said 'I can't'. It took me a while to understand why. Hammond or 'Vinny' as she called him, got her drunk one night and insisted she try something. He promised she would thank him and told her it was harmless. It was far from harmless.' As Vicky said it, her voice grew hard, 'It was heroine. Sara was sick but under pressure; later she tried it again and that was the hold Vince Hammond had on her, he kept her supplied. It was his way of keeping her; he liked to own things.

Do you know he actually likes to listen in on people? It's a kind of perverse hobby with him to hide a microphone thing, what's it called...? A bug?'

Tony nodded.

'And listen to conversations. I'm convinced that Hammond's not sane. He crawls with paranoia. Sara and I would check for bugs. It was a ridiculous way to live. I tried to persuade Sara to leave with me, I promised to get help for her. She pleaded with me not to make her, not only did she rely on Hammond for drugs but she was petrified of him, when he lost his temper he was capable of anything.

Sara's condition deteriorated, she lost weight and looked like hell. The heroine didn't even give her a high anymore she needed it to stay normal. Sometimes Hammond refused to give her any. First she would get irritable then tremble and sweat like a cold or something but a thousand times worse.

I hated Hammond but I couldn't leave her. I quit my job put my belongings in storage and gave up our flat. He made my skin crawl but I stayed and he liked me there. If he was in a good mood we'd go to restaurants, he enjoyed walking in with two women. I hated it, hated it but couldn't leave my little sister. A year passed, my God a year, trying to get Sara to leave, pretending I didn't know what was going on.'

Vicky was having trouble with the next part of her story, her voice shook, 'On that last night, Vince went out to a meeting. Sara had been begging him for more heroine but he was getting tired of her. He shook her off and told me to keep her out of his way. Sara hadn't had a fix for so long she was heavily into withdrawal.' Vicky swallowed, her voice was strained as if it were painful to talk, 'Heroine withdrawal can last for days; she had a fever, stomach cramps, violent pains, she kept being sick and going to the toilet, she was in a terrible state.

As Hammond drove off, Sara raced after him taking his second car. I ran outside in time to see her driving off. I ran down the drive and waved down a black cab and told the driver I needed to catch the car in front. I remember he thought it was a big joke, said he always wanted someone to say that. There was nothing funny about it, Hammond had a temper and I had seen it, he could be vicious, another reason why Sara wouldn't leave. She was terrified he would come after her.

When Hammond arrived at his meeting, he drove down to an underground car park. Sara got there in time to see him drive in. She saw the door in the wall, which lead to the lower level. I suppose she thought it was a quicker way down. She abandoned the car and ran in. I saw her go through the door, but it took a few seconds to pay the cab off. I rushed to the door. Sara had run down in the dark, I fumbled about for the light switch and followed her down the steps, but I was too late.

When Sara burst through the door in the sub-level, they thought it was a set up. Some kind of illegal arms deal was in progress, I had heard Hammond discussing it on the phone and I think he had a shipment in a lorry park somewhere. Anyway, I suppose things were pretty tense so when the door burst open, Hammond must have spun round and… and… shot her…! She died in my arms. I ran. Hammond shouted for me to stop but I ran.'

Tony nodded grimly, 'And that's why Hammond or one of his men tried to run you an' Ron off the road because you know he killed Sara and he probably thinks Ron knows too.'

Vicky nodded, 'And if he sees Ron, he'll kill him on the spot, Shades is a witness to that and… we have to get there!' She wanted to cry but there wasn't time. There should be time to grieve, this wasn't right, this wasn't fair, none of it was fair!

'Does Hammond own a big house like these?' Tony nodded at the grand looking homes they were passing.

Vicky was choked; to her Sara had just died. She nodded and managed to say, 'Yes, like these.'

'We may be too late. A house like that is bound to be alarmed, 'specially if this Hammond's an electronics nut and as paranoid as you think… bugs you say?' Tony shook his head. Vicky was quick, 'No, Hammond had it all ripped out because it kept going off and the new one he wants is so new only one company in the whole country sells it and he was having trouble getting one.' This one crumb of good luck gave her a little hope.

Tony pulled up at the gates leading to Vince Hammond's house and switched off the engine. Beyond the gates the house appeared quiet. He glanced at Vicky then got out to stand at the gates and looked through the bars. Vicky was desperate, she was still frightened of Tony but also terrified of what might be happening to Ron and this gave her courage. Making up her mind she scrambled out and joined Tony, 'We have to do something!' Tony turned to her, 'We can't go storming in there, perhaps Shades and Ron are fine. If we go crashing in at the wrong moment, anything could happen.'

Vicky felt almost hysterical with worry but knew she had to make sense or Tony would ignore her. She fought to keep her voice level, 'Anything could already be happening. Look, if Hammond knows others are involved, he may think twice before he does something.'

Something was indeed happening. The two men in the office were still talking while Ron and Shades stood tensely in the small alcove behind the curtains with their backs to the balcony door.

One voice, presumably Hammond, was giving the other man his orders, 'Put the money on the desk, Micky. So they paid up this time in full.'

'Yeah, no problem, I think you sending two of the boys with me did the trick.'

A contented snort then, 'These small businesses have to learn if they don't pay their insurance they're inviting accidents.' Micky laughed, 'That's right.' 'Turn around Micky, no one knows the combination but me.' 'Sure, Vince.' After a short pause, there was a click of a safe door closing.

'By the way you definitely got rid of the damaged car properly, didn't you?'

'Oh yeah, nothing to worry about, dumped it, torched it, (laughs) picked up a nice new one... powerful, got it from a long stay car park, won't be missed for a fortnight.'

'Good, right take your nice new car and go check on the truck.'

'It should be fine Vince, don't forget I slapped false plates on it after I nicked it.'

'Should isn't good enough, I want to *know* it's fine. Don't touch it just drive past and look it over and when you leave the lorry park check no-one follows you, got it?'

'Sure, sure no problem.'

'When you go out, tell the boys to do a sweep of the grounds. I'm not happy about the alarm system being out. Vicky's loose out there, thanks to you. She hasn't gone to the police because we would have had a visit, she might be trying something on her own, or with this guy she's hooked up with,' he paused then, 'who we still don't know anything about, again thanks to you.'

Behind the curtain Shades looked at Ron who was staring at the floor listening intently.

Hammond continued, his quiet voice hiding none of his anger, 'Your mistakes are adding up, Micky.' Eager to show his usefulness and change the subject Micky quickly said, 'I know you're unhappy about the alarm Vince, so I already told 'em to check the grounds.'

'*You* told them?'

'Yeah, I thought...'

If Ron and Shades hadn't been hiding they would have seen Micky take half a step back and if they had the same view as Micky they would have understood why.

'*I* do the telling, Micky, you do the doing, got it?'

'Yes Vince.'

There was another tense silence while Vincent pushed the point home by glaring into Micky's frightened eyes. Satisfied, he asked, 'You and the boys still got silencers on those pistols? We're not exactly in the middle of nowhere here.'

'Sure we do, like you said.' He nodded at Vince and patted his jacket pocket, Vince considered Micky for an uncomfortable moment. Was it time to replace him?

Shades glanced sideways at Ron, who looked green and not only because of the light filtering through the green curtains. He licked his own dry lips and listened hard.

Hammond snapped, 'The truck.' 'Yes Vince, I'll go right now.' He sounded eager to have an excuse to leave quickly. There was movement in the room, the light went out and Shades and Ron heard the door close. They relaxed and softly exhaled as if they had been holding their breath the whole time, which is what it felt like.

Shades opened the door and the two crept out onto the balcony. After the heat of the house, it felt colder than ever, not helped by the steady rain. They crouched low and looked down on the shadowy grounds, nothing. Shades whispered in Ron's ear, 'That Hammond told the other guy, Micky wasn't it?' Ron nodded.

'Just told that guy Micky to go and check some truck. We better wait till he leaves.' Ron just wanted to get the hell out, 'Let's run for it now.'

'No!'

Somewhere out in the dark an engine started, a moment later they watched a big silver car move off down the drive.

Outside the gates, Tony and Vicky saw the car's headlights. Tony sprang to the driver's side, 'Quick.' Vicky didn't need encouraging, she leapt into the passenger seat, taking a chance Tony drove the car down the street with the lights off and slid into the shadows between the streetlamps. Tony switched off the motor and focussed his attention on the rear view mirror. It was fifty-fifty which way the car would go. If it came their way the distinctive Chevrolet would be lit up, Vicky tensed and Tony knuckles grew white as he held the steering wheel.

The gates slid apart and headlights lit the road. Tony spoke slowly, 'He's going....' then finished quickly, 'the other way.'

'Oh,' Vicky breathed then, 'let's get back.'

Ron stared at the gap between the balcony and garage roof, 'It looks worse from here!' Shades didn't have much patience, the tension of the last few minutes had been quite considerable, even for an adventure-hungry screen hero like himself, 'Don't be such a wimp and jump, will ya!' Ron felt angry and this seemed to help, 'Okay, what are we waiting for then?' With that he stepped over the rail, tensed his legs then with all his strength, sprang. For a moment, there was a rush of wet, cold night air then, thump crack, he landed awkwardly on the roof. His foot had broken a tile and disappeared through up to the ankle.

Shades watched Ron struggle for a moment and raised his eyes to the rain. 'I don't believe it!' He too leapt for the roof. Having landed safely, Shades grabbed Ron's leg and pulled. Ron's foot came free and some fragments of broken tile trickled off the roof, but with the storm worsening there was little chance of anyone hearing. They were both soaked to the skin, clothes sticking to their bodies. The cold was paralysing, made worse by the knife-like wind, it hurt their ears and slashed at their bodies in vicious gusts. 'Jump!' Shades pointed to the patch of ferns beside the garage. Ron nodded and they jumped together. As they landed, a stern voice from behind said, 'Hold it right there.'

As one, they ran without looking back. There was a muted, spiteful short crack. They stopped quickly and held their arms up, guessing instantly what had made the strange noise. They turned slowly. One of Hammond's men had been sheltering from the rain under the porch at the garage end of the house. Ron and Shades had jumped down in front of him.

Tony and Vicky had returned to the gates on foot. Now drenched, they were standing looking through the bars. Suddenly, a sharp tap thud noise from behind made them turn. They were just in time to see a small piece of tarmac fall to the road. At the same instant some bark dropped from a tree on the other side of the road. For a moment neither moved, then everything happened at once. Tony's strong hands seized Vicky's small waist and pulled her toward him knocking the breath out of her. He moved both himself and her from the gate and out of sight of the house behind the wall. Vicky's frightened eyes stared up at Tony's face, he was silent and still held her. Vicky's eyes widened in horror, 'That was a bullet!' Tony remained silent but let go of her. 'Wasn't it?' She almost shouted the question. She received a short, clipped answer, 'Think so.' Vicky was almost hysterical, 'Tony, we must get in...! Oh my God... Oh my God, if he's shot Ron... Oh my God!'

Tony pulled a vicious-looking flick knife from his jacket and jammed it into the small slit in the panel that controlled the lock to the gates, hoping the wooden grip would be sufficient insulation. There was a buzz and a smell of burnt wire as the locking mechanism fused. The gates normally opened by sliding parallel with the wall inside. Tony pulled one gate and Vicky instantly sprang forward to pull with all her strength on the other gate. The big gates parted. Once they had moved wide enough for the car, Tony ran back jumped in and started the motor. Hot on his heels Vicky climbed in beside him.

'Get out, this isn't for you.'

By now Vicky was frantic with worry, frozen stiff and drenched to the skin. For a hot moment she forgot all about being frightened of Tony, 'Cut all the macho shit and drive the bloody car... *now*!' As she said 'now', she gritted her teeth and brought her fist down hard on the dashboard. Instantly, the engine stopped and all the lights went out. Vicky stared in horror at the dark dashboard. Tony opened his mouth and also stared, 'What did you do?' he demanded.

'Loose wire, Ron said there was a loose wire!'

Tony wrestled with the ignition key, nothing happened. Vicky hit the dashboard again even harder. Lights sprang on, the starter turned and the hot engine fired. Tony glared at her as he selected 'drive' and floored the accelerator. The wheels spun and the back of the car slewed around a little, then as the tyres bit, it straightened and they rocketed through the gate with headlights blazing.

'Keep down, there may be more shooting!' Tony shouted without taking his eyes off the drive, she crouched low in her seat.

Speeding up the drive, they could see all the house lights were on, clearly illuminating the scene, Ron and Shades standing with their hands behind their heads were facing them, standing close behind with guns drawn were two of Hammond's men. A very large man stood behind Ron and a smaller man behind Shades. A short distance away to the left stood Vince Hammond himself, blonde neat hair, tall, lean, clad in dark trousers, dark roll neck sweater and sports jacket. He also held a gun, which was trained on Ron and Shades.

They all turned as the Chevy tore toward them. Tony threw the car into an impressive skid that showered everyone with gravel, snatched the keys from the ignition and leapt out with surprising speed for his size. Since Hammond and his men were armed they hadn't expected this and for a precious moment, hesitated. Tony ran at the two guards, Hammond shouted, 'Hold it!' and raised his gun. While Hammond's attention was focussed on Tony who was closing on the first guard standing behind and slightly to the left of Shades, Vicky was also moving quickly, having sprung from the car, swept around it and flung her body at Hammond, her shoulder striking his and knocking him off balance. As they both fell the gun fired but the shot flew wide.

The first guard standing by Shades had expected Hammond to stop Tony and had done nothing. He now looked away from Hammond back at Tony in time to get the full force of Tony's fist square in the face, sending him toppling over backwards. The second bigger guard lifted his gun but Ron, catching the movement in the corner of his eye brought his arm back and cracked him hard on the nose with the back of his fist. Adrenaline and fear brought Vicky to her feet first. Fury launched Hammond to his feet a split second later. He swung wildly at Vicky, animal rage spoiling his aim. She managed to dodge the blow and tried to kick the gun from his hand. Unfortunately, in the moment her attention was on the gun Hammond seized the opportunity and with his free hand caught her with a left cross to the jaw. The force of the blow sent her sprawling back to the ground.

Ron witnessed Hammond strike Vicky and with murderous rage lunged forward. In that moment he would have killed Hammond if he had reached him. The big man behind Ron could do nothing to prevent him as Ron's blow had given Tony sufficient time to reach him and was at that moment attempting to wrestle the gun from his hand. Shades had run over to help but the man was nearly as big as Tony and it was proving no easy task.

Unluckily for Ron the first guard Tony had punched now regained his feet and as Ron hurtled past on his way to Hammond, the guard struck him on the back of the head with the butt of his gun. Ron crumpled and ploughed nose first into the gravel. Meanwhile, Shades and Tony were still busy with the second guard who was putting up quite a fight. During the struggle, Tony was knocked to the ground and the car keys fell from his pocket. The first guard saw this, ran over and snatched them up. Hammond saw Ron begin to rise groggily, 'Throw him in the boot!' he bellowed at the first guard who left Shades wrestling with his colleague and ran back to the staggering Ron who he grabbed and dragged to the car.

Vicky sat up in time to see the first guard open the boot and push Ron in. Still stunned, he fell heavily, the guard slammed the lid and locked it.

Vicky rose to her feet and started forward but Hammond seized her arm and bent it behind her back,

'Be still.' He hissed between gritted teeth. She stood on tiptoe to try and ease the pain in her arm. Having got Ron out of the way, the first guard started back to help his colleague still wrestling with Shades, but before he could reach him Tony who had got up angrier than he had gone down improved his mood by kicking the second guard between the legs from behind. The pain caused him to slump forward. As he bent double, Shades brought his knee up smashing him in the face. The guard toppled back and landed hard. Shades spun around and began to move towards Vicky.

Hammond gripped Vicky with one hand and tried to aim the gun with the other. Although in pain, she stamped her heel down hard on Hammond's foot, he cried out in pain. The first guard, who hadn't quite reached Tony and Shades, glanced back over his shoulder at his boss. In that split second Shades had closed the gap and took the opportunity to punch him in the stomach as he ran past. The guard doubled up and dropped the keys, with one hand gripping his stomach now in a stooped position made to pick them up but before he could, Tony, hot on Shades' heels kicked him in the face, fracturing his nose and hurling him backwards. Hardly breaking his stride, Tony scooped up the keys and followed his brother who was heading for Hammond and Vicky. Hammond levelled his gun at them again and fired, it was only Vicky's struggling that made him miss.

There was another shot, this time from the big second guard who had rolled over and was in a half-sitting position. Tony shouted, 'The car!' Shades hesitated and looked at Vicky then a shot from behind nicked his arm and another whistled past his head.

He realised there was nothing they could do but run for the car and come back for her. Shades dived in the passenger side and stayed low. At the same moment, Tony started the car and lying on his side resting his head on his brother's shoulder had enough of a forward view to accelerate fast in the direction of the guards, the big guard stopped trying to shoot and clumsily began to rise to his feet. Fearing Tony would mow him down, the smaller guard with the fractured nose, not having time to stand scrambled frantically on all fours to get out of the way. Tony hauled the car around at the last moment in a u-turn and sped roughly in the direction of the gates.

The first guard had recovered his senses enough to roll into a sitting position and pulled his gun. The second big guard fired from a standing position. Hammond's shots were hampered by Vicky but some hit the mark. Three guns shot at the car. By some miracle they didn't hit the fuel tank or the brothers but shot after shot ripped through the thin metal of the boot.

Vicky, thinking of Ron inside screamed, 'Stop! Stop! For God's sake, stop!' The guns continued to fire. The rear of the car was peppered with bullet holes, one of the rear lights exploded into spinning fragments, Vicky now hysterical tried to claw at Hammond's face. He stopped shooting and grabbed both her arms. She stood helpless and broken as Tony skidded off down the drive gravel spitting from the rear wheels. Shades stayed low as Tony drove with his foot hard on the floor. The 180 horsepower V8 engine hurled the car down the drive.

Hammond shouted to the guards, 'Stop shooting, get my car!' He flung Vicky to the ground, reached into his pocket for his key ring that operated the gates and pushed the button hard, then threw the keys to his men who were now both making for his car, 'Catch!' The keys landed in the gravel close to Hammond's car. The big guard grabbed them and lost no time getting in starting the engine and with his colleague in the passenger seat roared off after Tony.

Vicky remained on the wet ground half-lying, half-sitting in shocked silence. Ron was dead was all she could think as she stared at the disappearing Chevrolet.

At the end of the drive the damaged mechanism in the gate began to move jerkily. Tony's eyes were wide with horror as he saw the heavy iron gates begin to slide shut. He had accelerated to nearly forty-five miles an hour! The gates were shuddering and faltering but definitely closing. Hearing no further gunfire hitting the car Shades sat up cautiously in time to see the gates shutting, 'Oh shit!' He ducked down again. Tony held the wheel tightly and clenched his teeth. The gap between the iron gates now looked impossible. The Chevy thundered down the drive like a battering ram. From his crouched position, Shades glanced at his brother. Tony looked determined as he stared fixedly ahead. He was going through.

'Oh Christ, he's gonna do it,' Shades whispered as he screwed his eyes tight shut and waited for the impact. He heard the scream of tortured metal as the car sped through with nothing to spare, the gates having shaved off the paint down one side and tearing some metal trim from the other.

It was something of a shock even for Tony that they had made it, 'Wow!' Hitting the brakes he pulled the wheel hard to the right. The car skidded, mounted the pavement, ran along the path for a few hundred yards, narrowly missed two trees and bounced back on to the road.

Hammond's men reached the gate far too late and swerving to a halt jumped out and tried to force the gates apart by hand but it was no use, the circuitry had fused completely. All they could do was stare through the bars and watch Ron's car disappear into the miserable twilight of Thursday morning.

They drove slowly back to Hammond, who to put it extremely mildly was not happy. When he had finished venting his fury at the two wet and bleeding men who stood before him he ended his tirade with 'Lock her in the basement.' The big guard gripped Vicky and roughly hauled her away. She simply allowed herself to be taken. Ron was dead. Hammond shouted after them, 'And I want to keep an eye on her, you know what to do.' The guard nodded. Hammond glaring at the back of their heads followed them into the house. He was worried about Tony and Shades; he knew Tony's reputation, they wouldn't go to the police but this whole thing was messy. It would need careful handling and Hammond couldn't be sure who else knew he had killed Sara, so for now he would lock Vicky up and see what the brothers did.

Vicky was pushed into the house and down to the basement. She was of course familiar with the house but the basement had always been off limits. It was a large old house and there were a number of rooms below ground used only for storage. Vince Hammond had occasionally used it to store God knows what, evidently, preferring to keep really incriminating material off site. Vicky was taken to one of these rooms and shoved through the door with so much force that she fell to the floor. The big guard's disposition could never, even on a good day, be described as sunny and this was not a good day. The man had been punched and kneed in the face, also kicked forcefully between the legs. He yearned to hit, slash or kill something. Bending down he snatched up her small shoulder bag and left, slamming and bolting the door after him.

She sat and stared at the floor for some time, her mind struggling to absorb what had happened. It seemed too unreal somehow. Suddenly, the door opened and her bag was placed in the room. The door slammed shut again with the sound of the bolt sliding into place and heavy footsteps receding.

She was alone, really alone. Sara was gone, Ron was gone, she was completely on her own. Vicky felt so wretched it was almost unbearable. She looked about the room, it was dirty with old pieces of furniture scattered about, also some wooden crates, a stepladder, paint pots and various other bric-a-brac. There was no light bulb, but a faint, greyish light was coming from a small window set high up in the wall. The window itself was low to the ground if viewed from outside.

Stiffly, she got to her feet and scrambled onto some boxes. Standing on tiptoe she could see out. Reaching through the bars and rubbing some of the grime from the glass, she could make out the front drive. There was no way out through the window as the bars were too narrowly spaced. Holding the bars, Vicky looked down the long drive but from the low angle couldn't see the gates. She stared at the drive remembering the car hurtling down it with the gunfire punching holes in the boot where Ron lay. Letting go of the bars she sank to the floor. Misery washed over her with such force she felt death would be welcome, better than being here, feeling this hopeless unbearable sadness. She shivered, her coat, sweater and jeans were all soaked through.

A few miles away the battered Chevrolet pulled into one of the disused warehouses on the old industrial estate near the river. The low burble of the engine stopped abruptly, followed by the simultaneous clunks of doors opening. Shades and Tony got out slowly and plodded to the rear of the car. Shades looked pale, his arm was bleeding a little but that wasn't the reason for his lack of colour. The brothers stood quietly staring at the many bullet holes in the boot. Without a word Tony put the key in the lock and turned it. He hesitated for a moment then lifted the lid quickly. Shades looked away, 'Oh Jesus, no!' Tony stared down. Ron lay covered in blood. Without taking his eyes from Ron, Tony spoke quietly, 'He still seems to be breathing.' Shades looked back hopefully, 'Hey, do ya think there's a chance that...?' Tony whispered, 'No one loses that much blood and makes it.'

Ron was trying to speak, Shades bent to listen and answered softly, 'Yes, of course we will, you'll be alright.'

Vicky had retrieved her bag from across the room. She opened it and pulled out the small bear Ron had bought for her when they had stopped at the shops. She held it now, she held it very tight. Drawing up her knees, holding the bear, dropping her head and shutting her eyes, she quietly wept.

Outside was another grey, freezing, miserable day, the heavy rain during the night had disintegrated to a steady misty drizzle.

At the warehouse, the big grey car was still parked in the entrance. The wind blew rain in through the open door. Beneath the rear of the car a puddle had formed and into that puddle red liquid slowly dripped. Tony slammed the boot lid, 'Let's go!' He climbed in. The starter turned lazily then the low familiar burble could be heard as the engine fired. The car backed out and drove off. A thin, blue cloud lingered for a moment then all that remained to show they had been there was a small, reddish puddle just inside the door on the cold concrete floor.

PART ONE
CHAPTER 6
THURSDAY AFTERNOON 3:00

Vicky sat up with a jolt, looked around the dirty cellar room, then glanced at her watch but it was becoming too dark to see the face. Tilting it toward the weak, grey light coming from the small barred window she could make out three o'clock. She had cried herself to sleep exhausted by the strain of the last few hours it was the cold that had awoken her. Vicky began to think about Ron and felt like crying again but it was so cold it was hard to concentrate on much else, apart from the pain in her right cheek from Hammond's blow. Her teeth chattered and her body shivered. She would need to look around the room and find something to wrap around herself. It was important to look now; if left any longer it would be too dark to see anything. After all this was December so it would be completely dark by four thirty. Vicky rummaged around finding some cardboard boxes, which she broke down for something to sit on. They at least provided some insulation against the stone floor. Now, for something to cover herself. The window was so small and dirty and the sky outside so overcast, night was coming early to the small underground prison. It was now far too dark to see anything except very large objects. A chest of drawers stood against the wall. Opening the top drawer and very carefully putting her hand in, her fingers touched material, which she pulled. It seemed to be quite big. 'A towel? No, a blanket... No, too big for that.' Something made a metallic noise... 'Rings...? Curtain rings!' It was a large heavy curtain. She dropped it to the floor and felt for more. 'Yes, another one!' Pulling it out, she stooped to pick up the one on the floor and felt her way back to the cardboard boxes.

Wrapping the old dusty curtains around herself, she sat in the quickly darkening room. It was still cold but just tolerable. The need for protection satisfied, her mind recalled details of things she didn't want to think about. Vicky kept her eyes open and tried to look at the rapidly fading objects around her. When the light faded completely, she shut her eyes, lay still and tried to escape both thoughts and room with the only option left, sleep. The image of the car pulling away with bullets tearing holes in the boot returned to torment her. Not knowing what else to do, she curled up as tight as possible and lay still in the dark, a small bundle, hopeless and alone.

Upstairs in the light and warmth, Vince Hammond sat at his desk. He twiddled his thumbs and rocked gently from side to side in his swivel chair. He was not happy; this whole thing was messy, very messy. This was all Sara's fault. Why had he got mixed up with her in the first place? She wasn't even pretty. He stopped rocking and frowned. She had been when he first met her. Oh well. It was all going beautifully then the stupid bitch burst in on one of the biggest

140

deals he had ever made. The deal had gone bad. Illegal arms dealers like to keep their transactions very low profile. He snorted. They like to deal in guns but to see what a gun could do at close range... They didn't want to know. The arms dealers were the moneymen behind the murder. They dealt in supply, how the product was used was none of their business, leaving that to the hit men and terrorists. Hammond shook his head. When Sara hit the ground, they couldn't get out of there quick enough. Now he had a shipment of guns sitting in a stolen truck with no buyer, also a witness in the basement who could cause plenty of trouble. To top it off, there were three others involved, one of the three was dead, true.

Hammond pondered, would one less make it more complicated or easier? It all depended on what Big Tony and his brother did next. Hammond only knew Big Tony from rumour, he had been told that Tony and his brother were on the fringes of local dealings but not actively involved. Hammond wondered if that were true or whether, like himself the brothers kept their business very private. Something else to consider was this man Vicky had been with. By her reaction they had been close, and the way Tony came up the drive... Could this mean that Tony was good friends with the man as well? If this was true, Tony may want revenge, or perhaps he wasn't interested in the man or Vicky and had only got involved to rescue his brother. The brother! What the hell was Tony's brother Shades, doing breaking into his house? What was he after?

Hammond poured himself a drink and tried to reason it out again. He sat and rocked and thought. It was on the third trip to the decanter, he noticed it was only a quarter full. He frowned and returned to his desk.

In another part of the house, Micky alternated between gazing out of the window and nervously pacing the room. He had returned some time ago after checking all was well with the truck but finding all was certainly not well with Vincent, had quickly made himself scarce. When his boss was angry it was dangerous to be near, so Micky had taken refuge in what Vincent referred to as the security room. Although part of the house and accessed via a connecting door Vincent never visited, as the untidy room disturbed him. It was furnished with old leather chairs beaten into submission by heavy men dropping into them. A sticky table was strewn with cards, well-thumbed girlie magazines and a dartboard finished off the look nicely. The dubious charms of the room would never feature among the pages of glossy décor magazines unless grubby became the new look.

Micky wasn't alone but nobody in the room was in the mood for cards. Of the two men who shared the space with him one had a fractured nose and bruising, the other still had enough pain between his legs to spoil any hope of concentration. The atmosphere, usually full of swearwords and cigarette smoke was heavy and brooding. What Micky's colleagues were really in the mood for was to beat someone with a baseball bat, preferably Tony and Shades.

Hammond pushed the small intercom button that connected him to this room. Confident he would find

Micky there he wasn't surprised when a voice answered, 'Hello?'

'Micky, where's my special brandy?' Micky's answer was nervous and apologetic, his boss had had about as much bad news today as he could handle, 'It hasn't come.' From experience he knew if Vincent was unhappy it soon followed that people around him found themselves in a similar state. Hammond was predictably irritated, 'Well, get down to that supplier tomorrow and find out why and don't take any excuses Micky, I pay enough for the stuff.' 'Sure, Vince... tomorrow, first thing.' The intercom clicked off. Micky Slater had worked for him for a few years and was the only one permitted to call him by his first name and could enter the house without being summoned, which he rarely did. Micky was useful; he never asked questions. He was spiteful and as long as there was money in it, would do anything, up to and including murder. He was also aware that Micky was frightened of him and made sure it stayed that way. Recently, he had made mistakes. Perhaps Micky's time had come. There was too much going on at present, he would have to consider Micky's future and whether he had one.

Hammond ate alone in his large, neat, well-ordered kitchen and later strolled moodily around the cold colourless grounds. That evening found him back in his office dealing with another of his dubious enterprises. Finally, putting these tasks to one side and carefully locking the drawer his mind returned to the problem of guns and parked trucks.

At eleven o'clock the phone rang. Hammond, with his elbows resting on the arms of the chair thoughtfully stroked his lower lip with his thumb and watched it ring for a moment. Then with a quick movement he parted his hands, leaned forward and snatched it up. 'Hammond!' He barked. The voice at the other end was quiet and deep, 'This is Big Tony.' Hammond became coy, 'Who?' Tony wasn't in the mood for games, 'Come on Hammond, cut it out. We have things to discuss.'

'We do?'

'Yes, we do.' Tony was firm.

Hammond protested, 'I don't like doing business on the phone.'

'You admit we have business to discuss then?'

'I'm admitting to nothing.' He snapped, but Tony was quick too, 'Listen Hammond, you left me and my brother with a certain item in the boot of the car. I'm phoning you to see if you want us to handle it. Of course, if you would prefer I turn it over to someone else, that's fine, I'm sorry to have bothered you.'

'Hold it… I don't know what you're talking about but perhaps you'd better come to the house to straighten this misunderstanding out.'

'I want the girl to be there too.'

'What's she got to do with you?'

'Two things. First, if I take care of the problem in the boot, she could be trouble if she talks to anyone and it would be my neck. The second thing is, I may be in a position to help you convince her to keep quiet.' There was a moment's silence from Hammond, then, 'I'm not talking any more on the phone, come round tomorrow morning, nine o'clock.'

'Okay, nine then.'

Hammond sat and looked at the phone for a while after hanging up. He considered; things may be looking better. This Tony could be the answer. Then again, it may be a pack of lies and some kind of trick. Hammond decided to play things close, listen to Tony sure, but he wasn't admitting anything. After all, he had roughed up Tony's brother and during the latest scuffle outside, he felt sure he had seen Shades nicked by a bullet. Vincent sat and weighed the facts, what would Tony do? Vincent knew people could react strongly to that sort of thing because he had observed the way his parents reacted to his brother's death. They had cried a lot. Eight-year-old Vincent had wiped his eyes as he saw them do, copying them, wiping his eyes as if to brush away tears. Losing his brother had been something of an education for little Vincent. He soon learned that if he looked sad he got attention and presents. His first thought on hearing the news of his brother's death had been 'I get the big bedroom all to myself and I get his toys'. As it sank in, the possibility of double Christmas presents occurred to him. His brother's death had been hard for little Vinnie, hard to keep from smiling. Vincent wiped the smile off his face now as his mind returned to the present. No, this Big Tony character had plenty to have a grudge about, even if he had no connection with Vicky, after all he and his men had tried to shoot him. No mention of the police? Tony must have something to gain. Perhaps this Tony was a bigger operator than he suspected. The best thing was to wait and see what tomorrow brought. He drained his glass, went to bed and slept soundly.

PART ONE
CHAPTER 7
FRIDAY MORNING

Wakefulness brought with it the brutal reality of Vicky's situation and the utter misery that invariably followed. Ron was dead, her Ron, the only good thing to have happened since that cursed day Vincent Hammond had walked into her life. Vicky knew she was awake but postponed opening her eyes as long as possible. Finally giving up, the first thing she saw was the grubby ceiling. She shut them again quickly the reality of the situation was too much, far better to try for sleep and oblivion. But sleep wouldn't come, only images of Ron getting hit, the car pulling away and bullets tearing into the boot. She shook her head and forced her thoughts to shift to something else, now after rest her mind was clear, far too clear!

'Vicky, it hurts... it hurts,' the voice of Sara returned to haunt her, 'No!'

Vicky sat up quickly and opened her eyes. After sleeping for so many hours the luxury of unconsciousness was forbidden. She was cold, the curtains had definitely helped but it had been a very cold night in the unheated cellar. Struggling up stiffly she rubbed her hands vigorously over her thighs then massaged her upper arms, stretching on her toes and hopping up and down a little in an attempt to get warm and move the blood to numbed toes and fingers.

A sudden noise made her spin round, the heavy bolt on the door was being drawn back. A guard from the night before entered the room; the big stocky one.

Vicky instinctively took a step back; he certainly was ugly. Of course his aesthetic appeal hadn't been improved much by Ron's fist to his nose, nor Shades' knee in the face. The said nose was swollen and the eyes blackened, the short hair was black, bristly and stood up from his scalp. His face was fat with thick lips giving him the appearance of constantly pouting. Also, he didn't appear to have a neck, his head just disappeared into his bullish shoulders. Surprisingly, he still looked better than his smaller counterpart whose nose Tony had actually fractured.

'Here!' He held out a tray. She would have liked to kick it out of his hand and tell him where to shove it, but it had been hours since her last meal and it was far from certain if or when her next would be. So she edged closer and took it from him. He said no more and turned to leave.

'I need the bathroom.' Vicky announced curtly, the sharpness in her own voice surprised her. He turned and looked at her. Vicky stared back defiantly, she was so small she hardly posed a threat.

'Walk.' He pointed at the open door. Vicky placed the tray on a box and walked stiffly out of the room followed closely by the guard. She hesitated unsure of the direction. 'That way.' He gestured to the right.

She had been expecting to be taken upstairs, but instead was shown to a small WC in the basement.

He left her at the door. Inside, she cast about for either a weapon or means of escape but it was useless, no window, small sink, no mirror, hard, cracked soap. Before leaving she took the opportunity to wash her face and dab it dry with her coat. She sighed, walked out and was quickly returned to her prison, the bolt slid back into its keep, alone again with her thoughts, poor company.

There was a big tin mug of steaming tea, a small pot of jam and two hunks of bread sitting on the tray where she'd left it. She snorted while examining the plastic knife. They weren't taking any chances. Against her wishes, after quickly eating the bread and jam, she felt surprisingly better. This made her feel guilty, the two people closest to her in the whole world were dead, killed by the very people who were holding her and she felt better, no, not better, stronger! Yes, things were bad probably as bad as things could be but she was a strong woman and would get out of this somehow. When that happened they'd pay.

Swallowing the last piece of bread then washing it down with hot sweet tea, she was done feeling sorry for herself. Of course, the grief would return but, for now, she needed to be angry.

Suddenly there was the sound of a car. Quickly she climbed on to the boxes once more and tried to see out of the grimy window. The rain, that had never been far away over the last few days, had turned to sleet. The world outside had become grey, as if all colour had been washed from it. Out of the grim veil of slowly falling sleet a car faded into view. Her spirits were raised even more when the car stopped and Big Tony climbed out. He disappeared quickly out of sight toward the main entrance.

She waited in excited silence. Would there be shooting? Would there be police cars chasing up the drive? The minutes ticked by, nothing happened. She listened for shouts or the sound of fighting, but all was quiet. Vicky wasn't sure about Tony but in this awful house he was the closest thing to a friend, what was going on up there?

Suddenly, the bolt was pulled back, the heavy door hauled open and the big ugly guard stood solidly at the threshold. He held a gun, which waved in a gesture that obviously meant 'this way'.

Upstairs, Vicky was directed into the large lavishly decorated sitting room, which Hammond used for visitors when discussing business. There were sofas - one of which held Tony who appeared comfortable and relaxed - chairs and a desk in front of the Georgian window, seated behind the desk looking equally relaxed was Vincent Hammond. Big Tony turned to look at her as she entered. She stared at him his face was impassive then recalling what Ron had told her about knowing Tony's mood by the colour of his shirt, tried to remember what black meant.

Ignoring the look of hatred from the guard, Tony watched her carefully. Her eyes were red from crying, face pale, a bruise had formed on her cheek, hair unbrushed and she had the crumpled appearance of someone who had slept in their clothes, which of course she had. She gave Tony a faint smile. He stared back coldly. Again, she glanced at his shirt. Ron hadn't mentioned black, she didn't know what it meant, her bright face dimmed. Tony returned his attention to Hammond, 'Half then.' Hammond nodded.

Tony continued, 'and the rest when this part of the job is completed.' She stared in disbelief; he was doing a deal! Tony stood, moved to a case lying on a nearby table and flicked the catches. Vicky couldn't see what lay inside. He nodded curtly, 'Okay, by now my brother has already taken care of the problem in the car, soon there won't be anything more to worry about.' He eyed Vicky, she blinked this was the stuff of nightmares. Surely, it must be some kind of trick Tony was playing on Hammond? Her stomach tightened, she felt faint. Was it really possible this was what it seemed and Tony was taking her away to kill her? Then she remembered Shades, Tony possibly, but Shades? No, he was Ron's friend it was Shades who had helped Ron through the drinking after Jacqui died. Shades would never be a part of this.

Doubt must also have passed through Hammond's mind because he walked to the table and rested a hand on the case. He looked into Tony's face searching for a glimmer of a lie, 'We had your brother roughed up and you say he was nicked in the arm as you made your theatrical exit yesterday and now he's helping you?'

Tony stared back, his eyes still emotionless except for the faintest glint of anger, his voice was deep and hard, 'This is business! My brother is a businessman and he is as practical as me in these things. Yes, he got roughed up but we're in a rough business, he accepts that. In our line of work we deal with tough people, it's the way it is, that's all. Now we know who we're dealing with, there's no reason we can't work together. Us tidying up the boot is our way of showing good faith. Now we're doing our first paid job for you. We may discuss future jobs that could be mutually rewarding,' Tony showed a ghost of a smile, 'perhaps... very lucrative.'

Keeping his hand on the case, Hammond's eyes locked on Tony while he spoke. It was Hammond who broke the stare first, 'Hold on, let's not get ahead of ourselves and see how you handle this job first then we'll take it from there,' suddenly, he became charming, lifting his hand from the case he returned to his desk, 'I think we may have the same view, making money is the important thing, I like a man who keeps useless emotions from sound business.' Tony nodded, 'Sounds right and don't worry about Shades, he does what I tell him.' He picked up the case then looking at the guard said, 'Hands and feet then dump her on the back seat of my car.' The guard looked at Hammond who stared at Tony for a moment then apparently satisfied, he nodded. The guard dragged the shocked and speechless Vicky away.

Outside she struggled, the guard slapped her hard and in the cold air it stung. She felt a surge of anger and raised her hand to retaliate but he caught it, spun her around and slammed her against the car. Pulling some thin cord from his pocket, he tied her arms quickly behind her back. On opening the car door, he flung her face down onto the back seat. Without her arms to save her she landed heavily, knocking the wind out of her. She felt the cord tighten around her ankles. Fleetingly, it occurred to her that he had done this more than once, then the door slammed shut. Lying on her bag, which was uncomfortable, she wriggled about until she was on her back. The bag fell but wasn't lost as the long strap was still around her. Her face was still stinging from the slap but she was unable to rub it and lay still watching her breath rise in the chilly atmosphere.

Several uncomfortable minutes ticked past. Vicky tried to make sense of what she had heard. This must be a trick of Tony's to get her out... it must be! When Tony got in the car and they were safely on their way he would let her in on it.

Suddenly, there was a sound like the boot being opened, then a slam, yes, definitely the boot. Then the rear door opened and she had a brief glimpse of Tony then blackness, a car blanket had been thrown over her. The door slammed again, a second later the sound of the drivers door being opened. The car rocked as Tony got in. 'I'll phone you later tonight.' He was talking to Hammond, she imagined Hammond nodding. The door slammed shut and the engine started.

The sleet was settling on the frozen ground so the tyres made a crunching noise as the car made its way down the drive. After a few seconds it slowed, probably they were passing through the damaged gates. Then the car turned and accelerated. If Vicky could have seen Tony she would have noticed he carefully checked the mirrors several times as he drove.

Under the blanket she held her breath. If all this was indeed a rescue, at any minute Big Tony would laugh and say, 'Well, we got you out,' but as the car moved along the murky street, Tony remained silent. Vicky felt all hope of rescue fade to misery, 'Tony?' There was no reply. 'Tony?'

'What?'

'Where are we going?'

'Don't worry about it.'

'Tony... Ron, is he..., was he...?'

'Don't worry about Ron.'

Vicky fell silent Ron must be dead she didn't know why she had even asked. Her mind sharply returned to the immediate problem, *her own death.* The car slowed, turned and stopped. With the engine still running she heard the driver's door open. A sudden rush of cold air as the blanket was quickly removed. Tony's face was looking down at her. He... was *smiling.* He put his finger to his lips and held up a notepad, which read, 'Please don't say a word', he flipped a page, 'he's probably bugged you.' He raised his eyebrows as if asking 'Understand?'

Finding it all very hard to grasp she stared at him wide-eyed and nodded. He put his finger to his lips again and began to untie her. She sat up but stayed where she was on the rear seat. He got in and scribbled something else on his pad turned and held it up, 'Don't worry about what I say, play along, Okay?'

She nodded again. Before she could stop herself she blurted out suddenly, 'What about Ron?' Vicky covered her own mouth with her hand.

Tony turned again, 'Dead. Now shut up.' Vicky blinked and stared at him. He had spoken harshly but at the same time put his finger to his lips again and grinned, the combination wasn't reassuring it was unsettling and... creepy. Confused, she said no more.

They moved off. Soon the grey suburban streets gave way to a lonelier industrial landscape. She heard what sounded like a boat whistle blow; the

Thames couldn't be far. Tony spoke, 'Don't bother trying anything here. This area is going to be developed and all the warehouses are empty, waiting for the bulldozers. That means there's no-one about on the whole estate, so save your efforts.'

Doubt crossed her mind was this a rescue? Had Hammond planted a bug? Why keep up the pretence? Her mouth was dry her breathing quickened. Perhaps it was his way of keeping her quiet until he got her to this lonely spot. Then again, he had untied her. No! That didn't prove anything. He could be thinking if she felt safe she'd be no trouble right up to the last moment. *Her* last moment! Sudden panic swept over her, she must do something.

They slowed then leaving the public highway slipped past the decaying gates of the huge abandoned industrial estate. Ahead the roadway swept left, beginning at this bend a long white building striped with three blue lines, its paint faded and flaking, ran along the left hand side of the road. They drove a short distance alongside the building. Tony slowed and turned left into a courtyard and Vicky caught a glimpse of a weathered sign, 'Ice House Refrigeration'.

PART ONE
CHAPTER 8
FRIDAY MID-DAY

The car stopped. This was it. She wanted to run but something held her back, indecision made her hesitate. Tony got out, walked round, opened the rear door and stood blocking it, 'Keep still, I'm going to untie your legs.' Vicky glanced down at her already free legs, then up at Tony, who was smiling, the smile was an unnerving contrast to his tone of voice, 'Come on, get out!' She struggled out of the car feeling light-headed, perhaps this was a rescue but did she really trust Tony enough to bet her life on it? She thought of kicking him and again had the urge to run but he put his powerful arm around her shoulder and held her securely, was it to comfort or stop her escaping?

'That way!' Ahead was a warehouse door big enough for lorries it stood partly open, she looked around frantically for an escape route or someone to help her. Time was running out, if she went through that door she may never come out. She must do something but Tony was right the whole area was deserted, the centre of an industrial estate, just empty derelict warehouses. They walked through the door and into the gloom.

Her eyes darted around the interior. It was empty apart from some packing cases in the middle of an expanse of concrete floor.

Suddenly, she noticed at her feet just inside the door was a semi-frozen puddle of what looked like blood. In front of her was a raised loading bay to which a flight of iron steps ran, then up again to a high office that looked down on the warehouse floor. There was a wide iron door on the back wall behind the loading bay but she could never reach it. With no cover she would be an easy target and even if she succeeded, there was a hefty-looking padlock on it. Her eyes scanned for a possible weapon or some other way to escape but it was hopeless. The place was concrete except for the wall to her right, which was corrugated iron. Rusty holes in this wall let beams of light fall at steep angles on to the dirty floor. To her left was a second office, this one small and ramshackle. In its dirty decaying interior Shades stood alone watching Tony and Vicky through the filthy windows, ready to swiftly help if an opportunity presented itself. Further along the wall between the office and loading bay was another smaller door. This door was meant for people and not freight like the other one up on the bay but again the distance was too great and Tony would gun her down or catch her before she got ten feet.

Tony walked closely beside her, 'Right, hold it there.' He released her, she turned and looked up, he produced the pad from his pocket, scribbled and held it up, 'You're safe, put your fingers in your ears!' He flipped the pad over and wrote again, 'Vital to be quiet!!!' Pocketing the pad and pen his pulled a gun and took careful aim at the tin roof. Vicky covered her ears and screwed her eyes tight shut. Shades silently made his move.

'Good-bye, Vicky.' She flinched as the gunshot reverberated around the warehouse.

In his upstairs office Hammond smiled as he heard the shot on the radio set. It seemed that Tony had kept his word. Things were getting neater. No more Sara, no more Vicky and the man she had been with for the last few days also dead. The only people involved were Tony and his brother Shades. Now they had killed Vicky they were in deep. There was no chance of them going to the police. Who knows? Perhaps this Tony was the London connection Hammond needed to really start to operate. All in all, things were straightening out well. If he could set up another deal with the guns, he could still come out on top. Hammond leaned closer to the radio to try and make out if anything more was said.

Vicky opened her eyes. Someone was standing behind her, holding her around the waist with one arm and covering her mouth gently with their free hand. Tony again put a finger to his lips. Still the hand stayed over her mouth. She didn't struggle but stood in shocked silence as she watched Tony put the gun in the pocket of his long overcoat. He fished about and produced his trusty notepad and pen. He scribbled something on the pad then held it up for her to read, 'If Hammond has bugged you we want him to think you're dead, say nothing.' Tony flipped the page over and wrote some more, 'If he thinks you're dead, you're safe, Shades is standing behind you, say nothing. You could get us both killed if he thinks we double-crossed him. Do you understand?' Vicky read it and nodded. Tony looked at the person behind her and gave a nod. Very slowly, the hand was removed from Vicky's mouth. She turned and smiled at Shades who put his finger to his lips as Tony had done. Tony wrote some more and lightly tapped her on the arm making her turn. He held up the notepad again with one hand and pointed to the small ground floor office with the other. It read, 'Complete set of clothes in that room, take off everything and change. Put all clothes and possessions in bag. Say nothing.' She nodded again and as she turned from Tony squeezed Shades' arm and smiled weakly, took one step toward the office when Tony grabbed her arm. Startled, she stared up at him, he pointed at her feet. She frowned and shook her head. Tony looked at the ceiling in exasperation then he scribbled and turned the pad to her, 'Heels, concrete floor, CLIP CLOP!' She bent and slipped off her new zip-sided ankle boots. Tony held out his hand for the boots, she handed them over and padded away to change.

Vicky could not for the life of her see how Hammond had planted a bugging device on her, but after witnessing Ron's death, being frightened out of her wits and spending an uncomfortable night in wet clothes locked in a dark cellar, she suspected the brothers were thinking clearer than she was. In addition, she felt too grateful to them both to put up any argument.

While she was gone, Tony examined the boots closely, pulling and twisting the heel, it was obvious they were innocent new boots and no more. Satisfied, he set them down on the small pile of packing cases.

A few minutes later she returned, carrying a bag of her old clothes. She was now clad in jeans and sweater part of the small collection of clothes purchased on the recent shopping trip with Ron. All that protected her feet from the concrete floor were thick socks. They motioned her to sit on the packing cases then Shades said aloud to Tony, 'Help me with the chain.' They pulled a heavy chain from one of the packing cases and wrapped it noisily around the bundle of clothes. Tony winked at Shades, 'This will send her to the bottom and in a few months the body will rot and the tide will scatter the bones, no problem!' Vicky didn't particularly enjoy the rest of the conversation. She stroked her thumb nervously across the small object in her hand. As he straightened up, Tony noticed the movement. He stepped quickly toward her. She looked up at him, startled. Tony reached down and gently lifted her closed hand. She didn't want to let go but he frowned at her so she gave up the little bear. He examined it, noticing the stitching was rough on the bear's back he pulled out his flick knife. Vicky stood up and put her hand on Tony's and looking up at him, shook her head, it was the last link with Ron and she didn't want it destroyed. He gently removed her hand and turning the bear over showed her the uneven stitching. It surprised her she hadn't noticed it, then a sudden revelation, *of course*. She remembered her bag had been taken. At the time, she assumed they were simply searching it for sharp nail scissors or some weapon, later they had returned it. But it occurred to her now that Hammond had used it to hide his bug.

What a fool she had been! Hadn't she herself told Tony that Hammond did things like that! Before she

161

was dragged downstairs, Hammond had shouted to the guard 'I want to keep an eye on her, you know what to do.' It all made sense now.

Tony carefully cut some of the stitching away then stopped. Putting away his knife he reached into the bear and pulled out a small metal object, which he held up for Vicky to see, she stared at it then looked at Tony. He raised his eyebrows and came dangerously close to looking happy. Handing back the bear, he turned to Shades, 'Right then, let's get this lot into the boat.' He placed the bug in the bag and carried the bundle out of the warehouse.

As Vicky watched them go she suddenly felt very tired, she slipped her ankle boots back on and laid down on the packing cases. After the terrible pressure of the past few hours, the hard wood felt like a bed of feathers. She put an arm behind her head, gazed at the roof high above and began to cry.

Hammond listened to Shades' voice, 'We'll come back after dark and take the boat out.' Then the familiar baritone, 'She'll be safe enough down there, throw her down after three... one, two, three...' Hammond listened but the radio had gone dead. He switched it off and nodded to himself, 'Very good.' The bug was tough yes, but to be thrown into the hold of a boat with the weight of a body falling on top of it, even with the padding of the bear, he wasn't surprised the transmission had ceased. Now he would wait for Tony's phone call.

He finished the last of his favourite brandy, then looking disapprovingly at the decanter raised his eyebrows at Micky, who had been standing patiently enjoying the broadcast. Micky's smile vanished, 'I went down there early today. They say they'll be getting a case in soon.' He frowned, so Micky added, 'Vince, I tried all over town, I asked everywhere, no-one sells it,' he shrugged, 'I'm sorry.'

Shades looked at Tony and whispered, 'Do you think it's dead?'

'I should think so, you just whacked it with the best part of a tree five times.' He tipped the bag up, the clothes fell out and so did the bug in three pieces. Shades dropped the lump of wood and smiled. Not taking any chances, in case it wasn't the only bug the brothers said no more. Stuffing Vicky's coat, clothes and bag into an old rusty barrel they threw bits of rubbish on top to cover it. Then turning away from the barrel walked back towards the open warehouse door. Shades was relieved, 'So far, so good, let's get back to Vicky, poor kid she looks like hell.' They hesitated at the door, Vicky was crying. Tony gestured to his brother to go to her, Shades looked uncomfortable, 'I hate it when they cry,' he hissed at Tony, 'you go.' Tony shook his head, 'She's your friend's girlfriend, say something… er.. appropriate.'

In the end they both went. Tony tried first, 'Now come on, what's all this then? We got you out okay, you're not hurt.' Vicky didn't answer and continued to sob. Tony shrugged at Shades then waved his hand in a 'your turn, be my guest' attitude. Shades took a deep breath and began, 'Now, now, things aren't as bad as all that.' Vicky sat up and looked at Shades through red-rimmed eyes. 'They killed my sister, then they killed Ron. You didn't know my sister but Ron was your friend too!' Shades ran his hand over his mouth nervously and glanced at Tony for help.

163

Tony became interested in a small smudge of grey dust on his black shirt and began to examine it closely, it seemed unlikely he would receive further help from Tony, 'Some brother.' Tense situations involving drunks with bottles or punks with knives held little fear for him. Tense situations involving broken-hearted women who desperately needed kindness, care and sensitivity were frankly daunting.

Squaring his shoulders he decided to be brave, 'Look Vicky, I've got to talk to you and it's very important, see? I can't talk to you if you keep crying.' Vicky sniffed, wiped her eyes and took a deep breath. She exhaled somewhat jerkily but seemed to have control. Tony chipped in, 'That's the ticket.' Shades and Vicky glanced at him and he looked away. Shades ploughed on, 'Right.. mm.. good, now then…' He took her hand and patted it as he spoke which seemed to make him feel better. He was obviously nervous and it crossed Vicky's mind that Shades and Tony were trying to be gentle, sensitive and sweet but they had not had a lot of practice. Shades seemed to be working up to something, 'As I was saying, things aren't always as bad as they seem. You've been through a lot lately and we've been asked to try and make the next couple of minutes easy on you… pave the way, so to speak.' He seemed pleased with his newfound mastery of the English language.

'What's going to happen in the next few minutes?' Vicky asked quickly, she began to grow frightened again.

Shades belayed her fears fast, 'Oh nothing bad… something good…' he sighed and glanced at the roof for inspiration, finding none in the rusty heavens he continued, 'I'm not making a good job of this, I wish he could have done it himself.'

'Who?'

'Never mind that now… Er, what would you say if I said Ron wasn't exactly dead but just hurt very bad?' Vicky stared wide-eyed at him her mouth opened but nothing came out as her mind tried to absorb what Shades had said. Could there be a glimmer of hope? She managed to whisper 'Is he alive?' Shades nodded slowly and said quietly, 'Yes'. One little word fanned the glimmer of hope into a flame. Vicky, suddenly alive with energy gripped Shades' upper arms and held tight. Excitedly, she asked, 'How bad is he hurt?'

'Well, not that bad at all really.'

'Don't try to protect me, tell me how bad.'

'Couple of scratches.'

There was silence Vicky repeated slowly, 'A… couple of scratches?'

'Yes… and a bump' Shades confessed, 'I've not handled this too well, the idea was for me to ease the shock, you er…., look shocked.'

Vicky was fighting to remain calm, she felt faint, her cheeks prickled and she was conscious of her heartbeat. With great effort, she managed to ask mechanically, 'Shades, where is Ron?' Shades smiled and pointed to somewhere behind her. Vicky let go of Shades, stood up from the crates, looked down at her feet and took a moment to compose herself, smoothed her sweater, ran her tongue around her dry lips and tried to breathe evenly. Then looking up, she swallowed and began to turn slowly. There was a figure standing at the top of the iron staircase. Vicky stared, there was a sickening moment when her mind was not synchronised with the world around her. *It was Ron*. This was impossible! While keeping her eyes fixed on him in case he vanished, very slowly she began to walk towards him, she couldn't feel her legs, they seemed disconnected somehow.

He started down the stairs. Vicky walked faster then panicked, she could see him, she *must* get to him. She tore across the floor, '*Ron*!!' The shout echoed around the warehouse. By the time she reached him, he was at the bottom of the stairs. She stopped short. Her smile vanished. She had been through so much, if he disappeared now she would go mad.

He stared at her with deep concern, she didn't look well. Slowly, she reached out. Ron moved closer, too emotional himself to speak, he gazed at her pale little face, her brown eyes puffy and red rimmed from crying, wide in disbelief. He noticed the bruise on her cheek. Her fingertips touched his shoulders he was real, flesh and blood. She pulled him toward her, 'Ron, Ron, Ron, Ron, oh Ron!!!' Vicky sobbed and laughed at the same time, the flood of emotion was overwhelming for both of them.

They held each other tightly for a long time, not saying anything but in those moments, Ron knew she loved him as much as he loved her. When they turned, Tony and Shades had vanished having stepped outside to give them a little private time together.

A few minutes later, Vicky and Ron walked slowly from the warehouse tightly holding hands and headed towards Tony's car. Tony sat at the wheel, Shades in the passenger seat. Ron and Vicky climbed in behind them and Tony moved off. Vicky didn't know where they were going somehow it didn't seem important.

She couldn't stop staring at Ron, he was alive, it seemed unbelievable. Just a few faint scratches on his nose and chin where he'd hit the gravel were the only physical signs of his ordeal... a miracle! Linking her arm through his she rested her head on his shoulder. Later she would have a thousand questions but for now Ron was alive and that was all she wanted or needed.

PART ONE
CHAPTER 9
FRIDAY EVENING

In the flat above *The Blue Parrot*, Vicky relaxed having showered. On top of her clothes, she wore a bathrobe that belonged to Shades. She sat, warm and comfortable a very large brandy in one hand while the other rested on Finbar's head. The cat dozed on Vicky's lap, happy and content to have some company. Tony and Shades sprawled on the sofa opposite.

Ron came out of the bathroom he too dressed in a thick robe. Shades got up and handed him a brandy; Ron nodded and sat near Vicky. She gazed at him; it still didn't seem possible. Now the initial shock was fading, she was full of questions. 'Okay, don't take this wrong, but why aren't you dead?' He grinned and looked at Shades, who said, 'For a while there we thought he was, when we opened the boot he was covered in blood!' Vicky looked quickly at Ron, 'But you're not hurt, right?' He shook his head, 'No, I'm not hurt.' Vicky said in exasperation, 'Will someone please tell me what happened?' Ron smiled, 'Okay, sorry. Remember during the scuffle at Hammond's, I was cracked on the back of the head?' 'Of course I remember.' She shuddered, lifted her hand from

Finbar and slowly reached out towards his head, which he tilted toward her and said, 'It's just there, nothing to worry about, didn't even break the skin.' Very gently, she made little circular explorations with her fingertips then stopped, 'I can feel it, a little bump,' satisfied, she moved her hand away, 'and you're sure you feel alright?'

'I'm fine now I was a bit dazed at the time and before I could pull myself together they dumped me in the boot and slammed the lid. That was when I picked up the blood.' Vicky stared, 'You said you weren't hurt... you mean you cut yourself on something in the boot?'

'No... think back... after we got Hammond's phone number from the waiter at 'Nick's' we stopped off at that little village. I bought you that bear and we picked up some shopping.' She nodded, 'Yes.'

'In the shop you told me off for not having any fruit and veg in the flat. You tutted, waved your finger at me and said something like, 'In fact, you haven't got anything very healthy at all. I said junk always tastes better.'

'Yes and I thought I'd change your mind with a good meal as a thank you for everything.'

'Right, so after the village we went on to the library, then back to the flat with the shopping.' Smiling, Vicky reminded him quickly, 'And you fell over the cat.' Ron narrowed his eyes at the peacefully dozing Finbar, 'Yes, I fell over the cat. You said there was another bag still in the boot, the heavy one. But we never fetched it because we received the call from Tony to say there had been some trouble. The bag was still in the boot when I was thrown in. The bag was heavy because it

170

contained several cartons of tomato juice and pasta sauce. They were plastic and split open when I landed on them. Gave Shades and Tony a bit of a shock when they opened the boot. After being whacked over the head and thrown about in the boot as Tony made his getaway, I was still a bit groggy when they opened it. I tried to tell them it was only tomato juice, I mumbled something about food and healthy, Shades thought I said 'Help me' and I was rambling because I was bleeding to death. It was only when I got my breath back a few minutes later that I could explain. You should have seen their faces when I climbed out of the boot and told them 'I'm fine'!'

Vicky shook her head. 'I'm glad I didn't see you covered in red juice, I would have passed out. I still don't understand though, I saw lots of bullets hit the boot, they went right through, I could see the holes. I was on the ground near Hammond when they were shooting at your car, it was peppered with holes.'

Ron was smiling and nodding, 'Yes, the bullets punctured the boot alright and a lot of them went right through.' She frowned, 'But I still don't….'

'Remember Dave?'

'Dave? Oh Dave London, your welder friend.'

'That's right, he patched up the back of the car the morning after Hammond's men tried to run us off the road.'

'Yes, of course.'

'When we took the cup of tea down to him in the alley, he wasn't too happy because I told him to patch it because we needed the car. When he finished he said it was safe but didn't look too pretty. He also said he didn't have the right stuff and that he'd been doing some work down on the docks. What he meant was he only had heavy gauge metal in the van. So he patched up the car where the floor pan meets the boot with far thicker metal than was necessary. Just thick enough to stop a small calibre bullet anyway.'

'But Dave only patched a bit here and there. What about the shots that you said got through?'

'You know that whopping great toolbox of mine I helped Dave put back in the boot?'

'Mm.'

'It's got a number of holes in it now, but not right through. All the spanners and junk in it did the trick.' Vicky exhaled slowly and shook her head slightly in wonder, 'Wow, someone is watching out for you.' He nodded again, 'Pretty lucky.'

Still puzzled, she asked, 'How did you know Hammond would plant a bug on me?'

Shades answered this one, 'We weren't sure, I told Tony what we'd found in the office, the papers and stuff, then I mentioned the small table of electronic bits 'n' pieces and the radio receiver, which me and Ron thought was bugging equipment.'

Tony took over the story, 'I told Shades and Ron all about our conversation on the way to Hammond's after you remembered about your sister and everything. You mentioned Hammond liked to keep track of people using bugs, you said it was a perverse hobby of his. We all figured that he sure as hell would want to keep track of you and to be sure we got rid of you, so it seemed almost certain he would have you bugged to make sure we went through with it.'

Ron carried on, 'So we went back to my place to get me and you some clothes... er, and Finbar, then came straight here. I went mad trying to think of a way to get you out. Then I thought of getting Tony to phone Hammond and arrange a deal. I thought Hammond would trust Tony if he thought Tony had got rid of my body. I'm sorry we put you through all that. When we got you out, Tony couldn't tell you I was alive, not until we'd removed the bug. Even then, I didn't want to just walk in, you'd been through so much. I was worried about the shock.'

Vicky looked over at Shades, 'I thought Shades handled it very gently.' He looked embarrassed and got up to pour another brandy, 'Top up anyone?' Tony allowed himself a smile as he watched his brother. She turned her attention back to Ron, 'So what do we do now?' Ron looked at Tony for help, 'Well now, it's a little tricky. We're safe at the moment because Hammond thinks we're dead, but we can't hide here forever.' 'You can stay here as long as you need to.' Tony offered helpfully. Shades agreed, 'We've both got our own places, we use this flat sometimes because it's above *The Blue Parrot* and convenient if one or both of us are here late but we both have perfectly good homes not far away, it's no problem.'

Ron was relieved, 'That's good of you both but as I said we can't hide forever. I must think of something... we could go to the police.' The brothers looked uncomfortable. Ron explained, 'The trouble is, we haven't got much in the way of hard proof. We don't know what they did with Sara,' as he said it he instinctively took Vicky's hand and held it, 'it's really only our word against his and if we break cover and don't get him then we're back where we started, looking over our shoulders all the time. All we've really done is bought ourselves time.'

They sat thinking. Vicky suddenly exclaimed, 'It's been a hell of a day, I've been so much trouble.' Ron squeezed her hand, 'It's not your fault. Vince Hammond's the cause of it all.'

'I know but you've been knocked unconscious and nearly killed, Shades was nicked by a bullet, Tony risked his life crashing through the gates. I've put you all in danger. I don't want you to do any more. Perhaps it would be better if I got out of London and tried to make a life somewhere... perhaps we... I...' Ron put his arm round her, 'Come on, we're not going on the run, after some sleep we'll think of something and sort this thing out somehow, you'll see.' Vicky was obviously exhausted as they all were. Tony stood up, 'We're going to look in on the club then we'll be off, lock the front door after us. We'll be back in the morning, don't answer the phone or the door. We have a key so we can let ourselves in, there's food in the kitchen, help yourselves.'

Tony moved to the balcony door behind the curtains, he checked it was locked and removed the key, 'Right, the balcony door to the fire escape is locked, I'll leave the key here.' He placed the key on a shelf, 'Keep the curtains drawn, we'll go out the front door down through the club. The staff won't come up here they'll just lock up at the end of the night. Your car's out of sight in the lock-up in the yard. We'll take our cars out of the yard and lock the gate you'll both be safe here tonight so you can relax and get a good night's sleep.'

Vicky watched them prepare to leave, 'You're going to all this trouble, giving up your beds now... I...' Tony tried to reassure her, 'I told you, don't worry about us. I've got a great big solid Victorian house to keep the rain off my head.' Shades, obviously not impressed with great big solid Victorian houses, chipped in, 'And I've got a warm, draught-free modern apartment not too far away.' Tony, catching the dig, responded, 'My house isn't draughty, and it isn't a rabbit hutch either!'

'The apartment is perfectly big enough, I just don't have rooms I never use.' Before Tony could respond to that Vicky said quickly, 'Well, we certainly appreciate you both letting us stay, don't we Ron?'

'Really boys! I don't know what we would have done, thank you so much, both of you.' Tony waved his hand dismissively, 'It's no problem.' 'Yes, no problem.' Shades echoed. Ron shook hands with the brothers.

At the door Shades smiled at Vicky, 'Good night.' On a sudden impulse, she jumped up from the sofa and ran to the door, 'Thank you.' She kissed both brothers lightly on the cheek, stretching on her toes to reach Tony who bent slightly so she could reach. He nodded at her and Ron closed the door through which they heard Tony mutter, 'I do use all the rooms, you're jealous....' the rest of the conversation was lost as they walked away down the corridor and off to the club two floors below.

Vicky managed a smile, 'Like a couple of kids.'

'Not really, just brothers.' They returned to the sofa and sat down. 'Sara and I bickered a bit, like them I suppose, never over anything important,' her eyes shone with tears, 'oh Sara!' Vicky looked sadly at Ron, 'I can't believe she's gone.' He put his arm round her and held her tight, they sat in silence for a long time both thinking their own thoughts. Finally, Vicky sat up straight, took a deep breath and patted

Ron's leg as she stood up, then said quietly, 'You pick your friends well, Ron.' He nodded, 'Mm, they've been amazing, they said there's food in the kitchen, are you hungry?'

'I should be but... no, I only want to lie down.' She walked to one of the bedrooms. Ron lingered and looked at the other bedroom door. Then a voice came from the first bedroom, 'Are you staying up for a while?'

'No, I thought I'd get some rest too, it's been quite a day.' There was silence. He looked once more at the empty bedroom. Vicky called again, 'I'll leave the light on for a minute then.' Ron glanced quickly at the open door, he wasn't certain if he had interpreted that right. Slowly, he walked to her room. Without looking in, he whispered, 'I'm going to bed now, try not to worry, we're safe here.' He turned to go. Vicky's voice stopped him, it was soft and a little nervous, 'It's warmer in here,' she said simply. After their embrace at the warehouse Ron was left in no doubt they loved each other. How quickly this translated into sharing a bed he hadn't been sure, it seemed she was. He walked into the room, looked down at her and smiled, then reached for the lamp and turned it off. He undressed and slid in beside her. It was completely dark with the curtains drawn against London's nightglow. Ron felt her move closer and put an arm across his chest. He slid his arm around her waist as he turned toward her.

Vicky sighed, 'My God, Ron, I really thought you were dead.' She held him a little tighter. He was close enough to smell the scent of her hair and feel the warmth of her body. He kissed her on the forehead, she tilted her head and he could feel her breath on his face. Gently, she kissed his mouth, this was so right, so natural. They moved together, suddenly both feeling an intoxicating mixture of excitement and nervousness. It wasn't long before the nerves evaporated and the excitement soon merged into pleasure. Later, relaxed and content, warm in body and soul they fell asleep holding each other.

Outside, the city murmured to itself softly in the way that cities do, inside all was still and silent.

PART ONE
CHAPTER 10
SATURDAY MORNING

Vince Hammond was up very early; he had things on his mind. He knew Sara and her sister were dead, the man in the boot too, but he felt uneasy about Tony and his brother. He would have been a lot happier if they too were out of the picture. Having met Tony, he was convinced that Tony was no fool and would keep his mouth shut, so he was reasonably sure that apart from his people, who didn't count because they were *his* people, the only ones who knew the truth about recent events were the brothers. After all, if Tony had thought there was any chance that Vicky had talked to anyone else apart from the man in the boot, he wouldn't have agreed to dispose of her. Tony would be sure to contact him at some point today to collect the other half of his money for getting rid of her. It had never been his plan to get involved in killing people, but since he had shot Sara, the idea of dealing with problems that way seemed appealing.

Having slept on it, thoughts of working with Tony were gone. He had decided he didn't work with people, people worked for him and that was that. It occurred that if he did get rid of the brothers in such a way that the local underworld knew he was behind it that may suit him very well. It would make people jump when someone said, 'Vince Hammond sent me'; he liked the idea of his name alone terrifying people. Yes, he liked that idea a lot. Of course, he had considered the police problem but dismissed it, thinking and proving were worlds apart.

Hammond wasn't the only one up early; Vicky lay awake. She glanced at Ron sleeping peacefully beside her. Reaching out, she stroked his thick hair gently, which was surprisingly soft. Pulling up the covers, she snuggled down again breathing in deeply then out slowly, the worries of the day could wait. She was safe, Ron was safe, both warm and comfortable. Soon she drifted off again.

The next time Vicky woke was an hour or so later, to find herself alone. The room was bathed in cheerful light as morning sunshine passed through the yellow curtains. The bedroom was similar to the living room in that it was neat, tidy, very spacious and comfortable but again lacking in anything personal. She smiled, recalling how the brothers had bickered the night before. Probably the neutral style of the shared space was something they could both live with. If the flat represented a truce in a war of taste, the battlefield was indeed a rather elegant one.

She assumed Ron would be in the lounge or kitchen. Getting up, she dressed quickly in some of her clothes brought from the flat; pastel yellow sweater and jeans. On leaving the bedroom, she called for him, 'Ron, Ron, Ro…?' She noticed the balcony door which lead onto the fire escape, it was open a crack, a cold draught drifting in. She popped her head out and looked down, from there she could see the yard behind the club, the roof of the lock-up where Ron's Chevrolet was stored and Tony's car. The gate looked locked, Tony wasn't taking any chances. She wondered where they were, obviously not in the flat, possibly in the club somewhere?

Suddenly, she became aware of quiet murmuring, but was unable to make out what was being said, it sounded like Tony's voice. It was coming from somewhere above. Not only did the fire escape lead down to the yard but further steps lead up to the roof.

She ducked back in, put on Ron's slippers and Shades' robe over her clothes, curling her toes to stop the slippers falling off and pushing open the door, stepped onto the balcony.

Tony's voice grew louder as she ascended the steps, 'You are beautiful... yes you are!' Vicky was fascinated she could never have imagined Tony saying such sweet things. As her head appeared over the roof, she could see him with his back to her. At first she thought he was talking to himself, but creeping closer revealed he was holding a dove. Suddenly, there was cacophony of cooing beside her. Turning quickly she saw a coop, her sudden appearance had started the chorus. She turned back to find Tony staring at her. This time it wasn't Vicky who was nervous, Tony looked uncomfortable, 'They're not mine.' he said defensively. 'Oh, right,' Vicky nodded, 'mm', then added coaxingly, 'that one's very pretty.'

'Yes, she's my favourite,' he stopped himself, 'I mean they're a bit of a nuisance really but she's the best of a bad lot.' Vicky was charmed with the contrast between Tony's huge size and obvious strength in relation to that of the small fragile bird, who dozed contentedly in his powerful hands. As he talked, she noted his finger continued to gently stroke its small feathery chest.

'Who built the coop?'

'The coop? Ah, er, well, I did. Um, you see a couple started to nest here and well, if you're stuck with doves, you might as well have the place neat so I, so I...' his voice faded out. Vicky helped him, 'So you built the coop to sort of keep the roof tidy.'

'Yeah, course it didn't work... only had two to start with, now there's a load of the little buggers,' he moved closer to Vicky and spoke quietly as if confiding in her, 'only Shades and Ron know they're here, it's all a bit awkward. Me and Shades own *The Blue Parrot*. It can get a bit rough some nights and we have to have respect. There's nothing wrong with the little buggers... it's just not good for the image. I mean, it would be okay if they were vultures or something,' he chuckled nervously then looked serious again, 'but doves! Well, just doesn't go, see? I hope you understand.' Vicky nodded solemnly, trying not to laugh at the image that had popped into her head of a roof covered with vultures and Tony standing proudly with one on his arm. 'I understand, you can rely on me to be discreet.'

'Good, I wish the little buggers would sod off, but they won't.' She couldn't resist teasing, 'The coop, water and seed probably don't help.' Tony regarded the coop grimly, 'No.'

'Still, no harm done as long as no one finds out.' Relieved, Tony smiled, 'Well, that's what I say.'

When they had first met, she hadn't thought Tony capable of smiling. It was a surprise to find he was accomplished at it. The softened face was a glimpse behind the curtain at the real Tony Manning. Vicky understood why Ron liked these two curious characters. They could be tough, yes, but not tough all the way through with nothing left. Big Tony and Shades were princes among men with hearts as big as a house. She would never be nervous of Tony again, 'Do you know where Ron is?'

'Oh yeah, he's over there, I think he's thinking because I saw him wandering up and down with his hands behind his head, talking to himself. He does that when he's writing a tricky bit.' Tony pointed at a couple of chimneystacks and a cooling outlet for the club three floors below. The roof was smooth with a waist high boundary wall. It was certainly a good place to think, airy and quiet.

Vicky walked over to Ron, who was pacing restlessly. On seeing her, he stopped and smiled, 'Good morning.' He held out his arms and they hugged, 'You saw Tony's doves then?'

'Yes, you never said.'

'He's a bit shy about it.'

'If you had said something, I wouldn't have been so nervous of him for so long.'

'I didn't know you were frightened of Tony.'

'Well, I'm not now.'

'Oh, don't let the doves fool you, he can be tough if he needs to be, but he's not vicious or spiteful and if he likes you he'll do anything for you. Well, you know that.'

'Yes. Hey, there's one question you didn't answer about yesterday.'

'Mmm?' Ron raised his eyebrows.

'You once told me it was possible to tell Tony's mood by the colour of his shirt, shades of blue if he was down, dark maroon or red if he was angry, yellow or white if he was happy, you remember?' Ron nodded, 'I can't see today's, he's got his big coat on but I would guess a light blue, he's worried we don't have a plan, but he would never admit it.'

'Never mind that for now, when he came to Hammond's to rescue me he was wearing a black shirt. I racked my brains to figure out what that meant but you didn't mention black, did you?'

Ron laughed, 'No, I didn't.'

'So come on, Ron, what does black mean? It's not funny. At the time, I thought it was the shirt he killed people in.'

Ron threw his head back and laughed again. There hadn't been much laugh at in the last few days and Vicky found herself smiling too. When Ron managed to stop laughing, he shook his head, 'Oh dear.' Noticing the question still in Vicky's face, he gave in and explained, 'Tony only ever wears black,' he hesitated for effect, 'when he's playing poker.' Vicky raised her eyes to the sky in exasperation, 'Ah! I should have guessed.' When she looked back at him he was staring out across the city. The rapport between them so good now, she could almost read his thoughts and sensed a shift in Ron's mood, 'What's the matter?'

'I've been thinking.'

'Yes?'

'Yeah, em.'

'Come on, spit it out.' She smiled encouragingly. 'I've been thinking about this problem, about Vince Hammond.'

'Have you thought of something?'

'Yes, but I'm not sure if it's a good idea. I wanted to talk it over with you before I mentioned it to the others.' She nodded and said carefully, 'Okay,' sensing that Ron's idea bothered him and she may need to coax it from him, 'fire away... I mean, anything is worth talking over, as you say, we have to do something. Can't stay here forever pretending to be dead.' He nodded and leaned on the wall, 'Hey, are you cold?' He quickly turned to look at her. She was but didn't want to stop him by going inside in case he changed his mind about explaining, 'I'm okay, go on.' He turned to look at the skyline again and spoke without looking at her, 'During this business, something happened to me,' he smiled, 'first, I fell in love with you, that was the good bit,' his face grew serious again, 'at Hammond's when he hit you, I went for him. If I had got to him in that instant I think I could have killed him, you know that?' She nodded. 'But that was in the heat of the moment, I'm not a killer, I... answer me honestly, suppose we did go to the police and suppose they believed us and suppose we got Hammond put away. A lot of supposing I know. Would that be enough after all he's done?' Vicky thought for a moment then said simply, 'No.'

Ron continued to stare at the city, they were both silent, Vicky spoke first, 'Ron, don't imagine it's only you who's been changed by all this. When Hammond had me dragged off down to the basement I looked at him and I hated him. He killed Sara and at the time I thought he had killed you. If I had been given the chance then I would have killed him,' she fell silent thinking, then glancing over to see if Tony was still on the roof, she added quietly, 'Ron?' He turned to look at her, 'Yes?' 'Then again, when I thought Tony was going to kill me, I decided, if it came down to it, I would… I..'

'If you think your life's in danger, we're all capable of things we never thought possible.'

'I think I know what's on your mind Ron, but… I don't think I could… I don't know if I.. if… someone hurts someone you love, you may do anything to stop them in the heat of the moment. Like the way you felt when Hammond hit me. Or how I felt when I believed Tony was going to kill me, again in the heat of the moment in a kill or be killed situation. But I think, to plan it that takes a different kind of person. I mean I'd like to see the bastard dead, as I said there was a moment when I could have done it. But now, I don't know if it's in me. I feel guilty because I think it should be, he killed my sister. But to hold a gun, look him in the eye and pull the trigger, then watch him fall to the ground dead… I just don't know.' She looked distressed so Ron spoke quickly, 'I feel the same way, I'm not sure if that makes me strong or weak. As you say there was a moment; for me it was when I saw him hit you. If I'd got to him I would have crushed his throat with my bare hands, *at the time*. Without that anger to hold a gun, aim it and in cold blood execute him, I don't know. This is real not a play, not TV, real! As you say, it takes a different kind of person to plan it in advance. The problem is we have no evidence it's only our word. I'm almost certain they wouldn't convict and even if by some miracle they did, none of us are that old. Vincent Hammond would be released in our late thirties and I honestly believe he would come after us.'

'I *know* he would.' Vicky slid her arm around him and they both turned and looked out across the rooftops in silence. Ron was first to speak, his words came out slowly, as if feeling his way, ready to stop and say no more, 'What... if... I said, I knew a way?'

PART TWO
CHAPTER 11
SATURDAY MORNING
AFTER BREAKFAST

Tony stared at his empty breakfast plate then looked up at Ron who watched him carefully over his coffee cup. 'Okay Ron, it sounds good.'

Shades nodded in agreement, 'Yeah, I'm in.' Vicky looked concerned, 'Are you sure you're alright Shades?' He frowned in puzzlement. 'Your arm.' She prompted. 'Oh that, it's just a graze,' he added happily, 'the doc' reckons it'll leave a scar though, told him I fell over in the cellar tidying up.' Vicky shook her head. A gunshot scar on his arm would give him a lot of fun when he put on his serious face and told people he couldn't talk about it. His light attitude was not comforting given the violent forces they were attempting to control. This wasn't a game, uneasy, she spoke quickly, 'Look, I'm not happy about this, it seems too risky.'

Ron compressed his lips, he wasn't happy either, but it was all he had come up with. He tried to make light of it, 'It would make a lousy script for a book, even Max would think twice.' Vicky turned on him, 'This isn't a joke, Ron. You're relying a lot on luck.

This is dangerous, very dangerous,' she shook her head, 'the more I think about it the less I like it. I say leave it, there must be another way.'

Ron had never been one to make speeches but the spotlight was upon him. He judged his moment had arrived, 'I have taken more time than most to study people, you know, for my characters in the books, how they reason and what they may do in any given situation. I also have experience in game design, weighing risk and probabilities while being aware of the uncertainty factor.'

Vicky snapped with nervous irritation, 'You mean like rolling a dice?'

'Erm, I do admit random factors do play a part...' his maiden speech was cut unceremoniously short as Vicky interrupted hotly, 'Oh shut up! And don't try to be clever. You're just saying what I said. For this to work, you've got to be lucky, it's as simple as that.' Ron did shut up and folded his arms with the air of a child who had been told off. Shades, who was enjoying the whole thing enormously, raised his eyebrows and grinned at her, 'That's telling him.' Vicky turned her anger on him and stood up, 'And you're not helping, you know this is dangerous.' Tony smiled faintly as he watched his brother get reprimanded. He wiped it off quickly as Vicky turned to him. 'What do you really think, Tony?'

'There's no doubt it's a bit risky, but you can't stay in hiding forever and if you can think of another way, I'd be glad to listen.' Vicky couldn't, she sat down suddenly deflated and said quietly, 'I don't want to see any of you get hurt, that's all,' she glanced around, they were all watching her, she swallowed and continued, 'the thing is we are talking about arms dealers, terrorists, murderers as if it was normal… and people will die, not just Vincent Hammond, others. Once we start this thing we won't be able to stop it, are we sure?' Ron sighed heavily, 'About the killing?' Vicky nodded.

'We aren't going to kill anybody, on the day we aren't even carrying any weapons.'

'I know but…' She didn't know how to articulate her misgivings. Ron spoke slowly as he explained his own mixed emotions, 'It feels wrong because we aren't like them, Vincent Hammond, his men and the terrorists wouldn't hesitate to kill to get what they want.' Vicky nodded slowly. She knew it was true.

Tony leaned forward and rested his chin on his fists, 'We didn't go looking for this, they forced their way into our lives and they're not going to leave us alone. This won't go away, we have to make it.' Shades added, 'You're right, it is risky but Ron's plan is more dangerous to them. If we do nothing, it's more dangerous to us.' Vicky couldn't disagree, 'I know.'

Ron felt uncomfortable, he didn't want Vicky goaded into doing something she didn't agree with and quickly added, 'Look, for this idea to work all four of us must agree, if you don't want to do it, that's it, we won't.' Vicky ran her hand over her forehead and shook her head slightly, 'No, you're right and Shades has a good point, to do nothing is also dangerous.' Ron paused and looked at her, it seemed she was in. He began quietly, 'Right then, let's go over the details. From what Vicky has told us Hammond was going to make a deal with some illegal arms dealers, after the shooting, the deal went bad. Shades and I found some lists in his office, we

191

didn't have time to study them in detail but it looks like he's holding a small armoury. It could be he has them stashed in a truck somewhere, we heard him telling one of his men to check on a truck he seemed worried about. So the first part is for Tony to contact Hammond and arrange a meeting to collect the second part of the money for getting rid of Vicky. While he's there, he must talk Hammond into a deal with the guns. Now, that won't be easy so I think you should say something on the lines of…'.

PART TWO
CHAPTER 12
SATURDAY MORNING 11:45

The phone rang as Hammond was eating. He wiped his mouth, threw down the napkin and lifted the receiver to his ear, 'Hammond.'

'This is Tony.'

'Ah, I've been expecting your call.'

'The job you wanted sorted out is complete. If you're ready to close the deal, I can be over this afternoon.'

'It all went well, did it, no problems?'

'You've nothing to worry about Hammond, when I do a job I do it properly.'

'Good, good, well, I think this afternoon will be convenient, but I do have some things to do. You'd better make it after three thirty.'

'I'll be there at three forty-five.' Tony hung up.

Hammond pushed a button on the desk to summon Micky. A few seconds later, Micky entered the room. His sharp little eyes darted about he was always on his guard. Vincent Hammond was undoubtedly a shortcut to rich rewards, he had been in the past and would be in the future. However, he was a dangerous man to work for. Micky was also painfully aware that he had messed up lately. His strong sense of self-preservation was telling him his boss was not going to let his errors go unpunished.

'Ah Micky, good, sit down.' Micky sat.

'I've been thinking a lot and the more I think, the more I don't like it. Things need tidying up, so I've got a job for you.'

'Job, Vince?'

'Yes and you're going to like this one, it involves this Big Tony character.'

Micky's little eyes grew even smaller, 'Him.'

'You don't like him?'

'Nah, I don't like him or his scrawny brother.' Micky was remembering how Shades had put up a good fight in the yard behind *The Blue Parrot*. He was also recalling how Shades had shouted to the bouncers to 'get them'. The memory of how he and the others had run made him angry.

Hammond brought him back to the present, 'I think an accident, something like stumbling in front of a fast-moving vehicle.'

'London's a dangerous place, Vince.' Micky grinned.

Hammond stood up, moved around his desk and leaned on the front edge looming over the seated Micky, he appeared relaxed, Micky was not. Hammond carried on, 'After we've tucked Tony away we'll have to give his brother some thought,' he sniggered, 'pretty soon there will be only one name in London, Vince Hammond and you'll be part of the team. My team. I like the word 'team', Micky.' Micky nodded, 'The winning team, Vince!' Micky flinched as Hammond leaned forward, his face hard. Micky's frightened eyes looked into Hammond's grey ones. Suddenly, Hammond laughed, he flashed his yellow teeth and slapped Micky on the shoulder, 'The winning team…! I like that Micky. Don't do anything just yet I want to think about it some more. There's no rush now they've got rid of a body and killed someone for me, they're not going to run to the police. I thought it would give you something to look forward to.' Micky relaxed a little and laughed nervously, perhaps Vincent was going to let his recent failures slide but he wasn't convinced.

At *The Blue Parrot* everyone was busy, Shades had gone down to the bar on Ron's say so and was looking for a particular Irish customer who had been a regular feature of late. Given the clubs reputation, it seemed the place to fish.

Tony had gone to the basement to look for some items Ron would need. Vicky was searching for some binoculars Tony had said were somewhere in the flat, but Tony hadn't seen them since he last went to the races.

Ron was on the phone to Dave London the master welder. Vicky heard only Ron's side of the conversation and under different circumstances would have laughed. 'Look Dave, it doesn't matter where I've been, the point is will you help? Yes, no, look, forget the car! I know you don't like doing a patch job, I promise I won't tell anybody you just patched it,' Ron looked at Vicky and raised his eyes to the ceiling, 'yes… yes, when I have a bit more time you can do a proper job, I promise… I know about your reputation… oh for God's sake Dave you're like an old woman…! Sorry… sorry… sorry… don't hang up… well, I will if only you'll stop going on about the car… it's a feasibility study… no, I didn't think you would... you know I'm working on a book...? Well I am... yes, and one of the characters has got to escape quickly from a tight spot... if you'll shut up a minute, I'll tell you what it has to do with you... What I have to do is simulate the circumstances to see if what I'm writing is feasible, see? So I want you to do a bit of welding for me down at the old industrial estate... yes, the one near the river they're going to knock down, the old refrigeration plant..., mm, that's the one... Oh and Dave, bring that heavy gauge stuff you used on the car. Heavier if you've got it... now I want you to put thicker plates on a metal door that's already there, how long do you thing it will take?' There was a pause as Ron endured Dave's answer, 'I know you're not a clairvoyant,' Ron rolled his eyes at Vicky and shook his head slightly, 'roughly... forty-five minutes, give or take, okay, right, I'll meet you at the entrance tomorrow at seven-thirty... I know it's Sunday... Dave... Dave... *Dave*! This is important. Sunday's double time, yes? What...? You're joking, how much? Look, sod off... No, not you, Finbar's sharpening his claws on my leg. Get him off will you Vicky? Okay, Okay, I give in... yes... yes, I will... promise... seven-thirty... no, I'm not joking... mm... bye.'

Ron sat back and puffed out his cheeks. Vicky had stopped ransacking the chest of drawers and was sitting with Finbar on her lap.

'You'd better keep an eye on that bloody cat, if he gets a whiff of Tony's doves and goes up there, you'll find out how rough Tony can be.' Vicky nodded, 'Dave said he'd do it then.'

'Eventually, he's so temperamental.' She smiled, 'He's an artist you know and he's got a reputation to think of.'

'Yeah, he mentioned that. Do you know I had to promise I'd put him in my book under acknowledgements for technical help on welding?' Vicky giggled, 'I like Dave, he's alright,' she became serious, 'er, I found this in one of the drawers while I was looking for the binoculars.' She lifted a cushion to reveal a pistol. Even the sight of the gun had made her uncomfortable and she had gently placed a cushion over it until Ron finished his phone call. Of course, they had both seen Tony with it at the warehouse when he fired it at the roof. Ron had known about it even before, as it was part of the plan to rescue Vicky. But to see it lying casually in the flat was disturbing. He was still staring at it when suddenly the front door opened and Tony entered carrying a large cardboard carton, 'Is this the sort of stuff you wanted?' he set it down and glanced up at them immediately sensing the atmosphere, 'what's the matter?' Without taking his eyes off Tony, Ron moved to one side so Tony could see the sofa. Tony looked at Vicky, 'What?' Vicky glanced down at the gun.

'Oh that, so what?'

Ron asked timidly, 'Is it yours?' Tony looked him in the eye, 'No.' Ron was obviously uncomfortable so Tony shrugged and began to explain, 'Ron, don't make such a big thing about it, we got raided one night. The police had a tipoff there were drugs here, there weren't but they searched everybody anyway. When me and Shades closed up, we found the gun in one of the big plant tubs, someone must have dumped it when everyone was being searched. I just kept it, you never know,' Tony picked up the gun and slipped it in his pocket, 'is there anything in the box that you can use?'

Vicky scooped Finbar carefully off her lap and placed him on the sofa where he curled up and shut his eyes, apparently sharpening claws on people was quite taxing. She rummaged through the silly wigs, old clothes and junk.

Tony snapped his fingers, 'Oh yeah, when I was in the basement, I remembered where the binoculars are. They're in the wardrobe on the top shelf. My bedroom, that one.' Vicky nodded, 'Top shelf, right Tony, thanks.'

'I had them on the boat but they're not powerful enough, do you think they'll do Ron?'

'They don't need to be brilliant.' Vicky was fascinated by the contents of the carton, 'Why is all this stuff in the basement?' Ron grinned, '*The Blue Parrot* was a music hall then cinema and for a while it became a theatre. It didn't do very well. That's when Tony and Shades took it over and turned it into the club. I recently helped Shades clear up the basement. He was thinking of turning it into his own private cinema and showing his old movies, but when he looked into it, the big projectors cost a bomb. Anyway we put all the theatre junk in some boxes. Is there anything you could use?' She pulled a short black wig from a plastic bag, 'This looks to be in reasonable condition,' more rummaging, then, 'ah ha, jackpot, make-up kit and a black clutch bag, I'll need those.' Another exploration deep into the carton brought forth a little black dress and neatly folded with it a short delicate black lace scarf, they both smelt a little musty but like the wig they had been stored in a plastic bag so were clean. She peered at the label, 'Twelve, that's lucky.' She promptly disappeared into the bedroom to try it on.

'Tony, you'd better keep an eye on Shades, if he makes contact I don't like him talking to those guys without someone watching out for him. I've got some more phoning to do.' Tony nodded and left through the front door moving along the corridor and descending the stairs to a door, which opened behind the upstairs bar. He could see the whole club from there and Shades would be easy to watch.

Ron sat pondering exactly how to ask the theatre people for the help he needed. Picking up the phone, he was about to ring the theatre where his play was running when Vicky called from the bedroom, 'Ron!'

'Yes?'

'The dress fits… it's very short, shall I try the make-up and wig, sort of dress rehearsal?'

'I think that's a good idea. Perhaps you could pick the equipment up from the theatre, see if they recognise you.., be a good test. I'm just phoning now.'

'Okay.'

There were no further questions from the bedroom so Ron turned his attention to his phone call. He had as much trouble with the producer, Johnny Mitchell as he did with Dave. Finally, he managed to convince the man to calm down and promised to spend the whole day with him on Monday to straighten out the thousand little crises that had cropped up during his absence. He told the producer the same story that he had been deeply wrapped up in a new book. Flattering him by saying that 'as an artist he of course, would understand'. That did the trick. Ron went on to explain he was conducting a feasibility study on Sunday.

The producer didn't want to admit he didn't know what that was so he let Ron talk away about acting out the scene he was writing to see if it was possible. The producer was genuinely impressed and congratulated him on his thoroughness. Ron used this and asked if he could borrow some props with the understanding that he would return them on Monday, when he would spend all day at the theatre. He concluded by asking if he could talk to the special effects man, Tom Anderson. The answer was, 'Of course dear boy, glad to help. One thing though…'

Ron nodded, 'Yes, yes, of course, I would have anyway.' While he waited for Tom to be summoned, the thought crossed his mind that at this rate the acknowledgement pages of his new book would be thicker than the novel. The familiar voice of Tom the special effects man came on the line, 'Hello?'

'Oh Tom, it's Ron.'

'Ron, where've you been?'

'I've been working kind of hard on my new book, had to get some ideas down while I thought of them, you know, when it flows, it flows. Listen Tom, I need a favour, I've squared it with Johnny, I need to borrow some stuff 'till Monday.'

'Sure Ron, what kind of stuff?'

'I need some squiffs and a squiff detonator. I know you have some because you need them for the big shoot-out in scene four. Can you spare a few?'

Tom laughed, 'The word is squibs and yes, you can have some. What do you want 'em for?'

'Er, I'm a bit short on time. It's for a feasibility study, the producer will explain.'

'Oh... right, okay.'

'What kind of range has the detonator?'

'Depends on how long the wire is.' There was a pause. Ron had imagined this part would be easy, he didn't know he had to run wires. 'They're not triggered by radio then?'

'Yes, they can be, but we don't like to do it.'

'Why?'

'Because when we use radio, we use UHF and there's always the chance of them going off by accident. You know I've done film work?'

'Yes.'

'On set we use radios a lot so we shy away from using radio detonated squibs.' Ron was worried, 'If I said I must fire them by radio and I needed three hand-held walkie-talkies that didn't interfere with the squibs, could you help?'

'No Ron, use wires to be on the safe side, what about some of those mobile phones?'

'Have you seen the price? They're half-a-grand each! And it has to be reliable, I've heard people say they can't always get a signal. Anyway, I need to speak to two people at the same time, can't do that with a phone. The radios would be a sure thing over half a mile, wouldn't they?'

'Half a mile? Oh yes, I do have some and I'll put in a new set of batteries for you. Switched on they're good for a day.'

'That's great, I only need them for a couple of hours.'

'Well, that's not a problem.'

'Tom, these wires I've got to run...'

'Yes?'

'It's quite a long distance.'

Tom answered slowly, 'Okay.'

Dreading the answer, Ron took the plunge, 'It's about fifty yards from the squibs to my building, up five floors then about fifty feet across the roof.' Ron held the phone tightly and waited, this part of the plan was crucial.

'Mm, okay, fifty yards is one hundred and fifty feet, five floor building, twelve feet a floor that's sixty feet and fifty feet across the roof, that's two hundred and sixty feet total.'

'Yes, can it be done?'

'Well if you'd asked yesterday I'd have said no, but it's your lucky day.' Ron was so happy, 'Really?'

'Yes, just so happens I've got my van here today and I know there's some reels on board, I'll sort out three hundred foot reels for you, okay? They plug together.' 'Tom, you're a marvel.'

'Yes I know.'

'I'll send someone over to pick up the gear... oh and Tom?'

'Yes?'

'Put some instructions in, will you?' Tom laughed, 'Sure, it's really simple. Hey Ron, I want a mention in the book for this, now is that it?'

'Er yes, is Jane there?'

'Yeah, hang on.' The line went quiet. A few moments later Ron heard the breathless bubbly voice of Jane, the make-up lady. 'Hello Ron, where have you been? Naughty man, I've been worried.'

'Hello Jane, can't explain now, can you come round to *The Blue Parrot* tomorrow morning at eight-thirty? I know it's Sunday.'

'*The Blue Parrot*, are you hanging about in that rough place?'

'I'll explain it all if you come. It's a long story. I want you to make me up so my own mother wouldn't recognise me, make me old or something. Doesn't matter as long as I can't be recognised.'

'You know you're barmy!'

'It's possible, Jane,' he hesitated, in for a penny, 'tell you what, if you help I'll mention you in my new book.' 'Really?' she said excitedly.

'Yes.'

'Okay, I'm game for a laugh. You creative types are all mad.'

'Oh that's great, thank you Jane, how long will it take to make me up?'

'You want to look like someone else, you're not going for any particular look?'

'No, just so I'm not recognised by someone who knows me.'

'Weeeeell, a little under an hour perhaps.'

'Fantastic, and eight-thirty's okay for you?'

Chuckling at the other end of the line, 'I'll be there.'

'Thanks again Jane, see you tomorrow.' 'Bye.' She hung up. Ron shut his eyes; boy this wasn't easy! He didn't get much time to relax, because a raven-haired beauty leapt out of the bedroom. 'Ta da! What do you think?' Vicky did a twirl; she looked amazingly different. Her pixie cut blonde hair had disappeared, replaced by a spiky black wig. Her fine features had been completely hidden by an almost monstrous amount of make-up; she really did look a different woman. The black dress was indeed very short. Ron stood up and moved closer, she stood still as he walked around her, 'Wow!' He looked at her thick black eyebrows and red lipstick. She had delicately used shading to change the shape of her face and had managed to completely conceal the bruise on her right cheek.

'How did you learn to use make-up like that?'

'I told you when Sara and I were younger we did a bit of theatre work, only 'am dram' stuff and it didn't last long but you pick things up.' Suddenly, she looked sad, 'Oh Sara.' To distract her, he changed the subject, 'You'll catch pneumonia in that dress.' She smiled and looked down at her legs, 'It is a bit short, isn't it?' He nodded, 'Just a bit!' Ron looked thoughtful, 'could be handy though.'

'What do you mean?'

'It will draw attention from your face.'

'I'm not sure how to take that,' she tried to look stern, gave up and laughed. Then more seriously, 'I don't know if I feel too comfortable going out like this.'

'Are you having second thoughts about tomorrow, getting cold feet?' She was aware he was worried about the following day, to reassure him she reached out to squeeze his hand, 'I'm getting cold legs,' they both smiled, 'I didn't catch all of it from the bedroom, is everything okay?'

'Yes, it's all fixed up, Jane's coming over tomorrow and Tom, the effects man, is expecting someone to pick up the gear. So get yourself over to the theatre and say you've come to pick up some equipment from Tom.' Vicky went to fetch her old coat from the bedroom luckily Ron had remembered it when he and Shades retrieved her clothes from his flat. Her new warmer coat having been left at the warehouse, dumped in the old barrel with her other clothes and bag. This was the first time she had looked at it properly since her memory had returned. She paused, looked sadly at the faded red stain and bit her lip as she stroked it gently with her thumb. Blinking back the tears she swallowed, now wasn't the time. She couldn't do anything for Sara, but by God she could do something about Vince Hammond. Folding the coat over her arm she returned quickly to the living room in time to see Tony enter. He stared at her, for a fleeting moment he wondered who she was before he realised. Vicky turned to Ron, 'How am I going to get to the theatre? Your car's too distinctive and what with the dents and bullet holes I'd probably get stopped.' Ron frowned, 'Of course you can't and Tony's is known to Hammond, I'd better phone for a cab.'

Without taking his eyes off her, Tony pulled out some keys, 'This is a spare set, you'd better use Shades' car. It's next to mine in the yard, he won't mind.' 'Thanks, Tony,' Vicky took the keys slipped on her coat, picked up the short black scarf, quickly arranged it to conceal the bloodstain and nodded at them both, 'won't be long.' She disappeared through the balcony door to the fire escape then carefully descended to the yard behind the club. Tony stared at the closed door for a moment then turned to Ron, 'What's the idea of her dressing up like that?'

'I need someone to collect the equipment from the theatre and we can't take any chances Hammond hasn't got some of his men keeping an eye on this place, not for me and Vicky obviously, but he could be keeping tabs on you and Shades.'

'I should have gone and if I was followed, I could have lost them.'

'You have to meet Hammond, anyway Vicky and I thought a dress rehearsal would be a good idea, if she's not recognized at the theatre it will give her confidence. If Hammond or his men catch a glimpse of her, she won't be recognized. And between you and me I think she needs to be busy to keep her nerves under control.'

Tony nodded, 'Is she very worried?' Ron hesitated then looking Tony in the eye, 'We're *both* very worried.' Tony was unsurprised, 'Well, it'll keep you both sharp. What's next?'

'I've got to go down to the industrial estate to sort out the place we're going to use. I think the warehouse we used last time will work but I want to look it over again.' Tony looked concerned, 'Don't go on your own, if the place is being watched...'

'I don't know it is, I'm just trying to think of all the angles. When Shades has finished downstairs, we'll go together in his car. Vicky won't be long with the car, the theatre's not far. I'll keep low as we leave the yard and only sit up when Shades is sure we're not being followed. How's he getting on down there?' Tony shrugged, 'He made contact okay, he was still talking when I last looked.'

Now it was Ron's turn to be concerned, 'He's alright isn't he?'

'Oh yeah, yeah, everything seemed to be under control.'

'What do you mean 'seemed'?'

'Yes! Everything is under control, don't worry!'

'But I *do* worry Tony, these guys break kneecaps if you just tick 'em off a bit. I hope Shades sticks to what I told him to say.   God!   They're the unpredictable part of this whole plan, unfortunately, they *are* the whole plan.'

PART TWO
CHAPTER 13
SATURDAY AFTERNOON 3:35

Tony had left for Hammond's in his own car, Vicky hadn't returned from the theatre and Shades was still downstairs somewhere in the club.

Ron paced nervously, stopping occasionally to look out of the balcony window. The glorious bright morning had deteriorated and clouds scudded across the ice blue sky. As he watched, the heavens were soon the same grey cold colour as the buildings they looked down on. Sleet began to fall, perhaps fall was the wrong word, it seemed to move horizontally propelled by the sharp wind that cut the city.

It would be dark soon. Ron wanted desperately to get to the industrial estate before it was too dark to look the place over. In his mind, he felt the place Tony had taken Vicky would suit his plan but wanted to be sure, the last time he was there all his attention had been focussed on Vicky. They had one chance and everything had to be right. He turned from the window frowning, where the hell was Shades? He could feel the tension rising, what was happening down there? If Shades' part didn't work... it had to work, what was keeping him?

The front door opened suddenly and Shades came in, grinning all over his face. Ron's tension found a target, 'Where the bloody hell have you been?' Shades stopped grinning, 'I've been in the bar, where the bloody hell do you think I've been?'

'I told you to keep it simple, what were you telling them down there, your life story?' Shades was about to lose his temper but instead watched him carefully as Ron continued hotly, 'Do I have to do everything round here myself to be sure it's done right? Keep it simple, that's what I said. Do you think it's funny to keep me pacing about up here? Your brother thinks it's one big joke, I'm sure of that. This isn't the movies you know! The dead don't get up at the end of a scene, they stay dead!' Pausing, he passed a hand across his damp forehead over his hair and down the back of his neck where he tried to ease the tension in the steel wires that were once muscles, 'you're not Bogart no matter what you think. Christ Shades, I'm a bloody writer! You and Tony run a club! What the hell are we doing?' His voice had begun to quiver. Shades stood and let him go on, 'This is dangerous stuff, the people we're playing with would kill you, me, Vicky, like that.' He snapped his fingers, if truth be told he was a little startled at his own outburst, up until a moment ago he thought his emotions were under control.

Shades walked toward him and said quietly, 'Come on fruit, sit down a minute.' Ron allowed himself to be manoeuvred into a chair, he took a deep breath, 'I... I.. I don't mean to be ungrateful... you and Tony have been great in all this... it isn't really any of your concern... I mean, I do appreciate it. I'm just saying we need to be careful, that's all.' Shades touched him briefly on the shoulder, 'Yeah, sure Ron, you're right.'

Ron looked at Shades and spoke quietly as if imparting a secret. 'The thing is, I've been telling everyone what to do, like I'm writing a story and you're all characters. But if I get it wrong, someone may be killed... Vicky is looking to me for what to do, in a way, you all are. What if I'm trying to be clever and I do get one of you killed...? I don't know, perhaps the police are the answer, perhaps Vicky was right, this is too dangerous,' Ron slid his hands from his neck and palmed both cheeks with a long exhalation, 'sorry Shades.'

Shades leaned forward and punched Ron playfully on the arm. 'Come on Ronny boy, listen. Me and Tony aren't dummies y'know, we wouldn't agree to something that didn't have a chance. It's a good plan, it's simple. They do the dirty and we walk away nice and calm as you like. Look at the alternative; what if we do go to the police? We have no real evidence it's only our word. Hammond would get some smart lawyer and bang! He'd walk. Then all of us would be in for it; we'd all be looking over our shoulders. Ron, believe me, you're right. This is the only way. Come on, let me tell you how it went downstairs, I was so cool!' He was obviously pleased as punch.

Ron sat back and listened, having let off steam he felt a little better, in the back of his mind was still the worrying thought that Tony and Shades were loving every minute. 'Okay,' he nodded, 'Yes, come on then, what happened?'

'Oh by the way before I tell you, how did you know we had some Irish guy asking about guns? I wanted to ask you before but not in front of the others.'

Ron smiled, 'You told me you dope.'

'Me…! When? Look I didn't mention any names.'

'No, you didn't. Don't you remember when I first introduced you to Vicky? She said, 'You certainly get some odd characters in here.' You said something like… 'Yes, they're colourful all right, we've got thieves, cat burglars etc. Then you said you even had a guy with an Irish accent asking if the rumour about you and Tony being well connected was true and did it extend as far as arms. Vicky asked what you told him and you said it wasn't a good idea to upset these people. Instead of telling him to shove off you said you'd keep your ears open.'

'Yeah, I remember, cor you don't miss much do you?' Shades shook his head, 'You know I didn't mean it. Even if I had heard of any guns, I wouldn't have said anything, *The Blue Parrot* doesn't get involved with the customers, especially heavy duty stuff like the IRA.'

Ron was growing impatient again, 'So come on, are you going to tell me how it went or not?' Shades leapt enthusiastically back to his story, 'Oh yeah, sorry, well, I hung about for quite some time, then I saw the guy, but I didn't go straight to him. I glanced at him and gave a slight nod to show I remembered, real cool like. Then sat on a bar stool like I was keeping an eye on things, I played it really cool.'

'I got that bit Shades, you were cool,' then with a little more volume, 'what happened?' Irritated that Ron had interrupted his beautiful story, he responded quickly, 'Shut up. I'm getting to the good bit,' he shrugged, 'not that me being cool wasn't good.' Before Ron could erupt, Shades continued, 'After a while he came over and made some conversation like, 'It's busy for this time of day' or something. I asked him if he'd had any luck with his search. He hadn't, so in an off-hand kind of way I said that in my line of work, we meet all sorts and a certain customer had mentioned in a roundabout way that he had some shooters. I told him that I didn't know this guy and if I passed on the number I wanted nothing to do with it. For all I knew it could be a con, in no way would I vouch for the seller as I didn't know him. I told him the guy had pulled a pony out of his pocket and said if I sent him any business, he'd be grateful. I added that I didn't know where this guy operated or anything. All I had was a phone number; I was told it was good only for a couple of days and that the other party would be on the line between 11pm and 12pm only. I explained that tonight was the second night so it was up to him. The Irish guy asked for the number, I gave it to him and repeated I wanted no involvement. He got a bit suspicious and asked what I was afraid of, so I gave him some line about this kind of thing being out of my league. But twenty-five pounds was twenty-five pounds, a nice little drink for passing on a phone number but I would leave the heavy stuff to the big boys. This seemed to amuse him, he smirked at me and said he thought me and Tony were big operators, I told him we just own the club and can't control who comes in. He nodded, threw his drink back and left.'

Ron said thoughtfully, 'Seems okay, we'd better be sure we're at the phone box at eleven.' Shades frowned, 'Are you sure it's the right number?' Ron nodded, feeling relieved that first contact had gone well. He smiled, 'Yes, I'm sure, in the early days before I began to make a name for myself, I didn't have a phone. I used the phone box on the corner of my road all the time. If I had an important call, I'd say, 'You can reach me at nine' then I would hang about outside the box and wait,' he shook his head, 'I made some of the most important deals that changed my life on that phone.'

The balcony door opened and Vicky entered carrying a box, 'Sorry I was so long. Jane, the make up lady caught me and asked a million questions. I think Tom the effects man told her you were sending someone over, she ambushed me.' Vicky's eyes widened in surprise, 'Do you know she recognised me beneath all this paint! I told her I was supposed to be unrecognisable, she waved her hand and said, "Oh darling it's my job, no one else would", and she was right, no one else did. She's burning to know what you're up to. I fobbed her off by saying I wasn't sure myself but thought it was either some kind of publicity stunt to promote the play or a big joke you were playing on someone. Anyway, she said she would see you tomorrow and expects you to explain the mystery.'

Ron smiled, it was so exciting to see her again, which he knew was ridiculous, she had been gone only a short time. Since Jacqui died, Ron had worked hard to ward off the constant feeling of loneliness. Now of course, he could allow himself to miss somebody he cared for, because he could look forward to their return. He took the box, 'That's great, well done. Don't worry about Jane, she's right, no one else would recognise you.' She nodded, convinced, then added, 'There's three cable reels still in Shades' car, I couldn't carry it all up.'

'That's fine, Shades and I are going to look at the warehouse, we'll carry them up when we come back. I think it would be better if you stayed here, okay?' Vicky squinted at herself in the mirror, 'Yes, I can get this gunk off my face. Be careful.'

'We're alright, our bit's easy, but I'm a bit concerned about Tony, he's the one walking into the lion's den.' Vicky frowned slightly, 'Mm,' turning to Shades, she smiled, 'here's your car keys, I hope you don't mind, Tony said it would be alright.' Shades took the keys, 'Sure, no problem.' Vicky turned to hang up her coat then hesitated, no, she'd take it into the bathroom and scrub the stain. A thought suddenly occurred to her and she spun round, 'Oh, how did it go in the bar?' Shades had been staring at Vicky's legs and she had caught him, he glanced quickly at the ceiling then back at Vicky flustered, 'A...? Er, oh, er... What?'

'I said, how did you get on at the bar?'

'Oh the bar! Yes, it's all fixed up. After we've looked the warehouse over, we come back here then later we're driving round to the phone box to wait for the call. Then we all meet back here again.' The way Shades was staring at Vicky was making her uncomfortable, she said briskly, 'Good! Right then... I'm going to change,' glancing meaningfully at Shades, 'this look really isn't me, I'll see you later,' she kissed Ron, 'stay safe.' Ron smiled and nodded as Vicky disappeared into the bathroom. Shades looked at Ron, 'Lipstick!' Ron frowned, 'What?' 'Lipstick! She's left her mark.' Shades pointed to his own cheek. Ron wiped his face, 'You can say that again.' He hesitated. Shades frowned at him, 'What's the matter now?'

'It's going to be pretty dark in the warehouse by the time we get there.'

'It's okay, we've got my car headlights and there's a small torch in the glove compartment. Come on, let's go.'

They let themselves out through the balcony door and Shades locked it behind him.

PART TWO
CHAPTER 14
SATURDAY EVENING 4:40

Tony had been at Hammond's for nearly an hour, Hammond was playing the charming host which given the circumstances was unsettling. He chatted freely and Tony let him talk. In spite of the relaxed appearance, he had to be careful. It was obvious he was gently probing Tony to see what he knew about Vicky. Tony realised he would need to think on his feet and spin Hammond some kind of credible story before he could even begin to discuss new business.

Tony had not expected any serious problems conversing with Vince Hammond but something wasn't right, Hammond wasn't right. There was an aura about the man that was disturbing, Tony felt it, and worryingly, did not understand it. All the familiar lines of non-verbal communication that usually informed him of so much were mute, this had never happened before and was disconcerting. Of course, during his first encounter when collecting Vicky, Tony had been aware something was odd. Tony would never admit the reason he had underestimated the problem was simply because he had been so concerned about Vicky and needed to concentrate hard to hide the fact. He hadn't fully appreciated how different Hammond was to what would be considered normal. Now without Vicky as a distraction, Tony was in no doubt he was dealing with something he'd never encountered before and was struggling to understand it.

He studied the smiling Vince Hammond sitting opposite behind his desk. Mr Hammond was outwardly wrapped conservatively enough appearing very smart and neat in grey sports jacket, pale blue sweater and grey trousers with almost dangerously sharp pleats. Even seated, it was clear he was tall but not broad, the hair very light no doubt blonde as a child, cut close and well groomed. What his teeth lacked in length they made up for in quantity, he appeared to have too many for the size of his mouth. He smiled too much, the friendly facade ruined by cold grey eyes. He had pushed an extremely large Scotch into Tony's hand, which he hadn't drunk, but wanted to, this meeting was a lot more stressful than he had anticipated.

'Come on Tony, I can call you 'Tony'? We are business colleagues now, drink!'

'I have to be careful Mr Hammond.' Imperceptibly, the charming smile faltered, 'With me?'

'I have the car with me, I like to keep a low profile with the law. Doesn't do to invite trouble.' The smile was fully restored, he waved his hand dismissively, 'Police, ha... And do drop the 'Mr Hammond'. My close business colleagues call me 'Vince'.'

'Okay Vince, thank you for the drink but I really have to be careful.' Vince studied Tony to see if there was anything behind the statement. Satisfied, he became animated again, 'Well, I don't have to worry about the police, cheers,' he swallowed his Scotch, 'ah, I like a good Scotch... prefer brandy really but I'm out. I like quality and why not, eh? If a man has money, why shouldn't he have the best?'

'Since you've touched on the subject of money, do you have the second part of our agreement?'

Hammond became serious, 'I like a man who talks straight.'

Tony decided a prod may provoke an interesting reaction, 'Then I'm asking you straight, do you have the money?' In spite of his statement about liking straight talk, Hammond didn't care for Tony's tone but let it pass, 'Of course, of course,' he reached under a nearby table, pulled out a briefcase and tossed it to Tony, 'here!' Tony caught it and clicked open the locks. Hammond made a show of being offended, 'I assure you it's all there.' Tony glanced at him then reached in and flicked the edge of a pile of banknotes with his thumb, 'Of course.' Hammond settled back comfortably in his chair and lit a cigar, the smoke curled round his yellow teeth and drifted away. He considered Tony for a moment, he intended to get his money back also get rid of the brothers but not until he understood the whole picture and even then not immediately. He would act, or get Micky to act, only when he was sure they were of no further value. 'You still haven't told me exactly what your brother was doing in my house with his friend,' he paused, 'who was he?'

Tony had on his best poker face but behind the mask was thinking fast, 'I don't know.'

'What connection had he with your brother then?'

'Why are you so interested?'

219

Hammond smiled, 'A man in my position needs to know things,' the smile evaporated and the voice grew hard, 'I can't have people breaking into my private office without knowing why.'

To gain more thinking time Tony nodded at the cigar, 'I don't have any concerns about one of those.'

Vincent regarded his own cigar then swiftly flipped the lid on the box and spun it round for Tony to help himself, his voice pleasant once more, 'Be my guest.' Tony took one. Considering it, he commented, 'I see what you mean about having the best.' Stripping the cellophane he was about to bite off the end when a genuinely horrified Vincent said quickly, 'Please!' and pushed a cigar cutter across the desk. Vincent was more than capable of watching Micky snap somebody's fingers without a care in the world, but to tear into the finest Cuban with one's teeth he considered barbaric. 'Of course, sorry,' Tony clipped and lit the cigar. He had a story just about straight in his head but the question was would Hammond believe it? 'Okay, why did my brother break into your office?' Vincent leaned forward a little and waited.

'I told him to.' Hammond was surprised, 'You?'

'Yes.'

'Why?'

'Okay Hamm… Vince, this is the story. I can see you won't let up until I've answered your questions so I'll cut all the bullshit and tell you straight. When I've finished I have new business to talk over, so here it is. As you know, me and Shades run *The Blue Parrot* and as you say men in our position need to be… in touch with what's going on. Now, you're new and for some reason no one was talking. The

220

word was you were new in London and you could be heavy, there were vague rumours that you were squeezing some of the small businesses, pay up or something bad will happen.' Hammond smiled. He liked to hear his reputation was building.

'I have some interests in this town myself,' Tony lied, only he and Shades knew they were straight everyone else thought they were clever. It was a reputation the brothers thoroughly enjoyed. Tony continued, 'We wanted to know more about you but you don't walk up to a stranger and start discussing the kind of business we're in. You need to know who you're dealing with, so we had a problem. One night, this crazy woman walks in out of the rain and starts crying on the bar. We were going to throw her out when this guy says she's with him. Anyway, he quietens her down so we let them stay but keep an eye on her. It looked like this guy was trying to pick her up, seen it a million times, she's all excited and dramatic and says she's lost her memory. As long as he's buying drinks, who cares.

At the end of the night they leave together. Next time they appear it's lunchtime. They bug the life out of Shades, asking if anything unusual has been happening locally, had he heard anything about a woman called Sara. The guy tells Shades his friend still can't remember anything and they're trying to piece together her past. Shades tells them he runs a bar not a public information service and they either buy a drink or leave, so they leave.

Next thing happens, you send three of your boys round in ski masks and rough up Shades, asking about the woman and her friend. One of the heavies said something like 'Hammond will want some answers'.'

There was a momentary flare of anger in Vincent's eyes. His people were making too many mistakes. Tony apparently didn't notice and smoothly continued his story, 'That gets us thinking that it may be the same Hammond we're interested in. We feel we have to get to the bottom of what the hell is going on, but we're not sure how to do it because as I said, no one's talking. Then we have a bit of luck. Some time later the guy and woman come back, he's been drinking. This time they say the woman's remembered something and that a man named Hammond may be trying to kill them. That's when we get really interested. This guy has a couple more drinks and says he's going to break into this Hammond's place to find out who the hell he is. It looks like a good opportunity to find out who you are and what's going on. If it goes wrong we can get out fast and leave the guy to face the music, so I tell Shades to tag along. I keep an eye on the girl outside.

In they go, the guy because he thinks someone is trying to kill him and his new girlfriend and Shades because we want to know more about the new face and find out why you had him roughed up. Then things get a bit out of hand, the rest you know. It didn't work out too bad though, we did you a favour, made some problems go away,' he nodded at the case, 'we made some money. Now we have a chance to talk new business.' Tony sat back and pretended to relax, he wasn't sure if Hammond had believed all of it, some of it or none of it. He couldn't read his face.

Hammond made no comment, five long seconds ticked by. Then he said slowly, 'You mentioned new business.' Since he had changed the subject, Tony took it as a good sign that he was willing to let the

222

explanation stand, at least for now. He took a deep breath, this was the main reason he was there, 'My brother tells me that when he was in your office he saw some papers that led him to believe you may have a shipment of items somewhere. Would you be interested if I said I may be in a position to find you a buyer?'

Vince had mixed feelings. On the one hand he wanted to have Tony dragged outside and given a pretty good going over as a warning to others who considered messing in his affairs. On the other hand, since the arms dealers had pulled out, he was stuck with a shipment of guns sitting in a lorry. The longer he had them on his hands, the higher the chance of them being discovered or even stolen. He had a lot of investment tied up with those guns. Sure, the Russian skipper seemed happy to get them off his hands and the price had been good, but he hadn't exactly given them away. The idea was a quick, lucrative deal. He wasn't supposed to have the guns for more than a few hours.

Carefully placing his cigar in the ashtray Vincent steepled his fingers and rested the tips on his mouth, 'Mm... and are you that buyer?'

'No, no not me, I have no use for them but in *The Blue Parrot* you get to hear lots of things and meet all kinds. You'd really be surprised the people who come to drink, to talk,' Tony hesitated, 'are you choosey who buys what you're selling? I mean do you care who points them at who?' Tony had only asked to see how Vincent would react, he got his answer fast, without hesitation. 'I'm a businessman. A buyer is a buyer, I have no prejudices, one man's money is as good as the next.'

223

'That's a very modern approach, Vince.' Hammond looked sharply at Tony, he didn't like to be mocked, but Tony's face was expressionless. 'Who's the buyer then?'

'They're not shy but they are careful. If I was to say they were from across the water and not fans of the UK Government, I think you'd understand their caution.'

'That description fits a good many groups and countries.'

'Let me narrow it down for you, this particular piece of water that separates us is only twelve miles wide.'

'Oh, them.'

Tony was very interested in Vincent's reaction to finding out that the guns would be used against his own country, 'Still no problem?' If he had to label Vincent's response, he would have described it as boredom at having to repeat himself, 'I told you, a buyer is a buyer.'

'Do you want me to contact them on your behalf?'

Vince shook his head his voice firm, 'I do my own negotiations.' Tony was eager to smooth him over, 'Yes, I understand that, all I want to do is set up the meet. I don't think they would like it if I just handed over their name and number. They'd be happier if I said I had someone who could deliver what they want and you wanted to meet.' Vincent was suspicious, 'And what do you get out of it?'

'Since we handled the mess in the boot for you as a sign of good faith. Then we did our first paid job with the girl. As business colleagues I don't think a small cut is out of the question to set this deal up for you.'

The pleasant veneer vanished, 'How much?'

'We're not greedy… say ten per cent of the take.'

'That still works out to be a lot of money for making a couple of phone calls.'

'It's not just that, is it? You're paying for my contact. It's not easy to talk to these people, the trust I have built up and…' Vince interrupted, 'Okay, okay, you made your point, how soon can it happen?'

'Fast, very fast. You could have the whole thing wrapped up by tomorrow night, the guns off your hands and a nice fat profit, no problem.' The idea of shifting the guns fast appealed to Vince, who was growing increasingly concerned about having such valuable merchandise sitting in a lorry park and in a stolen truck to boot. Sure, Micky had slapped some of his false plates on it, but if anyone checked, the big white truck did not look much like a Ford Granada. 'Okay, say I was interested in a quick deal, how would it work?'

Inside, Tony breathed a sigh of relief. This was the last hurdle, then he could get the hell out of there. Hammond may smile a lot but this man was dangerous, perhaps even unstable. 'It would be quite simple. I would inform the party concerned you were interested in negotiating a deal. They would contact you direct by phone tonight, to set up the where and the when. I'm certain they'll act quickly. The rest is up to you.'

'And for that you get ten per cent?'

'For that and for any future customers or deals I find. After all, as I said, *The Blue Parrot*'s a funny place. Weekends are the disco party people but during the week there's a different set altogether, lots of business is discussed and drunk to,' he smiled, 'we really do get all kinds.'

'You say tonight, they'll phone tonight?' Tony nodded, 'Tonight… it'll probably be very late, maybe close to midnight but yes, if it's on, I better get going now. I've got some calls to make. Also, you'd better give me a break down on the guns, exactly how many, what type, do you supply ammunition and so on. And note down your office phone number.'

Vincent stared at Tony, who found it hard not to break eye contact first. It seemed as if he was trying to extract the truth just by staring at him. Tony did well to return his gaze steadily. It was Hammond who broke first. Looking down at his desk he slowly pulled open the top drawer. Tony tensed but remained still. Hammond reached into the drawer then hesitated. Again he glanced at Tony, who looked back calmly. Tony never looked for nor started trouble however, with regard to violence, he was capable of returning, with interest, any aimed at him. Hammond could not see Tony's hands. One gripped the arm of his chair hard, the other had slipped into his pocket and firmly held the pistol, which was levelled at Hammond's crotch. If he tried anything, Tony would make damn sure he regretted it, fast. Vince glanced down at the drawer and quickly pulled out a piece of paper. Reaching for a pen he began to scribble.

While he wrote Tony swallowed and quietly took a deep steadying breath. 'Okay Tony, I'll wait for that call.' Standing up, Hammond held out the list for Tony to take. Tony removed his hand from his pocket and slid his sweating palm over his knee in an attempt to dry it as he stood. Taking the list, he folded and pocketed it. Vincent became charming again, stretching out his hand to grasp Tony's firmly. The coldness of his grip surprised Tony but his face betrayed nothing as Vincent looked hard at him once more. Tony released the hand, 'I'll be in touch.'

Vincent remained silent. He appeared to be thinking and nodded slowly. Perhaps Tony was useful alive, then again, perhaps not. He was glad he had told Micky to hold off. The brothers needed further thought. For him, people were not human, they were merely assets to be used or problems to be disposed of. In his mind, Tony hovered between the two. Since he had shot Sara he was warming to his new role. Vincent said thumbs up they live, Vincent said thumbs down, they die. The smile broadened at the idea of having the power of life and death. Hammond's smile brought Tony no comfort. It was those eyes again. 'Take a cigar with you.'

'Thanks.' Tony took the cigar, placed it carefully with the list in his inside pocket and nodded. The silent smiling Vincent watched him move to the door. As Tony reached it, Hammond's loud stern voice halted him, 'Tony!' He turned slowly one hand gripping the door handle very tightly. Hammond's expression had suddenly become glacial, Tony waited, 'Use a cigar cutter, won't you.' The mouth smiled again, taking pleasure in the shadow of concern on Tony's face. Quickly, Tony replaced it with a ghost of a smile, nodded curtly and closed the door carefully as he left.

Vince Hammond regarded the door and shook his head slowly, amazing, absolutely amazing! At first he had wondered if the brothers were something special because of the rumours, but no, they were just like the common herd. The fact Tony had even asked the questions, did he care who bought the guns, did he care who points them at whom. If Vincent thought of other people at all which wasn't often, he never ceased to marvel how weak and restrained they were, seeing obstacles to their objectives where in fact, there were none. Again, he thanked whatever strange stars were present at his birth that made him different, that made him superior.

Outside, Tony climbed into his car and drove out through the newly mended gates, he glanced in the mirror more than once but no one had followed. A few hundred yards along the road he pulled over and took a few deep breaths. Christ he was pleased to be out of there. He ran his hands over his face and rubbed his tired eyes, leaning back in the seat, 'Phew.' He felt drained. There was a couple of moments towards the end he'd been certain Hammond hadn't believed a word he said. Tony shook his head, the way the man looked at him, cold like a shark. He winced as he remembered the handshake even the guy's skin was cold... 'Jesus.' He wasn't going to dwell on it, he had played his part and as far as he could tell, Hammond had gone for it. Taking the paper he'd been given from his pocket he examined it and raised his eyebrows, 'Two hundred!' Tony started the car and headed for *The Blue Parrot*.

Having made their trip to the industrial estate Ron and Shades were also returning.

Vicky looked up as the balcony door opened. It was Tony. She had changed out of her disguise and looked more comfortable in jeans and jumper. 'Tony... How did it go, you were a long time, I was worried.' Tony headed straight for the drinks table and poured himself a generous brandy. 'He's a careful man your Vincent Hammond, had to spin him quite a yarn. Think he's pretty desperate to get rid of the guns. As far as I can tell he believed me, now he's waiting for a call from the buyers.' Before Vicky could respond, Ron and Shades arrived carrying the reels of wire Vicky had left in the car. Ron carried one and Shades the other two. They put them down quickly and began to rub life back into cold fingers. Anxious to talk to Tony, Ron asked quickly, 'How did you get on with Hammond?'

'As I was telling Vicky, he took some convincing but seemed to have gone for it by the time I left. He's waiting for a call. I've got a list here with exactly what he's selling.'

Ron continued to rub his hands, 'Good, good, brrrr, the temperature is really dropping, it's going to be well below tonight. I wish we didn't have to go back out.' He took the piece of paper from Tony and read it, 'Bloody hell, he's not mucking about, is he?' Ron passed the paper to Shades who studied it for a few seconds and gave a low whistle, 'Two hundred AKMS's, new and in the boxes with thirty rounds apiece,' there was a moment's thoughtful silence then Shades said happily, 'it went well at the industrial estate.' Ron agreed, 'Yes, it looks okay, we had a good look around.' Shades added, 'We did it mostly with the car headlights and a small torch, but from what we could see the building we used last time is perfect,' he smiled at Vicky, 'we dragged all those packing cases you sat on out of the way so it's all ready for the truck.' Ron carried on, 'Yes and we checked the distance from the squibs to Shades' firing point and I think three hundred feet will be plenty.' Vicky interrupted, 'What exactly is an AKMS?' Ron answered, 'It's a rifle, first made in the USSR I believe.' He looked at Tony for confirmation, Tony nodded, 'You've heard of the AK47?' Vicky shook her head. 'Well, it's a famous Russian rifle, the AKM is a slightly more modern version, the AKMS is the same except it has a folding butt stock. A bit easier to conceal, probably just what our friends from over the water will be looking for.'

Vicky shuddered, 'It's a different world out there, I don't believe I'm discussing gun shipments and IRA like it's normal or something.' Ron sat next to her, he smiled again, 'Everything seems to be coming together, hey, is anyone hungry?' There was a chorus of assent. Although deeply concerned about the dangerous plan she suddenly made up her mind to show support and be brave, Vicky slapped her thighs and stood up, 'I'll see what's in the kitchen.' They both disappeared.

Tony and Shades opened the big box Vicky had collected earlier and read the instructions Tom had scribbled. Shades called loudly, 'Hey Ron, it says here we've got to drill holes for the squibs, where are we gonna get the power from to...' he hesitated, 'forget it! I've cracked it,' turning to Tony and lowering his voice he asked, 'when we put the club's toolkit together, we got one of those battery drills, didn't we?' Tony nodded, 'We'd better charge it up, there's a big box of masonry bits in the kit where we did some work after the fit out.' Shades smiled, 'Good, we'll need them.'

They both checked the three walkie-talkies, everything they needed seemed there. Carefully, they examined the three hundred foot reels. Linking them together seemed simple. They joined using jumper connectors Tom had included in the box.

Half an hour later they all sat down with trays to eat, everyone felt upbeat. Vicky was still worrying about Ron, who unbeknown to her was worried enough for them both, but on the whole their spirits were high.

After dinner, Shades checked his watch, 'We'd better get over to your flat to wait for the call. How much are we going to tell the IRA we want for the guns?' Ron ran his hand over his chin thoughtfully and looked questioningly at Tony, 'What do you think how much do they go for?'

'Brand new... I'd say between three and four hundred pounds each. Hammond's got two hundred so that's...' Tony looked at the ceiling and squinted. Vicky helped, 'That's sixty to eighty thousand pounds, wow!' Tony stared at her, he appeared less than happy to have been helped. Catching his look, Vicky began to inspect her fingernails. Tony turned back to Ron, 'Yeah, tell 'em eighty thousand.' Ron regarded Tony for a moment, he had to ask, 'How do you know this?' Tony leaned back and put his hands behind his head, he wore the faintest of smiles. Pointing at the floor, indicating the club below he said quietly, 'As I always say we get all kinds of people in *The Blue Parrot* and they talk about all kinds of things. Ron nodded, the brothers certainly lived in a different world, he turned to Vicky, 'It's time... we won't be long.' They took Shades' car.

At 10:45, Ron and Shades pulled up on the corner by the phone box a few hundred yards from Ron's flat. Shades switched off the engine and glanced at Ron, 'Now we wait, I suppose.'

'Yup, now we wait, I hope they phone.' Shades was confident, 'They'll phone, they want guns an' they want 'em bad.'

'Hope so.' They sat quietly and watched the snow silently falling. The street was deserted. Ron mused how the snow made even the old, grey street look picturesque. The chilly breeze caused the snow to swirl here and there creating miniature whirlwinds. He looked up at the streetlights, big flakes were dancing around the lamps, glowing like icy orange fireflies. He gazed at the familiar buildings in the road, one or two fingers of yellow light escaped here and there, reaching out they gently touched the snowy ground. All was quiet, all was still. Ron knew the lights were probably left on for security reasons, his was the only residential property in the vicinity. A car rounded the bend and laboured past, then stillness again.

Suddenly, the phone rang. Even in its box the abrupt ring sounded loud. Ron scrambled out quickly, crossed the pavement to the phone box and snatched up the receiver, 'Yes?'

'We understand you may be able to supply something we want.'

Keeping his voice level, 'Yes, I've been expecting your call.' The voice seemed impatient, 'Let's get to it, what are you selling and how much?'

'We have two hundred AKMS, thirty rounds apiece, brand new and boxed up. The price is eighty thousand cash. The deal is you take them fast.' The line was silent for a moment then the voice spoke again, 'You say fast... when?'

'Tomorrow afternoon.'

'That many guns take up a lot of room. How would it be done?'

'They're in a truck. We would meet. You bring the cash, we bring the truck. We meet at a quiet place, do the deal. You leave with the truck. How you handle it from there is your affair.' The man on the phone was being cautious, 'What about the truck? Is it stolen? We don't want to get a couple of miles down the road and get pulled.' Ron had no idea but his creativity won through, 'We have made arrangements, the truck won't be missed for a week. After you've dropped off the consignment and finished with the truck, park it and make a quick call to us. We collect it, we've disconnected the speedo' so the mileage won't be noticed and we'll even top up the tank, no one will know it's ever been moved.'

'We ring you on this number?' Ron answered fast, 'No, this number is good only for tonight.'

'What, through Shades or Tony then?' Eager to disassociate the brothers from the picture, Ron snapped, 'No, they're not part of this organisation and we may not use them again. We don't like to have a pattern. Like you, we need to be very careful. You will be given a new number on completion of the deal.' So far, to Ron's amazement he had dominated the conversation, it helped that he was imagining himself as the hero Max Carter in his books. Suddenly, the conversation ended abruptly, 'Stay by this number.' There was a click, Ron hadn't expected this, he hung up slowly and looked out of the phone box at Shades, who was furiously biting his nails,

Ron shrugged at him. Shades climbed out of the car and crossed eagerly to the phone box, 'What happened?'

'They hung up.'

'Didn't they like the deal?'

'I thought they did, then suddenly he said 'stay at this number' and hung up.' Shades considered, 'Perhaps it's a bigger deal than they thought, this guy isn't senior enough to make a decision like this. It's a lot of guns. He's probably talking to someone else.'

'Maybe so,' Ron looked grave then added slowly, 'suppose they're on to us and they're tracing the call somehow.' They stared at each other and at that moment were caught in the headlights of an approaching truck. It was moving close to the kerb in an unusual way. Ron shouted, 'It's going to hit us!' He dived out of the phone box with Shades behind him. They both hit the snow-covered pavement hard, rolling over in time to see the gritting lorry skirt smoothly around Shades' car and continue on its way, the driver totally unaware of the panic he had caused. Shades hauled himself to his feet and glared at Ron who was also struggling up while brushing snow from his coat, 'This is between you an' me, right?' He spoke through clenched teeth. Ron readily agreed, 'Right!'

As they walked back to squeeze into the phone box again, Shades was muttering, 'If it got out I was scared of a gritting lorry, I'd never hold my head up in *The Blue Parrot* again,' then louder to Ron, 'now just calm down will you?' At that very moment the phone rang and they both jumped. Shades turned his back on Ron and glared out of the phone box, partly in embarrassment, partly in annoyance at himself for not being more like Bogart. Ron gripped the receiver, forcing his voice to sound calm, 'Yes?' 'We agree, give us the details.' Ron thrust a thumbs-up in front of Shades' nose who turned to listen as Ron told them about the industrial estate and carefully explained which warehouse, 'It's white with three blue lines on the left after the big sweeping left-hand bend. Park in the roadway outside the entrance to the courtyard. Look for the sign, 'Ice House Refrigeration'. We'll be inside with the truck, you'll get the chance to look the guns over and we'll have our man there to check the money. We meet at twelve o'clock on the dot. Not before or after, but twelve. If we see you snooping about before, it's off, okay?'

It was obvious to Ron that the voice on the phone preferred to give orders than take them. It said curtly, 'Okay, twelve o'clock…' there was a pause, the voice added, 'This better be straight or we'll be… unhappy, get it?'

'It's straight, tomorrow then?' The voice was silent. When it did speak it was ominously quiet, 'Tomorrow.' There was a click and the phone went dead. Ron slouched against the box, 'Wow, I'm too old for this sort of thing.'

'You're twenty-nine, don't be such a wimp.'

'Well, I feel too old for this sort of thing.'

'Oh shut up, be happy they're coming.' Ron smiled, 'Twelve o'clock, I can't believe this is working.'

It was almost eleven thirty when the headlights of Shades' car swept across the snow-covered yard behind *The Blue Parrot*. Two figures hurried up the fire escape to the private flat. As they entered the warmth was a relief. They brushed snow off themselves and hung up their coats. Ron complained, 'It's bloody cold out there.' Vicky had two brandies ready, handing them one each she asked, 'What happened, did they ring?' Ron cupped his brandy and smiled, 'They rang.' 'And?' Shades answered, 'Twelve tomorrow, all set.' Vicky turned back to Ron, 'It's just the call to Hammond then.' Ron sipped his brandy, 'Just the call, I'll warm up a bit first.' She was suddenly concerned, 'Ron, your voice!'

'It's not a problem, Hammond's never heard me speak, so he can't recognise my voice.' She nodded but remained unsettled, even being in the room while someone spoke on the phone to Vince Hammond was unnerving.

A few miles away the man himself sat alone in his office. Tony had told him to expect the call late so he was unconcerned as the clock approached midnight. He felt rather pleased with himself, among his curious collection of attributes, confidence was a plentiful commodity. He had been certain he would find a way out of his gun problem and was now on the brink of a new deal. While he awaited the promised phone call he indulged himself in a mental time travel, looking back over his career, which was based on the simple concept of achieving what he wanted by removing anything in his way.

Ice cream! It had all begun with ice cream. Golden-headed Vincent, the little boy who wanted a cornet with a chocolate flake. The obstacle to this particular tasty goal took the form of a smaller boy in front of him, taking his time to study the pictures of various ice creams on offer adorning the ice cream van. While the driver was distracted Vincent had shoved the child forcefully on the back of the head with as much power as his seven year old arms could deliver, smashing the little boy's face against the side of the van. The resulting bloody nose had flowed like raspberry topping as the boy staggered aside. The ice cream vendor had turned in time to see young Vincent step up, 'Nose bleed, a ninety-nine please.'

Adult Vincent smiled, to show such promise! Such decisive action at a young age, his success had only been a matter of time. Returning to the present he rested his gaze on the phone.

Everyone sat quietly as Ron dialled the number. An unruffled confident voice answered, proclaiming to be Vincent Hammond. Ron nodded to his audience and began to speak, 'I believe someone has told you we are interested in what you're selling.' Hammond answered, 'Someone has contacted me, yes. If I sell or not depends on whether we can reach an agreeable price.'

'We do want your product and we aren't a small organisation, I'm sure we could meet any reasonable price.'

Ron looked at Tony, who blinked and nodded encouragingly. Ron continued, 'We are told you have two hundred items to sell and thirty consumable accessories per item.' Hammond was smooth, 'Yes, that sounds about right.' Ron pushed, 'And what kind of price were you thinking to secure these items.' Hammond dropped the smooth tone his voice became flat and uncompromising, 'One hundred thousand.'

'Since we're taking them fast and in bulk, I'm sure you can do better than that.' Hammond was stubborn, 'A hundred grand that's the sum, take it or leave it.'

'If we agreed, could the items be delivered ready to move say, on a truck that we could leave at a prearranged location for you to dispose of?'

Hammond was quick, obviously, he did want to get the guns off his hands, 'Yes, that could be arranged.'

'We would need to move quickly, can you deliver them on pallets, with a pallet lifter?'

'Again, that's not a problem.' Ron ran with it, 'We'd like to close this deal tomorrow.' 'Sounds good.' Hammond was unable to conceal his eagerness.

'Can you be at the old industrial estate down by the river by eleven thirty with the items?'

'Industrial Estate?'

'The one due for demolition down by the old docks, off Nelson Road.'

'I'll find it.'

'Okay, this is what you do. At eleven thirty, drive the lorry onto the industrial estate down the main roadway and around the sweeping left-hand bend. There's a long white building with three blue lines on your left. Drive along the road until you see a courtyard to that building marked 'Ice House Refrigeration'. Turn into the courtyard and in front of you is a warehouse, which is the loading bay for the building, drive in there. Don't forget, eleven thirty. If we see anyone snooping around before then, the deal's off, okay?'

'I'll be there.'

Ron could tell Hammond was slightly relieved. He judged it was a good time to tell him about the examination. 'I will of course, be bringing an expert to look the items over before we close the deal, we will want to crack open a couple of boxes, have a crowbar handy.' Hammond regained his charm, 'I have nothing to hide, look all you want. Just bring the cash.' Ron was easing into his part now and put a little ice into his voice, 'We'll have the money, be there on time with the items ready to move.'

'It'll be there, eleven thirty.' Ron closed the conversation, 'Tomorrow then.' 'Tomorrow' was the reply. Ron hung up and everyone relaxed, Tony raised his glass, 'Tomorrow!' which was joined by three more and in chorus they toasted, 'Tomorrow!' Shades commented, 'Of course, all this wouldn't be necessary if you got rid of Hammond.' Ron looked at Vicky then at Shades. In a serious voice he asked, 'And you would do it, would you?'

Shades shifted in his chair, 'Not me no, but there are people that come to *The Blue Parrot*... for the right price...' Ron shook his head, 'No! Look, one, we would probably get caught and two, if we didn't the killer would have something on us; and three, this way we don't hurt anyone. All we do is bring two violent factions together, give them a nudge they do the rest. What's the saying? *If you live by the sword, you shall die by the sword.* There's personal revenge too, I'll admit that and why not? The IRA robbed Vicky of her parents and Hammond murdered her sister, tried to kill me, paid to have Vicky murdered and you beaten up. Why the bloody hell shouldn't there be revenge?'

The atmosphere had suddenly grown uncomfortable. Ron was tense. Vicky was thinking of both Sara and her parents, it had been a long night for all of them. Tony broke the moody silence, 'Look, I'm sure we've done the right thing, if Hammond found you both still alive he'll come after you, then me an' Shades for double-crossing him. It's time we put it to bed. Tomorrow's a big day we need to be sharp. We'll be back at six-thirty in the morning.' The atmosphere thawed as they all shook hands. Vicky whispered her thanks to Tony, she even hugged Shades. The brothers said goodnight and left.

Ron and Vicky were soon in bed, the room softened with only one bedside light illuminating it. They sat propped up holding hands and resting their tired heads on respective pillows. Ron was living the next day in his head and checking for problems. Without the distractions of the busy day, Vicky was brooding about her sister and riding emotional waves that varied between regret, anger and sorrow. On the crest of regret she suddenly burst out, 'I should have done something!'

Ron was jolted back to the present and quickly turned to her. Vicky's eyes brimmed with tears, 'I should have done something to save her.' The tears overflowed, Ron released her hand and brushed them away then taking her hand once again, 'What could you do?' With a slight shake of the head, she sniffed, 'I don't know,' an angry wave rolled in, 'I was there a year, a year, I had time, I should have got her out, made her leave.' It hurt Ron to see her so upset but was at a loss for what to say. Vicky frowned, reliving the experience, 'He could be charming for days, even when he was being nice there would be an underlying tension in the air. It was like walking on eggshells, Sara would beg me not to upset him. If something didn't go his way he could be spiteful, his mood could change in a moment. Sometimes Sara would have a bruise on her arm or face, she was terrified of him. I tried and tried to make her leave but she thought he would come after her, I think he would have too. She was so unhappy but pretended to be happy to please him,' a wave of anger peaked, 'and there was the heroine!'

To save Vicky the pain of recounting it Ron said gently, 'Tony told me everything you said in the car while you were driving over to Hammond's to rescue Shades and me. We discussed it while we were trying to plan a way of rescuing you.'

Vicky was silent, then after a little thought, 'I've heard about women who put up with being bullied, I've always imagined they were weak. I never in a million years believed I'd be in a situation like that. Running around after him, Sara pleading with me to be nice to him, don't upset him, smile, keep him happy. I did too, to protect Sara. It was like acting in a twisted play; unreal, not like living,' anger lost its energy and was quickly replaced by regret, 'I should have done something!' she said again, half to herself. 'Oh Vicky, it's hard to see what, the man's a monster with a bunch of paid thugs backing him up. What could anybody do?' Regret faded and in its place sorrow rose, 'But I was her big sister Ron, I should have protected her somehow.' She turned to face him and they hugged for a few moments then Ron pulled away slightly to look into her face, 'If tomorrow goes as it should he won't be smiling at the end of the day I promise you that, now come on, you're tired.'

'I am.' She lowered her pillow and lay flat with a huge sigh. He leaned over and switched off the lamp. At first the room appeared to be completely black but as Vicky's eyes grew accustomed to the darkness she became aware of the faint green glow from the bedside clock and Ron's vague outline next to her in the dark still sitting up thinking and sipping his brandy.

Vicky turned on her side, 'Come on Ron, knock it off, there's nothing more you can do. You must be exhausted too.' She put her hand on his arm. He was trying so hard to hide it but she knew he was very worried, they would need luck for the plan to work, some of the variables were unpredictable and dangerous and they both knew it. She tried to reassure him, 'It'll be alright.' He turned to look at her and could dimly make out her face. He swallowed the last of his brandy, put down the glass and patted her hand still resting on his arm, 'Yes, it'll be alright,' after a pause, 'I'll tell you Vicky, I'll tell you honestly, I think you saved me that night in the rain, not the other way around.' She shook her head, squeezed his arm and snuggled down. He sat for a moment and looked at her, then gently stroked her forehead. She murmured sleepily, 'My mother used to do that.' Vicky's exhaustion was hot on the heels of her grief for Sara, soon it caught up and overtook. Finally, she escaped into merciful dreamless sleep.

Ron sat awake for some time, but finally he too lay down. Tony was right, tomorrow was a big day, he was so tired. It wasn't long before his breathing became deep, as worries for the following day melted into the soft, ever-shifting world of dreams, which tiredness deepened into oblivion.

PART TWO
CHAPTER 15
SUNDAY MORNING 5:30

Ron had woken early. Outside it was still dark, there had been a heavy snowfall overnight. He stood alone in the living room, holding his coffee cup in both hands staring out into the blackness as his thoughts turned inward. Today was going to be a long one, his stomach was already beginning to churn. People were going to die today and he had arranged it, everything was set. He felt little remorse for the people, he was certain they would kill him or anyone else if it suited them, but he had a part to play and was already nervous. People he cared about were relying on him.

Vicky was still asleep so to hear a voice Ron muttered aloud to make himself feel better, 'Come on Ronny! Get it together,' then after a thoughtful pause, 'for Vicky.' He smiled as he thought of her, in spite of all the trouble she had brought, Vicky was the best thing to happen to him since Jacqui died and he was happier than he would have thought possible. He sat down hugging his coffee and gazing vacantly at the carpet, all this had to work, for her sake... for all their sakes.

He looked up suddenly, sensing he was being watched, Vicky stood in the doorway, 'Couldn't you sleep?' she asked, smiling at him. He shrugged, 'It's a big day.' Vicky's concern showed in her voice, 'Ron, you will be careful, won't you?' Her smile faded as her mind ran quickly through some unpleasant what ifs. He moved to her and put his arms around her, 'Of course, try not to worry. Today we'll get this thing done, then... then there'll be time for us.'

'If anything should go wrong, I don't know if I... What I...'

'Shh, shh, nothing is going to go wrong, we've gone over the whole plan. The only really dangerous part is when I back away from Hammond and he won't understand what's happening until it's too late, then I'll be safe.'

'Yes, I know but... oh, just come back.'

'Come on, come on, it'll be alright, promise.'

She looked up at him searchingly and would have been shocked to discover how much effort Ron's confident expression was costing him, 'Aren't you even nervous?' 'No... er, yes... well, a bit.' He lied.

'I'll be glad when this is over I know that!' Vicky shook her head. In an attempt to ease the tension and lift the mood Ron switched on the kitchen radio, they drank more coffee and ate some toast. Neither felt like eating but Vicky pointed out they couldn't afford to feel faint later on, not today. They sat together on the sofa, then at six-fifteen, Ron stood up, 'We'd better get dressed, the boys'll be here at six-thirty.'

A little before six-thirty there was a knock at the front door. Although the door was accessible only from the club below, Ron hesitated with his hand on the lock then a familiar deep voice said, 'It's me, Tony.' With relief, Ron opened the door. Tony and Shades entered both in jeans and heavy coats, Tony's a World War II sheepskin flying jacket (the river would be extra cold), Shades wearing a long, grey wool coat and carrying a huge holdall. They nodded curtly and sat down. Vicky came out of the bedroom wearing thick sweater, jeans tucked into ankle boots and carrying her old beige coat over her arm, which she threw on the sofa and sat next to Ron.

They all looked at each other each trying to gauge how the others were feeling. Shades and Tony weren't in a chatty mood; this was their chance. Instead of merely watching a plot unfold from the safety and comfort of a seat, this was real. The danger was real. They were the cast in a story without an ending, they must try to create their own, but there were no guarantees, life had no respect for Hollywood gloss. On the reality side of the thin silver screen, stories could end unfairly or brutally, no matter how much the players wished otherwise. They knew it and relished that uncertainty and danger with nervous excitement.

Shades unzipped his holdall and pulled out a big powerful torch, 'Will this do?' Ron took the torch and examined it, flicking it on and off a few times, 'Fine, good.' He stood, put the torch back in the holdall and placed it on the floor with the box of effects Vicky had collected from the theatre.

The radio murmuring in the background bleeped six-thirty, Tony checked his watch, 'I know this sounds corny but timing is important.' They all looked at their watches, Vicky complained, 'Hey, I don't have one, I put it in the bundle you and Shades

245

threw away.' Tony walked to a drawer, rummaged about then turned to her, 'Here, it's old but it works.' He handed her an old digital watch and she slipped it on. Tony looked at his own watch, 'I've got six thirty-one... now!' Everyone adjusted their watches and looked up. Tony glanced at Ron. Taking his cue, Ron ran through the sequence of events, 'Okay, I'll go over it once more. I'm to meet Dave at seven-thirty to get the welding done then back here by eight-thirty for Jane. Hammond and the guns are supposed to arrive at eleven-thirty and the IRA has been told twelve.

Tony, how long do you need to drive to the dock and get *The Grey Lady* ready?' Tony ran a finger over his bottom lip and grimaced, he didn't want to worry Ron, 'It won't take too long to get there even in the snow, but the engine may need some coaxing to start, 'specially in this weather, it's been a bit temperamental lately,' seeing Ron's horrified face he added quickly, 'don't worry, it won't let you down, I'll leave with you to be sure, it'll give me lots of time.'

Ron nodded, not entirely happy with the revelation of a temperamental boat engine to add to his worries, 'Right, you leave with me then, once you get it started take her round to the industrial estate waterfront. Remember, when Vicky gives you the signal it's three short blasts on the foghorn. The second time she calls you it's two blasts, the last time Shades will call and it's one blast. That close to the river no one's going to think twice about a boat horn. Shades, on the last blast you have to judge it so that I have two or three seconds to say my line. We'll figure out the exact timings when we get down there, then hit the squibs. Tony, as soon as you hear them go off, pull the anchor and get the boat round to the mooring slip by the old boat yard. Vicky, when you hear the squibs go off start the engine. I've timed it, so I know I'll be out of the door in give or take fifteen seconds. Meanwhile, Shades will have climbed down from the roof, collected the detonator, reeled up the wires and made his way to Tony. Then you two go back to the dock and pick up the car. We all meet back here. Any questions?' No one answered. Vicky felt a surge of nervous energy it was really going to happen. She stood up suddenly needing to be busy, 'Does anyone want a coffee?' The brothers nodded, 'Please, thank you.'

'Ron, another one?'

'Please.'

Tony spoke to Ron, 'I know the industrial estate is only ten minutes but it's been snowing hard, I'd give it a bit longer.'

'Yes, good idea.'

Vicky soon returned with a tray of coffee. Further conversation was sparse punctuated by long contemplative silences. At seven o'clock Ron put down his cup and rose to his feet, 'Right then, I'm off to meet Dave.' 'Here!' Shades tossed his car keys, Ron caught them with both hands, 'Thanks,' turning back to Tony, 'don't forget your walkie-talkie.' Looking at Shades and Vicky, Ron added, 'I'll see you both back here at eight-thirty.'

Tony slipped the walkie-talkie into his pocket, everything was set, everything was said. Now all they had to do was follow it through. Tony and Ron left together through the balcony door and descended the fire escape to the yard.

Vicky and Shades looked at each other. Reading the anxiety on Vicky's face, he asked in his best Bogart voice, 'Got any more of that Java sweetheart?' She threw a cushion at him and smiled glad to have him there. He would help keep her nerves under control.

Outside in the snowy car park, Big Tony shook hands with Ron, he was serious but his eyes sparkled. Ron got the distinct and worrying impression he was enjoying himself. 'Good luck, Ron.' Ron tried to speak but his mouth was dry and he only managed a nod. This cool nod without a lot of talk impressed Tony who didn't realise Ron was so nervous he felt sick. They separated, Tony to his car and Ron took Shades'. With a final glance at each other they climbed into their cars. Two motors turned over slowly and fired, thick clouds of steamy white gas billowed from the exhausts as they edged out of the yard and swung off in different directions.

Ron pushed a cassette into the tape player and music filled the car. He was a little surprised it was opera that swelled from the speakers. He glanced at the other three tapes that lay in the centre console near the gearshift, all opera. Shades often did and said things that surprised him, it followed his musical tastes would be unpredictable. He remembered the brothers were half Italian, perhaps that explained it. Ron knew nothing of opera but somehow the energy and passion suited his mood. He let it play and held the steering wheel firmly as he thought of Hammond. He knew this was dangerous and they were rough people who would snap bones without giving it a thought. Ron shrugged, to hell with them. Their violence was what he was relying upon.

He made good progress despite the snow and arrived a little ahead of time. As the industrial estate came into view he could see Dave's van, he was also early, good. Ron rolled down the window and leaned out of the car, 'Hey, Dave!'

Dave, who had been blowing on his fingers and expecting Ron's Chevrolet, looked up, 'I gotta be mad this is me only day off. Where's the car?'

'Don't worry about it, follow me okay?' Dave mumbled, 'Yeah, yeah, keep your knickers on.' He started the van's engine and followed Ron into the estate. Ron drove along the main roadway around the sweeping left hand bend. The familiar white and blue refrigeration plant flashed past on his left. They swung left again into the courtyard marked 'Ice House Refrigeration' and parked in front of the warehouse doors to the loading bay, the same warehouse Tony had taken Vicky. Ron got out, pulled the heavy sliding door wide and waved at Dave to drive in.

Inside, Dave switched off the engine and jumped out, steel toe-capped boots clapping down on the hard concrete floor with an echo, 'What's the job then? And exactly why did you want me 'ere at this time of the mornin'?'

'I told you Dave, I'm conducting an experiment to see if something is feasible for my new book.'

'Is this the one I'm gonna get a mention in?'

'Yes, that's the one. Now, you don't want me to tell you all about my idea, do you? If I do, you won't enjoy it because you'll know how it ends.' Dave snorted, 'S'pose so,' he admitted grudgingly, then peering at Ron and narrowing his eyes, 'you cut yourself shaving?' Ron's answer was slightly exasperated, 'Never mind my chin, can we make a start?' Dave became brisk and business like, 'Fine with me, I left a nice warm 'ouse to be 'ere and I think I'd like to get back to it, so what d'ya want me to do?'

'Right, you see this metal door over here?' Ron pointed to the small door set in the concrete wall on the left between the small office and the steps that led up to the loading bay.

'Yeah.'

'Do you think it could stop a bullet?' Dave walked over and examined it, 'Nah, too thin innit.'

'That's what I thought, can you weld a plate to it, then fit a bolt on the other side?' Dave put his hand on his chin, 'I 'aven't got a plate that big but I can weld three bits across it. The gear in the van's a bit thicker than I 'ad last time.' He checked the hinges, 'It's a solid steel frame. If I beef up the hinges, it should take the weight. As far as the bolt goes, I dunno, I've got a lot of bits 'n' pieces in the van, I'll 'ave to 'ave a butchers.' Ron smiled, 'Good man! Want some help?'

'Yeah, and just 'cos you're 'elping, don't think I'm gonna knock anything off the bill. Sunday mornin' is still Sunday mornin'.' He stopped and looked hard at Ron as a thought struck him, 'Are you actually gonna take pot shots at it?' Ron shrugged, 'No... maybe. Look Dave, I'm timing how long this takes to do, you know, for accuracy in the book. Can we please get on with it?' Dave shook his head, 'Mad.'

At the flat Shades having dropped his coat on the sofa with Vicky's, peeled off his sweater and sat opposite her in shirtsleeves cradling a fresh coffee. She still appeared anxious and the waiting wasn't helping. Shades was smiling at her over his mug, 'This is nice, thanks, try not to worry.'

'I am worried, I'm particularly worried that you're not worried! You do realise how dangerous this is, don't you.'

To make her laugh Shades adopted his silly gangster voice, 'Look Baby, Ma and Pa Manning didn't raise no dummies ya know, me and Tony do get it.'

'Is that your surname?'

He resumed his normal voice, 'Yup, Tony Manning, Shades Manning.'

'Shades isn't your real name?'

'It's the only one I answer to.'

She watched him and waited. He was silent. He considered, they were all depending on each other, she was right, this would be dangerous, perhaps even life or death, 'You won't tell?' She crossed her heart.

'Even Ron doesn't know.'

'Between us,' she reassured him. Still he hesitated, then making up his mind leaned forward and whispered in her ear, her eyes widened in surprise, 'Really?'

'Mm really,' she didn't appear convinced so he explained, 'Tony and me are half Italian, Dad was English, Mama Italian. I nearly didn't make it as a baby. It means 'gift from God''.

'Wow,' realising he didn't share this information with just anybody she added, 'thank you Shades.' He nodded and drank his coffee.

'So, Manning is your Dad's surname?'

'Aha.'

She laughed, 'That doesn't have a meaning then?' Shades put down his coffee carefully and smiled, 'Actually, it does.'

'Really!'

'Yes, it's Norse in origin and before you ask, no, I'm not telling you.' She frowned and adopted a joke pout.

'Pout all you like, I'm not telling, look it up if you're that nosey.' Vicky's expression became serious again, she sighed, 'When this is all over, I will... I wish it was all over now.' After a thoughtful moment she brightened a little making an effort to be strong and asked, 'While we're talking about names why did you smile when you heard my name was Blaine, what was that all about 'being more suited to a hero than a heroine'? It was one of the first things you said to me.' He laughed, 'Ah! Well, in *Casablanca*, Bogart is the hero and his name was Richard Blaine, Ricky Blaine, Vicky Blaine,' still smiling he managed to look slightly serious, 'you did turn out to be a hero... at least to Ron.'

'I love Ron,' she said quietly. Shades' smile widened and he nodded, it wasn't news. He had guessed by the way they looked at each other even before they themselves had been sure. 'You're good for each other, I'm really pleased.' Vicky smiled shyly then the smile faded and her brown eyes looked steadily at Shades, 'I know you're doing your best to distract me, to stop me worrying,' she paused, 'bless you Shades.' He shook his head slightly as if to say, forget it. Vicky murmured half to herself, 'I wonder how they're getting on.'

A few miles away, Tony had parked and was trying to coax the old boat engine into life, 'Come on baby, you know you want to.' The oily black mass of pipes and wires squatted sulkily in the bowels of Tony's boat and did an excellent job of pretending it didn't want to, it growled at him as he tried the starter yet again, rrrrrrh, rrrrrrrh. He ran a hand over his face and sighed, then looked out at the grey overcast sky. It wasn't snowing but snow wasn't far away. He gave a sideways glance at the open cover of the engine compartment. He'd checked all the connections, primed the fuel lines having removed an air lock and cleaned one or two already cleaned components.

Perhaps bribery would work, 'What if I promised you that new fuel pump?' Having made his promise he hesitated, the battery didn't have too many tries left in it. Tony pushed the starter button and held his breath. Rrrrrrh... VROOOOOM. 'I thought you'd say that.' Lighting a celebratory cigar, he cast off the lines, then settling himself in the draughty cabin, grasped the throttle and with a grin rammed it forward. Out here on the boat he could be himself, the engine note rose and the bow lifted out of the water. Tony spun the wheel and the boat bounced away from the dock, kicking up ice cold spray as it plunged on. He spun the wheel again and the hull cut a slice of water and flung it to the right as the vessel changed direction then roared off roughly toward the old industrial estate waterfront. He had plenty of time so planned to amuse himself and carve up the still water near the dock. Glittering spray arced into the air made silver against the lead grey sky.

The shower of sparks ceased abruptly, 'What?' Dave flipped up his mask. Ron tried again, 'I said, is it going to take much longer?' Dave snapped down his mask and in a muffled voice muttered, 'It takes as long as it takes… longer if I gotta keep stopping to answer dumb questions.'

Ron paced, his shadow dancing across the floor, brought to life by the flashes of weird blue-white light as Dave welded. He stopped pacing and watched the shadows. If it hadn't been for that bolt of blue-white light at the precise moment he looked out of the window, he would never have seen Vicky crouching in the alley. He was sure he was doing the right thing this simply must work! Suddenly, he became aware of Dave speaking. 'Sorry Dave, what?'

'I said it's done.' Ron walked eagerly over to the door to examine it. To be on the safe side, Dave had even welded the hinges to the metal frame. Ron reached out to touch it but Dave slapped his hand away, 'It's still hot, you stupid sod.'

''Course it is, sorry. Well, it looks like a great job, thanks Dave.'

'See if you still thank me when you get my bill for dragging me outta bed on a Sunday morning.' He chuckled, obviously not a morning kind of person, but now he had been up a while, the thought of planting a hefty bill on Ron had revitalised his sense of humour, 'Oh, by the way, I gave that idea of yours some thought.' Ron stared back blankly. Dave elaborated, 'You know, about signing my work.'

'Ah.'

'What d'ya reckon about little copper tags with my signature etched into 'em, pot-riveted under the motors?'

Ron had said it only as a joke, which had now gone too far to admit to. He opened his mouth, nothing came out. Finally, 'Er, yes, it's a thought isn't it?'

'Mm, 'tis. When I 'ave a crack at fixin' your Chevy prop'ly, it could be my first signed work.' Ron did not dare tell him he could add a broken taillight, missing chrome door trim and bullet holes to the long list of problems. Dave's first signed work was shaping up to be a possible masterpiece. He nodded, 'Sure, Dave, sure, we'll think about it when I've got more time. Right now I've got some other things to set up for this feasibility study so I'd better get going.' He glanced again at his watch, eight-twenty. 'Okay Ron, now ring me, right?' Ron promised and they both left.

It had taken Ron longer at the warehouse than planned and not all the roads were clear which added five minutes to the normal fifteen minute journey time so he didn't get back to the flat above *The Blue Parrot* until eight-forty. Vicky greeted him nervously, 'Everything's alright, isn't it?' He reassured her, 'Yes, took Dave a bit longer than I thought, you know what a perfectionist he is. Did Jane come?' Then looking round he added, 'And where's Shades?' Vicky, relieved Ron was back, suddenly giggled. He smiled, 'What's the joke?'

'Shades went to hide in the kitchen but Jane followed him,' Vicky lowered her voice, 'I think Jane has taken a real fancy to him.' Ron breathed quietly, 'No!' Vicky whispered, 'Yes! It's handy really, because she's lost all interest in whatever you're up to.' He shook his head, 'How is Shades handling it?'

255

'You know what he's like, he's trying to be cool like one of his gangster heroes but Jane just thinks he's cute. You'd better go and rescue him.'

'Yes, we're a bit behind schedule. Dave insisted on telling me he's thought of a way of signing his work. Little copper tags etched with his signature, I ask you!' Vicky laughed, 'Serves you right for making fun of him.'

PART TWO
CHAPTER 16
SUNDAY MORNING 8:41

Jane peered closely at Ron who was perched on a stool in the small kitchen. Vicky and Shades looked on waiting for the show to begin. Jane pointed at Ron's face as she spoke, 'You've got some small scratches on your face this stuff may sting a bit, okay?'

'No problem Jane, slap it on.' She nodded and corrected Ron's advice gently, 'I don't slap things on people. I apply carefully what's required using the appropriate method.' Ron grinned and Jane went about her work chatting happily. After fifteen minutes Ron was unable to concentrate on what Jane was saying, he suddenly spotted a problem with his plan and needed a quick solution, 'Might work.' He'd spoken so quietly no one had noticed, then with more volume he halted Jane's stream of chat with, 'Excuse me Jane, I need to ask Shades something while I think of it.' 'Go for it.' She suspended work to rummage in her magic box of potions for some vital item. Ron turned to look at Shades, 'Have you got any brooms in the Club?'

It was unexpected, 'Brooms?'

'Yes.'

'Er.. yes. Why?'

'If you have three, can you put them in the car boot please?' Shades was puzzled, 'Three, I'm sure we have, there's all sorts of gear in the cleaners' room behind one of the downstairs bars.'

Jane had found what she wanted and gently turned Ron's head away from Shades to face forward. She was attempting to apply carefully what was required, using the appropriate method, when Ron, wondering if Shades had any questions, shifted slightly in an attempt to glance in his direction. It earned him a sharp reprimand, 'Now sit still Ron, how can I do my stuff if you keep fidgeting?' Jane caught Shades smiling, 'And you can wipe that grin off your face, laddie!' She waved a make-up brush at him threateningly.

Shades took an instinctive step back and flipped Finbar's water bowl all over the kitchen floor. 'Oh look what he's done now. Men, I ask you, what would they do without us?' Jane looked at Vicky, tutted and threw her head up then turning her attention to Ron, 'Ronny! I said keep still, this stuff has to dry.'

Vicky saw Shades shake his wet foot then loosen his tie in exasperation and glare at Jane, who was prattling away about how she 'knew this man once who was so clumsy…' The rest of the story was lost as Vicky steered Shades out of the kitchen into the living room. The kitchen door swung gently shut. Ron saw them go but Jane was in full flow and didn't notice.

In the quiet safety of the living room, Vicky and Shades sat down. 'Wow, she's so annoying!' He did his Bogart grimace, 'A broad like that needs a strong man.'

'Stronger than you!' She giggled. Shades was about to argue then conceded, 'Yeah...' he shrugged, 'probably right!' Finbar jumped onto his lap and Shades calmed himself by stroking Finbar's soft black fur. He liked Shades... cats know, his calming effect soon restored most of Shades' cool, 'What does Ron want with three brooms?' Vicky shook her head slightly, 'I don't know.'

'I'd better go and put them in the car, could be important... don't see how though.' He placed Finbar on the empty seat beside him, picked up his coat and moved to the front door. Vicky pointed to his thick sweater left on the sofa, 'Do you need that?'

'No, won't be long.' He gave a short wave and slipped out.

Suddenly, alone without the distraction of company or activity, worry and sadness slipped from the shadows. Vicky's anxiety propelled her to her feet, unable to be still she moved restlessly about the flat. Somehow it felt wrong to return to the kitchen and Jane's bubbly banter. Pausing a moment to gaze through the balcony door at the depressingly grey sky she sighed, by tonight it would all be over, tonight seemed a long way away.

As Vicky looked up at the featureless grey heavens they became her own silver screen onto which her mind projected images of Sara, her Sara, alive with youthful energy chatting about all the things she planned to do and places she hoped to visit.

In the kitchen Jane laughed at something, the laughter gently drifted Vicky's mind further back in time to the child Sara. To long hot summers they shared, filled with light and laughter, playing all day on the Devonshire moors, the smell of heather, stretching out in late afternoon on the warm sweet grass, Vicky stroking her sister's hair as she napped.

The bright image darkened into shadow as the scene formed of the woman Sara lying on a concrete floor and Vicky stroking her hair for the last time.

She turned quickly from the window and faced the terrifyingly empty room. For her, the muffled voices from the kitchen faded completely. The emptiness felt unlike anything she had ever experienced. Her sister would never come into this, or any other room. She yearned so much to see her that Vicky could almost imagine Sara sitting there on the sofa... at nearly the same moment that Sara looked at her and smiled Vicky suddenly found herself staring at an empty seat. For an instant, the grief and despair was smothering. She began to panic, when suddenly, Jane's muffled voice came back to her, bringing with it some sense of normality. Vicky clung on. The room once more became merely an empty room. Vicky sat down and sighed, there had been so little time to even begin to come to terms with the enormity of her loss.

She was so pleased to see Shades when he returned a few moments later, exclaiming with relief, 'Oh, it's good to see you.' He laughed, 'It's nice to be missed, but I've only been gone a few minutes.' She shrugged, slightly embarrassed, 'I'm being silly.'

'No, it's only nerves, it's natural.'

'Are you nervous then?'

Shades was, but even to himself he had labelled it as excitement and buried it. Vicky's anxiety on the other hand was plain to see, his response was calculated to make her smile, "'Course not! Heroes don't get nervous, did you ever see James Stewart or Bogart look nervous when they charge in and save the day?'

'Oh, shut up.'

They sat and talked for a while. Now she was used to him, she understood why Ron found him interesting; he was funny and quick. He knew what to say and when to say it to make her laugh. She was determined to play her part, after all, they were all doing this for her and she wasn't about to let them down. Vicky glanced at her watch, 'Right, you sit there and relax, I have to change into my disguise... just in case.'

'Yeah, I'll sit here,' he glanced nervously at the kitchen door, Jane's voice could be heard chattering to Ron as she worked, 'er... you won't be long, will you?'

'No, my disguise doesn't have to be as good as Ron's. I'm not getting close to Hammond. Hopefully, he won't see me at all, but the terrorists will, so we don't want them remembering a blonde, do we? Ron said he wants to play it as safe as he can.' She disappeared, leaving Shades to stroke Finbar and prepare himself for another encounter with Jane.

Twenty minutes later she reappeared wearing her disguise, grateful to be busy once again. The hair was black and spiky, the make-up fearsome, the disguise certainly worked. The woman who sat opposite Shades now looked nothing like Vicky. He gestured at the kitchen door, 'She's still got him in there, poor sod!' Vicky couldn't resist the opportunity to entertain herself and said slowly, 'You know,

Shades…' He looked at her, 'Mm?' 'I think she fancies you.' She sat back wickedly to enjoy his reaction, it didn't disappoint. He stopped stroking Finbar and looked alarmed, 'No!' She smiled and nodded, 'Yes!'

'Are you sure? I mean, how can you tell?' He composed himself and lowered his voice an octave. He was Shades, this was no way to carry on, 'What I mean is… oh, er, what makes you think a thing like that?' Too late he tried to sound casual. Vicky pointed at Finbar who had sat up to see why the stroking had stopped, Shades resumed and Finbar lay down again.

'A woman can tell these things. Anyway, what if she does? She's a nice girl, isn't she?'

'Yeah, she's okay, apart from that hair which looks like an explosion in a bedspring factory and the fact that she *never* stops talking.'

'Oh that's cruel, Jane's got a heart of gold, you can tell. She's a little nervous, I think that's why she chats so much. It would do you good to have a girlfriend.'

'Not her! She doesn't stop, had me pinned to the kitchen wall and wouldn't let up, wouldn't even let me finish a complete sen…..' Suddenly, the door burst open and Jane came bounding into the room, 'Okay, sh, sh, sh everyone sh, meet the mystery man!' With a theatrical flourish she presented… the kitchen door. All three of them stared, Jane yelled, 'Come on, Ron, your audience awaits.'

An elderly man slowly entered the room, a great deal older than Ron. The top of his head was bald and the small amount of hair either side, grey. His face lined and when he smiled deep furrows gathered around his eyes. He was smiling now, 'What do you all think?' It was only the voice that identified him Shades stared at him then at Jane. He was genuinely impressed and removing Finbar, rose to his feet for a closer inspection. Ron stood still as Shades circled him, 'That is amazing, I would have passed him by in the street,' he looked again at Jane as if seeing her for the first time, 'you really know your job, don't you?'

Jane flashed a small embarrassed smile and galloped on, 'I've been doing it long enough, I should do by now.' She pushed her big round spectacles back on her nose and explained, 'Really, this was an easy one, Ronny just said he didn't want to be recognised. Most of the time I have to create something, you know, make him evil, make him sad, make him handsome, oh, sometimes I think they think I'm a witch, not a make-up artist.'

Shades smiled then noticing Vicky watching him, quickly wiped it off. Turning his attention back to Ron he asked, 'How did you create the wrinkles?' Jane beamed, happy he seemed interested in her work, 'That's easy, it's liquid latex, comes in a bottle. You pull the skin tight around the eyes and forehead and paint it on. When it dries it contracts, bingo, lots of wrinkles, puts years on him doesn't it?' Shades shook his head, 'Really amazing, what about the rest? You didn't shave his head did you?' Jane tutted and shook her head, 'Silly boy, 'course not,' she was pleased to talk about her work and enthusiastically explained, 'the bald head and grey side-pieces are stuck on. I've used make-up on the bald patch and on his face. The moustache is also glued on, I coloured it to match the grey side-pieces. I put the colouring on with a toothbrush. There's nothing clever about it, it's my job.' Jane looked a little bashful and smiled at Shades. If anything about Jane made Shades more uncomfortable than her shouting at him, it was her smiling at him. He coughed and swallowed, 'Excuse me, erm, time's getting on, 's time we got going.'

He bent down to quickly gather up the equipment. Reaching into the large holdall he pulled out a strong canvas bag into which he placed two of the three hundred foot wire reels. The last of the reels was placed carefully on top of a canvas rucksack that was neatly folded in the bottom of the holdall with the remaining equipment. Finally, he zipped up both bags and pulled on his sweater.

Ron checked his watch, nine thirty-five, Hammond was due at the warehouse at eleven-thirty, 'Look Jane, thanks a million, we've got to go now, what do I owe you?' He reached in his rear pocket for his wallet.

'Oh don't be silly, it didn't take long, you always bring cakes to rehearsals, anyway,' She looked at Shades who was preparing to leave, 'I like meeting new people.' Then to Vicky who she suddenly became aware of, 'Oh, you've changed too!' Ron continued quickly to prevent Jane asking any questions, 'I'll see you next week, I'll bring extra nice cakes and tell you how it all went.' As all three hurried to put on their coats, Vicky slipped her small clutch bag into her pocket, the boys picked up a bag each and they all piled hastily through the balcony door.

Jane called, 'How what all went...? Ron, you never told me why you wanted it done! Ron!' He called back, 'No time, no time,' as his voice grew fainter, he called up from the yard, 'When you've packed up, let yourself out and don't let Finbar escape, bye, bye!' All three of them waved and disappeared into Shades' car. Jane, who had taken a step onto the cold balcony ducked back into the warm flat and closed the door. She dropped onto the sofa and spoke to Finbar, who was looking sadly into the kitchen at his water dish. Where were they all rushing off to, and why the disguise? She shrugged, 'They say that brilliance borders on insanity. Ron has an excuse, he's an artist, but the other two are as batty as he is. I must stop hanging about with people like them or I'll start talking to myself.'

'Meeeeaaaaww!'

'What's your problem, darling? Oh, no water, ah, hang on a minute.' Jane filled his bowl, gave him a pat, collected her equipment and let herself out through the front door. The Club wasn't open yet for the lunchtime customers but the staff were in and it was a lot safer than struggling down the slippery fire escape.

In the car the atmosphere was tense, Shades drove, Ron and Vicky sat together behind him. Ron put his arm around Vicky and gave a reassuring squeeze, 'Soon be over.' She nodded her mouth dry, she couldn't tell him how frightened she felt, he needed her support, his was the most dangerous part of the plan. Ron was putting on a brave face, but felt queasy the only thing that prevented him from throwing up was the thought of doing it in front of them.

Shades made an attempt to break the silence and said brightly, 'I'll be watching you Ron, don't worry.'

They arrived at the industrial estate at nine-fifty. As Shades drove through the gate Ron leaned forward and rested a hand on his shoulder, 'Can we stop a moment?' 'Sure.' Shades brought the car to a gentle halt fifty yards beyond the gate.

Ron turned to Vicky, 'I know you've been here before, but I'm guessing you weren't taking in much.' She gave a short humourless laugh, 'I was a little distracted.'

'Yes, things may happen fast, you should be familiar with the layout. This is the main roadway, it winds right through the industrial estate. Ahead you see it curves off to the left?'

'Yes.'

'The old refrigeration plant is big, it starts at that bend and runs alongside the roadway until the turn into its courtyard and loading bay. We're going there in a minute.'

'Yes, I remember, it's a left turn, *Ice House Refrigeration.*'

'That's right. Now you see these two small alleys ahead of us on the left?'

'Mm.'

'They run parallel with each other and join at the end in a tight horseshoe bend, so it's possible to drive into the first one down to the end, around the bend and come out of the second one back to this road.'

'I understand.'

'Let's go, Shades and show Vicky the door.'

Shades moved off and cautiously turned left into the first alley. The crunching of snow under the tyres seemed louder in the confined space. The alley was strewn with rubbish but nothing large enough to hinder their journey. They drove slowly past doors and windows on either side, some broken, all old, dirty and abandoned. On reaching the end Shades stopped the car. Ahead, the road curved to the right in a long bend. 'That,' Ron said, pointing to it, 'eventually, takes you to the side of the loading bay where Hammond is going to be, you don't want to go down there. You need this, sharp horseshoe turn here,' he pointed to the right and almost behind them. Shades hauled the wheel hard right and nosed the car around in a sharp u-turn, then drove down the second alley, now heading back in the direction of the main roadway from which they had begun. Before reaching the end, he stopped once again, this time by a small door set into the wall.

Ron pointed at the door as he spoke, 'Vicky, this is the door I'll come through. There's a maze of passages behind it but it leads to the warehouse and loading bay. Now, after the IRA leave you, come and park here, start the motor when you hear the squibs go off. I'll come running out in around forty-five seconds. If I don't come out in one minute tops I want you to go.'

She looked distressed so Ron added fast, 'I don't see why I won't, but you have to know what to do if something goes wrong. It may be Hammond or one of his men that come through the door and you mustn't be here!' Vicky nodded feeling a little light-headed. Shades drove the short distance to the end of the alley, turned left onto the roadway, travelled along it and around the sweeping bend at the end. A few hundred yards along the now familiar sign, *Ice House Refrigeration* appeared on the left. Shades turned in and parked in the wide courtyard in front of the warehouse that housed the loading bay. They all got out, Shades retrieved the radios from the holdall and handed one to Ron who switched it on, 'Tony, can you hear me, over?'

There was a hiss of static, then Tony's clear voice, 'It's bloody freezing out here, over.'

'Tony, this is Ron again, I'm going to turn my radio off, see if you can hear Shades, over.'

'Okay Ron, over.'

Shades turned on his radio and spoke, 'Tony, this is Shades, can you hear me, over?' There was a second hiss of static from Shades' radio then again, the clear voice, 'Yes, loud an' clear, over.'

Ron switched on his radio again, 'Okay Tony, I want you to try the foghorn to make sure I can hear it from here. Don't bother to answer just hit it... now! From somewhere over the rooftops in the direction of the river they heard the wail of Tony's foghorn. 'Good, I heard it loud and clear. Don't forget, hit it three times when Vicky gives you the first signal, then twice when she calls you the second time and once when Shades signals, over.' Tony responded, 'Okay Ron, no problem, over.'

'Tony, we're going to get set up here, we'll give you a call when we're done. Keep your set switched on, out.'

'Okay got that, listening out.'

Ron returned the radio to the car. Shades hauled the large box from the big holdall that Tom the effects man had leant them. Ron considered the concrete wall opposite the warehouse and courtyard on the other side of the main roadway, 'That wall still looks good in the daylight, if I can get them to park here just in the courtyard entrance, with the warehouse in front and the concrete wall behind, we're in business.

Come on you two, Shades, grab the drill.' Shades stared at Ron in horror, 'The drill?' Ron looked alarmed, 'Yes, the drill Shades, the battery drill, you said you had one, I thought you picked it up this morning as you came up through the Club.' Shades' face was deadly serious he reached slowly into the holdall then with a big smile he produced the drill, 'That got you going, didn't it?' Ron stared at him, he wasn't smiling. Shades looked to Vicky for help and received none, 'I was only trying to lighten the mood a bit.' Neither Ron nor Vicky commented; they just stared. He got the message, 'Sorry.'

With Ron carrying the box and Shades the drill they all walked out of the courtyard and crossed the main roadway to the concrete wall. Ron set down the box and opened it. He glanced at Tom's instructions again to be sure, 'It doesn't seem too bad. Shades, you drill a line of holes deep enough to take these,' he held up a squib, 'along the wall at regular intervals... er, say a couple of feet apart. Vicky, you push the squibs into the holes, I'll wire them to the firing box. Then Vicky, you follow us along and hide them as best you can, poke some dirt or rubbish into the holes, okay?' They both nodded and set to work.

Twenty minutes later, they stood back and surveyed the wall. Only a close examination would reveal the squibs. The wires connecting the squibs to the firing box were so thin that even from a short distance they were undetectable. The firing box that controlled the squibs Ron had placed on the ground near the wall. 'Okay Shades, drive round to the alley behind this wall and take the firing box from me.'

'Right.' Shades got in the car and backed out of the courtyard. He drove a short distance further along the roadway and disappeared round a right-hand bend. Vicky helped Ron drag some old wooden pallets into a pile near the wall. He scrambled on top and pulled up the last pallet, which he propped against the wall before climbing up the slats like a ladder. By that time Shades had driven around to the other side of the concrete wall, parked and was standing on the car roof, this raised him within arms reach of the top of the wall. He looked up at Ron and called, 'Ready!' Ron climbed down and held out his arms for Vicky to pass up the firing box, being careful not to jerk the wires. Ron walked back up his makeshift ladder and stretched over the wall. Shades took the box and placed it carefully on the roof then climbed down, picked up the box from the roof and set it on the ground. Ron had judged the wire length just right, looking down at Shades from the top of the wall he called, 'That's great, right come back round.' He scrambled off the pallets. Shades drove back around to Ron's side to find him and Vicky had finished dismantling the pile and distributing the pallets.

'Right Shades, get the brooms out of the boot and we'll brush the snow about to hide the footprints best we can.' Shades laughed, broom mystery solved, 'Ah.' He swiftly fetched the brooms and the three of them brushed snow as they slowly backed away from the wall. The ground looked disturbed but a quick glance wouldn't reveal any footfall. Shades looked doubtfully at the tyre tracks stretching away along the roadway, 'What about the car tracks?'

'There's nothing we can do about that, as long as they don't go examining the wall,' Ron glanced at Vicky, 'I'm sure they won't.' She regarded the wall and ground, 'Wouldn't have thought so.' Ron

270

clapped his hands and rubbed his cold fingers together, 'Right, let's put the brooms back in the boot and get the torch.' Shades hesitated, 'What about the footprints we're going to leave up to the warehouse door and into the loading bay?' Ron shook his head, 'Not worried about that, it won't stop them going in, they may be a bit more curious but the main thing is they stay away from that wall.'

Having completed their work outside, they walked into the warehouse, Ron carrying the torch. He stopped and stood thinking with his back to the open door. To their right was the corrugated iron wall peppered with rusty holes shooting tiny beams of light into the space. Ahead, the loading bay and high above was the deserted office on the rear wall. The big iron door up on the bay was rusted and padlocked. To Ron's left was the concrete wall and a small office. On the same wall between the office and the iron steps, which led up to the bay was the small door Dave had reinforced.

Ron crossed the wide floor to the little door set in the concrete wall and opened it. A long hall of doors stretched away into the darkness. When the food refrigeration plant had been operating, it was a busy thoroughfare used by all the workers. It had bustled with people pushing trolleys and coming on and off shifts, now it was silent and dark. Ron switched on the torch stepped through and shut the door. It closed easily and the heavy bolt Dave had fitted slid into its keep. He turned off the torch placed it on the ground and felt for the bolt in the dark, found it and slid it open and closed a few times. Then opened the door and stepped through. He tried to open the door fast, having done so, jumped inside and bolted it as quickly as possible then felt for the torch. He found it without difficulty and switched it on. This done, again he unbolted the door and rejoined the others. Ron stood regarding the door for a moment his thoughts were broken by Vicky, 'Ron, the time's getting on.' 'Right,' Ron leaned back inside, placed the torch on the floor and shut the heavy door then turning to Shades, 'let's check the timing, it's vital you fire the squibs at the right moment.'

'Yes.'

'Now, when you see me light my cigar, it means that everything is alright and I want you to fire the squibs. I need time to get to the door before you do, so let's see how long it takes from the time I go into the warehouse,' he walked back to the entrance, 'this has got to be really accurate so time me, both of you, from when I say now, ready?' They both raised their wrists and stared at their watches. 'Now!' He walked from the entrance to the reinforced door, mumbled some lines and shouted, 'Now! How long was that?' Shades looked up, 'Fifteen seconds.'

Ron looked at Vicky for confirmation, 'Yes, fifteen seconds.'

'Very good, it takes fifteen seconds to walk to the door and say my lines, so Shades, as soon as I disappear into the warehouse, time it, then start the fireworks. After that, don't hang about, get down the fire escape reeling up the wire as you go, run over to your side of the wall, grab the firing box, pull out the wires and hotfoot it to the docks, Okay?'

'No problem, got it.'

'Good, and Vicky?' She repeated her part back to him, 'I check in with Tony when I see them coming. I check in again when they leave me. When they're out of sight, I drive round to the small door on the side of the plant you showed me on the way in. I switch off the engine and wait. When I hear the squibs I start the engine. You come out and we drive off fast, down the alley, turn right and out of the estate.'

Ron was sharp, 'You've forgotten something.'

She looked at him almost sulkily, knowing which part he meant but said flatly, 'No.'

He was patient but firm, 'If I don't come out between forty-five seconds and a minute after you hear the squibs fire, I'm not coming. I told you it takes that amount of time to pass through the passages from the warehouse to the side door. I know because we timed it twice when Shades and I looked the place over, there's no point you sitting there. I'll probably come running out, but if I don't, I really want you to go.' 'Alright.' She said quietly without making eye contact.

'I mean it Vicky, go, as I said it could be Hammond or one of his men that comes out and this will all be for nothing.' She looked at the ground and whispered, 'I know.'

Ron wasn't convinced she would leave but time was short and they still had work to do. He picked up the radio, 'Tony, this is Ron. We've planted the squibs, Shades has to run the wires up to the roof then we're all getting into position, over.'

'Okay Ron, check in when you're in position, out.'

'Will do, Tony, out. Let's go.'

When they reached the car, Shades pulled his rucksack from the holdall. He quickly placed two reels of wire, connecting jumper cables, radio, binoculars and trigger switch in it and swung it onto his back. With his hands now free, he picked up the third reel. He squinted up at the nearby rooftop, which looked down on the wall and the courtyard, 'Better get up there, see you when it's over. I'll walk along the tyre tracks so I won't leave a trail. Good luck, Ron.'

Vicky looked on as the two friends shook hands she felt her stomach tighten as she caught the look of concern on Shades' face. He turned to her and grinned, 'And you drive carefully.' She tried to smile, 'Yes, we'll see you later.' Shades hesitated, she looked cold and worried, 'There's a car blanket in the boot, Vicky.' Without waiting for an answer, he gave Ron a final nod and walked away, taking care to walk in the tyre tracks as he moved off down the roadway, to make his way around to the firing box behind the concrete wall.

On reaching the firing box Shades connected the wires and paid out the reel as he moved towards the tall derelict building that looked down on the roadway. When the reel ran out he plucked the next one from his rucksack connected it with the jumper cables and continued. The last reel he added halfway up the fire escape was long enough to cross the roof with fifteen feet to spare.

Meanwhile, Ron and Vicky had climbed into Shades' car, reversed into the roadway and headed out of the estate. They turned right onto the public highway, drove a few hundred yards and pulled over to the kerb. Reversing, Ron swung the car into a small alley where he stopped and shut off the engine. He nipped out, fetched the blanket from the boot and handed it to a grateful Vicky. He smiled, 'Shades, the tough guy.' Vicky managed a weak smile, 'With all that's going on.' She arranged the thick blanket so it covered her but kept her arms on the outside. She hoped desperately Ron wouldn't revisit the 'if I don't come out leave without me' scenario Vicky doubted she would be able to leave. If he pressed it she would have to lie to avoid worrying him, she hated the thought of doing that.

From the shadowy alley they could see the estate entrance, Ron checked the time, ten-fifty, 'We'll give Shades another five minutes to run the wires up to the roof, God I hope they're long enough.' Vicky was concentrating on breathing evenly to control her nerves. They sat quietly and the time dragged. At ten fifty-five, Ron scooped the radio from the rear seat, 'Tony! Shades! Can you both hear me? Shades first, over.'

'Shades, loud an' clear, over.'

'Tony, no problem, over.'

'Shades, are you in position on the roof?' A pause then…

''Look at me ma, top of the world!''

Tony keyed his mike, 'James Cagney, *White Heat*, closing scene.'

Shades answered, 'Give that man a cigar.'

'No need, I've got one.' Tony grinned.

Ron glanced at Vicky's worried face, 'Guys! Stop messing about, you're making Vicky nervous.'

On the boat Tony stopped grinning, he knew instantly Ron really wanted to say '… us nervous.' He keyed his mike again, 'Time to go to work, over.'

Shades picked up both what he said and what he meant and responded simply with, 'Check, over.'

Hearing the exchange Ron tried to smile at her, 'They're fine.' He put his hand on her blanketed knee and she covered his hand with her own. Suddenly, doubt welled up and she exclaimed, 'Are we doing the right thing?' Ron tried hard to think of a suitable line a hero might say but could hide nothing from her, she could read his face too well even under his disguise, the eyes can't lie. He admitted, 'I don't know.' Then he twisted his hand palm up and held her hand tightly.

'Oh Ron.'

'Come on, it's nearly time, soon be all over,' he gave her hand a final squeeze and picked up the radio, 'Shades, describe what you can see from there, over.'

'I can see the courtyard in front of the warehouse and the warehouse door. I can see along the main roadway down to the bend, the old refrigeration plant is only single storey down there so I can see about two hundred yards of the road after the bend.' To make Ron feel better he added, 'That means when they arrive I'll probably be able to give you two or three seconds' notice before they round the bend, over.'

'That's great, we're in position in the alley and can see the entrance to the estate clearly. Okay fellas, looks like we're all set, out.' Ron checked his watch, ten fifty-nine. Hammond would be there in thirty-one minutes. The radios were silent. Vicky held Ron's hand, squeezing it from time to time but saying nothing. The minutes crawled past.

Shades put down his binoculars, turned up his collar, drove his hands deep into his pockets and waited.

Out on the boat, Tony searched for another cigar, then remembering he had transferred Hammond's gift to his heavy flying jacket, reached into his pocket. He stripped off the cellophane and smiling broadly, bit off the end and spat it over the side.

Ron gazed out at the white street. Suddenly, he froze. A silver car rounded the corner; they slid down in their seats as it passed. He could clearly make out Hammond in the front passenger seat with three more in the rear. The car left the highway and turned into the estate. Ron radioed, 'Hammond's here, there's four guys in the car with him!' As he was talking, a truck swung wide around the corner. Ron added, 'The truck's behind them, over.'

Shades responded, 'Okay Ron, over.'

They watched as the truck followed the car into the estate. A few seconds later, Shades' voice came over the radio, 'I can see them coming down the roadway, okay they've rounded the bend... they're driving toward me... oh, the truck's appeared behind them. The car's slowing... yes they've seen the sign... the car's turned into the courtyard in front of the warehouse, it's stopped. Three guys are getting out the back... the truck's pulled in behind them. Two guys are opening the warehouse doors wider, they've gone in... the third guy is waving the car in, it's moving into the warehouse, the truck's following... The third guy is standing by the door looking about, keeping lookout I suppose. You were right, they didn't notice the ground, over.'

'Okay Shades, we're moving into position. Tony, did you get all that? Over.'

'Got it, good luck Ron.'

Having swapped places Vicky drove the car to the entrance of the estate and parked so the car partially blocked it. She switched off the engine and released the bonnet catch. They got out and Ron lifted the bonnet, 'Now, watch what I do.' He leaned into the engine compartment and pulled off one of the small wires leading to the coil. 'See that? Now the engine will turn over, but it won't start. Don't push the accelerator or you'll flood it and don't turn it over too much or you'll flatten the battery. When they've gone, pull the bonnet and push that wire back on. Probably, none of this is necessary but in case they seem suspicious you can turn it over and show them it won't start.'

'You've tried to think of everything, look don't worry about me, it's you who's taking the big risks. You will be careful, won't you?' She threw her arms round him, he looked at her serious face. She was beautiful, even beneath all the heavy make-up. 'It'll be alright and I will be careful, promise.' They hugged. Ron glanced at his watch, eleven thirty-three, 'I've got to go.' He hated leaving her.

Vicky watched him walk briskly through the gate and along the main roadway. She took a deep breath and exhaled slowly. She must hold it together for a while yet. She slipped into the car and picked up the radio, 'Ron's on his way in, over.' Shades answered, 'Okay Vicky, over.'

Ron was having similar misgivings, he muttered to himself, 'Think of Max… yes, for the next few minutes I *am* Max, how would *he* play it?'

Vicky was cold, she jumped when Shades' voice crackled from the radio, 'I can see him walking down the roadway,' then after a few minutes, 'he's entered the courtyard and is walking to the warehouse door. Someone's at the door, they're talking. Ron's going in, he's... gone, over.'

Vicky didn't answer, there was nothing to do now but wait. They were committed there was no turning back. She felt a stomach-churning queasy sensation, like the tense anticipation on a slowly rising rollercoaster before it launches downward on its terrifying journey. And like a rollercoaster there was no getting off or stopping, on it to the end, she needed to hold on tight and hope.

Ron was led over to meet 'Mr Hammond' who stood by the tail of the truck. As he approached bravely decided to take control of the conversation from the start, 'Mr Hammond, I assume.' Hammond smiled, 'Yes, I'm Hamm...' Ron took pleasure in cutting him short, 'Are the guns in there?' indicating the truck. Hammond didn't like being interrupted and gave a curt nod. Ron pointed to one of Hammond's men, 'You! Open it up.' The man looked at his boss for instructions. Hammond stared steadily at Ron, who desperately wanted to look away but forced himself not to and even raised his eyebrows in an expression that clearly said, 'What are you waiting for?' Without taking his eyes off Ron, Hammond snapped, 'Do it.' The man pulled the heavy bolts and the doors swung wide. A light flickered on in the roof of the truck, illuminating several crates on pallets. Ron climbed up, 'Crowbar,' he ordered. Someone found one and handed it up. He split open a crate and pulled out a Russian doll. Oh God, Hammond had set him up. This was some kind of trick. Hammond had guessed his plan and he'd walked right into a trap.

Stay in character, for all they knew he had people outside somewhere. If they killed him in here, they themselves were trapped. In Ron's highly charged state of mind thoughts flashed, *stay in character, stay in character and see what happens next, don't blow it.* He swung round and as viciously as he could, snarled, 'What are you trying to pull?'

Hammond's answer was dangerously quiet in an effort to keep his temper, 'Look under the dolls.'

Ron probed and found a thick layer of cardboard, under this some packing then a gun. The relief was overwhelming. He pulled it from its wooden rest and stood in the doorway of the truck to examine it. His hand shook slightly but luckily they didn't seem to notice. Without looking up, he asked, 'They're all the same?'

'All the same,' was the flat answer. Hammond asked suspiciously, 'Where are the rest of you?'

Ron looked sharply at him, 'We're very careful men, Mr Hammond, there's no need for you to see anyone but me up close.' He said it quietly, but managed an edge to his voice. For a bizarre moment, it crossed Ron's mind he may be doing the wrong job and if he were to get out of this alive, perhaps he should try an acting career. There had been no foghorn from the river so the IRA hadn't yet arrived. He began to look over the other crates, 'I want to open another one you have no objection?'

Hammond swept his hand in an exaggerated 'be my guest' gesture. Ron split another crate and made a big show of examining the guns, he knew he had to time it right. While his hands were in a crate, unseen by the others he checked his watch, eleven forty-two. He walked to the back of the truck, 'I want two crates off-loaded.' Hammond stared at Ron impassively for a long moment, then very much on his guard, 'Why?'

'Because I want to roll them outside to show my people.'

'Why can't they come in here?' Ron adopted his sharp tone again, 'Because my people don't want to come in here. Look Mr Hammond, I'm happy the consignment is okay. All I want is a sample put outside so they can look for themselves. Remember, you're asking them to part with a great deal of money.'

Vicky leaned under the dashboard and whispered into the radio, 'Tony, they're here... they're early! Over.' Tony responded by blasting the foghorn three times.

'Here I go, wish me luck, you both better stay quiet 'till I call you, okay?' Tony's voice, 'Good luck.' Shades' voice, 'Good luck.' To be safe Vicky turned the volume right down and slid the radio under the passenger seat then sat up.

Ron felt a quiver of panic. The IRA were coming, Vicky could only hold them up maybe three minutes at best. He must convince Hammond to roll the crates outside now! Hammond regarded him with distrust. Ron would have preferred to be more calm, taken his time and not push, but he had no time, 'My people sent me in to check the merchandise, I'm satisfied the guns look sound, now all I want is to run out two crates to show them a sample. In exchange, I'll bring the money for you to check, after all Mr Hammond a contact like you is valuable, you are in a position to get more?'

'It's possible.' Ron pressed, 'Then why should we want to do anything that may jeopardise future business?' Hammond was not entirely convinced, after what seemed like an eternity he said reluctantly, 'Very well.' It took all Ron's control not to show his huge relief. He stood quietly and watched Hammond's men roll two pallets to the tailgate and lower the trucks electric ramp. Ron pointed to the warehouse door, 'Put them out there in the courtyard just this side of the gate.'

Vicky thanked the men who had arrived in two cars and pushed her car away from the estate entrance to the kerb a little way along the road. The men returned to their cars but one lingered, he looked her up and down and liked what he saw.

Vicky attempted to sound both bored and slightly fed up, 'I'll phone for a cab, this old thing's my boyfriend's,' she pointed at Shades' big old car, 'he loves it, ha, well he can come and get it.' As she reached in for the clutch bag that lay on the passenger seat the man leaned forward and squeezed her bottom hard. She withdrew quickly and straightened up, Vicky felt a sudden surge of hot energy, the muscle in her right arm tensed and her eyes flamed as she glared at the grinning man who stood before her. He was blissfully unaware how close he'd come to having that grin slapped off his ugly face, for Vicky, in spite of her size was quite capable of delivering a surprisingly powerful teeth-rattling slap and indeed had done so on more than one occasion. She did nothing. Her triumph of self-control owed much to the happy thought that this man who grinned so smugly was about to have a very, very bad day. 'Oh, now that's naughty.' This brought a smile to her face, which the man totally misinterpreted.

'Maybe you should get a new boyfriend and a new car,' he leered. She stared at his pointed scrawny face he had acne scars and his hair was greasy. For Ron she thought, 'Well, if you ever get down to 'The George' you may see me there.' 'The George' was a small local pub Vicky had never been in but guessed it was popular. She and Ron had driven past it on their way to *The Blue Parrot*, she'd noticed queues outside waiting to be admitted, mostly young people. She guessed this man didn't go there, he didn't look the yuppie type.

'*The George*, a? You might be lucky, darlin'.' Vicky kept smiling but as she turned her back and walked away mouthed 'yuk' to herself.

A couple of the others who were standing by their car waiting for Vicky's admirer shook their heads and she heard one of them ask, 'Quite finished?'

They all returned to their cars and drove cautiously through the gate. As soon as they disappeared Vicky sprang back to the car, dived under the seat and retrieved the radio, 'Tony, they're on their way.' She instantly heard the distant sound of the foghorn blow twice.

The crates were in position less than a foot inside the entrance to the courtyard and Ron was at the warehouse door talking to Hammond when with relief he heard the second signal. He knew he had maybe ten seconds before the cars rounded the corner, 'As I said, I work for very careful people, when I give them the signal to come forward, none of you move.' Hammond wasn't happy but he had come this far,

283

'Right.' With Hammond and his men looking on, Ron hurried across the courtyard to the road and looked to the right. He knew at this moment, the IRA had entered the industrial estate and would appear around the bend imminently. As he had guessed, their suspicion meant they drove slowly, scanning the empty buildings as they passed.

Vicky had slid the wire back on the coil and was now listening intently to the radio.

Out on *The Grey Lady*, Tony held his radio to his ear.

On the roof Shades gripped his radio tightly, 'Okay, this is it Tony, when I say now, hit the horn. From up here I can see the cars coming down the roadway just before they round the bend, get ready, right, give Ron the signal, *now*!'

Immediately, there was a single blast that echoed round the estate, nobody but Ron paid it any attention everyone knew the river was nearby. He knew the cars would round the bend at any moment. Ron raised his hand and brought it down in a sweeping motion. Almost instantly, the cars appeared. As Hammond and his men looked on, it appeared as if Ron has given a signal to some hidden colleague for the cars to drive up.

Ron moved closer to the packing cases. When the cars were between the cases of guns on his side of the road and the planted squibs on the other side of the road he stepped forward and raised a hand. The cars halted the engines silenced. He waited patiently for what seemed like an age. Abruptly, the silence was broken by a series of metallic clicks as the car doors opened simultaneously. The group approached him, he could feel his heart pounding and hoped he could keep his voice level, 'Hello gentlemen,' silence, he pretended not to notice the atmosphere was as frosty as the weather and continued, 'I'm sure you wish to examine the consignment thoroughly, Mr Hammond is over there by the truck with the rest of the guns.' He gestured behind him and across the courtyard to the warehouse, the truck was barely visible in the relative gloom. 'This is a sample for you to look over, I'm sure you'll be satisfied. In exchange, we would like to examine a sample of the money. Then I'll come back and if you wish you can open any further crates you like. When we're all satisfied, we leave with the money; you leave with the truck. As I told you it won't be missed for a week, make a call telling us where it is, leave the key in the exhaust and we'll deal with it.' Ron felt pleased with the way he had kept outwardly calm. The man who now regarded him did not look so impressed. He was without doubt, the hardest-looking character Ron had ever seen. He had a slab of a face, the nose had obviously been broken at least once, his hair was short and his eyes were no more than slits. He stared at Ron, who had the sickening feeling he hadn't believed a word. 'Why is Mr Hammond standing over there and why am I talking to you?' He pointed at Ron's chest with a thick finger.

'I'm only here to carry the money and introduce the deal. You're perfectly free to talk to Mr Hammond when you check out the rest of the guns.' There was an uncomfortable silence then abruptly the man said, 'The case!' He kept his eyes on Ron as another man brought a briefcase. To Ron's relief, he looked down and flicked open the lid. Reaching in, he stopped as if changing his mind then turning to Ron, 'You choose the bundles.' He watched carefully as Ron put his right hand in and began to remove some wads of money, cradling them in his left arm. He could feel the palms of his hands sticky with sweat, despite the freezing air. One bundle, two bundles, three, four. He reached in for another, but the man brought the lid of the case down on his fingers and squeezed, smiling as he watched Ron's face. He leaned forward only inches from Ron and whispered, 'Enough. Now stay in sight all the time and don't try to be smart or we'll come calling... Get it?' Ron spluttered, 'Yeah.' The man released the pressure and Ron removed his bruised fingers. 'Remember, stay in sight.' Ron nodded. Still holding the money in his left arm, he slowly moved his right hand to his pocket. He stopped as he caught the dangerous look on the man's face. 'Smoke,' Ron said as he very, very slowly pulled a pack of cigars from his pocket and fumbled with them. He had meant to have one out of the box ready, but had forgotten, now he was trying awkwardly to extricate a cigar one-handed from the box. The man was amused at Ron's nervousness. He took the cigars from him and put one in his own mouth, hesitated, then stuck one in Ron's mouth. He lit his own and smiling, held out the match. Ron leaned forward and lit his own cigar. He held out his free hand for the packet, the man slowly put it in his own pocket, then exhaled, blowing smoke in his face. Ron turned and walked away slowly.

During the conversation, Ron's back had been turned toward Hammond and his men so they weren't sure what had been happening. For a moment, Hammond hadn't liked what little he could see but now Ron, who Hammond believed to be part of the IRA, was approaching with a sample of the money, he felt better. Some of the IRA men were examining the guns while others watched Ron.

Meanwhile, Vicky had driven onto the estate, travelled the short distance from the entrance and eased the car into the first of the two alleys as Ron and Shades had shown her. At the end there was the choice of either a gentle bend that curved off toward the loading bay and ran along the outside of the bay's corrugated iron wall, or a sharp right horseshow bend. She manoeuvred the big car around the horseshoe bend and as before rolled to a halt beside the small door through which Ron intended to escape. She had parked only for a few minutes but to her time appeared to stretch and drag itself from minute to minute. In the shadowy alley the light had a bluish tint. The car soon cooled, she shivered slightly both from the cold and nervous tension. The engine needed to be silent as she wanted to be sure to hear both Tony's signal and the squibs fire. Ahead, she could clearly see the end of the alley and a small section of the main roadway. The plan was to drive out of the alley, make a quick right and on through the gate, leaving the estate as fast as possible, then aim the car for warmth, coffee and safety. For the moment, there was nothing for her to do but wait. Vicky tapped the steering wheel. Shades' voice came over the radio, 'He's got the money and he's given the signal all's okay. Fifteen seconds after he disappears into the warehouse I hit the fireworks. Stand by, out.'

Aboard *The Grey Lady,* Tony was feeling tense. This was something of a new experience and he didn't like it. He was aware his part was important and that no-one could handle the boat the way he could, however his part was the safest, this fact gave him no comfort, indeed if anything it heightened his stress. Tony's fingers drummed the boat's throttle control as he looked out across the water.

Vicky tilted her head back looked at the roof lining and her breath rising in the cold air, and concentrated on breathing evenly while she waited for the sound of gunfire.

Shades' finger hovered over the detonator button.

Ron's mouth was dry and his legs felt shaky as he walked through the warehouse door. In his head, he began to count, '1, 2...'

Up on the roof, Shades was also counting, '...3, 4, 5...'

Hammond started to move towards Ron, puzzled why he was heading for the small door in the wall and not him. Hammond stopped, 'Where're you going?' Ron looked at him but remained silent, he continued to count, '...10, 11...'

Shades licked his top lip nervously, '...12, 13...'

Ron stopped at the door then still looking at Hammond said, 'Why pay when we can take?'

Shades pushed the button.

A volley of gunfire exploded along the wall behind the IRA men. They dived for cover, some behind gun crates, others behind cars. They pulled handguns and fired into the dimness of the warehouse. Hammond's men scattered and began to return fire. Outside, the bullets ricocheted around the courtyard walls smacking holes in rusty barrels. Fragments of wood exploded from discarded pallets, bullets nicked the packing cases and punched holes in the cars. The terrorists continued to fire almost blindly into the open warehouse door, inside Hammond's men were pinned down. Bullets pinged and ricocheted off the concrete walls. There was an explosion of glass as the front and back windows of Micky's stolen car disintegrated.

As soon as Vicky heard the squibs fire, she started the engine and stared at her watch, 'Thirty seconds more.' She glanced across at the door. Shots rang out as real gunfire continued to burst from both sides.

All but one of Hammond's men had retreated further from the warehouse door. The terrorists continued to fire into darkness, shot after shot rained through the open door. Explosions of noise amplified by the concrete buildings reverberated around them. One of Hammond's men who had edged his way round to the door tried to push it closed but caught a shot in the kneecap and screamed as his leg buckled. He fell in plain view across the doorway and caught two more bullets in the chest. The scream outlived the man and continued echoing around the deserted buildings seconds after he lay silent.

Hammond's men knowing there was no way out, began to panic, they fired frantically. An IRA man took a shot full in the face shattering his teeth to exit the back of his skull, he fell forward, dead before he hit the ground.

Vicky stared at the door, still no Ron. She glanced at her watch. It was now forty-five seconds since the squibs had fired. Ron should be out! But the long seconds piled one upon the other and towered into terrifying minutes, still no Ron. She revved the engine, 'Come on, come on…!' Snatching up the radio, she shouted, 'Shades!' But he had thrown his radio into the rucksack. Shades was sure, deserted area or not, all the gunfire would soon have police sirens screaming onto the estate. He was busy frantically reeling up the three hundred feet of wire, unplugging the separate reels and throwing them into his rucksack as he descended the fire escape.

Vicky got no reply only static, she felt sure something had gone wrong, 'SHADES!' this time, it was almost a scream.

Tony's voice answered, 'Vicky, this is Tony, is Ron not out yet?'

'No! And it's been,' she checked her watch again, 'a minute and a half.' There was silence, then Tony said without apparent emotion, 'You'd better get out of there.'

'NO, I won't leave Ron!' She screamed and threw the radio onto the back seat.

Two of his thugs were dead and Hammond himself was hunched in a corner like a frightened animal. It left only Micky, the driver and one other. Micky had edged toward the truck and vanished from view. The driver was positioned near the rear of the truck trying to use it for cover and taking pot shots at the terrorists through the open door. The remaining man was in front and slightly to the driver's right, he was planning another attempt at shutting the door but the last person to try that was dead so he was moving very cautiously.

Suddenly a shot ripped an ugly gash in the driver's arm, he screamed, jerked his arm to the right, the pain caused him to clench his hand pulling the trigger, which was unfortunate for his colleague in front of him who he shot in the back.

Shocked at what he had done, the driver took one step forward. A second bullet grazed his other arm. Angrily, he lifted his gun and fired wildly. A shot tore through the ear of Vicky's admirer, blood gushed, hardly life threatening but nonetheless painful. He gritted his teeth and sent an answering volley of fire into the warehouse. The driver felt a stab in his leg, a tear in a main artery is both unpleasant and spectacular. Hammond watched the driver try in vain to stem the flow of blood with his hand. No one was left to shoot. Soon, the terrorists would swarm through the door.

Suddenly, he heard the truck motor turning over and realised Micky was going to attempt to crash out. One of the four rear tyres exploded as a bullet tore into it. Hammond bolted to the truck and pulled himself up into the passenger seat. He didn't know what would happen next, but to stay in the warehouse was suicide. Micky was revving the engine and hauling the wheel, oddly he didn't seem to be aiming for the door.

Vicky was sobbing and screaming for Ron, her knuckles white as she gripped the wheel. Almost insane with tension and frustration, she revved the engine and stared at the door. Rational thought and behaviour had been eroded by the consuming need to see Ron safe. The natural primeval responses to extreme stress, fight or flight, were tipping heavily toward the former. Vicky balanced on the razor edge of reason at the very brink of losing control, leaping from the car, running through the door and dragging Ron to safety. Even given her slight size, with the adrenaline and energy she now possessed, she may well have succeeded. But at the very moment she tensed her leg muscles to do it the door burst open. Ron staggered out and blinked in the light for a moment then put his hand to his face shielding it from the relative glare. Seeing the car, he wrenched open the door and leapt in.

Vicky stared at him momentarily stunned, then the scales slammed down on the side of flight, which translated instantly into the physical act of her accelerator foot hitting the floor, at the same instant dropping the clutch. Shades' car skidded on the snowy ground and snaked off with engine screaming. She hauled the wheel to the right and the car slewed broadside around the corner and onto the main roadway. Vicky was too frantic to ease off the accelerator so the car didn't straighten. Rather than travelling along the roadway to exit the estate, it skidded and swung into the first alley that ran parallel with the second. The car careered into some dustbins and rocketed on then, around the right hand bend, missing the sharp horseshoe turning that would have taken her in a circle back past Ron's exit door and onto the main roadway.

Ron tried to keep his voice calm, 'You have to slow down so we can get back to the roadway. This is taking us down the side of the warehouse, we're going back towards the terrorists, you must calm down,' he took a deep breath and exhaled slowly, 'look… calm,' Vicky eased her foot off the accelerator, Ron smiled, 'that's it, nice and ca *aaaaaaaaaaah*!' He screamed, his eyes open wide in terror.

A few hundred yards ahead, the corrugated iron wall had exploded. Shrieking sheets of rusty metal were flying in all directions as the truck smashed through the rusty wall and lurched towards them. In the narrow alley there was nowhere to go. Vicky and Ron froze. Coming to her senses, she stamped on the brake, with the wheels locked and the car still sliding forward she rammed the gearshift into reverse, slamming the accelerator pedal once more to the floor. The car shuddered, stopped and began to move backwards the engine at full throttle, tyres biting through the thin dusting of snow and smoking as they spun on the tarmac. They stared horrified as the truck bore down on them.

Micky's original idea was to punch a hole in the rusty wall, abandon the truck and make a run for it.

Finding that he could keep driving, he was not hanging about and like Vicky, had his foot hard down.

Vicky, with a magnificent piece of instinctive driving managed to reverse the car at fantastic speed and negotiated the bend before the truck hit, slamming into them with a tremendous jolt. The car was hurled backwards as the truck burst out of the alley onto the roadway it swung to the right and sped toward the gate. Vicky had no chance of turning but luckily there was another small alley opposite, they careered backwards into it for several hundred yards before finally stopping. Miraculously, there were only some minor scuffs and heavy dents in the front bumper. They sat staring straight ahead stunned and panting for air. Neither spoke. Vicky prised her stiff hands from the steering wheel. Ron let go of the dashboard and stared at the small indentations his nails had left. 'Are you alright?' Vicky nodded, 'You?'

'Yeah, we, er… better get out of here.'

As they emerged from the alley and turned left onto the roadway they could see the truck. It had overturned trying to make the turn out of the estate onto the public highway and lay on its side. Someone was climbing out of the cab, as they drew closer they could see it was Hammond. They didn't stay to see what happened next, but flashed through the gates, swerved around the truck, raced down the public highway and headed for *The Blue Parrot*.

Ron retrieved the radio from the back seat and tried to raise Tony and Shades but they were out of range.

PART TWO
CHAPTER 17
SUNDAY AFTERNOON 12:55

Both Ron and Vicky had removed their make-up and showered quickly. Now she sat on the sofa in sweater and jeans, emotionally drained, staring blankly at the floor.

'Here!' Ron handed her a drink, she took it with barely a nod and with the other hand continued stroking Finbar. 'Come on Vicky, we'll think of something.' He ended lamely. She lifted her head and looked at him mournfully, 'Oh Ron,' she breathed, 'I can't go through any more, I can't put you through any more, we failed that's all. We tried and we failed, and where's Shades and Tony? We got back twenty minutes ago and they're still not here.'

'They have to go and moor the boat before they drive back, they'll be here any minute.' On queue Shades and Tony came through the balcony door stamping their feet and blowing into their hands. Shades laughed with relief, 'Hey Ron, you made it!' He swung the rucksack from his shoulder placed it carefully on the floor and smiled at Vicky, who looked uncomfortably from Shades back to the floor.

Shades' smile faded, he turned to Ron and spoke slowly, 'You are okay, aren't you?'

'Mm.'

Happy, Shades slapped him on the shoulder and became animated again, 'Tony told me the last thing Vicky said was that you hadn't come out then we moved out of range. So it worked did it?'

The brothers hung up their coats, Shades sat on the sofa opposite Ron and Vicky slightly puzzled at their lack of enthusiasm. Tony tossed his car keys in a drawer near the door and joined Shades. Tony nodded at Ron, 'So come on, what happened to you?' Ron spoke wearily, 'Oh, er... Well, during the transaction, the IRA leader squashed my hand in the briefcase as a kind of warning,' Vicky was concerned, he reassured her quickly, 'It's fine now, only a bit bruised,' he brightened a little, 'getting through the door was a piece of cake, Hammond didn't have a clue what was going on. I walked over to it, he began to follow, I just had time to say, 'Why pay when you can take' and Shades fired the squibs, the timing was beautiful. They dived for cover, I nipped through the door and bolted it. It was a good job Dave reinforced it because the first thing they did was fire at the door, I heard the shots hit it. I was full of adrenaline and in the dark I made a grab for the torch. I managed to scoop it up, but because my hand was hurting, I picked it up awkwardly and dropped it. Something must have jarred loose because I couldn't get the damned thing to come on. I heard someone rattle the door trying to come after me, or escape, but Dave's huge bolt wasn't letting anyone through. I had to grope my way down the passage in the dark and it took a bit longer.' Finishing his story he looked sadly at his drink and was silent.

Shades and Tony looked at each other then at the two depressed people opposite them. Nothing Ron had said so far explained the gloom. Tony took a deep breath and asked the question, 'Okay, out with it! What else happened?' Vicky sighed and without enthusiasm explained, 'I got us out of there pretty fast,' the brothers nodded, 'I drove too fast and skidded, we ended up going down the side of the loading bay, the truck crashed out through the corrugated wall. I'm sorry, your car's got a few scuffs and some dents in the bumper I'm afraid.' Shades snorted and waved his hand as if that was the least of his worries. Vicky finished her story, 'The truck got out but overturned trying to leave the estate. As we drove past it...' her voice was now shaking, the brothers grim-faced, waited patiently, 'we saw Hammond climbing out,' she stopped, then close to tears burst out, 'it's all been for nothing!'

The tension and the disappointment were all too much, Ron put his arm around her, he could have cried himself. He had really tried and the last few hours had been rough. Vicky held up a trembling hand to indicate she was all right but was too upset to say any more.

Ron looked at Tony and Shades, 'As the truck smashed out we could hear gunfire, so the IRA were still shooting. I don't know if any were killed. Hammond's out there and so are a few very angry terrorists. I've really got you all into something, haven't I?' It had been his plan, it hadn't worked so it was his fault. He stood and paced, 'This was all my idea and now I've put your lives at risk. Thought I was so smart, get Hammond and his bunch of thugs together, get the IRA there, give them a nudge and wham! They would wipe each other out, just like that. It was supposed to be so neat, we wouldn't kill anyone, they would do it all themselves!'

Nobody spoke, they sensed there was more to come, they were right. Ron's tension and guilt gave way to anger, 'And why not? Hammond tried to kill me, he tried to kill Vicky, he *did* kill Sara,' he glanced at Vicky, 'the IRA murdered Vicky's parents, not these actual men but that didn't matter it was setting things straight,' he paused, ran his hand over his head and held the back of his neck thinking a moment, then, 'Vicky tells me her father was researching blood disorders, leading his field! How many other people have died because Vicky's father wasn't able to continue his work?' Ron was almost shouting now, 'No, this was justice and for this service the bastards would actually pay us,' he pointed at the pile of money on the table, 'but it didn't work like that and it's my fault.' He shook his head dismissively, holding out both arms palms up in exasperation, 'Vicky's right, it's all been for nothing.'

Deeply upset, he crossed to the balcony door, folded his arms tightly and looked out at the dark brooding sky. The view through the pane was as depressing as the view of their future.

Tony spoke, 'So we were unlucky. It *was* a good plan and we could have got rid of Hammond. The police would have found the bodies and the guns and assumed an arms deal had gone wrong and they'd killed each other. Now we have to think.' Vicky had been thinking, 'The police! Ron, your fingerprints will be on the guns, the door and the torch you left behind!'

'No they won't.'

'But you didn't have gloves.'

'While Jane was focussed on Shades,' here Shades rolled his eyes, Ron explained, 'I borrowed some of that liquid latex she used to give me the wrinkles and dabbed my fingertips in it in the bathroom.' Vicky managed to a weak smile, 'Tony's right, you did come up with a clever plan, you really thought of everything, no one could have guessed they would leave through the wall!' Ron didn't look any happier he felt the weight of failure rested squarely with him he had let them down. Looking at his sad face Tony added, 'The thing is Ron we're all adults and we all went along with it because it was a good idea, just back luck. As I said, we have to think.'

Ron slowly returned to Vicky and sat down, 'But Tony, Hammond will think you set him up, God knows what he'll do and the IRA may come after Shades. I've contacted people at the theatre, it won't be long before Hammond finds out who I am, that I'm not dead and Vicky too. It's only a matter of time, however you look at it it's a hell of a mess and there's no point saying it's not.'

Nobody said anything everyone was trying to think of a way out, with the possible exception of Shades, who suddenly announced, 'I'm hungry.' Everyone looked at him and Vicky gave a short laugh. Shades shrugged, 'Well, I am.' Tony frowned, 'Don't remember when I last ate, I think it was yesterday.' Vicky looked at Ron, 'We've only had a slice of toast each all day.'

Ron was grateful for any opportunity, no matter how small, to do something for the people he felt he had let down so badly. He sprung to his feet, 'I'll get lunch.' Before Vicky could stop herself she asked, 'Is that a good idea?' 'I do know how to cook,' Ron answered, a little offended, 'I didn't bother much only for me.' He huffed off to the kitchen, Vicky watched him go then looked at the brothers, 'Ron's cooking,' after a thoughtful pause, 'you fellows really are tough.' Shades smiled. Vicky pointed to the shelf near the door, 'While I think of it, I left your car keys there.'

'Thanks.' Shades got up and slipped them in his coat that hung near the door.

In the kitchen, Ron threw everything into an enormous pot. With only a few ingredients on offer he tried very hard and an hour or so later they were eating a sort of stew, which was surprisingly good. After, they lounged about, full up and very tired.

It was Ron who spoke first, 'We have to do something!' Nobody disagreed with that, the question was, what? Everyone looked at each other hopefully, but no one had any ideas. The afternoon had slipped into early evening, although only four-thirty it was completely dark outside. The mood had grown serious and gloom had settled on the group. Vicky massaged the back of her neck, tipped her head to one side and groaned, 'Oh, what a mess!' She stared at the floor and continued to rub her aching neck. Ron turned to her, 'You look exhausted, I know you had a quick shower but why don't you have a soak in the bath then get some rest.' She considered, 'Mm, a hot bath.' Conscious of being a guest she glanced at Shades. He nodded, 'Yeah, go on, it'll make you feel better, take a drink with you.' Tony added, 'There's candles in there and matches.'

At the moment Tony mentioned his bath candles Ron had been looking at Vicky. Being careful to keep his head turned in her direction his eyes swept over her head and slid down to his right to rest on Tony for a moment, then in a low curve up to Vicky's eyes to wait for her reaction. Sensibly, Vicky made no comment saying simply, 'Right, I think I will.' She got up stiffly and trudged off to the bathroom.

Tony, who appeared to have his mind elsewhere, noticed nothing and offered Ron a brandy. Shades and Ron talked in low voices about the possible consequences of the failed plan. Tony said very little and seemed distracted, so much so that Ron finally asked, 'What is it Tony?' Tony's expression told him he was holding something back and seemed unsure whether to share it. Shades knew his brother well and Tony wasn't a man to be hurried. Finally, he spoke, keeping his voice low, not wanting it to penetrate the bathroom, 'I've always been able to read people, it's helped me in life, in business,' he snorted, 'in poker. I can look them in the eye and I just know. I can tell real tough characters from fakes, I know when people are lying to me. I can look people up and down and I know. *But*, I'll tell you both straight, your Vince Hammond scares the crap out of me!' There was silence, Ron and Shades were deeply shocked, Ron had felt completely confident with Tony's ability to handle Vince Hammond. To find Tony so unsettled after meeting him was stunning. After all, he managed *The Blue Parrot*. He was no stranger to the varied peculiarities of the varied and peculiar public at large, who in the case of some of the Clubs patrons,

301

by rights should not be at large at all. The stunned silence lengthened.

Tony asked, 'You know why he plants listening devices on people?' They shook their heads, finally Ron speculated, 'I don't know, doesn't trust anyone?'

'He doesn't trust himself.'

'I don't get it.'

'He can't read people, no empathy, the way he thinks is so alien to normal people he can't guess what they'll do.'

'Why does he frighten you so much, I've seen you throw bigger people than him out of the club?' Ron felt he had to ask but wasn't sure he wanted to know the answer, when he got it he was sure he didn't want to know the answer.

'Because Vince Hammond is a psychopath.' He let the statement hang in the air for a moment, then hammered it home with, 'The real thing. I've come across people who were slightly that way, but he's special, one hundred per cent undiluted psychopath. That means he's totally free to do whatever he wants, there's nothing to hold him back, the normal restraints of behaviour aren't there, he's capable of anything. Once he's pieced it together his only reason for living will be to come after us!' Ron swallowed, his mouth suddenly dry.

'I didn't want to go into it in front of Vicky she's been through enough.' Ron shot a quick look at the bathroom door, 'I think she knows, I think I did too really,' he paused, 'it's still shocking to hear you say it.' Tony's voice remained quiet, 'We have to be honest about what we're dealing with here.' Ron fell silent, even Shades looked grave, without doubt the situation was extremely perilous. Tony shrugged, 'I feel bad telling you but you had to know, it could make a real difference to what we do next, I'm sorry Ron.'

Some time later Vicky emerged from the bathroom looking pink clad in a robe and followed by a swirl of steam. The boys had got nowhere and talked themselves round in circles; a moody silence prevailed. Vicky flopped down next to Ron, 'Come up with anything?' she asked without much hope, Ron didn't answer the question, then in an attempt to dispel the mood said making an effort to sound bright, 'Hey, anyone fancy a coffee?' Realising the effort, everyone said yes.

The rest of the evening passed slowly, with little conversation much thought and no small amount of worry.

Finally, Tony rose pulled the curtains and turned to the others, 'Look, I don't think anything will happen tonight, but to be safe, I think we all better stay here. Me and Shades will take the double bed in my room. Vicky can have Shades' room, you don't mind the sofa do you Ron?'

Vicky answered for Ron, she spoke quietly not meeting Tony's eyes, 'Ron doesn't have to use the sofa.' This simple statement tripped Tony up, the attraction between Ron and Vicky had been obvious but even he hadn't realised it had bloomed so quickly. He glanced at Ron, who was smiling at Vicky. 'Oh, right, mm, good.' Shades couldn't resist another opportunity to use his favourite Bogart line, ''is this the start of a beautiful friendship?'' He grinned. 'Shut up,' Tony snapped, Shades' grin widened. Then to try and lift the mood before they turned in

Tony offered, 'Perhaps we'll come up with something after some sleep. Could be the police will pick up Hammond. Maybe they'll link the overturned truck with him and he left his car there. Anyway, it's been quite a day and we'll think more clearly in the morning.'

It was only nine o'clock but nobody objected to an early night. All the stress had left everyone feeling exhausted. Ron got up wearily and touched Tony and Shades on the shoulder, 'Thanks guys.' They all said goodnight.

Outside, the wind had sprung up driving the freshly falling snow into heaps against doorways and windowsills. Streets looked flat as snow packed against kerbs.

In the upstairs flat, it wasn't long before they were all asleep. The flat was still and queit, apart from the soft murmur of people in *The Blue Parrot* below. Occasionally, a voice would rise above the others but quickly die down. Gradually the club grew silent as customers drifted away and the bar staff locked up.

Finbar slept peacefully on his bundle of beer towels that Tony had brought up for him from the bar.

Given their exhaustion, it should have been a peaceful night, but it wasn't.

PART TWO
CHAPTER 18
MONDAY MORNING 4:00

At the top of the fire escape outside the flat above *The Blue Parrot*, a shadow moved as it worked silently on the balcony door. In the dark living room there was a faint click from behind the curtains that covered the door. A large shape bulged in the curtains as something entered the room. The silhouette of a man slid from behind the curtains. He stood motionless, then a small torch flicked on, its narrow beam explored the room. In the other hand a thin stiletto blade glinted silver in the torchlight. The man crossed to an open door, the torch revealed the kitchen. He moved to another door, which was closed. The light went out, pocketing the torch he slowly turned the handle, silently opened the door and slipped into the room.

The faint green glow from the digital clock on the bedside table was enough to make out two figures in the bed. The man crossed to the bed and looked down at Vicky, she opened her eyes suddenly and stared straight into the nightmarish green face of Vincent Hammond, with a look of sheer euphoria he raised the knife with both hands and plunged.

Vicky sucked a gulp of air and stared wide-eyed into the darkness. She had sat up and her splayed fingers dug deep into the mattress, her blood pounding in her ears as if she had been running for her life. She swallowed and her eyes darted around the still room, satisfied, she lowered herself back onto the pillow breathing deeply. A nightmare, just a nightmare, the relief was overwhelming. She wiped the back of her trembling hand across her damp forehead and lay still waiting for her heart to slow. Lying with her eyes open staring into darkness, she knew this thing was far from over, perhaps not even the worst of it. Checking the digital clock beside her, 4:02 then turning her head, Vicky could vaguely see Ron in the darkness. He had been so kind. Now he loved her so there was a reason, but when he first found her she'd been a stranger and he had still helped her. What had she given him? Nothing but trouble since the day they had met. He had been shot at, beaten over the head and now he was practically on the run.

Vicky looked across the room to the dim shape of the door. Shades and Tony were out there. Ron was lucky to have such friends. She pictured Tony the day she had caught him up on the roof by the dove coop. The way he held that dove, the way he talked to it. Big mean Tony with a heart as big as a house. And Shades, Mr Cool, a real roughneck, who was scared stiff of Jane Flutter the make-up lady and made little jokes to make her feel better when he could see she was frightened. None of them complained, they had accepted her problems as their own. It was not fair. It was time she sorted out her own life. Sara's last words drifted through her mind again, 'It hurts Vicky, it hurts.' She shook her head quickly and tried to lose the image.

She lay thinking for some time then swinging her legs out of bed, sat on the edge bent her head and ran a hand through her hair. God, how she hated Hammond! *Hated him*! She imagined him dying at her feet. Yes, at her feet, whimpering. She narrowed her eyes and compressed her lips. Rising anger eclipsed the fear, yes, in that moment Vicky believed she could do it. For Sara, Ron, Tony, Shades and herself.

Swiftly and silently, gathering her clothes from a chair, she took a few steps toward the door. A thought halted her, 'What about after?' She hesitated at the door and speculated, her mind made up, opened the door and slipped out; after didn't matter. After Ron would be safe and the nightmare would be over. Hammond dead was all that mattered. She could end this thing now, tonight, today, what the hell.

In the living room, she dressed quickly by the light of a small lamp and moved to the coat hooks by the door to feel in Tony's flying jacket pockets. The search produced a card with the clubs phone number, she needed that but it wasn't what she was looking for. Switching off the lamp she crossed to Tony's bedroom where he and Shades were sleeping. Peering round the door she strained her eyes to see. The bedroom had an identical bedside clock and its faint green glow was enough to make out some of the room. There was something dark on the chair near Tony's side of the bed on top of his yellow (the day had begun in high spirits) shirt. Holding her breath she crept into the room toward the chair. Yes! It was Tony's gun. Carefully, she picked it up, it felt heavy and cold in her hand. Then glancing at Tony she very nearly dropped it in fright. Tony was looking at her with narrowed eyes. Rooted to the spot she stared back, not knowing what to do. Unable to bear the way he stared at her, Vicky decided to confess her plan hoping he would not be too angry. She was about to speak when unbelievably Tony turned over and mumbled. Vicky leaned against the wall for a moment to steady herself, before creeping from the room.

Back in the living room she could breathe and tried to swallow but her mouth was too dry. She stood resting her hand on the edge of the sofa to compose herself and waited for her heartbeat to return to normal. Tony slept with his eyes open! She'd heard of people who do that but had never seen it.

A search in Shades' coat pocket brought forth the bunch of car keys and a little small change she would need that for the 'phone, 'Yes!' Feeling determined, she snatched a tea towel from the kitchen, wiped the gun over then fumbled with it until the magazine ejected. The bullets were given the same treatment and the magazine snapped back in, only her prints would be on the gun.

Donning her boots and coat then leaving via the balcony door she found the cold brutal, the rush of freezing night air that lay in wait didn't merely nip but sank its icicle teeth in deep and held on. Undeterred, Vicky cautiously descended the fire escape feeling her way more than seeing. On reaching the bottom, the deep drifts of snow made it hard to walk. The sun wouldn't be up for hours yet and the world glowed eerily as the lights of the city reflected in the fresh snow, which also muffled any noise. A tense silence prevailed, like the hush of an audience before a play's opening act.

Vicky was breathing hard when she reached Shades' car. After touching the frozen metal of the fire escape her fingers were now numb and stiff, she fumbled clumsily with the keys, finally managing to unlock the door but it was frozen shut. She pulled hard, it finally wrenched open with a crack so loud she looked up quickly at the balcony, nobody had heard. The interior light came on, she found a window scraper and after pushing the loose snow away with her arm frantically scraped the windows clear of ice, little shavings showered her hands. She climbed quickly behind the wheel and crossed her arms putting her frozen red fingers under her arms to regain some feeling.

The interior light faded and she sat in the freezing darkness. Reaching for the ignition key she hesitated, would it start? She frowned. Did she really want it to? Turning the key, the answer to both questions was yes. The terrible tension and fear would end and all she needed to do to make this happen was to simply move a finger, to squeeze a trigger and instantly she'd be free, everyone would be safe. She settled herself into the driving seat and decisively plunged the car into reverse then touched the accelerator causing the wheels to whine as the car skidded backwards. She stopped and pulled the wheel hard, then selected first. Again, the wheels fought for grip as the car moved forward. Struggling out, Vicky plodded through the snow and pulled on the frozen bolts that held the gates shut. Luckily, in their haste Tony and Shades hadn't snapped the padlocks closed. However, it required all her strength

309

to shift the frozen bolts in their keeps, the lower bolt requiring a sharp kick to free it. She hauled the gates wide dragging them through the snow and stumbled back to the car, again glancing up at the fire escape. She climbed in quickly and moved off, bumping out of the yard as the headlights flicked on. The twin beams of light stretched out across the snow-covered road, touching a building opposite then swept across it as the car turned right and its red taillights disappeared into the darkness.

Ron turned over and reached for Vicky but instead of finding her waist his arm came down on empty bed. He opened his eyes, 'Vicky?' He sat up and looked about. Quickly getting up he reached for his robe and moved to the bedroom door, then peering out, 'Vicky?' he hissed in a loud whisper. The living room was empty and dark. Rubbing his eyes he wandered into the kitchen, 'Vi...' No one was there apart from Finbar slumbering atop his beer towels. Ron became fully awake as panic began to stir. He turned at the sound of a door opening, 'Vicky?' A deep voice answered, 'No, Tony.' Ron returned to the living room, 'Tony, Vicky's not in the flat,' Tony was silent Ron couldn't see his face in the almost dark room, 'I said Vi...'

'My gun's gone.' For a moment, both remained still as the full impact of this hit home. Ron shouted, 'Hammond...! I've got to stop her!' He ran to the bedroom to dress, while Tony dived back to his own room. Lights blazed on, Ron was ready first, rushing back to the living room he frantically searched for car keys until he remembered Tony had thrown his in a drawer. He snatched the keys ran to the balcony door, flung it wide and dashed out.

Recklessly skidding and slipping down the metal steps of the fire escape, he heard Tony's voice calling from the flat above to wait but had no intention of losing a single second. He reached Tony's car as Tony got to the top of the steps. With one swipe Ron removed the snow from the windscreen and scratched wildly at the icy frost beneath with both hands using his nails, then unlocked, climbed in and jammed the key into the ignition. The engine turned over, coughed and caught. Tony had descended the lethal steps more sensibly and by the time he reached the ground Ron was already moving out of the yard. Tony called again for him to wait but the car disappeared in a cloud of exhaust gas. Tony turned and shouted up to Shades who had appeared at the top of the fire escape, 'Find Ron's car keys... *fast*! Shades whipped back into the flat.

Ron drove fast, too fast for the snow-covered streets. He nearly lost control on a couple of bends but not knowing what kind of start Vicky had on the ten minute journey to Hammond's, he pushed it to the limit. For all he knew he was already too late. A few near misses forced him to stop and clear the windscreen properly of ice. This wasted further precious seconds but there was no choice. He scrambled in and motored on.

As he drove, his mind tormented him with images of what would happen to Vicky if he didn't stop her. Most likely she would be gunned down before getting anywhere near Hammond. A strange woman in the grounds of his house with a gun in her hand, Hammond would have no trouble talking his way out of that. What if by some miracle, she did get to him? After all that had happened Ron had little doubt she would do it.

He skidded round a bend. As he fought to straighten the car it rocked from side to side, the wheels losing grip, he had little choice but ease off the power to regain control. As soon as the car steadied, he hit the accelerator and drove madly on. Okay, so if she killed him, then what, prison? Hammond had murdered her sister but it was unlikely the police would ever find a body. Vicky may serve only a few years, but he couldn't imagine her surviving prison, even when they eventually released her in five or ten years, her character would be changed forever. Supposing she got away with it, had her revenge? He shook his head. She was no killer. What would happen when it was over and all that remained was grief for Sara? She may handle it, feeling she did the right thing, however, to engineer a situation where greed for money and selling guns to terrorists would rid the world of Vincent Hammond was very different to looking him in the face and pulling the trigger.

The car slid dangerously coming out of a bend and Ron came terrifyingly close to a head-on crash. The other car blazed past headlights on full beam, horn blaring the sound rising then abruptly falling as the Doppler effect diminished the pitch. What was wrong with him? He could drive better than this! But he had no feel for the car. The paradox was he yearned to reach Vicky in time and for that he must drive fast. To do this, he must put her out of his mind and think only of driving.

It was nearly five in the morning, the roads were almost deserted, it was still dark and the cold was petrifying. Concentrating as hard as he could, it was impossible to prevent the car from sliding around bends and snaking down the slick streets where the snow had compacted into sheet ice but at least the drifting was more controlled. Unfortunately, with over nine thousand miles of road in the Greater London area, even working flat out, gritting lorries rarely reached all the suburbs before it thawed so progress was frustratingly slow.

Tony and Shades were having frustrations of their own. Ron's old car hadn't been started since Thursday, nearly four days ago, plus Tony did not have Ron's knack. The car had refused to start and now the battery was flat. Tony kicked the door shut adding yet more to Dave's job list and Ron's bill, then glared at Shades and said with hopeless exasperation, 'There's nothing we can do.' Shades blew on his hands, stamped his feet and shivered, 'What about a cab?' Tony shook his head, 'By the time we get there it will all be over one way or another.' Shades rolled his head back, looked at the dark sky and sighed, 'Oh Vicky!'

Vicky had stopped a short walk from Hammond's house. Switching off the engine she climbed out, locked the car and checked her watch. Five o'clock. After looking up and down the street to ensure there was no one about, she bent down quickly and pushed the car keys into the exhaust pipe.

She had noticed a phone box on the corner of the last street so pulling her coat tightly around her and knotting the belt she pushed her hands deep into the pockets, her cold fingers closed on the small card with the club's number while the other hand held the gun. She hunched her shoulders against the cold and began to trudge towards the phone box.

At the flat, Tony handed his brother a mug of coffee, they sat cradling their drinks in mournful silence.

Shades spoke first, 'I know why she did this.' Tony looked at him moodily over his mug. 'She wants to finish it on her own and protect us.' Tony nodded, 'Poor kid. Unless Ron gets there first she'll end up either dead or up for murder.'

The phone rang, they stared at it for an instant then Tony leapt to his feet, spilling his coffee on the carpet and made a grab for the receiver with his free hand as he thumped down the mug with the other, 'Yes?'

'Tony, it's Vicky.' Tony put his hand over the mouthpiece and hissed, 'It's her.' Shades rose quickly and stepped closer. Tony spoke as soothingly as he could, 'Now listen, Vicky...' But Vicky wouldn't let him talk, 'Look Tony, I don't have much time so you must listen to me, I won't let any of you risk your lives anymore, I'm going to finish it today. I have your gun, I know it's not registered in your name or anything and there's only my fingerprints on it because I've wiped it and the bullets. I've parked your car near Hammond's, the keys are in the exhaust pipe, pick up the car later today. It's in...' she looked around and spotted a road sign, 'it's in Palmerstone Road. Thank you for all your help, tell Ron I..., tell Ron not to worry.'

Tony replaced the receiver slowly and turned to Shades, 'She hung up.'

Vicky stepped out of the phone box and exhaled slowly. She thought of Ron, imagining the life they could have had and hated Hammond more. Tightly gripping the gun in her pocket, she walked briskly down the road toward his house. Her face stung as the vicious wind chilled her and the freezing air hurt her lungs. Stopping at the end of the road that ran past Hammond's gates, the question was how to get over the wall? She glanced down the road at the gate and debated if it was better to simply ring the bell. Hammond's men would be shocked to see her alive and probably take her straight to him. If she was not searched that would be the easiest way. Vicky was of course unaware that Hammond's hand picked small army of thugs had been neatly pruned back by gunfire into the shape of Micky.

Although it was very early, Vincent Hammond was still awake having been up all night. After struggling home with Micky the day before, there had been plenty to keep him from sleep. His anger had raged white hot, it was only now finally in the small hours that Vincent's fury burned low enough for rational thought not to be incinerated in pure hatred. A plan, a course of action had begun to form in his mind. Since even he realised he couldn't take on the IRA, so all his fury and driving need for revenge had sharply focussed on the brothers. As for the IRA, in future he would steer clear of them, assuming that they left him alone now. It was odd that the older man had walked in with the money. He shrugged, checking the guns were there and how many men they had to deal with before they attacked, yes that must be it. Double-crossing bastards and the brothers had set him up!

He paced about in his office, it was more than the loss of the money he had invested in the guns. He could not afford to lose his burgeoning reputation. Reasoning he could get it all back if Shades and Tony should meet with an accident and if it was circulated they had double-crossed him. Yes, that could work out well, his reputation in the city would be saved, even enhanced. He would savour planning the brothers' short futures. He considered, although he wanted them out of the way it should not be anything quick, no that wouldn't do. One, they had to suffer and two, they had to know before it was over who was behind it. But all that would be later, business first, then revenge.

The plan's details were crystalizing fast and as they did so he cooled rapidly and even smiled with the anticipation of the scheme's fruitful and painful conclusion. Of course he would need to find replacements first, he hated new people around him. His whole team wiped out in the shoot out, trapped in the warehouse that was annoying. Only he and Micky had made it out, crawling from the wreckage after the truck overturned. He was glad Micky had survived he'd made some mistakes lately but was useful. If it had not been for Micky the car and the truck could have been traced back to him, he smiled again, Micky could enter and start any vehicle quicker than most people could with a key, then slap on false plates and bingo, unlimited supply of vehicles. Yes, Micky had many uses. The thought of

Micky reminded him, he glanced at the empty brandy decanter. Suddenly, he remembered the case of brandy that had finally arrived by courier the night before. A drink! He would have a drink. He was Vincent Hammond and he would turn this thing around. Okay, so the big arms deal was a disaster, he would recover and when he came out of this, his reputation would be so great that his extortion racket would be more lucrative than ever.

What if it was five in the morning? He did what he wanted and what he wanted right now was a drink, then after some food and sleep he could work on the details and begin. He ran his tongue over his bottom lip, where had Micky put the case? He remembered he had screamed at Micky to leave him alone when he had come to tell him it had arrived. Micky had probably left it in the hall or kitchen.

He found both Micky and the brandy case in the kitchen, Micky seated at the kitchen table staring into space, thinking. He flinched as the door opened suddenly then relaxed slightly, relieved to see Vincent looking more in control, 'Join me for a drink Micky? Then after some sleep we go to work.' Micky smiled, 'You got a plan, Vince?' 'I've got a plan Micky.' As usual Vincent's smile was anything but comforting, Micky kept quiet and waited. With no scruples and the ability to carry out whatever was asked of him, including breaking bones, made him a valuable asset that Hammond recognised and paid a healthy salary. One thing he admired about Vincent, his clear thinking was usually profitable, if not always legal and sometimes not always painless for any human obstacles. The fact he had a plan was a sure sign of future employment and rich pickings. But Micky needed to be careful, working for Vincent Hammond carried certain risks, his moods could change quickly in the same way a storm could turn a pleasant day's sailing into a life-threatening situation and Micky did not want to end up man overboard. The recent storm, however, appeared to have passed.

Vincent paused in his attempt to open his brandy crate and looked up at Micky, 'I'm thinking about running a club, I feel the brothers could be persuaded to take on a partner. Later after their accident I'll run it alone, then we focus attention on our insurance business.'

At first glance, there appeared little difference between the unpleasant characters of Micky Slater and Vincent Hammond, but in fact they were very different. Vincent was driven by a need to acquire money, power and respect, fear being close enough to respect in his mind. If to achieve his goals he needed to instruct Micky to break people's fingers or worse, Vincent simply did not care. Micky on the other hand, enjoyed hurting people and viewed that aspect of his employment as something of a perk. His greed for money, although healthy, came a close second. The prospect of dealing with Tony and Shades was without doubt a thing to savour.

Micky smiled broadly, 'People pay us to ensure continuing good health.' 'No Micky people pay me, I pay you.' Micky's smiled faltered, 'Sure Vince, that's what I meant.'

Outside, Vicky rested her shaking hands on the railings of the gate. She had steadied her nerves, in a moment she would be face to face with Vincent Hammond and was going to shoot him. At the same instant Vicky raised her hand to push the bell she was caught in the glare of car headlights. Turning, she put her hand to her forehead to shield her eyes and squinted into the light. A car surged toward her and slid to a halt a few feet from the gate. The door opened, 'Vicky!' It was Ron's voice. 'Ron, you shouldn't have come!' 'Vicky, you can't do this!' She shook her head, 'I can, I *must*!'

'We'll think of another way.'

'No! What if you're killed next time?'

Ron had been relieved to reach her but it was upsetting to see how distressed she was. The intense cold, stress and desperation had conspired to rob her of any vestige of colour. The face that stared back at him with wide frightened eyes was disturbingly white, he noticed also her hands were quivering. His mind flashed back to how she'd looked the night he found her in the alley, 'Look, there must be another way, I tell you what, we'll go away, leave London, leave England even!'

'No Ron, why should we? Anyway what about Tony and Shades? We can't leave them to face what we've started.'

'You'll be killed in there and if not, you'll go to prison I...' his voice broke a little, 'I can't lose you! Please give me the gun.' Vicky looked confused, then suddenly her anger faded to despair and exhaustion for she knew in her heart the moment had passed, she no longer possessed the power to go through with it. Dropping the gun in the snow her legs folded under her. Tears filled her eyes, blurring her vision. She put a hand out to steady herself Ron took it and knelt down in the snow with her. He hugged her tightly and rocked her gently. With her face buried in his chest her voice was muffled as she sobbed, 'Oh Ron, what are we going to do?'

The question was never answered. Suddenly, the earth-shattering blast of a mighty explosion tore through the silence. He instinctively lay flat, taking Vicky down with him, he covered her head with his hands the best he could. She managed to look sideways in time to witness a monstrous ball of fire curl up into the dark sky. Even from where they lay, the hot shockwave could be felt. As the huge ball of flame began to dissipate, small fragments of roof tile and splinters of wood began to rain down. Flying shards of glass momentarily lit by the dying fireball fell to earth embedding in the snowy ground. Vicky put her head down and shut her eyes tightly. Ron moved as close to her as he could and tried his best to protect her as flaming debris fell all around. One small piece landed on his arm causing a tiny flame to flicker on the sleeve. Hastily he patted it out. Tiny pieces of shattered house had been hurled hundreds of feet into the air and it was a while before it was safe to stand.

Ron got to his feet first and stared in disbelief. Where a large, solid house had stood moments before, now the centre had completely vanished, replaced by twisted metal, fire and rubble. Without taking his eyes from it, he leaned down, caught Vicky's hand and helped her to her feet. After the initial shock, Ron collected himself and looked about his feet in the snow for the gun, finding it, he picked it up swiftly and slipped it into his pocket. He pulled Vicky toward him and they clung to each other, 'It's over.' He whispered. The relief was so immense that Vicky both cried and laughed. They held each other for a long moment, Ron blinked back tears of relief, she was safe, they were all safe.

People from nearby houses began to gather at the gates to stare at the burning ruins. The distant sound of approaching sirens could be heard. Soon Vicky and Ron were just two more faces in the crowd peering through the bars of the gates, their stunned features lit by the fire as it engulfed the remains.

PART TWO
CHAPTER 19
TWO WEEKS LATER
CHRISTMAS EVE 7:30PM

The heart of Ron's gas fire burned a deep crimson. Orange tendrils drifted up as it shimmered and rippled with waves of heat. Finbar lay curled on his rug in front of it luxuriating in the warmth truly content after reclaiming his cherished spot. He purred loudly as he dozed and his nose twitched a little.

The air was filled with the wonderful aroma of turkey and roast potatoes. Vicky was quietly humming 'Silent Night' as she put the last touches to the Christmas tree. Her smile was comically and hugely exaggerated in a large red Christmas bauble as she leaned into the tree. After some minor adjustments, 'Yes, perfect.' She sat back on her heels to admire the work. It wasn't possible to look at the rich warm colours without feeling happy. Then glancing at the time, seven thirty-one, she called, 'They'll be here any minute.' Ron could also be heard singing in the kitchen, mercifully, he paused to answer, 'All under control.' She smiled, gave the tree a final scrutiny, satisfied she stood up and smoothed her new dress, it was knee-length, dark red velvet with a delicate high lace collar with matching wrist-length sleeves, a hidden zip secured the back. The outfit was complemented by dark red, kitten heel suede shoes. The only jewellery was a pair of crystal earrings in the shape of tiny Christmas trees, a gift from Ron. As she moved her head they danced and sparkled. She had really wanted to dress up. This meal was the first time they were to receive guests as a couple and everything had to be perfect.

The doorbell rang, Ron called from the kitchen, 'Can you get it? I'm just pulling the turkey out.'

'Okay.' Vicky walked eagerly to the door and opened it. Shades and Big Tony stood outside looking a little bashful, they were not accustomed to dinner invitations.

'Come in, come in, oh you both look cold.' Vicky hugged them and pretended not to notice Tony colour slightly.

The two removed their coats. Tony carried a briefcase, which he placed by the sofa. Ron came out of the kitchen looking hot and holding a tea towel. He had a sparkle in his eyes, partly due to the sherry he had been sipping all afternoon. 'Hello boys, perfect timing,' he wiped his hands on the tea towel and shook hands, 'come on, sit down.'

Vicky poured them a drink and Ron ran back and forth to the kitchen bringing platefuls of delicious Christmas dinner. He placed them on the small pine table he and Vicky had moved from the kitchen and temporarily relocated between the back of the second sofa and the bay window. Ron finished placing the food, stood back and announced, 'Dinner is served.' They all took their seats. Vicky noted the brothers had dressed for the occasion, both looked smart but she was especially pleased to see Tony in a creamy yellow shirt and a rich brown tie with a delicate gold pattern. She laughed out loud as she compared the well dressed brothers to the happy little specimen in the t-shirt with 'Ho, Ho, Ho' emblazoned across the chest who sat beside her. Ron glanced at her and beamed, he was a scruffy creature but he was her scruffy creature.

They sat eating and chatting and with a couple of generous glasses of wine under his belt, even Tony loosened up. The tree was politely given the praise it richly deserved, Ron confessed although he'd helped, it had been under direction and was Vicky's vision. Ron raised his glass and they toasted the tree. He was in excellent spirits, so much so he kept grinning and insisting the others pulled crackers with him. Both he and Vicky sported party hats. Vicky handed Tony and Shades a hat each, the brothers stared at her, Tony spoke for them both, 'No!' Vicky poured herself another glass of wine, 'You have to, it's Christmas,' she announced.

The atmosphere grew a little tense. Ron stopped chewing and watched Tony. Shades looked to his brother for what to do. Tony was frowning at Vicky who appeared to be immune and smiled back happily. After all they had been through together, she felt completely comfortable with them both, but especially with Tony. The encounter by the dove coop had somehow been a turning point. In her eyes, he would always be a kind and gentle man. In turn, Tony liked Vicky very much and believed her to be brave and caring. He shared Shades' opinion that she and Ron needed each other and belonged together, consequently, Vicky could get away with things other mortals would never dream of.

Tony pointed his finger at her and spoke slowly, 'If one word gets out I'll earn that fee I took from Hammond.' Still she smiled sweetly. Carefully, he picked up his paper hat and slowly put it on, then glared at Shades who quickly followed suit. Tony held up his glass to Vicky and *smiled*! 'Cheers!' Ron put down his fork and stared at Vicky, then swallowing his mouthful of food, blinked. A woman's powers were indeed awesome.

After dinner, they slumped on the sofas too full to move, each cupping a glass of brandy.

Shades pointed at the empty table, 'I know you can make a stew, but I never knew you could cook like that, Ron.'

'That's what comes with living on your own, oh I can knock up a good roast with the best of them.' Vicky shook her head, 'I can't believe it's all over, it doesn't seem possible that two weeks ago we were hiding out, frightened and...' Ron interrupted, 'Believe it...' he hiccupped, 'it's over.' Vicky turned to Shades, 'Did you hear any more from your Irish friend?'

''Frankly my dear, I don't give a damn.'' Ron smiled, 'Oh, *Gone With The Wind*! One of your mum's favourites,' he added, for extra points. Tony, not wanting to be left out, chipped in, 'Nineteen thirty-nine.' Vicky was slightly irritated and a good deal more than slightly the soberest, 'Even I know that one. Come on Shades, seriously, I'm worried about them. They may think there's a score to settle.' Shades' expression became a little more sober, even if the same couldn't be said for the rest of him, 'He

326

surfaced a week ago.' Vicky looked alarmed but Shades explained calmly, 'It wasn't a problem. He wanted the word put about, making it clear to everyone, what happens to people who cross them. Mind you, truthfully, I was a bit uncomfortable to see him. But you have to remember that as far as he was concerned, all I did was put him in touch with Hammond. I made it clear at the time I didn't know what kind of guy he was. They lost a few grand but not the lot. Ron only lifted a sample of the money. I mean, a fair chunk but not all of it. Anyway, I don't think the money was as important to them as the harm to their reputation if they hadn't dealt with Hammond.' Ron sipped his brandy, 'What did he actually say?'

'He said the transaction was disappointing and things hadn't worked out. However, as it was Christmas and to show no hard feelings, they had sent him a big crate of brandy by special delivery, since the word was it was his favourite.' Vicky was relieved, 'Was that it?'

'It was enough for me!'

Vicky shook her head, 'No, I mean, was that it? He didn't say he had anything against you?'

'No, it looks as if they believed I was only passing on a number I'd been given.' Tony added, 'We've been following the papers, it seems that the police think it was an arms deal gone bad; two factions shooting it out. They're patting themselves on the back because they recovered all the guns from the overturned truck. As for the explosion, of course it made the news but since it first happened, there's been no mention of it. I don't think they're exactly grieving over Vince Hammond being killed. They must have known he was up to all kinds of shady schemes, but knowing and proving are different things. One thing's for sure, this Christmas will be a lot happier for all the family businesses in this area without Vincent Hammond squeezing them for money.'

Vicky was visibly relieved, 'Thank you for that, Tony it's a huge relief. Ron and I have been avoiding the news, we've been out of touch.'

Tony nodded and after a pause, added, 'There's something else... me and Shades have been talking it over. There's a possibility that, inadvertently, we all may have saved a good many lives.' Vicky frowned slightly, 'I don't understand.'

'Hammond's house blew up around five in the morning.'

'Yes.'

'The bomb must have been delivered late afternoon or early evening the day before, in that big crate of brandy the IRA told Shades about. It couldn't have arrived later than five or six; legitimate couriers don't deliver much after that. Hammond would have been suspicious.' Tony looked at Shades as he picked up his drink, 'Tell them what we figured.'

Shades took up the story, 'The shoot-out happened a little after twelve. From noon to five or six in the evening is not long enough for them to get explosives, put a bomb together, disguise it as a crate of booze and deliver it, so...' he raised his eyebrows, waiting for Vicky or Ron to reach the same conclusion he and Tony had. Vicky answered slowly in a half-question, half-statement, 'So... they already had a bomb?'

'Mm, if they hadn't used it on Hammond's house, it would probably have been used somewhere else in London. That close to Christmas, the streets are packed.' Vicky opened her mouth in shock and glanced at Ron. He looked stunned and said, 'Vicky and I saw it explode, it was *massive.*' Remembering she had lost her parents in a terrorist attack, Ron looked at her with concern. She was gazing at the floor, her eyes unfocussed, thinking of that terrible New Year's Eve so long ago. Ron watched her; that was nearly nineteen years ago, she had been only five. Suddenly, she took a deep breath, straightened slightly and raised her eyes. That was then, this is now. Ron saw the change and smiled. She was a strong, brave, sensible, loving woman and he was a lucky man. She clapped her hands, 'Okay, come on that's enough, we did the right thing and that proves it. Think about it, we stopped Hammond's reign of terror on local businesses, prevented a shipment of guns falling into the hands of terrorists, got justice for Sara and now it seems, prevented a bomb being used on the streets of London. It's over and I don't want to think about it anymore today, it's Christmas Eve.' There was a general nodding and smiling of agreement.

She stood up and moved to the tree, then kneeling down, 'Oo, Santa's been already, look!' She lifted a parcel from under the tree and passed it to Tony then quickly did the same for Shades and sat back down next to Ron, 'Come on, open them!'

Ron put his arm around her, she leaned into him and they both watched the brothers. Vicky picked up a cushion and hugged it, relishing the moment, 'Go on Tony, you first.' Tony smiled and opened his present carefully, Vicky commented excitedly, 'They're proper nautical ones, quite powerful, for the boat.' Tony pulled the binoculars from the box and held them up, 'Thank you both very much, they're really great.' Vicky felt a little moved, she sensed they didn't get many presents and Tony looked delighted, 'Go on Shades.'

He opened his, then stared at them blankly, 'It's a joke, right? Can't be real?'

''Tis.'

'No.'

'Yes.'

Ron added, 'Should be, it cost enough.' Vicky hit him with the cushion, 'Shut up.' He laughed. Cheeky street-wise joking Shades, tough co-owner of *The Blue Parrot* looked at that moment like a child on Christmas morning, 'It's really real?' he whispered as he gazed at the framed and signed black and white photograph of Humphrey Bogart. Ron confirmed it's authenticity, 'Picked it up from a London auction house, it's got all the proper provenance and everything, came direct from a man whose father actually worked on the set of some of Bogart's films. It was Vicky's idea.' After staring at it for a long time Shades murmured, 'Thank you.' Then regaining some of his cool put down his present and raised his glass to Vicky, '"Here's looking at you, kid."' Everyone chimed, '*Casablanca*!' They laughed, raised their glasses and toasted.

By now Ron teetered precariously on the verge of what some might describe as being totally chateau-ed, but for all that he was extremely amiable and happy, unaware that both he and Vicky were about to become even happier.

Placing his gift to one side, Tony announced, 'We have a little present for you too.' He seemed pleased with himself reaching for the briefcase he placed it on his knees and flicked the latches. Hesitating for a moment to raise the drama, he reached in and pulled out several bundles of banknotes, which he tossed casually onto the coffee table. Vicky and Ron stared open mouthed, she was the first to speak, 'I don't understand.'

'This is the money Hammond gave me for getting rid of you, plus the sample Ron took from the IRA.' Ron found his voice, 'We can't accept all this.' He glanced at Vicky who shook her head and agreed, 'It doesn't belong to us, you both did so much.'

Tony grinned, 'Well I didn't earn it, I was supposed to take care of the pair of you, look how well you both are.' They all stared at the bundles of banknotes. It was Shades this time who broke the contemplative silence, '"It's the stuff that dreams are made of."'

Turning to him Vicky raised her eyebrows but before she could comment Tony jumped in with, '*The Maltese Falcon.*' Shades smiled, 'Whose line?' Without hesitation, Tony answered, 'Bogart, closing scene.' Shades laughed, 'Ha, you got it.' Tony looked smug.

Ron gestured at the heap of notes, 'Guys! What are we going to do?' No one answered so he suggested slowly, 'We could split it I suppose.' He looked at Vicky who was smiling and nodding in agreement, 'Yes, we all played a part.' Shades had a far away look in his eyes of things to come. In that moment he had already spent his share of 'the stuff that dreams are made of' to make a particular dream a

331

reality.   He raised his eyes from the money and beamed at Vicky and Ron, 'Sounds good.' Tony gave a deep laugh, 'I think it's what Vince would have wanted.'

They all stood, touched glasses and in chorus toasted, 'Merry Christmas!'

EPILOGUE

After all the excitement and drama, Vicky and Ron enjoyed a blissfully quiet Christmas together. Of course, Sara was never far from Vicky's thoughts, however, she was determined to give Ron a happy Christmas after all he had done for her. She also knew Christmas could be difficult for him too.

Their conversation at 'Nick's' restaurant had stayed with her. Ron had come through a lot of pain to reach his hard-won insight of 'not letting today turn into tomorrow's regrets'. She wanted them both to remember their first Christmas together as a happy one and smile.

Ron was also mindful that Vicky must be finding this first Christmas without her sister heart breaking and was equally determined to give her the best Christmas he could.

The harder each tried to please the other, the happier they themselves became. Eventually, they both enjoyed a particularly lovely Christmas, each having put aside their own troubles to be kind to the other. Consequently, it could be argued with some confidence that the spirit of Christmas burned more brightly in that small South London flat than almost anywhere you could care to mention.

Vicky kept her word and insisted on repaying the loan. Ron told her it wasn't necessary and was informed gently but firmly 'it was a point of principle'.

Over Christmas both made plans for their respective windfalls, it was Ron who spoke of it first. A few days after Christmas he announced suddenly he was going out to arrange a New Year's surprise and disappeared. Vicky had taken advantage of his absence to retrieve Dave London's number from under the fridge magnet and call him. She had smiled as she removed the blue fabric belt from her pyjamas to put in her bag, then she had phoned for a cab and slipped out.

By chance that afternoon, they had returned simultaneously, like secretive children, both delighted with the afternoon's work.

The belated Christmas gifts were exchanged that very evening as they were sitting by the fire. Both took the form of mysterious envelopes. Vicky had opened hers first and was thrilled to find two tickets for a winter cruise a week after New Year's Day. Her only reservation was concern for Finbar. Ron had felt they all deserved and needed a holiday, even Finbar. He explained Finbar was to have his holiday with Jane where, no doubt, he would be fussed over and thoroughly spoilt. Vicky was delighted.

Ron's envelope had been uniquely decorated with a faint oily thumbprint. The unpromising envelope however, held within pure joy, at least for Ron. He had discovered a receipt from Dave and a brief note formally accepting the job, it read, '*I undertake all repairs to the bodywork on the '57 Chevrolet Bel Air belonging to Ronny Moon and will oversee the engine work and re-spray in baby blue, colour matched to the fabric sample provided, signed Dave London, Master Welder'.*

Vicky had remembered the colour was his favourite. She had worked extremely hard for Ron's gift. It had taken all her powers of persuasion to bring Dave safely down to earth after he had surveyed the bullet holes and damage suffered by the car, as it sat miserably in the lock-up behind *The Blue Parrot*. For Ron, she had endured a lengthy lecture by Dave on care and consideration for automotive classics. It stopped only because she cleverly asked if it was possible to see the etched copper signature tags that were to be pot riveted beneath his artistry. Ron had opened his mouth to tell her it was too much. Guessing what he was about to say she had given him what Ron had come to refer to as her look. Ron still found it amazing and slightly mystifying how much information Vicky could pack into 'The Look'. The translation read 'I'm doing this my way! Or we can talk about it for a long time, then, I'm doing this my way.' Wisely, he had said nothing and kissed her thank you.

Tony not only kept his promise to *The Grey Lady* about the new fuel pump, but also paid for a complete engine overhaul.

Shades asked Dave to take care of the minor repairs to his own car and had plenty left to buy an impressive film projector system to show old movies on his very own silver screen. He set it all up in the basement of the club and told Ron and Vicky they were always welcome to the monthly late night showings, which he said was for the 'cultured few'.

On New Year's Eve, Shades and Tony threw a big party at *The Blue Parrot*. Everyone was there, including the crew from the theatre as Ron's special guests. The show had moved from the suburbs to the West End, where it was even gathering a cult following. Ron declared it a double celebration.

Tony stood resplendent in his brightest yellow shirt, puffing a cigar while leaning on the rail in the almost deserted upstairs bar. Looking approvingly at the packed dance floor below, he could see Ron dancing with Vicky, both deliriously happy. She looked up and waved wildly as Ron's request *Brown-Eyed Girl* blasted from the Club's speakers, Tony raised an arm in acknowledgement and smiled down. The loud music had woken the Club's sophisticated lighting system; a kaleidoscope of patterns and colours pulsated and flashed in all directions. A huge mirror ball had been lowered from its home high up in the Club's cavernous ceiling, it flung multi-coloured spots of light into the darkest corners as it sparkled and rotated majestically.

Scanning the busy bars Tony could make out Dave London. Having swapped his overalls for a jacket, Dave looked almost smart. He had even scrubbed nearly all of the dirt from his nails especially for the occasion. He was having a wonderful time arguing a technical point with Tom the effects man, about how in the movies any welding was always carried out with the flame set all wrong.

As Tony turned his attention back to the dance floor, he laughed out loud as he spotted Shades, who had been pounced upon for a dance partner by Jane Flutter.

The music pumped out from the powerful disco on the raised platform at the rear of the Club, mixing with the murmur of conversation and laughter. Glasses clinked and champagne corks popped. High above the disco, dominating the rear wall, the giant blue neon sign flashed on and off in time with the music, *The Blue Parrot*, *The Blue Parrot*, *The Blue Parrot*.

The End
…. or to be more accurate for Ron and Vicky,
The Beginning.

Thank you for reading *Bolt From The Blue*. Please tell your friends and leave positive feedback on Amazon. In doing so, you will be helping not only myself but self-publishing authors, creative writing and books in general. And giving hope and support to those who struggle with dyslexia on a daily basis, proving that all things are possible.

Clifford

Acknowledgments

To my mum for bringing me here.

To Sally Boehme for making it worth coming, also for her invaluable encouragement, advice and typing skills.

To my friend Dr Graham Baker Phd MA MSc PGCE BA(Hons) for proof reading this book.

To my friend Dr Frances Warren, who stood in the pouring rain to model for my cover painting.

To Nancy Smith my Adult Education teacher, who was wonderfully patient and generous with her time. It was she who diagnosed my severe dyslexia and once cheerfully informed me, 'Not to worry, I know I can help you, I mean you'll never write a book or anything, but we'll definitely improve that spelling!' Thank you Nancy, you helped me more than you'll ever know.

I would like very much to thank you, the reader. A kindred spirit and fellow armchair adventurer, who loves books and derives so much simple pleasure from reading.

Fictional Acknowledgments

To my characters because I promised them:

Dave London, welding genius, a true artist of
unparalleled skill.

Jane Flutter, a make-up artist of the highest calibre
for her generous help and patience.

Tom Anderson, whose advice on special effects
was special indeed.

Johnny Mitchell, the producer who gave Ron's
first play wings.

Printed in Great Britain
by Amazon

78278742R00203